LORD PETER

Mysteries by Dorothy L. Sayers

Busman's Honeymoon
Clouds of Witness
The Documents in the Case
The Five Red Herrings
Gaudy Night
Hangman's Holiday
Have His Carcase
In the Teeth of the Evidence
Lord Peter: The Complete Lord Peter Wimsey Stories
Lord Peter Views the Body
Murder Must Advertise
Strong Poison
Unnatural Death
The Unpleasantness at the Bellona Club
Whose Body?

LORD PETER

THE COMPLETE
LORD PETER WIMSEY STORIES

DOROTHY L. SAYERS

BOURBON STREET BOOKS

An Imprint of HarperCollinsPublishers
www.harpercollins.com

A hardcover edition of this book was published in 1972 by Harper & Row Publishers, Inc. It is here reprinted by arrangement with the Estate of Anthony Fleming.

HarperCollins books may be purchased for educational, business, or sales promotional use. For information, please e-mail the Special Markets Department at SPsales@harpercollins.com.

First Perennial Library edition published 1987.
First Harper Paperbacks edition published 1995.
First Perennial edition published 2001.
First Bourbon Street Books edition published 2013.

Library of Congress Cataloging-in-Publication Data is available upon request.

ISBN 978-0-06-227548-6 (pbk.)

23 24 25 26 27 LBC 15 14 13 12 11

CONTENTS

INTRODUCTION

by James Sandoe

Lord Peter's first recorded utterance is "Oh, damn!" as he remembers his forgetfulness and asks a cab driver to go back to 110 Piccadilly for the Brocklebury sale catalogue, since he had hoped to pick up a book or two. But there is his mother on the telephone asking him to see what can be done for luckless little Mr. Thipps, who is embarrassed by an unknown dead man in his bathtub "with nothing on but a pair of pince-nez." *Whose Body?*, subtitled The Singular Adventure of the Man with the Golden Pince-nez (1923), began the succession.

In this first chronicle we had a good deal: Peter himself; Freddy Arbuthnot, mild and engaging; the splendid Dowager Duchess, Peter's extremely apposite mother; the quietly splendid Bunter (obviously related to Jeeves); Parker of the Yard who was later to become Peter's brother-in-law; that formidable defender, Sir Imprey Biggs; the sedulous Sugg (Miss Sayers' Inspector Lestrade whom she invented, to discard) and who else that delighted us after that?

Miss Sayers herself reread *Whose Body?* without much admiration,* a judgment characteristically severe and (characteristically?) lofty. We need not agree.

Clouds of Witness (1926) followed and set Lord Peter the problem of his amiable if foolish brother the Duke of Denver (married to a shrew, Helen) accused of murder and tried before the House of Lords, a rare but remarkable occasion. A number of old friends persist happily and we have a fuller chance to meet others including that correct solicitor Mr. Murbles. There is even a glimpse of Denver's son, Peter's young nephew, identified as Pickled Gherkins. Much later, as an Oxford undergraduate, he will fall (understandably) in love with Harriet Vane. Lord Peters flies across the Atlantic to make his climactic appearance before the assembled Lords. It was at that date no casual event.

There followed *The Dawson Pedigree (Unnatural Death,* 1927), one of Miss Sayers' cunningest puzzles but just as memorable for introducing us to the breathless Miss Climpson, one of the most energetically emphatic correspondents in history.

Miss Climpson is not recruited for the singular excitements comprising *The Unpleasantness at the Bellona Club* (1928), that exceedingly staid military fellowship so startled on Armistice Day by the demise of General Fentiman, but Mr. Murbles is present, correct and concerned as always. And it is here that we have one of our glimpses of the pleasing Marjorie Phelps, who is Lord Peter's entree to Chelsea, "a pleasant-looking young woman with curly hair and a blue overall heavily smudged with clay" whose statuette of Peter amuses him decidedly.

The dozen adventures comprising *Lord Peter Views the Body* (1928) followed; and as they are before you in this volume, you may make such additions to these reminiscing notes as they seem to stimulate. I find them as delightful as ever.

Strong Poison (1930) is rich on many scores. We meet again

*"Gaudy Night" in *Titles to Fame,* edited by Denys Kilham Roberts (London, 1937).

the reporters, Salcombe Hardy and Waffles Newton, Sir Impey, Marjorie Phelps, Lady Mary Wimsey (not yet married to Parker), the chilly Duchess and the pleasant if opaque Duke of Denver together with Freddy Arbuthnot, engaged now to Rachel Levy (see *Whose Body?*). We also meet Harriet Vane, who at the beginning of the novel is on trial, charged with the murder (by arsenic) of her trying lover, Philip Boyes. Peter is fiercely (nay, frantically) sure that she is innocent, and what follows proves that he is right. But he is also in love with the lady, who has no taste for his pity and refuses him without dashing his hopes entirely.

In the same year was published a much too-little-known novel, *The Documents in the Case*, which Miss Sayers wrote in collaboration with Robert Eustace, a physician and mystery writer who had earlier been one of Conan Doyle's fellow contributors to *The Strand Magazine*. It is for about half of its course an epistolary tale of considerable teasing charm but a tale of detection that does not involve Lord Peter (for all that Sir James Lubbock is invoked) and hence a sort of stepchild in the succession, however regrettably.

Miss Sayers never quite explained why, having boxed Lord Peter up in this understandable passion for the poised Harriet, she postponed dealing with it. There is no hint of Harriet in *The Five Red Herrings* (published in the United States first as *Suspicious Characters*, 1931), a sort of apogee among tales of timetable detection involving alibis of the kind Freeman Wills Crofts had been occupying himself with for years. I find it a dry tale in remembrance but reread it each time with pleasure in its human engagements, which oil the mathematics of train schedules. Its setting is Scotland and it is brightly and vigorously peopled for all that its schematics seem to dominate.

Harriet Vane returned to the scene and to Peter's fierce concern in *Have His Carcase* (1932), a monumentally if not very fruitfully long novel which was as much about the wooing of Harriet as about the corpse that Harriet discovered on a coastal rock between Lesston Hoe and Wilvercombe. At the

end of this slightly tiresome stretch of self-indulgence we are
as sure of Lord Peter's interest in Harriet as before but still
hanging romantically on a cliff.

Miss Sayers was to keep us there for two novels more, because this second involvement of Lord Peter and Harriet is
nowhere invoked in the two tales that follow. The first of them
was *Murder Must Advertise* (1933), in which Miss Sayers played
pretty games with a world (publicity) that she knew as a paid
practitioner. A lot of old friends and acquaintances are there
(Lady Mary is now married to Parker and Freddy to Rachel)
and there are such new acquaintances as young Ginger, whose
"catapult" (we should call it a slingshot) is vital to the action.

The other interloper between our glimpses of Lord Peter's
prolonged wooing was "changes rung on an old theme in two
short touches and two full peals," a tale that is many readers'
favorite, *The Nine Tailors* (1934). Fenchurch St. Paul in the fen
country is Miss Sayers' setting, and its criminal concerns are,
of course, ingeniously wound in the ancient art of change-
ringing. It is a long, complex, very rich tale with astonishingly
little dependence on the stock company which Miss Sayers
had by that time evoked. Sugg is mentioned in passing (as retired) and Parker is briefly apparent, but our concern is much
more with the villagers and their gentle clergyman, a scholarly
soul, Rector Venables.

I see that I have overlooked that second collection of short
stories, *Hangman's Holiday* (1933), in which we have a few
more short stories about Lord Peter, the first appearances of
that shrewd old character, Mr. Montague Egg, "traveling representative of Plummet & Rose, Wines and Spirits, Piccadilly." He has a keen remembrance of the apothegms
contained in the *Salesman's Handbook* and an even sharper regard for the vagaries of human nature. The alert reader of
those few tales concerning Lord Peter will find references to
Freddy Arbuthnot, Parker, The Soviet Club, Peter's nephew,
Gherkins (Viscount St. George, to the correct), and other
friends and acquaintances.

Nowadays we can move readily from *Strong Poison* to *Have*

His Carcase to *Gaudy Night* and then to *Busman's Honeymoon*.
But Miss Sayers' first readers had a very long wait before
coming to the singular excitements of *Gaudy Night* (1935),
which never in its considerable length ever finds need to discover excitement in a corpse. There is ample engagement
without a body.

It is pre-eminently an Oxford novel and, in spite of Miss
Sayers' disclaimers, a Somerville novel, set amongst the tight
academic and nonacademic concerns of the college. Here
Peter returns to his active pursuit of Harriet (who, in the last
line, succumbs in suitable Latin), but it is all delightful if un-
sentimental nostalgia.*

The last of the Lord Peter novels was *Busman's Honeymoon*,
A Love Story with Detective Interruptions (1937), which
began life as a play written by Miss Sayers and Muriel St.
Claire Byrne and was later translated into a film starring
Robert Montgomery as Lord Peter, Constance Cummings as
Lady Harriet and Sir Seymour Hicks as Bunter. Miss Sayers,
always precise, describes it fairly, and through its course she
invokes all sorts of old friends from the splendidly garrulous
Dowager Duchess to "Mrs. Merdle,"† the ninth Daimler of
that name.

So far as Lord Peter is involved there is very little more to
record. He is twice apparent in the collection of stories called
In the Teeth of the Evidence (1939), a volume involving Mr. Montague Egg again, and a number of those detective and crime
stories which dot the other volumes, often happily. But a good
many readers have never met the ultimate tales about Lord
Peter, which have not until now been gathered among her
own tales. "Striding Folly" is welcome but less memorable
than "The Haunted Policeman," which begins as Peter views
his firstborn with incredulity. The adventure that follows is
trivial, if agreeable: the event is some sort of climax.

---

*Readers with proper curiosity will be interested at the glimpses of Dorothy L. Say-
ers in Vera Brittain's *Testament of Youth* (1933).
†The name may come from Dickens. See *Little Dorrit*.

There are glimpses of the Wimseys through the earlier war years in Miss Sayers' contributions of "The Wimsey Papers" to the English newspaper *The Spectator*. And there was at least one projected Lord Peter novel, *Thrones, Dominations*, which was never published, probably never written.

Meantime, the remarkable Miss Sayers (Mrs. Atherton Fleming) had had a number of other interests, all of them literate, many of them scholarly and none of them worth the omission or neglect they are bound to receive here. She began publication as a poet and, more specifically as a Christian poet (see *Op.1:* Oxford, 1916), and translated the fragments of *Tristan in Brittany* from the Anglo-Norman poet Thomas (1929 in publication, although the translation must have been done much earlier).

Her critical study of Wilkie Collins never got itself written, unfortunately (although her bibliography graces the *Cambridge Bibliography of English Literature*). She wrote some lively verse plays, including variations on the Faust theme (*The Devil to Pay;* 1939).

The crown of her creativity and of her scholarship came, certainly, with her translation of Dante's *Divine Comedy* (Penguin commissioned it; Hell appeared in 1949, Purgatory in 1955 and Paradise, completed by her friend Barbara Reynolds, after her death and in 1962). The concern with Dante is further expressed in at least two other volumes, *Introductory Papers on Dante* (1954) and *Further Papers on Dante* (1957).

Our purpose here has been for the most part to recall just that part of Dorothy L. Sayers' much more varied career than concerns Lord Peter Wimsey. These affectionate notes have suggested some of her other (and, to her, more important) concerns. The curious reader may discover notes toward a bibliography *(Bulletin of Bibliography,* May/August 1944) sadly incomplete but symptomatic.

Meantime, what you have here are all of the stories about Lord Peter, a lively assembly which suggests the Sayers sense of responsibility toward a "medium" (the tale of detection) which she wrote with skill and reviewed with acuity. She wrote ingeniously, wittily and cleanly (in spite of the *longeurs* of *The Five Red Herrings* and *Have His Carcase; Gaudy Night* is long but I detect no fat on its frame), and with as deep a responsibility to the tale of detection as she brought to the tale of salvation while translating Dante.

LORD
PETER

THE ABOMINABLE HISTORY OF
THE MAN WITH COPPER FINGERS

The Egotists' Club is one of the most genial places in London. It is a place to which you may go when you want to tell that odd dream you had last night, or to announce what a good dentist you have discovered. You can write letters there if you like, and have the temperament of a Jane Austen, for there is no silence room, and it would be a breach of club manners to appear busy or absorbed when another member addresses you. You must not mention golf or fish, however, and, if the Hon. Freddy Arbuthnot's motion is carried at the next committee meeting (and opinion so far appears very favourable), you will not be allowed to mention wireless either. As Lord Peter Wimsey said when the matter was mooted the other day in the smoking-room, those are things you can talk about anywhere. Otherwise the club is not specially exclusive. Nobody is ineligible *per se*, except strong, silent men. Nominees are, however, required to pass certain tests, whose nature is sufficiently indicated by the fact that a certain distinguished explorer came

to grief through accepting, and smoking, a powerful Trichi-
nopoly cigar as an accompaniment to a '63 port. On the other
hand, dear old Sir Roger Bunt (the coster millionaire who
won the £20,000 ballot offered by the *Sunday Shriek*, and used
it to found his immense catering business in the Midlands)
was highly commended and unanimously elected after declar-
ing frankly that beer and a pipe were all he really cared for in
that way. As Lord Peter said again: "Nobody minds coarse-
ness but one must draw the line at cruelty."

On this particular evening, Masterman (the cubist poet)
had brought a guest with him, a man named Varden. Varden had
started life as a professional athlete, but a strained heart
had obliged him to cut short a brilliant career, and turn his
handsome face and remarkably beautiful body to account in
the service of the cinema screen. He had come to London from
Los Angeles to stimulate publicity for his great new film,
Marathon, and turned out to be quite a pleasant, unspoiled person — greatly to the relief of the club, since Masterman's guests
were apt to be something of a toss-up.

There were only eight men, including Varden, in the
brown room that evening. This, with its panelled walls, shaded
lamps, and heavy blue curtains was perhaps the cosiest and
pleasantest of the small smoking-rooms, of which the club possessed half a dozen or so. The conversation had begun quite
casually by Armstrong's relating a curious little incident which
he had witnessed that afternoon at Temple Station, and Bayes
had gone on to say that that was nothing to the really very odd
thing which had happened to him, personally, in a thick fog
one night in the Euston Road.

Masterman said that the more secluded London squares
teemed with subjects for a writer, and instanced his own singular encounter with a weeping woman and a dead monkey,
and then Judson took up the tale and narrated how, in a
lonely suburb, late at night, he had come upon the dead body
of a woman stretched on the pavement with a knife in her side
and a policeman standing motionless near by. He had asked if
he could do anything, but the policeman had only said, "I

wouldn't interfere if I was you, sir; she deserved what she got." Judson said he had not been able to get the incident out of his mind, and then Pettifer told them of a queer case in his own medical practice, when a totally unknown man had led him to a house in Bloomsbury where there was a woman suffering from strychnine poisoning. This man had helped him in the most intelligent manner all night, and, when the patient was out of danger, had walked straight out of the house and never reappeared; the odd thing being that, when he (Pettifer) questioned the woman, she answered in great surprise that she had never seen the man in her life and had taken him to be Pettifer's assistant.

"That reminds me," said Varden, "of something still stranger that happened to me once in New York — I've never been able to make out whether it was a madman or a practical joke, or whether I really had a very narrow shave."

This sounded promising, and the guest was urged to go on with his story.

"Well, it really started ages ago," said the actor, "seven years it must have been — just before America came into the war. I was twenty-five at the time, and had been in the film business a little over two years. There was a man called Eric P. Loder, pretty well known in New York at that period, who would have been a very fine sculptor if he hadn't had more money than was good for him, or so I understood from the people who go in for that sort of thing. He used to exhibit a good deal and had a lot of one-man shows of his stuff to which the highbrow people went — he did a good many bronzes, I believe. Perhaps you know about him, Masterman?"

"I've never seen any of his things," said the poet, "but I remember some photographs in *The Art of Tomorrow*. Clever, but rather overripe. Didn't he go in for a lot of that chryselephantine stuff? Just to show he could afford to pay for the materials, I suppose."

"Yes, that sounds very like him."

"Of course — and he did a very slick and very ugly realistic group called Lucina, and had the impudence to have it cast in solid gold and stood in his front hall."

"Oh, that thing! Yes—simply beastly I thought it, but then I never could see anything artistic in the idea. Realism, I suppose you'd call it. I like a picture or a statue to make you feel good, or what's it there for? Still, there was something very attractive about Loder."

"How did you come across him?"

"Oh, yes. Well, he saw me in that little picture of mine, *Apollo comes to New York*—perhaps you remember it. It was my first star part. About a statue that's brought to life—one of the old gods, you know—and how he gets on in a modern city. Dear old Reubenssohn produced it. Now, there was a man who could put a thing through with consummate artistry. You couldn't find an atom of offence from beginning to end, it was all so tasteful, though in the first part one didn't have anything to wear except a sort of scarf—taken from the classical statue, you know."

"The Belvedere?"

"I dare say. Well, Loder wrote to me, and said as a sculptor he was interested in me, because I was a good shape and so on, and would I come and pay him a visit in New York when I was free. So I found out about Loder, and decided it would be good publicity, and when my contract was up, and I had a bit of time to fill in, I went up east and called on him. He was very decent to me, and asked me to stay a few weeks with him while I was looking around.

"He had a magnificent great house about five miles out of the city, crammed full of pictures and antiques and so on. He was somewhere between thirty-five and forty, I should think, dark and smooth, and very quick and lively in his movements. He talked very well; seemed to have been everywhere and have seen everything and not to have any too good an opinion of anybody. You could sit and listen to him for hours; he'd got anecdotes about everybody, from the Pope to old Phineas E. Groot of the Chicago Ring. The only kind of story I didn't care about hearing from him was the improper sort. Not that I don't enjoy an after-dinner story—no, sir, I wouldn't like you to think I was a prig—but he'd tell it with his eye upon you as if he suspected you of having something to do with it. I've known women do that and I've seen men do it to women and seen the women squirm, but he was the only man that's ever given *me* that feeling. Still, apart from that, Loder was the most fascinating fellow I've ever known. And, as I say, his house surely was beautiful, and he kept a first-class table.

"He liked to have everything of the best. There was his mistress, Maria Morano. I don't think I've ever seen anything to touch her, and when you work for the screen you're apt to have a pretty exacting standard of female beauty. She was one of those big, slow, beautifully moving creatures, very placid, with a slow, wide smile. We don't grow them in the States. She'd come from the South—had been a cabaret dancer he said, and she didn't contradict him. He was very proud of her, and she seemed to be devoted to him in her own fashion. He'd show her off in the studio with nothing on but a fig-leaf or so—stand her up beside one of the figures he was always doing of her, and compare them point by point. There was literally only one half inch of her, it seemed, that wasn't absolutely perfect from the sculptor's point of view—the second toe of her left foot was shorter than the big toe. He used to correct it, of course, in the statues. She'd listen to it all with a good-natured smile, sort of vaguely flattered, you know. Though I think the poor girl sometimes got tired of being gloated over that way. She'd sometimes hunt me out and confide to me that what she had always hoped for was to run a restaurant of her own, with a cabaret show and a great many cooks with white aprons, and lots of polished electric cookers. 'And then I would marry,' she'd say, 'and have four sons and one daughter,' and she told me all the names she had chosen for the family. I thought it was rather pathetic. Loder came in at the end of one of these conversations. He had a sort of a grin on, so I dare say he'd overheard. I don't suppose he attached much importance to it, which shows that he never really understood the girl. I don't think he ever imagined any woman would chuck up the sort of life he'd accustomed her to, and if he was a bit possessive in his manner, at least he never gave her a rival. For all his talk and his ugly statues, she'd got him, and she knew it.

"I stayed there getting on for a month altogether, having a thundering good time. On two occasions Loder had an art spasm, and shut himself up in his studio to work and wouldn't let anybody in for several days on end. He was rather given to that sort of stunt, and when it was over we would have a party, and all Loder's friends and hangers-on would come to have a look at the work of art. He was doing a figure of some nymph or goddess, I fancy, to be cast in silver, and Maria used to go along and sit for him. Apart from those times, he went about everywhere, and we saw all there was to be seen.

"I was fairly annoyed, I admit, when it came to an end. War was declared, and I'd made up my mind to join up when that happened. My heart put me out of the running for trench service, but I counted on getting some sort of a job, with perseverance, so I packed up and went off.

"I wouldn't have believed Loder would have been so genuinely sorry to say good-bye to me. He said over and over again that we'd meet again soon. However, I did get a job with the hospital people, and was sent over to Europe, and it wasn't till 1920 that I saw Loder again.

"He'd written to me before, but I'd had two big pictures to make in '19 and it couldn't be done. However, in '20 I found myself back in New York, doing publicity for *The Passion Streak*, and got a note from Loder begging me to stay with him, and saying he wanted me to sit for him. Well, that was advertisement that he'd pay for himself, you know, so I agreed. I had accepted an engagement to go out with Mystofilms Ltd. in *Jake of Dead Man's Bush*—the dwarfmen picture, you know, taken on the spot among the Australian bushmen. I wired them that I would join them at Sydney the third week in April, and took my bags out to Loder's.

"Loder greeted me very cordially, though I thought he looked older than when I last saw him. He had certainly grown more nervous in his manner. He was—how shall I describe it?—more *intense*—more real, in a way. He brought out his pet cynicisms as if he thoroughly meant them, and more and more with that air of getting at you personally. I used to think his disbelief in everything was a kind of artistic pose, but I began to feel I had done him an injustice. He was really unhappy, I could see that quite well, and soon I discovered the reason. As we were driving out in the car I asked after Maria.

" 'She left me,' " he said.

"Well, now, you know, that really surprised me. Honestly, I hadn't thought the girl had that much initiative. 'Why,' I said, 'has she gone and set up in that restaurant of her own she wanted so much?'

" 'Oh! she talked to you about restaurants, did she?' said Loder. 'I suppose you are one of the men that women tell things to. No. She made a fool of herself. She's gone.'

"I didn't quite know what to say. He was so obviously hurt in his vanity, you know, as well as in his feelings. I muttered the usual things, and added that it must be a great loss to his work as well as in other ways. He said it was.

"I asked him when it had happened and whether he'd finished the nymph he was working on before I left. He said, 'Oh, yes,' he'd finished that and done another—something pretty original, which I should like.

"Well, we got to the house and dined, and Loder told me he was going to Europe shortly, a few days after I left myself, in fact. The nymph stood in the dining-room, in a special niche let into the wall. It really was a beautiful thing, not so showy as most of Loder's work, and a wonderful likeness of Maria. Loder put me opposite it, so that I could see it during dinner, and, really, I could hardly take my eyes off it. He seemed very proud of it, and kept on telling me over and over again how glad he was that I liked it. It struck me that he was falling into a trick of repeating himself.

"We went into the smoking-room after dinner. He'd had it rearranged, and the first thing that caught one's eye was a big settee drawn before the fire. It stood about a couple of feet from the ground, and consisted of a base made like a Roman couch, with cushions and a highish back, all made of oak with a silver inlay, and on top of this, forming the actual seat one sat on, if you follow me, there was a great silver figure of a nude woman, fully life-size, lying with her head back and her arms extended along the sides of the couch. A few big loose cushions made it possible to use the thing as an actual settee, though I must say it never was really comfortable to sit on respectably. As a stage prop for registering dissipation it would have been excellent, but to see Loder sprawling over it by his own fireside gave me a kind of shock. He seemed very much attached to it, though.

" 'I told you,' he said, 'that it was something original.'

"Then I looked more closely at it, and saw that the figure actually was Maria's, though the face was rather sketchily done, if you understand what I mean. I suppose he thought a bolder treatment more suited to a piece of furniture.

"But I did begin to think Loder a trifle degenerate when I saw that couch. And in the fortnight that followed I grew more and more uncomfortable with him. That personal manner of his grew more marked every day, and sometimes, while I was giving him sittings, he would sit there and tell one of the most beastly things, with his eyes fixed on one in the nastiest way, just to see how one would take it. Upon my word, though he certainly did me uncommonly well, I began to feel I'd be more at ease among the bushmen.

"Well, now I come to the odd thing."

Everybody sat up and listened a little more eagerly.

"It was the evening before I had to leave New York," went on Varden. "I was sitting—"

Here somebody opened the door of the brown room, to be greeted by a warning sign from Bayles. The intruder sank obscurely into a large chair and mixed himself a whisky with extreme care not to disturb the speaker.

"I was sitting in the smoking-room," continued Varden, "waiting for Loder to come in. I had the house to myself, for Loder had given the servants leave to go to some show or lecture or other, and he himself was getting his things together for his European trip and had had to keep an appointment with his man of business. I must have been very nearly asleep, because it was dusk when I came to with a start and saw a young man quite close to me.

"He wasn't at all like a housebreaker, and still less like a ghost. He was, I might almost say, exceptionally ordinary-looking. He was dressed in a grey English suit, with a fawn overcoat on his arm, and his soft hat and stick in his hand. He had sleek, pale hair, and one of those rather stupid faces, with a long nose and a monocle. I stared at him, for I knew the front door was locked, but before I could get my wits together he spoke. He had a curious, hesitating, husky voice and a strong English accent. He said, surprisingly:

" 'Are you Mr. Varden?'

" 'You have the advantage of me,' I said.

"He said, 'Please excuse my butting in; I know it looks like bad manners, but you'd better clear out of this place very quickly, don't you know.'

" 'What the hell do you mean?' I said.

"He said, 'I don't mean it in any impertinent way, but you must realize that Loder's never forgiven you, and I'm afraid he means to make you into a hatstand or an electric-light fitting, or something of that sort.'

"My God! I can tell you I felt queer. It was such a quiet voice, and his manners were perfect, yet the words were quite meaningless! I remembered that madmen are supposed to be extra strong, and edged towards the bell—and then it came over me with rather a chill that I was alone in the house.

" 'How did you get in here?' I asked, putting a bold face on it.

" 'I'm afraid I picked the lock,' he said, as casually as though he were apologizing for not having a card about him. 'I couldn't be sure Loder hadn't come back. But I do really think you had better get out as quickly as possible.'

" 'See here,' I said, 'who are you and what the hell are you driving at? What do you mean about Loder never forgiving me? Forgiving me for what?'

" 'Why,' he said, 'about—you *will* pardon me prancing in on your private affairs, won't you— about Maria Morano.'

" '*What* about her, in the devil's name?' I cried. 'What do you know about her, anyway? She went off while I was at the war. What's it to do with me?'

" 'Oh!' said the very odd young man, 'I beg your pardon. Perhaps I have been relying too much on Loder's judgement. Damned foolish; but the possibility of his being mistaken did not occur to me. He fancies you were Maria Morano's lover when you were here last time.'

" 'Maria's lover?' I said. 'Preposterous! She went off with her man, whoever he was. He must know she didn't go with me.'

" 'Maria never left the house,' said the young man, 'and if you don't get out of it this moment, I won't answer for *your* ever leaving, either.'

" 'In God's name,' I cried, exasperated, 'what do you mean?'

"The man turned and threw the blue cushions off the foot of the silver couch.

" 'Have you ever examined the toes of this?' he asked

" 'Not particularly,' I said, more and more astonished. 'Why should I?'

" 'Did you ever know Loder make any figure of her but this with that short toe on the left foot?' he went on.

"Well, I did take a look at it then, and saw it was as he said—the left foot had a short second toe.

" 'So it is,' I said, 'but, after all, why not?'

" 'Why not, indeed?' said the young man. 'Wouldn't you like to see why, of all the figures Loder made of Maria Morano, this is the only one that has the feet of the living woman?'

"He picked up the poker.

" 'Look!' he said.

"With a lot more strength than I should have expected from him, he brought the head of the poker down with a heavy crack on the silver couch. It struck one of the arms of the figure neatly at the elbow-joint, smashing a jagged hole in the silver. He wrenched at the arm and brought it away. It was hollow, and, as I am alive, I tell you there was a long, dry arm-bone inside it!"

Varden paused, and put away a good mouthful of whisky.

"Well?" cried several breathless voices.

"Well," said Varden, "I'm not ashamed to say I went out of that house like an old buck-rabbit that hears the man with the gun. There was a car standing just outside, and the driver opened the door. I tumbled in, and then it came over me that the whole thing might be a trap, and I tumbled out again and ran till I reached the trolley-cars. But I found my bags at the station next day, duly registered for Vancouver.

"When I pulled myself together I did rather wonder what Loder was thinking about my disappearance, but I could no more have gone back into that horrible house than I could have taken poison. I left for Vancouver next morning, and from that day to this I never saw either of those men again. I've still not the faintest idea who the fair man was, or what became of him, but I heard in a roundabout way that Loder was dead—in some kind of an accident, I fancy."

There was a pause. Then:

"It's a damned good story, Mr. Varden," said Armstrong— he was a dabbler in various kinds of handiwork, and was, indeed, chiefly responsible for Mr. Arbuthnot's motion to ban wireless— "but are you suggesting there was a complete skeleton inside that silver casting? Do you mean Loder put it into the core of the mould when the casting was done? It would be awfully difficult and dangerous—the slightest accident would have put him at the mercy of his workmen. And that statue must have been considerably over life-size to allow of the skeleton being well covered."

"Mr. Varden has unintentionally misled you, Armstrong," said a quiet, husky voice suddenly from the shadow behind Varden's chair. "The figure was not silver, but electro-plated on a copper base deposited direct on the body. The lady was Sheffield-plated, in fact. I fancy the soft parts of her must have been digested away with pepsin, or some preparation of the kind, after the process was complete, but I can't be positive about that."

"Hullo, Wimsey," said Armstrong, "was that you came in just now? And why this confident pronouncement?"

The effect of Wimsey's voice on Varden had been extraordinary. He had leapt to his feet, and turned the lamp so as to light up Wimsey's face.

"Good evening, Mr. Varden," said Lord Peter. "I'm delighted to meet you again and to apologize for my unceremonious behaviour on the occasion of our last encounter."

Varden took the proffered hand, but was speechless.

"D'you mean to say, you mad mystery-monger, that *you* were Varden's Great Unknown?" demanded Bayes. "Ah, well," he added rudely, "we might have guessed it from his vivid description."

"Well, since you're here," said Smith-Hartington, the *Morning Yell* man, "I think you ought to come across with the rest of the story."

"Was it just a joke?" asked Judson.

"Of course not," interrupted Pettifer, before Lord Peter had time to reply. "Why should it be? Wimsey's seen enough queer things not to have to waste his time inventing them."

"That's true enough," said Bayes. "Comes of having deductive powers and all that sort of thing, and always sticking one's nose into things that are better not investigated."

"That's all very well, Bayes," said his lordship, "but if I hadn't just mentioned the matter to Mr. Varden that evening, where would he be?"

"Ah, where? That's exactly what we want to know," demanded Smith-Hartington. "Come on, Wimsey, no shirking; we must have the tale."

"And the whole tale," added Pettifer.

"And nothing but the tale," said Armstrong, dexterously whisking away the whisky-bottle and the cigars from under Lord Peter's nose. "Get on with it, old son. Not a smoke do you smoke and not a sup do you sip till Burd Ellen is set free."

"Brute!" said his lordship plaintively. "As a matter of fact," he went on, with a change of tone, "it's not really a story I want to get about. It might land me in a very unpleasant sort of position— manslaughter probably, and murder possibly."

"Gosh!" said Bayes.

"That's all right," said Armstrong, "nobody's going to talk. We can't afford to lose you from the club, you know. Smith-Hartington will have to control his passion for copy, that's all."

Pledges of discretion having been given all round, Lord Peter settled himself back and began his tale.

"The curious case of Eric P. Loder affords one more instance of the strange manner in which some power beyond our puny human wills arranges the affairs of men. Call it Providence—call it Destiny—"

"We'll call it off," said Bayes; "you can leave out that part."

Lord Peter groaned and began again.

"Well, the first thing that made me feel a bit inquisitive about Loder was a casual remark by a man at the Emigration Office in New York, where I happened to go about that silly affair of Mrs. Bilt's. He said, 'What on earth is Eric Loder going to do in Australia? I should have thought Europe was more in his line.'

" 'Australia?' I said, 'you're wandering, dear old thing. He told me the other day he was off to Italy in three weeks' time.'

" 'Italy, nothing,' he said, 'he was all over our place today, asking about how you got to Sydney and what were the necessary formalities, and so on.'

" 'Oh,' I said, 'I suppose he's going by the Pacific route, and calling at Sydney on his way.' But I wondered why he hadn't said so when I'd met him the day before. He had distinctly talked about sailing for Europe and doing Paris before he went on to Rome.

"I felt so darned inquisitive that I went and called on Loder two nights later.

"He seemed quite pleased to see me, and was full of his forthcoming trip. I asked him again about his route, and he told me quite distinctly he was going via Paris.

"Well, that was that, and it wasn't really any of my business, and we chatted about other things. He told me that Mr. Varden was coming to stay with him before he went, and that he hoped to get him to pose for a figure before he left. He said he'd never seen a man so perfectly formed. 'I meant to get him to do it before,' he said, 'but war broke out, and he went and joined the army before I had time to start.'

"He was lolling on that beastly couch of his at the time, and, happening to look round at him, I caught such a nasty sort of glitter in his eye that it gave me quite a turn. He was stroking the figure over the neck and grinning at it.

"None of your efforts in Sheffield-plate, I hope,' said I.

" 'Well,' he said, 'I thought of making a kind of companion to this, *The Sleeping Athlete*, you know, or something of that sort.'

" 'You'd much better cast it,' I said. 'Why did you put the stuff on so thick? It destroys the fine detail.'

"That annoyed him. He never liked to hear any objection made to that work of art.

" 'This was experimental,' he said. 'I mean the next to be a real masterpiece. You'll see.'

"We'd got to about that point when the butler came in to ask should he make up a bed for me, as it was such a bad night. We hadn't noticed the weather particularly, though it had looked a bit threatening when I started from New York. However, we now looked out, and saw that it was coming down in sheets and torrents. It wouldn't have mattered, only that I'd only brought a little open racing car and no overcoat, and certainly the prospect of five miles in that downpour wasn't altogether attractive. Loder urged me to stay, and I said I would.

"I was feeling a bit fagged, so I went to bed right off. Loder said he wanted to do a bit of work in the studio first, and I saw him depart along the corridor.

"You won't allow me to mention Providence, so I'll only say it was a very remarkable thing that I should have woken up at two in the morning to find myself lying in a pool of water. The man had stuck a hot-water bottle into the bed, because it hadn't been used just lately, and the beastly thing had gone and unstoppered itself. I lay awake for ten minutes in the deeps of damp misery before I had sufficient strength of mind to investigate. Then I found it was hopeless—sheets, blankets, mattress, all soaked. I looked at the armchair, and then I had a brilliant idea. I remembered there was a lovely great divan in the studio, with a big skin rug and a pile of cushions. Why not finish the night there? I took the little electric torch which always goes about with me, and started off.

"The studio was empty, so I supposed Loder had finished and trotted off to roost. The divan was there, all right, with a screen drawn partly across it, so I rolled myself up under the rug and prepared to snooze off.

"I was just getting beautifully sleepy again when I heard footsteps, not in the passage, but apparently on the other side of the room. I was surprised, because I didn't know there was any way out in that direction. I lay low, and presently I saw a streak of light appear from the cupboard where Loder kept his tools and things. The streak widened, and Loder emerged, carrying an electric torch. He closed the cupboard door very gently after him, and padded across the studio. He stopped before the easel and uncovered it; I could see him through a crack in the screen. He stood for some minutes gazing at a sketch on the easel, and then gave one of the nastiest gurgly laughs I've ever had the pleasure of hearing. If I'd ever seriously thought of announcing my unauthorized presence, I abandoned all idea of it then. Presently he covered the easel again, and went out by the door at which I had come in.

"I waited till I was sure he had gone, and then got up—uncommonly quietly, I may say. I tiptoed over to the easel to see what the fascinating work of art was. I saw at once it was the design for the figure of *The Sleeping Athlete*, and as I looked at it I felt a sort of horrid conviction stealing over me. It was an idea which seemed to begin in my stomach, and work its way up to the roots of my hair.

"My family say I'm too inquisitive. I can only say that wild horses wouldn't have kept me from investigating that cupboard. With the feeling that something absolutely vile might hop out at me—I was a bit wrought up, and it was a rotten time of night—I put a heroic hand on the door knob.

"To my astonishment, the thing wasn't even locked. It opened at once, to show a range of perfectly innocent and orderly shelves, which couldn't possibly have held Loder.

"My blood was up, you know, by this time, so I hunted round for the spring-lock which I knew must exist, and found it without much difficulty. The back of the cupboard swung noiselessly inwards, and I found myself at the top of a narrow flight of stairs.

"I had the sense to stop and see that the door could be opened from the inside before I went any farther, and I also selected a good stout pestle which I found on the shelves as a weapon in case of accident. Then I closed the door and tripped with elf-like lightness down that jolly old staircase.

"There was another door at the bottom, but it didn't take me long to fathom the secret of that. Feeling frightfully excited, I threw it boldly open, with the pestle ready for action.

"However, the room seemed to be empty. My torch caught the gleam of something liquid, and then I found the wall-switch.

"I saw a biggish square room, fitted up as a workshop. On the right-hand wall was a big switchboard, with a bench beneath it. From the middle of the ceiling hung a great floodlight, illuminating a glass vat, fully seven feet long by about three wide. I turned on the floodlight, and looked down into the vat. It was filled with a dark brown liquid which I recognized as the usual compound of cyanide and copper-sulphate which they use for copper-plating.

"The rods hung over it with their hooks all empty, but there was a packing-case half-opened at one side of the room, and, pulling the covering aside, I could see rows of copper anodes—enough of them to put a plating over a quarter of an inch on a life-size figure. There was a smaller case, still nailed up, which from its weight and appearance I guessed to contain the silver for the rest of the process. There was something else

I was looking for, and I soon found it—a considerable quantity of prepared graphite and a big jar of varnish.

"Of course, there was no evidence, really, of anything being on the cross. There was no reason why Loder shouldn't make a plaster cast and Sheffield-plate it if he had a fancy for that kind of thing. But then I found something that couldn't have come there legitimately.

"On the bench was an oval slab of copper about an inch and a half long—Loder's night's work, I guessed. It was an electrotype of the American Consular seal, the thing they stamp on your passport photograph to keep you from hiking it off and substituting the picture of your friend Mr. Jiggs, who would like to get out of the country because he is so popular with Scotland Yard.

"I sat down on Loder's stool, and worked out that pretty little plot in all its details. I could see it all turned on three things. First of all, I must find out if Varden was purposing to make tracks shortly for Australia, because, if he wasn't, it threw all my beautiful theories out. And, secondly, it would help matters greatly if he happened to have dark hair like Loder's, as he has, you see— near enough, anyway, to fit the description on a passport. I'd only seen him in that Apollo Belvedere thing, with a fair wig on. But I knew if I hung about I should see him presently when he came to stay with Loder. And, thirdly, of course, I had to discover if Loder was likely to have any grounds for a grudge against Varden.

"Well, I figured out I'd stayed down in that room about as long as was healthy. Loder might come back at any moment, and I didn't forget that a vatful of copper sulphate and cyanide of potassium would be a highly handy means of getting rid of a too-inquisitive guest. And I can't say I had any great fancy for figuring as part of Loder's domestic furniture. I've always hated things made in the shape of things—volumes of Dickens that turn out to be a biscuit-tin, and dodges like that; and, though I take no overwhelming interest in my own funeral, I should like it to be in good taste. I went so far as to wipe away any finger-marks I might have left behind me, and then I went back to the studio and rearranged that divan. I didn't feel Loder would care to think I'd been down there.

"There was just one other thing I felt inquisitive about. I tiptoed back through the hall and into the smoking-room. The silver couch glimmered in the light of the torch. I felt I disliked it fifty times more than ever before. However, I pulled myself together and took a careful look at the feet of the figure. I'd heard all about that second toe of Maria Morano's.

"I passed the rest of the night in the armchair after all.

"What with Mrs. Bilt's job and one thing and another, and the inquiries I had to make, I had to put off my interference in Loder's little game till rather late. I found out that Varden had been staying with Loder a few months before the beautiful Maria Morano had vanished. I'm afraid I was rather stupid about that, Mr. Varden. I thought perhaps there *had* been something."

"Don't apologize," said Varden, with a little laugh. "Cinema actors are notoriously immoral."

"Why rub it in?" said Wimsey, a trifle hurt. "I apologize. Anyway, it came to the same thing as far as Loder was concerned. Then there was one bit of evidence I had to get to be absolutely certain. Electro-plating—especially such a ticklish job as the one I had in mind—wasn't a job that could be finished in a night; on the other hand, it seemed necessary that Mr. Varden should be seen alive in New York up to the day he was scheduled to depart. It was also clear that Loder meant to be able to prove that a Mr. Varden had left New York all right, according to plan, and had actually arrived in Sydney. Accordingly, a false Mr. Varden was to depart with Varden's papers and Varden's passport, furnished with a new photograph duly stamped with the Consular stamp, and to disappear quietly at Sydney and be retransformed into Mr. Eric Loder, travelling with a perfectly regular passport of his own. Well, then, in that case, obviously a cablegram would have to be sent off to Mystofilms Ltd., warning them to expect Varden by a later boat than he had arranged. I handed over this part of the job to my man, Bunter, who is uncommonly capable. The devoted fellow shadowed Loder faithfully for getting on for three weeks, and at length, the very day before Mr. Varden was due to depart, the cablegram was sent from an office in Broadway, where by a happy providence (once more) they supply extremely hard pencils."

"By Jove!" cried Varden, "I remember now being told something about a cablegram when I got out, but I never connected it with Loder. I thought it was just some stupidity of the Western Electric people."

"Quite so. Well, as soon as I'd got that, I popped along to Loder's with a picklock in one pocket and an automatic in the other. The good Bunter went with me, and, if I didn't return by a certain time, had orders to telephone for the police. So you see everything was pretty well covered. Bunter was the chauffeur who was waiting for you, Mr. Varden, but you turned suspicions — I don't blame you altogether — so all we could do was to forward your luggage along to the train.

"On the way out we met the Loder servants *en route* for New York in a car, which showed us that we were on the right track, and also that I was going to have a fairly simple job of it.

"You've heard all about my interviews with Mr. Varden. I really don't think I could improve upon his account. When I'd seen him and his traps safely off the premises, I made for the studio. It was empty, so I opened the secret door, and, as I expected, saw a line of light under the workshop door at the far end of the passage."

"So Loder was there all the time?"

"Of course he was. I took my little pop-gun tight in my fist and opened the door very gently. Loder was standing between the tank and the switchboard, very busy indeed — so busy he didn't hear me come in. His hands were black with graphite, a big heap of which was spread on a sheet on the floor, and he was engaged with a long, springy coil of copper wire, running to the output of the transformer. The big packing-case had been opened, and all the hooks were occupied.

" 'Loder!' I said.

"He turned on me with a face like nothing human. 'Wimsey!' he shouted, 'what the hell are you doing here?'

" 'I have come,' I said, 'to tell you that I know how the apple gets into the dumpling.' And I showed him the automatic.

"He gave a great yell and dashed at the switchboard, turning out the light, so that I could not see to aim. I heard him leap at me—and then there came in the darkness a crash and a splash—and a shriek such as I never heard—not in five years of war—and never want to hear again.

"I groped forward for the switchboard. Of course, I turned on everything before I could lay my hand on the light, but I got it at last—a great white glare from the floodlight over the vat.

"He lay there, still twitching faintly. Cyanide, you see, is about the swiftest and painfullest thing out. Before I could move to do anything, I knew he was dead—poisoned and drowned and dead. The coil of wire that had tripped him had gone into the vat with him. Without thinking, I touched it, and got a shock that pretty well staggered me. Then I realized that I must have turned on the current when I was hunting for the light. I looked into the vat again. As he fell, his dying hands had clutched at the wire. The coils were tight round his fingers, and the current was methodically depositing a film of copper all over his hands, which were blackened with the graphite.

"I had just sense enough to realize that Loder was dead, and that it might be a nasty sort of look-out for me if the thing came out, for I'd certainly gone along to threaten him with a pistol.

"I searched about till I found some solder and an iron. Then I went upstairs and called in Bunter, who had done his ten miles in record time. We went into the smoking-room and soldered the arm of that cursed figure into place again, as well as we could, and then we took everything back into the workshop. We cleaned off every finger-print and removed every trace of our presence. We left the light and the switchboard as they were, and returned to New York by an extremely roundabout route. The only thing we brought away with us was the facsimile of the Consular seal, and that we threw into the river.

"Loder was found by the butler next morning. We read in the papers how he had fallen into the vat when engaged on some experiments in electro-plating. The ghastly fact was commented upon that the dead man's hands were thickly coppered over. They couldn't get it off without irreverent violence, so he was buried like that.

"That's all. Please, Armstrong, may I have my whisky-and-soda now?"

"What happened to the couch?" inquired Smith-Hartington presently.

"I bought it at the sale of Loder's things," said Wimsey, "and got hold of a dear old Catholic priest I knew, to whom I told the whole story under strict vow of secrecy. He was a very sensible and feeling old bird; so one moonlight night Bunter and I carried the thing out in the car to his own little church, some miles out of the city, and gave it Christian burial in a corner of the graveyard. It seemed the best thing to do."

THE ENTERTAINING EPISODE OF
THE ARTICLE IN QUESTION

The unprofessional detective career of Lord Peter Wimsey was regulated (though the word has no particular propriety in this connexion) by a persistent and undignified inquisitiveness. The habit of asking silly questions—natural, though irritating, in the immature male—remained with him long after his immaculate man, Bunter, had become attached to his service to shave the bristles from his chin and see to the due purchase and housing of Napoleon brandies and Villar y Villar cigars. At the age of thirty-two his sister Mary christened him Elephant's Child. It was his idiotic inquiries (before his brother, the Duke of Denver, who grew scarlet with mortification) as to what the Woolsack was really stuffed with that led the then Lord Chancellor idly to investigate the article in question, and to discover, tucked deep within its recesses, that famous diamond necklace of the Marchioness of Writtle which had disappeared on the day Parliament was opened and been safely secreted by one of the cleaners. It was by a continual and personal badgering of the

Chief Engineer at 2LO on the question of "Why is Oscillation and How is it Done?" that his lordship incidentally unmasked the great Ploffsky gang of Anarchist conspirators, who were accustomed to converse in code by a methodical system of howls, superimposed (to the great annoyance of listeners in British and European stations) upon the London wavelength and duly relayed by 5XX over a radius of some five or six hundred miles. He annoyed persons of more leisure than decorum by suddenly taking into his head to descend to the Underground by way of the stairs, though the only exciting things he ever actually found there were the bloodstained boots of the Sloane Square murderer; on the other hand, when the drains were taken up at Glegg's Folly, it was by hanging about and hindering the plumbers at their job that he accidentally made the discovery which hanged that detestable poisoner, William Girdlestone Chitty.

Accordingly, it was with no surprise at all that the reliable Bunter, one April morning, received the announcement of an abrupt change of plan.

They had arrived at the Gare Saint-Lazare in good time to register the luggage. Their three months' trip to Italy had been purely for enjoyment, and had been followed by a pleasant fortnight in Paris. They were now intending to pay a short visit to the Duc de Sainte-Croix in Rouen on their way back to England. Lord Peter paced the Salle des Pas Perdus for some time, buying an illustrated paper or two and eyeing the crowd. He bent an appreciative eye on a slim, shingled creature with the face of a Paris *gamin*, but was forced to admit to himself that her ankles were a trifle on the thick side; he assisted an elderly lady who was explaining to the bookstall clerk that she wanted a map of Paris and not a *carte postale*, consumed a quick cognac at one of the little green tables at the far end, and then decided he had better go down and see how Bunter was getting on.

In half an hour Bunter and his porter had worked themselves up to the second place in the enormous queue—for, as usual, one of the weighing-machines was out of order. In front of them stood an agitated little group—the young woman Lord Peter had noticed in the Salle des Pas Perdus, a sallow-faced man of about thirty, their porter, and the registration official, who was peering eagerly through his little *guichet*.

"Mais je te répète que je ne les ai pas," said the sallow man heatedly. *"Voyons, voyons. C'est bien toi qui les as pris, n'est-ce pas? Eh bien, alors, comment veux-tu que je les aie, moi?"*

"Mais non, mais non, je te les ai bien donnés là-haut, avant d'aller chercher les journaux."

"Je t'assure que non. Enfin, c'est évident! J'ai cherché partout, que diable! Tu ne m'as rien donné, du tout, du tout."

"Mais puisque je t'ai dit d'aller faire enregistrer les bagages! Ne faut-il pas que je t'aie bien remis les billets? Me prends-tu pour un imbécile? Va! On n'est pas dépourvu de sens! Mais regarde l'heure! Le train part à 11 h. 20 m. Cherche un peu, au moins."

"Mais puisque j'ai cherché partout—le gilet, rien! Le jacquet rien, rien! Le pardessus—rien! rien! rien! C'est toi—"

Here the porter, urged by the frantic cries and stamping of the queue, and the repeated insults of Lord Peter's porter, flung himself into the discussion.

"P't-être qu' m'sieur a bouté les billets dans son pantalon," he suggested.

"Triple idiot!" snapped the traveller, *"je vous le demande—est-ce qu'on a jamais entendu parler de mettre des billets dans son pantalon? Jamais—"*

The French porter is a Republican, and, moreover, extremely ill-paid. The large tolerance of his English colleague is not for him.

"Ah!" said he, dropping two heavy bags and looking round for moral support. *"Vous dites? En voilà du joli! Allons, mon p'tit, ce n'est pas parce qu'on porte un faux-col qu'on a le droit d'insulter les gens."*

The discussion might have become a full-blown row, had not the young man suddenly discovered the missing tickets—incidentally, they were in his trousers-pocket after all—and continued the registration of his luggage, to the undisguised satisfaction of the crowd.

"Bunter," said his lordship, who had turned his back on the group and was lighting a cigarette, "I am going to change the tickets. We shall go straight on to London. Have you got that snapshot affair of yours with you?"

"Yes, my lord."

"The one you can work from your pocket without anyone noticing?"

"Yes, my lord."

"Get me a picture of those two."

"Yes, my lord."

"I will see to the luggage. Wire to the Duc that I am unexpectedly called home."

"Very good, my lord."

Lord Peter did not allude to the matter again till Bunter was putting his trousers in the press in their cabin on board the *Normania*. Beyond ascertaining that the young man and woman who had aroused his curiosity were on the boat as second-class passengers, he had sedulously avoided contact with them.

"Did you get that photograph?"

"I hope so, my lord. As your lordship knows, the aim from the breast-pocket tends to be unreliable. I have made three attempts, and trust that one at least may prove to be not unsuccessful."

"How soon can you develop them?"

"At once, if your lordship pleases. I have all the materials in my suitcase."

"What fun!" said Lord Peter, eagerly tying himself into a pair of mauve silk pyjamas. "May I hold the bottles and things?"

Mr. Bunter poured three ounces of water into an eight-ounce measure, and handed his master a glass rod and a minute packet.

"If your lordship would be so good as to stir the contents of the white packet slowly into the water," he said, bolting the door, "and, when dissolved, add the contents of the blue packet."

"Just like a Seidlitz powder," said his lordship happily. "Does it fizz?"

"Not much, my lord," replied the expert, shaking a quantity of hypo crystals into the hand-basin.

"That's a pity," said Lord Peter. "I say, Bunter, it's no end of a bore to dissolve."

"Yes, my lord," returned Bunter sedately. "I have always found that part of the process exceptionally tedious, my lord."

Lord Peter jabbed viciously with the glass rod.

"Just you wait," he said, in a vindictive tone, "till we get to Waterloo."

Three days later Lord Peter Wimsey sat in his book-lined sitting-room at 110A Piccadilly. The tall bunches of daffodils on the table smiled in the spring sunshine, and nodded to the breeze which danced in from the open window. The door opened, and his lordship glanced up from a handsome edition of the *Contes de la Fontaine*, whose handsome hand-coloured Fragonard plates he was examining with the aid of a lens.

"Morning, Bunter. Anything doing?"

"I have ascertained, my lord, that the young person in question has entered the service of the elder Duchess of Medway. Her name is Célestine Berger."

"You are less accurate than usual, Bunter. Nobody off the stage is called Célestine. You should say 'under the name of Célestine Berger.' And the man?"

"He is domiciled at this address in Guilford Street, Bloomsbury, my lord."

"Excellent, My Bunter. Now give me *Who's Who*. Was it a very tiresome job?"

"Not exceptionally so, my lord."

"One of these days I suppose I shall give you something to do which you *will* jib at," said his lordship, "and you will leave me and I shall cut my throat. Thanks. Run away and play. I shall lunch at the club."

The book which Bunter had handed his employer indeed

bore the words *Who's Who* engrossed upon its cover, but it was to be found in no public library and in no bookseller's shop. It was a bulky manuscript, closely filled, in part with the small print-like handwriting of Mr. Bunter, in part with Lord Peter's neat and altogether illegible hand. It contained biographies of the most unexpected people, and the most unexpected facts about the most obvious people. Lord Peter turned to a very long entry under the name of the Dowager Duchess of Medway. It appeared to make satisfactory reading, for after a time he smiled, closed the book, and went to the telephone.

"Yes—this is the Duchess of Medway. Who is it?"

The deep, harsh old voice pleased Lord Peter. He could see the imperious face and upright figure of what had been the most famous beauty in the London of the sixties.

"It's Peter Wimsey, duchess."

"Indeed, and how do you do, young man? Back from your Continental jaunting?"

"Just home—and longing to lay my devotion at the feet of the most fascinating lady in England."

"God bless my soul, child, what do you want?" demanded the duchess. "Boys like you don't flatter an old woman for nothing."

"I want to tell you my sins, duchess."

"You should have lived in the great days," said the voice appreciatively. "Your talents are wasted on the young fry."

"That is why I want to talk to you, duchess."

"Well, my dear, if you've committed any sins worth hearing I shall enjoy your visit."

"You are as exquisite in kindness as in charm. I am coming this afternoon."

"I will be at home to you and to no one else. There."

"Dear lady, I kiss your hands," said Lord Peter, and he heard a deep chuckle as the duchess rang off.

"You may say what you like, duchess," said Lord Peter from his reverential position on the fender-stool, "but you are the youngest grandmother in London, not excepting my own mother."

"Dear Honoria is the merest child," said the duchess. "I have twenty years more experience of life, and have arrived at the age when we boast of them. I have every intention of being a great-grandmother before I die. Sylvia is being married in a fortnight's time, to that stupid son of Attenbury's."

"Abcock?"

"Yes. He keeps the worst hunters I ever saw, and doesn't know still champagne from sauterne. But Sylvia is stupid, too, poor child, so I dare say they will get on charmingly. In my day one had to have either brains or beauty to get on — preferably both. Nowadays nothing seems to be required but a total lack of figure. But all the sense went out of society with the House of Lords' veto. I except you, Peter. You have talents. It is a pity you do not employ them in politics."

"Dear lady, God forbid."

"Perhaps you are right, as things are. There were giants in my day. Dear Dizzy. I remember so well, when his wife died, how hard we all tried to get him — Medway had died the year before — but he was wrapped up in that stupid Bradford woman, who had never even read a line of one of his books, and couldn't have understood 'em if she had. And now we have Abcock standing for Midhurst, and married to Sylvia!"

"You haven't invited me to the wedding, duchess dear. I'm so hurt," sighed his lordship.

"Bless you, child, *I* didn't send out the invitations, but I suppose your brother and that tiresome wife of his will be there. You must come, of course, if you want to. I had no idea you had a passion for weddings."

"Hadn't you?" said Peter. "I have a passion for this one. I want to see Lady Sylvia wearing white satin and the family lace and diamonds, and to sentimentalize over the days when my fox-terrier bit the stuffing out of her doll."

"Very well, my dear, you shall. Come early and give me your support. As for the diamonds, if it weren't a family tradition, Sylvia shouldn't wear them. She has the impudence to complain of them."

"I thought they were some of the finest in existence."

"So they are. But she says the settings are ugly and old-fashioned, and she doesn't like diamonds, and they won't go with her dress. Such nonsense. Whoever heard of a girl not liking diamonds? She wants to be something romantic and moonshiny in pearls. I have no patience with her."

"I'll promise to admire them," said Peter — "use the privi-lege of early acquaintance and tell her she's an ass and so on. I'd love to have a view of them. When do they come out of cold storage?"

"Mr. Whitehead will bring them up from the Bank the night before," said the duchess, "and they'll go into the safe in my room. Come round at twelve o'clock and you shall have a private view of them."

"That would be delightful. Mind they don't disappear in the night, won't you?"

"Oh, my dear, the house is going to be over-run with policemen. Such a nuisance. I suppose it can't be helped."

"Oh, I think it's a good thing," said Peter. "I have rather an unwholesome weakness for policemen."

On the morning of the wedding-day, Lord Peter emerged from Bunter's hands a marvel of sleek brilliance. His prim-rose-coloured hair was so exquisite a work of art that to eclipse it with his glossy hat was like shutting up the sun in a shrine of polished jet; his spats, light trousers, and exquisitely polished shoes formed a tone-symphony in monochrome. It was only by the most impassioned pleading that he persuaded his tyrant to allow him to place two small photographs and a thin, foreign letter in his breast-pocket. Mr. Bunter, likewise immaculately attired, stepped into the taxi after him. At noon precisely they were deposited beneath the striped awning which adorned the door of the Duchess of Medway's house in Park Lane. Bunter promptly disappeared in the direction of the back entrance, while his lordship mounted the steps and asked to see the dowager.

The majority of the guests had not yet arrived, but the house was full of agitated people, flitting hither and thither, with flowers and prayer-books, while a clatter of dishes and cutlery from the dining-room proclaimed the laying of a sumptuous breakfast. Lord Peter was shown into the morning-room while the footman went to announce him, and here he found a very close friend and devoted colleague, Detective-Inspector Parker, mounting guard in plain clothes over a costly collection of white elephants. Lord Peter greeted him with an affectionate hand-grip.

"All serene so far?" he inquired.

"Perfectly O.K."

"You got my note?"

"Sure thing. I've got three of our men shadowing your friend in Guilford Street. The girl is very much in evidence here. Does the old lady's wig and that sort of thing. Bit of a coming-on disposition, isn't she?"

"You surprise me," said Lord Peter. "No"—as his friend grinned sardonically—"you really do. Not seriously? That would throw all my calculations out."

"Oh, no! Saucy with her eyes and her tongue, that's all."

"Do her job well?"

"I've heard no complaints What put you on to this?"

"Pure accident. Of course I may be quite mistaken."

"Did you receive any information from Paris?"

"I wish you wouldn't use that phrase," said Lord Peter peevishly. "It's so of the Yard—yardy. One of these days it'll give you away."

"Sorry," said Parker. "Second nature, I suppose."

"Those are the things to beware of," returned his lordship, with an earnestness that seemed a little out of place. "One can keep guard on everything but just those second-nature tricks." He moved across to the window, which overlooked the tradesmen's entrance. "Hullo!" he said, "here's our bird."

Parker joined him, and saw the neat, shingled head of the

French girl from the Gare Saint-Lazare, topped by a neat black bandeau and bow. A man with a basket full of white narcissi had rung the bell, and appeared to be trying to make a sale. Parker gently opened the window, and they heard Célestine say with a marked French accent, "No, nossing today, sank you." The man insisted in the monotonous whine of his type, thrusting a big bunch of the white flowers upon her, but she pushed them back into the basket with an angry exclamation and flirted away, tossing her head and slapping the door smartly to. The man moved off muttering. As he did so a thin, unhealthy-looking lounger in a check cap detached himself from a lamp-post opposite and mouched along the street after him, at the same time casting a glance up at the window. Mr. Parker looked at Lord Peter, nodded, and made a slight sign with his hand. At once the man in the check cap removed his cigarette from his mouth, extinguished it, and, tucking the stub behind his ear, moved off without a second glance.

"Very interesting," said Lord Peter, when both were out of sight. "Hark!"

There was a sound of running feet overhead — a cry — and a general commotion. The two men dashed to the door as the bride, rushing frantically downstairs with her bevy of brides-maids after her, proclaimed in a hysterical shriek: "The diamonds! They're stolen! They're gone!"

Instantly the house was in an uproar. The servants and the caterer's men crowded into the hall; the bride's father burst out from his room in a magnificent white waistcoat and no coat; the Duchess of Medway descended upon Mr. Parker, demanding that something should be done; while the butler, who never to the day of his death got over the disgrace, ran out of the pantry with a corkscrew in one hand and a priceless bottle of crusted port in the other, which he shook with all the vehemence of a town-crier ringing a bell. The only dignified entry was made by the dowager duchess, who came down like a ship in sail, dragging Célestine with her, and admonishing her not to be so silly.

"Be quiet, girl," said the dowager. "Anyone would think you were going to be murdered."

"Allow me, your grace," said Mr. Bunter, appearing suddenly from nowhere in his usual unperturbed manner, and taking the agitated Célestine firmly by the arm. "Young woman, calm yourself."

"But what is to be *done*?" cried the bride's mother. "How did it happen?"

It was at this moment that Detective-Inspector Parker took the floor. It was the most impressive and dramatic moment in his whole career. His magnificent calm rebuked the clamorous nobility surrounding him.

"Your grace," he said, "there is no cause for alarm. Our measures have been taken. We have the criminals and the gems, thanks to Lord Peter Wimsey, from whom we received inf—"

"Charles!" said Lord Peter in an awful voice.

"Warning of the attempt. One of our men is just bringing in the male criminal at the front door, taken red-handed with your grace's diamonds in his possession." (All gazed round, and perceived indeed the check-capped lounger and a uniformed constable entering with the flower-seller between them.) "The female criminal, who picked the lock of your grace's safe, is—here! No, you don't," he added, as Célestine, amid a torrent of apache language which nobody, fortunately, had French enough to understand, attempted to whip out a revolver from the bosom of her demure black dress. "Célestine Berger," he continued, pocketing the weapon, "I arrest you in the name of the law, and I warn you that anything you say will be taken down and used as evidence against you."

"Heaven help us," said Lord Peter; "the roof would fly off the court. And you've got the name wrong, Charles. Ladies and gentlemen, allow me to introduce you to Jacques Lerouge, known as Sans-culotte—the youngest and cleverest thief, safe-breaker, and female impersonator that ever occupied a dossier in the Palais de Justice."

There was a gasp. Jacques Sans-culotte gave vent to a low oath and cocked a *gamin* grimace at Peter.

"*C'est parfait,*" said he; "*toutes mes félicitations, milord,* what you call a fair cop, *hein*? And now I know him," he added, grinning at Bunter, "the so-patient Englishman who stand behind us in the queue at Saint-Lazare. But tell me, please, how you know me, that I may correct it *next time.*"

"I have mentioned to you before, Charles," said Lord Peter, "the unwisdom of falling into habits of speech. They give you away. Now, in France, every male child is brought up to use masculine adjectives about himself. He says: *Que je suis beau!* But a little girl has it rammed home to her that she is female; she must say: *Que je suis belle!* It must make it beastly hard to be a female impersonator. When I am at a station and I hear an excited young woman say to her companion, "*Me prends-tu pour un imbécile*"—the masculine article arouses curiosity. And that's that!" he concluded briskly. "The rest was merely a matter of getting Bunter to take a photograph and communicating with our friends of the Sûreté and Scotland Yard."

Jacques Sans-culotte bowed again.

"Once more I congratulate milord. He is the only Englishman I have ever met who is capable of appreciating our beautiful language. I will pay great attention in future to the article in question."

With an awful look, the Dowager Duchess of Medway advanced upon Lord Peter.

"Peter," she said, "do you mean to say you *knew* about this, and that for the last three weeks you have allowed me to be dressed and undressed and put to bed by a *young man?*"

His lordship had the grace to blush.

"Duchess," he said humbly, "on my honour I didn't know absolutely for certain till this morning. And the police were so anxious to have these people caught red-handed. What can I do to show my penitence? Shall I cut the privileged beast in pieces?"

The grim old mouth relaxed a little.

"After all," said the dowager duchess, with the delightful consciousness that she was going to shock her daughter-in-law, "there are very few women of my age who could make the same boast. It seems that we die as we have lived, my dear."

For indeed the Dowager Duchess of Medway had been notable in her day.

THE FASCINATING PROBLEM OF
UNCLE MELEAGER'S WILL

You look a little worried, Bunter," said his lordship kindly to his manservant. "Is there anything I can do?"

The valet's face brightened as he released his employer's grey trousers from the press.

"Perhaps your lordship could be so good as to think," he said hopefully, "of a word in seven letters with S in the middle, meaning two."

"Also," suggested Lord Peter thoughtlessly.

"I beg your lordship's pardon. T-w-o. And seven letters."

"Nonsense!" said Lord Peter. "How about that bath?"

"It should be just about ready, my lord."

Lord Peter Wimsey swung his mauve silk legs lightly over the edge of the bed and stretched appreciatively. It was a beautiful June that year. Through the open door he saw the delicate coils of steam wreathing across a shaft of yellow sunlight. Every step he took into the bathroom was a conscious act of enjoyment. In a husky light tenor he carolled a few bars of *"Maman, dites-moi."* Then a thought struck him, and he turned back.

"Bunter!"

"My lord?"

"No bacon this morning. Quite the wrong smell."

"I was thinking of buttered eggs, my lord."

"Excellent. Like primroses. The Beaconsfield touch," said his lordship approvingly.

His song died into a rapturous crooning as he settled into the verbena-scented water. His eyes roamed vaguely over the pale blue-and-white tiles of the bathroom walls.

Mr. Bunter had retired to the kitchen to put the coffee on the stove when the bell rang. Surprised, he hastened back to the bedroom. It was empty. With increased surprise, he realized that it must have been the bathroom bell. The words "heart-attack" formed swiftly in his mind, to be displaced by the still more alarming thought, "No soap." He opened the door almost nervously.

"Did you ring, my lord?" he demanded of Lord Peter's head, alone visible.

"Yes," said his lordship abruptly. "Ambsace."

"I beg your lordship's pardon?"

"Ambsace. Word of seven letters. Meaning two. With S in the middle. Two aces. Ambsace."

Bunter's expression became beautified.

"Undoubtedly correct," he said, pulling a small sheet of paper from his pocket, and entering the word upon it in pencil. "I am extremely obliged to your lordship. In that case the 'indifferent cook in six letters ending with *red*' must be Alfred."

Lord Peter waved a dismissive hand.

On re-entering his bedroom, Lord Peter was astonished to see his sister Mary seated in his own particular chair and consuming his buttered eggs. He greeted her with a friendly acerbity, demanding why she should look him up at that unearthly hour.

"I'm riding with Freddy Arbuthnot," said her ladyship, "as

you might see by my legs, if you were really as big a Sherlock as you make out."

"Riding," replied her brother, "I had already deduced, though I admit that Freddy's name was not writ large, to my before-breakfast eye, upon the knees of your breeches. But why this visit?"

"Well, because you were on the way," said Lady Mary, "and I'm booked up all day and I want you to come and dine at the Soviet Club with me tonight."

"Good God, Mary, why? You know I hate the place. Cooking's beastly, the men don't shave, and the conversation gets my goat. Besides, last time I went there, your friend Goyles plugged me in the shoulder. I thought you'd chucked the Soviet Club."

"It isn't me. It's Hannah Marryat."

"What, the intense young woman with the badly bobbed hair and the brogues?"

"Well, she's never been able to afford a good hairdresser. That's just what I want your help about."

"My dear child, I can't cut her hair for her. Bunter might. He can do most things."

"Silly. No. But she's got—that is, she used to have—an uncle, the very rich, curmudgeony sort, you know, who never gave any-one a penny. Well, he's dead, and they can't find his will."

"Perhaps he didn't make one."

"Oh, yes, he did. He wrote and told her so. But the nasty old thing hid it, and it can't be found."

"Is the will in her favour?"

"Yes."

"Who's the next-of-kin?"

"She and her mother are the only members of the family left."

"Well, then, she's only got to sit tight and she'll get the goods."

"No—because the horrid old man left two wills, and, if she can't find the latest one, they'll prove the first one. He ex-plained that to her carefully."

"Oh, I see. H'm. By the way, I thought the young woman was a Socialist."

"Oh, she is. Terrifically so. One really can't help admiring her. She has done some wonderful work—"

"Yes, I dare say. But in that case I don't see why she need be so keen on getting uncle's dollars."

Mary began to chuckle.

"Ah! But that's where Uncle Meleager—"

"Uncle *what?*"

"Meleager. That's his name. Meleager Finch."

"Oh!"

"Yes—well, that's where he's been so clever. Unless she finds the new will, the old will comes into force and hands over every penny of the money to the funds of the Primrose League."

Lord Peter gave a little yelp of joy.

"Good for Uncle Meleager! But, look here, Polly, I'm a Tory, if anything. I'm certainly not a Red. Why should I help to snatch the good gold from the Primrose Leaguers and hand it over to the Third International? Uncle Meleager's a sport. I take to Uncle Meleager."

"Oh, but Peter, I really don't think she'll do that with it. Not at present, anyway. They're awfully poor, and her mother ought to have some frightfully difficult operation or something, and go and live abroad, so it really is ever so important they should get the money. And perhaps Hannah wouldn't be quite so Red if she'd ever had a bean of her own. Besides, you could make it a condition of helping her that she should go and get properly shingled at Bresil's."

"You are a very cynically-minded person," said his lordship. "However, it would be fun to have a go at Uncle M. Was he obliging enough to give any clues for finding the will?"

"He wrote a funny sort of letter, which we can't make head or tail of. Come to the club tonight and she'll show it to you."

"Right-ho! Seven o'clock do? And we could go on and see

a show afterwards. Do you mind clearing out now? I'm going to get dressed."

Amid a deafening babble of voices in a low-pitched cellar, the Soviet Club meets and dines. Ethics and sociology, the latest vortices of the Whirligig school of verse, combine with the smoke of countless cigarettes to produce an inspissated atmosphere, through which flat, angular mural paintings dimly lower upon the revellers. There is painfully little room for the elbows, or indeed for any part of one's body. Lord Peter—his feet curled under his chair to avoid the stray kicks of the heavy brogues opposite him—was acutely conscious of an unbecoming attitude and an overheated feeling about the head. He found it difficult to get any response from Hannah Marryat. Under her heavy, ill-cut fringe her dark eyes gloomed somberly at him. At the same time he received a strong impression of something enormously vital. He had a sudden fancy that if she were set free from self-defensiveness and the importance of being earnest, she would exhibit unexpected powers of enjoyment. He was interested, but oppressed. Mary, to his great relief, suggested that they should have their coffee upstairs.

They found a quiet corner with comfortable chairs.

"Well, now," said Mary encouragingly.

"Of course you understand," said Miss Marryat mournfully, "that if it were not for the monstrous injustice of Uncle Meleager's other will, and mother being so ill, I shouldn't take any steps. But when there is £250,000, and the prospect of doing real good with it—"

"Naturally," said Lord Peter, "it isn't the money you care about, as the dear old bromide says, it's the principle of the thing. Right you are! Now supposin' we have a look at Uncle Meleager's letter."

Miss Marryat rummaged in a very large handbag and passed the paper over.

This was Uncle Meleager's letter, dated from Siena twelve months previously.

My Dear Hannah, When I die—which I propose to do at my convenience and not at that of my
family—you will at last discover my monetary worth.
It is, of course, considerably less than you had
hoped, and quite fails, I assure you, adequately to
represent my actual worth in the eyes of the discern-
ing. I made my will yesterday, leaving the entire sum,
such as it is, to the Primrose League—a body quite
as fatuous as any other in our preposterous state, but
which has the advantage of being peculiarly obnox-
ious to yourself. This will will be found in the safe in
the library.

I am not, however, unmindful of the fact that your
mother is my sister, and you and she my only surviving relatives. I shall accordingly amuse myself by
drawing up today a second will, superseding the other
and leaving the money to you.

I have always held that woman is a frivolous animal. A woman who pretends to be serious is wasting
her time and spoiling her appearance. I consider that
you have wasted your time to a really shocking extent.
Accordingly, I intend to conceal this will, and that in
such a manner that you will certainly never find it unless by the exercise of a sustained frivolity.

I hope you will contrive to be frivolous enough to
become the heiress of your affectionate

                              Uncle Meleager

"Couldn't we use that letter as proof of the testator's intention, and fight the will?" asked Mary anxiously.

" 'Fraid not," said Lord Peter. "You see, there's no evidence here that the will was ever actually drawn up. Though
I suppose we could find the witnesses."

"We've tried," said Miss Marryat, "but, as you see, Uncle
Meleager was travelling abroad at the time, and he probably
got some obscure people in some obscure Italian town to witness it for him. We advertised, but got no answer."

"H'm. Uncle Meleager doesn't seem to have left things to chance. And, anyhow, wills are queer things, and so are the probate and divorce wallahs. Obviously the thing to do is to find the other will. Did the clues he speaks of turn up among his papers?"

"We hunted through everything. And, of course, we had the whole house searched from top to bottom for the will. But it was quite useless."

"You've not destroyed anything, of course. Who were the executors of the Primrose League will?"

"Mother and Mr. Sands, Uncle Meleager's solicitor. The will left mother a silver teapot for her trouble."

"I like Uncle Meleager more and more. Anyhow, he did the sporting thing. I'm beginnin' to enjoy this case like anything. Where did Uncle Meleager hang out?"

"It's an old house down at Dorking. It's rather quaint. Somebody had a fancy to build a little Roman villa sort of thing there, with a veranda behind, with columns and a pond in the front hall, and statues. It's very decent there just now, though it's awfully cold in the winter, with all those stone floors and stone stairs and the sky light over the hall! Mother said perhaps you would be very kind and come down and have a look at it."

"I'd simply love to. Can we start tomorrow? I promise you we'll be frivolous enough to please even Uncle Meleager, if you'll do your bit, Miss Marryat. Won't we, Mary?"

"Rather! And, I say, hadn't we better be moving if we're going to the Pallambra?"

"I never go to music halls," said Miss Marryat ungraciously.

"Oh, but you must come tonight," said his lordship persuasively. "It's so frivolous. Just think how it would please Uncle Meleager."

Accordingly, the next day found the party, including the indispensable Mr. Bunter, assembled at Uncle Meleager's house. Pending the settlement of the will question, there had seemed every reason why Mr. Finch's executrix and next-of-kin should live in the house, thus providing every facility for what Lord Peter called the "Treasures hunt." After being introduced to Mrs. Marryat, who was an invalid and remained in her room, Lady Mary and her brother were shown over the house by Miss Marryat, who explained to them how carefully the search had been conducted. Every paper had been examined, every book in the library scrutinized page by page, the walls and chimneys tapped for hiding-places, the boards taken up, and so forth, but with no result.

"Y'know," said his lordship, "I'm sure you've been going the wrong way to work. My idea is, old Uncle Meleager was a man of his word. If he said frivolous, he meant really frivolous. Something beastly silly. I wonder what it was."

He was still wondering when he went up to dress. Bunter was putting studs in his shirt. Lord Peter gazed thoughtfully at him, and then inquired:

"Are any of Mr. Finch's old staff still here?"

"Yes, my lord. The cook and the housekeeper. Wonderful old gentleman they say he was, too. Eighty-three, but as up to date as you please. Had his wireless in his bedroom, and enjoyed the Savoy bands every night of his life. Followed his politics, and was always ready with the details of the latest big law-cases. If a young lady came to see him, he'd like to see she had her hair shingled and the latest style in fashions. They say he took up crosswords as soon as they came in, and was remarkably quick at solving them, my lord, and inventing them. Took a ten-pound prize in the *Daily Yell* for one, and was wonderfully pleased to get it, they say, my lord, rich as he was."

"Indeed."

"Yes, my lord. He was a great man for acrostics before that, I understood them to say, but, when crosswords came in, he threw away his acrostics and said he liked the new game better. Wonderfully adaptable, if I may say so, he seems to have been for an old gentleman."

"Was he, by Jove?" said his lordship absently, and then, with sudden energy:

"Bunter, I'd like to double your salary, but I suppose you'd take it as an insult."

The conversation bore fruit at dinner.

"What," inquired his lordship, "happened to Uncle Meleager's crosswords?"

"Crosswords?" said Hannah Marryat, knitting her heavy brows. "Oh, those puzzle things! Poor old man, he went mad over them. He had every newspaper sent him, and in his last illness he'd be trying to fill the wretched things in. It was worse than his acrostics and his jig-saw puzzles. Poor old creature, he must have been senile, I'm afraid. Of course, we looked through them, but there wasn't anything there. We put them all in the attic."

"The attic for me," said Lord Peter.

"And for me," said Mary. "I don't believe there was anything senile about Uncle Meleager."

The evening was warm, and they had dined in the little viridarium at the back of the house, with its tall vases and hanging baskets of flowers and little marble statues.

"Is there an attic here?" said Peter. "It seems such a—well, such an un-Attic thing to have in a house like this."

"It's just a horrid poky little hole over the porch," said Miss Marryat, rising and leading the way. "Don't tumble into the pond, will you? It's a great nuisance having it there, especially at night. I always tell them to leave a light on."

Lord Peter glanced into the miniature impluvium, with its tiling of red, white, and black marble.

"That's not a very classic design," he observed.

"No. Uncle Meleager used to complain about it and say he must have it altered. There was a proper one once, I believe, but it got damaged, and the man before Uncle Meleager had it replaced by some local idiot. He built three bay windows out of the dining-room at the same time, which made it very much lighter and pleasanter, of course, but it looks awful. Now, this tiling is all right; uncle put that in himself."

She pointed to a mosaic dog at the threshold with the motto, "Cave canem," and Lord Peter recognized it as a copy of a Pompeian original.

A narrow stair brought them to the "attic," where the Wimseys flung themselves with enthusiasm upon a huge heap of dusty old newspapers and manuscripts. The latter seemed the likelier field, so they started with them. They consisted of a quantity of crosswords in manuscript—presumably the children of Uncle Meleager's own brain. The square, the list of definitions, and the solution were in every case neatly pinned together. Some (early efforts, no doubt) were childishly simple, but others were difficult, with allusive or punning clues; some of the ordinary newspaper type, others in the from of rhymed distichs. They scrutinized the solutions closely, and searched the definitions for acrostics or hidden words, unsuccessfully for a long time.

"This one's a funny one," said Mary, "nothing seems to fit. Oh! it's two pinned together. No, it isn't—yes, it is—it's only been pinned up wrong. Peter, have you seen the puzzle belonging to these clues anywhere?"

"What one's that?"

"Well, it's numbered rather funnily, with Roman and Arabic numerals, and it starts off with a thing that hasn't got any numbers at all:

> " 'Truth, poor girl, was nobody's daughter;
>   She took off her clothes and jumped into the water.' "

"Frivolous old wretch!" said Miss Marryat.

"Friv—here, gimme that!" cried Lord Peter. "Look here, I say, Miss Marryat, you oughtn't to have overlooked this."

"I thought it just belonged to that other square."

"Not it. It's different. I believe it's our thing. Listen:

> " 'Your expectation to be rich
>   Here will reach its highest pitch.'

That's one for you, Miss Marryat. Mary, hunt about. We *must* find the square that belongs to this."

But, though they turned everything upside-down, they could find no square with Roman and Arabic numerals.

"Hang it all!" said Peter, "it must be made to fit one of these others. Look! I know what he's done. He's just taken a fifteen-letter square, and numbered it with Roman figures one way and Arabic the other. I bet it fits into that one it was pinned up with."

But the one it was pinned up with turned out to have only thirteen squares.

"Dash it all," said his lordship, "we'll have to carry the whole lot down, and work away at it till we find the one it *does* fit."

He snatched up a great bundle of newspapers, and led the way out. The others followed, each with an armful. The search had taken some time, and the atrium was in semi-darkness.

"Where shall I take them?" asked Lord Peter, calling back over his shoulder.

"Hi!" cried Mary; and, "Look where you're going!" cried her friend.

They were too late. A splash and a flounder proclaimed that Lord Peter had walked, like Johnny Head-in-Air, over the edge of the impluvium, papers and all.

"You ass!" said Mary.

His lordship scrambled out, spluttering, and Hannah Marryat suddenly burst out into the first laugh Peter had ever heard her give.

> *"Truth, they say, was nobody's daughter;*
> *She took off her clothes and fell into the water,"*

she proclaimed.

"Well, I couldn't take my clothes off with you here, could I?" grumbled Lord Peter. "We'll have to fish out the papers. I'm afraid they've got a bit damp."

Miss Marryat turned on the lights, and they started to clear the basin.

"Truth, poor girl—" began Lord Peter, and suddenly with a little shriek, began to dance on the marble edge of the impluvium.

"One, two, three, four, five, six—"

"Quite, quite demented," said Mary. "How shall I break it to mother?"

"Thirteen, fourteen, *fifteen*!" cried his lordship, and sat down, suddenly and damply, exhausted by his own excitement.

"Feeling better?" asked his sister acidly.

"I'm well. I'm all right. Everything's all right. I *love* Uncle Meleager. Fifteen squares each way. Look at it. *Look* at it. The truth's in the water. Didn't he say so? Oh, frabjous day! Calloo! callay! I chortle. Mary, what became of those definitions?"

"They're in your pocket, all damp," said Mary.

Lord Peter snatched them out hurriedly.

"It's all right, they haven't run," he said. "Oh, *darling* Uncle Meleager. Can you drain the impluvium, Miss Marryat, and find a bit of charcoal. Then I'll get some dry clothes on and we'll get down to it. Don't you see? *There's* your missing crossword square — on the floor of the impluvium!"

It took, however, some time to get the basin emptied, and it was not till the next morning that the party, armed with sticks of charcoal, squatted down in the empty impluvium to fill in Uncle Meleager's crossword on the marble tiles. Their first difficulty was to decide whether the red squares counted as stops or had to be filled in, but after a few definitions had been solved, the construction of the puzzle grew apace. The investigators grew steadily hotter and more quickly covered with charcoal, while the attentive Mr. Bunter hurried to and fro between the atrium and the library, and the dictionaries piled upon the edge of the impluvium.

Here was Uncle Meleager's crossword square:

Truth, poor girl, was nobody's daughter;
She took off her clothes and jumped into the water.

ACROSS

I.1   Foolish or wise, yet one remains alone,
'Twixt Strength and Justice on a heavenly throne.

XI.1   O to what ears the chink of gold was sweet;
The greed for treasure brought him but defeat.

"That's a hint to us," said Lord Peter.

I.2   One drop of vinegar to two of oil
Dresses this curly head sprung from the soil.

X.2   Nothing itself, it needs but little more
To be that nothingness the Preacher saw.

I.3   Dusty though my fellows be,
We are a kingly company.

IV.3   Have your own will, though here, I hold,
The new is *not* a patch upon the old.

XIV.3   Any loud cry would do as well,
        Or so the poet's verses tell.

I.4   This is the most unkindest cut of all,
        Except your skill be mathematical.

X.4   Little and hid from mortal sight.
        I darkly work to make all light.

I.5   The need for this (like that it's cut off short)
        The building of a tower to humans taught.

XI.5   "More than mind discloses and more than
        men believe"
        (A definition by a man whom Pussyfoot doth
        grieve).

II.6   Backward observe her turn her way,
        The way of wisdom, wise men say.

VII.6   Grew long ago by river's edge
        Where grows today the common sedge.

XII.6   One of three by which, they say,
        You'll know the Cornishmen alway.

VI.7   Blow upon blow; five more the vanquished
        Roman shows
        And if the foot slip one, on crippled feet one
        goes.

I.8   By this Jew's work the whole we find,
        In a glass clearly, darkly in the mind.

IX.8   Little by little see it grow
        Till cut off short by hammer-blow.

VI.9   Watch him go, heel and toe,
        Across the wide Karroo!

II.10   In expectation to be rich
        Here you reach the highest pitch.

VII.10 Of this, concerning nothing, much —
        Too often do we hear of such!

XII.10 O'er land and sea, passing on deadly wings,
        Pain to the strong, to weaklings death it
        brings.

I.11   Requests like these, however long they be,
        Stop just too soon for common courtesy.

XI.11   Caesar, the living dead salute thee here,
         Facing for thy delight tooth, claw, and spear.

I.12   One word had served, but he in ranting vein
         "Lend me your ears" must mouth o'er Caesar
         slain.

X.12   Helical circumvolution
         Adumbrates correct solution.

I.13   One that works for Irish men
         Both by word and deed and pen.

"That's an easy one," said Miss Marryat.

IV.13   Seven out of twelve this number makes com-
         plete
         As the sun journeys on from seat to seat.

XIV.13   My brothers play with planets; Cicero,
         Master of words, my master is below.

I.14   Free of her jesses let the falcon fly,
         With sight undimmed into the azure sky.

X.14   And so you dine with Borgia? Let me lend
         You this as a precaution, my poor friend.

I.15   Friendship carried to excess
         God him in a horrid mess.

XI.15   Smooth and elastic and, I guess,
         The dearest treasure you possess.

DOWN

1.I   If step by step the Steppes you wander
         through
         Many of those in this, of these in those you'll
         view.

"Bunter," said Lord Peter, "bring me a whisky-and-soda!"

11.I   If me without my head you do,
         Then generously my head renew,

            Or put it to my hinder end —
            Your cheer it shall nor mar nor mend.

1.II   Quietly, quietly, 'twixt edge and edge,
            Do this unto the thin end of the wedge.

10.II   "Something that hath a reference to my
            state?"
            Just as you like, it shall be written straight.

1.III   When all is read, then give the world its due,
            And never need the world read this of you.

"That's a comfort," said Lady Mary. "It shows we're on the right lines."

4.III   Sing *Nunc Dimittis* and *Magnificat* —
            But look a little farther back than that.

14.III   Here in brief epitome
            Attribute of royalty.

1.IV   Lo! at a glance
            The Spanish gipsy and her dance.

10.IV   Bring me skin and a needle or a stick —
            A needle does it slowly, a stick does it quick.

1.V   It was a brazen business when
            King Phalaris made these for men.

11.V   This king (of whom not much is known)
            By Heaven's mercy was o'erthrown.

2.VI   "Bid όν καὶ ἦμ όν farewell?" Nay, in this
            The sterner Roman stands by that which is.

7.VI   This the termination is
            Of many minds' activities.

12.VI   I mingle on Norwegian shore,
            With ebbing water's backward roar.

6.VII   I stand a ladder to renown,
            Set 'twixt the stars and Milan town.

1.VIII Highest and lowliest both to me lay claim,
            The little hyssop and the king of fame.

"That makes that point about the squares clear," said Mary.

"I think it's even more significant," said her brother.

9.VIII   This sensible old man refused to tread
          The path to Hades in a youngster's stead.

6.IX   Long since, at Nature's call, they let it drop,
          Thoughtlessly thoughtful for our next year's crop.

2.X   To smallest words great speakers greatness give;
          Here Rome propounded her alternative.

7.X   We heap up many with toil and trouble,
          And find that the whole of our gain is a bubble.

12.X   Add it among the hidden things —
          A fishy tale to light it brings.

1.XI   "Lions," said a Gallic critic, "are not these."
          Benevolent souls — they'd make your heart's blood freeze.

11.XI   An epithet for husky fellows,
          That stand, all robed in greens and yellows.

1.XII   Whole without holes behold me here,
          My meaning should be wholly clear.

10.XII   Running all around, never setting foot to floor,
          If there isn't one in this room, there may be one next door.

1.XIII   Ye gods! think also of that goddess' name
          Whose might two hours on end the mob proclaim.

4.XIII   The Priest uplifts his voice on high,
          The choristers make their reply.

14.XIII   When you've guessed it, with one voice
          You'll say it was a golden choice.

1.XIV   Shall learning die amid a war's alarms?
          I, at my birth, was clasped in iron arms.

10.XIV At sunset see the labourer now
Loose all his oxen from the plough.
1.XV Without a miracle it cannot be —
At this point, Solver, bid him pray for thee!
11.XV Two thousand years ago and more
(Just as we do today),
The Romans saw these distant lights —
But, oh! how hard the way!

The most remarkable part of the search — or so Lord Peter thought — was its effect on Miss Marryat. At first she hovered disconsolately on the margin, aching with wounded dignity, yet ashamed to dissociate herself from people who were toiling so hard and so cheerfully in her cause.

"I think that's so-and-so," Mary would say hopefully.

And her brother would reply enthusiastically, "Holed it in one, old lady. Good for you! We've got it this time, Miss Marryat" — and explain it.

And Hannah Marryat would say with a snort:

"That's just the childish kind of joke Uncle Meleager *would* make."

Gradually, however, the fascination of seeing the squares fit together caught her, and, when the first word appeared which showed that the searchers were definitely on the right track, she lay down flat on the floor and peered over Lord Peter's shoulder as he grovelled below, writing letters in charcoal, rubbing them out with his handkerchief and mopping his heated face, till the Moor of Venice had nothing on him in the matter of blackness. Once, half scornfully, half timidly, she made a suggestion; twice, she made a suggestion; the third time she had an inspiration. The next minute she was down in the mêlée, crawling over the tiles, flushed and excited, wiping important letters out with her knees as fast as Peter could write them in, poring over the pages of Roget, her eyes gleaming under her tumbled black fringe.

Hurried meals of cold meat and tea sustained the ex-

hausted party, and towards sunset Peter, with a shout of triumph, added the last letter to the square.

They crawled out and looked at it.

"All the words can't be clues," said Mary. "I think it must
be just those four."

"Yes, undoubtedly. It's quite clear. We've only got to look
it up. Where's a Bible?"

Miss Marryat hunted it out from the pile of reference
books. "But that isn't the name of a Bible book," she said. "It's
those things they have at evening service."

"That's all you know," said Lord Peter. "I was brought up
religious, I was. It's Vulgate, that's what that is. You're quite
right, of course, but, as Uncle Meleager says, we must 'look a
little farther back than that.' Here you are. Now, then."

"But it doesn't say what chapter."

"So it doesn't. I mean, nor it does."

"And, anyhow, all the chapters are too short."

"Damn! Oh! Here, suppose we just count right on from
the beginning—one, two, three—"

"Seventeen in chapter one, eighteen, nineteen—this must
be it."

Two fair heads and one dark one peered excitedly at the
small print, Bunter hovering decorously on the outskirts.

*O my dove, that art in the clefts of the rock, in the covert of the
steep place.*

"Oh, dear!" said Mary, disappointed, "that does sound
rather hopeless. Are you sure you've counted right? It might
mean *anything.*"

Lord Peter scratched his head.

"This is a bit of a blow," he said. "I don't like Uncle Meleager half as much as I did. Old beast!"

"After all our work!" moaned Mary.

"It must be right," cried Miss Marryat. "Perhaps there's
some kind of anagram in it. We can't give up now!"

"Bravo!" said Lord Peter. "That's the spirit. 'Fraid we're in for another outburst of frivolity, Miss Marryat."

"Well, it's been great fun," said Hannah Marryat.

"If you will excuse me," began the deferential voice of Bunter.

"I'd forgotten you, Bunter," said his lordship. "Of course you can put us right—you always can. Where have we gone wrong?"

"I was about to observe, my lord, that the words you mention do not appear to agree with my recollection of the passage in question. In my mother's Bible, my lord, it ran, I fancy, somewhat differently."

Lord Peter closed the volume and looked at the back of it.

"Naturally," he said, "you are right again, of course. This is a Revised Version. It's your fault, Miss Marryat. You *would* have a Revised Version. But can we imagine Uncle Meleager with one? No. Bring me Uncle Meleager's Bible."

"Come and look in the library," cried Miss Marryat, snatching him by the hand and running. "Don't be so dreadfully calm."

On the centre of the library table lay a huge and venerable Bible—reverend in age and tooled leather binding. Lord Peter's hands caressed it, for a noble old book was like a song to his soul. Sobered by its beauty, they turned the yellow pages over:

In the clefts of the rocks, in the secret places of the stairs.

"Miss Marryat," said his lordship, "if your Uncle's will is not concealed in the staircase, then—well, all I can say is, he's played a rotten trick on us," he concluded lamely.

"Shall we try the main staircase, or the little one up to the porch?"

"Oh, the main one, I think. I hope it won't mean pulling it down. No. Somebody would have noticed if Uncle Meleager had done anything drastic in that way. It's probably quite a simple hiding-place. Wait a minute. Let's ask the house-keeper."

Mrs. Meakers was called, and perfectly remembered that about nine months previously Mr. Finch had pointed out to her a "kind of a crack like" on the under surface of the stair-case, and had had a man in to fill it up. Certainly, she could point out the exact place. There was the mark of the plaster filling quite clear.

"Hurray!" cried Lord Peter. "Bunter—a chisel or some-thing. Uncle Meleager, Uncle Meleager, we've *got* you! Miss Marryat, I think yours should be the hand to strike the blow. It's your staircase, you know—at least, if we find the will, so if any destruction has to be done it's up to you."

Breathless they stood round, while with a few blows the new plaster flaked off, disclosing a wide chink in the stonework. Hannah Marryat flung down hammer and chisel and groped in the gap.

"There's something," she gasped. "Lift me up; I can't reach. Oh, it is! it is! it *is* it!" And she withdrew her hand, grasping a long, sealed envelope, bearing the superscription:

POSITIVELY THE **LAST** WILL AND TESTAMENT OF MELEAGER FINCH

Miss Marryat gave a yodel of joy and flung her arms round Lord Peter's neck.

Mary executed a joy-dance. "I'll tell the world," she pro-claimed.

"Come and tell mother!" cried Miss Marryat.

Mr. Bunter interposed.

"Your lordship will excuse me," he said firmly, "but your lordship's face is all over charcoal."

"Black but comely," said Lord Peter, "but I submit to your reproof. How clever we've all been. How topping everything is. How rich you are going to be. How late it is and how hungry I am. Yes, Bunter, I will wash my face. Is there anything else I can do for anybody while I feel in the mood?"

"If your lordship would be so kind," said Mr. Bunter, producing a small paper from his pocket, "I should be grateful if you could favour me with a South African quadruped in six letters, beginning with Q."

NOTE: The solution of the crossword will be found on page 289

THE FANTASTIC HORROR OF THE

CAT IN THE BAG

The Great North Road wound away like a flat, steel-grey ribbon. Up it, with the sun and wind behind them, two black specks moved swiftly. To the yokel in charge of the hay-wagon they were only two of "they dratted motor-cyclists," as they barked and zoomed past him in a rapid succession. A little farther on, a family man, driving delicately with a two-seater side-car, grinned as the sharp rattle of the o.h.v. Norton was succeeded by the feline shriek of an angry Scott Flying-Squirrel. He, too, in bachelor days, had taken a side in that perennial feud. He sighed regretfully as he watched the racing machines dwindle away northwards.

At that abominable and unexpected S-bend across the bridge above Hatfield, the Norton man, in the pride of his heart, turned to wave a defiant hand at his pursuer. In that second, the enormous bulk of a loaded charabanc loomed down upon him from the bridgehead. He wrenched himself away from it in a fierce wobble, and the Scott, cornering melodramatically, with left and right foot-rests alternately skimming the tarmac, gained a few triumphant yards. The Norton leapt forward with wide-open throttle. A party of children, seized with sudden panic, rushed helter-skelter across the road. The Scott lurched through them in drunken swerves. The road was clear, and the chase settled down once more.

It is not known why motorists, who sing the joys of the open road, spend so much petrol every week-end grinding their way to Southend and Brighton and Margate, in the stench of each other's exhausts, one hand on the horn and one foot on the brake, their eyes starting from their orbits in the nerve-racking search for cops, corners, blind turnings, and cross-road suicides. They ride in a baffled fury, hating each other. They arrive with shattered nerves and fight for parking places. They return, blinded by the headlights of fresh arrivals, whom they hate even worse than they hate each other. And all the time the Great North Road winds away like a long, flat, steel-grey ribbon—a surface like a racetrack, without traps, without hedges, without side-roads, and without traffic. True, it leads to nowhere in particular; but, after all, one pub is very much like another.

The tarmac reeled away, mile after mile. The sharp turn to the right at Baldrock, the involute intricacies of Biggleswade, with its multiplication of sign-posts, gave temporary check, but brought the pursuer no nearer. Through Tempsford at full speed, with bellowing horn and exhaust, then, screaming like a hurricane past the R.A.C. post where the road forks in from Bedford. The Norton rider again glanced back; the Scott rider again sounded his horn ferociously. Flat as a chessboard, dyke and field revolved about the horizon.

The constable at Eaton Socon was by no means an anti-motor fiend. In fact, he had just alighted from his pushbike to pass the time of day with the A.A. man on point duty at the cross-roads. But he was just and God-fearing. The sight of two maniacs careering at seventy miles an hour into his protectorate was more than he could be expected to countenance—the more, that the local magistrate happened to be passing at that very moment in a pony-trap. He advanced to the middle of the road, spreading his arms in a majestic manner. The Norton rider looked, saw the road beyond complicated by the pony-trap and a traction-engine, and resigned himself to the inevitable. He flung the throttle-lever back, stamped on his squealing brakes, and skidded to a standstill. The Scott, having had notice, came up mincingly, with a voice like a pleased kitten.

"Now, then," said the constable, in a tone of reproof, "ain't you got no more sense than to come drivin' into the town at a 'undred mile an hour? This ain't Brooklands, you know. I never see anything like it. 'Ave to take your names and numbers, if *you* please. You'll bear witness, Mr. Nadgett, as they was doin' over eighty."

The A.A. man, after a swift glance over the two sets of handlebars to assure himself that the black sheep were not of his flock, said, with an air of impartial accuracy, "About sixty-six and a half, I should say, if you was to ask me in court."

"Look here, you blighter," said the Scott man indignantly to the Norton man, "why the hell couldn't you stop when you heard me hoot? I've been chasing you with your beastly bag nearly thirty miles. Why can't you look after your own rotten luggage?"

He indicated a small, stout bag, tied with string to his own carrier.

"That?" said the Norton man, with scorn. "What do you mean? It's not mine. Never saw it in my life."

This bare-faced denial threatened to render the Scott rider speechless.

"Of all the—" he gasped. "Why, you crimson idiot, I saw it fall off, just the other side of Hatfield. I yelled and blew like fury. I suppose that overhead gear of yours makes so much noise, you can't hear anything else. I take the trouble to pick the thing up, and go after you, and all you do is to race off like a lunatic and run me into a cop. Fat lot of thanks one gets for trying to be decent to fools on the road."

"That ain't neither here nor there," said the policeman. "Your licence, please, sir."

"Here you are," said the Scott man, ferociously flapping out his pocket-book. "My name's Walters, and it's the last time I'll try to do anybody a good turn, you can lay your shirt."

"Walters," said the constable, entering the particulars laboriously in his note-book, "and Simpkins. You'll 'ave your summonses in doo course. It'll be for about a week 'ence, on Monday or thereabouts, I shouldn't wonder."

"Another forty bob gone west," growled Mr. Simpkins, toying with his throttle. "Oh, well, can't be helped, I suppose."

"Forty bob?" snorted the constable. "What do *you* think? Furious driving to the common danger, that's wot it is. You'll be lucky to get off with five quid apiece."

"Oh, blast!" said the other, stamping furiously on the kick-starter. The engine roared into life, but Mr. Walters dexterously swung his machine across the Norton's path.

"Oh, no, you don't," he said viciously. "You jolly well take your bleeding bag, and no nonsense. I tell you, I *saw* it fall off."

"Now, no language," began the constable, when he suddenly became aware that the A.A. man was staring in a very odd manner at the bag and making signs to him.

" 'Ullo," he demanded, "wot's the matter with the— bleedin' bag, did you say? 'Ere, I'd like to 'ave a look at that 'ere bag, sir, if you don't mind."

"It's nothing to do with me," said Mr. Walters, handing it over. "I saw it fall off and—" His voice died away in his throat, and his eyes became fixed upon one corner of the bag, where something damp and horrible was seeping darkly through.

"Did you notice this 'ere corner when you picked it up?" asked the constable. He prodded it gingerly and looked at his fingers.

"I don't know—no—not particularly," stammered Walters. "I didn't notice anything. I—I expect it burst when it hit the road."

The constable probed the split seam in silence, and then turned hurriedly round to wave away a couple of young women who had stopped to stare. The A.A. man peered curiously, and then started back with a sensation of sickness.

"Ow, Gawd!" he gasped. "It's curly—it's a woman's."

"It's not me," screamed Simpkins. "I swear to heaven it's not mine. This man's trying to put it across me."

"Me?" gasped Walters. "Me? Why, you filthy, murdering brute, I tell you I saw it fall off your carrier. No wonder you blinded off when you saw me coming. Arrest him, constable. Take him away to prison—"

"Hullo, officer!" said a voice behind them. "What's all the excitement? You haven't seen a motor-cyclist go by with a little bag on his carrier, I suppose?"

A big open car with an unnaturally long bonnet had slipped up to them, silent as an owl. The whole agitated party with one accord turned upon the driver.

"Would this be it, sir?"

The motorist pushed off his goggles, disclosing a long, narrow nose and a pair of rather cynical-looking grey eyes.

"It looks rather—" he began; and then, catching sight of the horrid relic protruding from one corner, "In God's name," he inquired, "what's that?"

"That's what we'd like to know, sir," said the constable grimly.

"H'm," said the motorist, "I seem to have chosen an uncommonly suitable moment for inquirin' after my bag. Tactless. To say now that it is not my bag is simple, though in no way convincing As a matter of fact, it is not mine, and I may say that, if it had been, I should not have been at any pains to pursue it."

The constable scratched his head.

"Both these gentlemen—" he began.

The two cyclists burst into simultaneous and heated disclaimers. By this time a small crowd had collected, which the A.A. scout helpfully tried to shoo away.

"You'll all 'ave to come with me to the station," said the harassed constable. "Can't stand 'ere 'oldin' up the traffic. No tricks, now. You wheel them bikes, and I'll come in the car with you, sir."

"But supposing I was to let her rip and kidnap you," said

the motorist, with a grin. "Where'd you be? Here," he added, turning to the A.A. man, "can you handle this outfit?"

"You bet," said the scout, his eye running lovingly over the long sweep of the exhaust and the rakish lines of the car.

"Right. Hop in. Now, officer, you can toddle along with the other suspects and keep an eye on them. Wonderful head I've got for detail. By the way, that foot-brake's on the fierce side. Don't bully it, or you'll surprise yourself."

The lock of the bag was forced at the police-station in the midst of an excitement unparalleled in the calm annals of Eaton Socon, and the dreadful contents laid reverently upon a table. Beyond a quantity of cheese-cloth in which they had been wrapped, there was nothing to supply any clue to the mystery.

"Now," said the superintendent, "what do you gentlemen know about this?"

"Nothing whatever," said Mr. Simpkins, with a ghastly countenance, "except that this man tried to palm it off on me."

"I saw it fall off this man's carrier just the other side of Hatfield," repeated Mr. Walters firmly, "and I rode after him for thirty miles trying to stop him. That's all I know about it, and I wish to God I'd never touched the beastly thing."

"Nor do I know anything about it personally," said the car-owner, "but I fancy I know what it is."

"What's that?" asked the superintendent sharply.

"I rather imagine it's the head of the Finsbury Park murder—though, mind you, that's only a guess."

"That's just what I've been thinking myself," agreed the superintendent, glancing at a daily paper which lay on his desk, its headlines lurid with the details of that very horrid crime, "and, if so, you are to be congratulated, constable, on a very important capture."

"Thank you, sir," said the gratified officer, saluting.

"Now I'd better take all your statements," said the superintendent. "No, no; I'll hear the constable first. Yes, Briggs?"

The constable, the A.A. man, and the two motor-cyclists

having given their versions of the story, the superintendent turned to the motorist.

"And what have you got to say about it?" he inquired. "First of all, your name and address."

The other produced a card, which the superintendent copied out and returned to him respectfully.

"A bag of mine, containing some valuable jewellery, was stolen from my car yesterday, in Piccadilly," began the motorist. "It is very much like this, but has a cipher lock. I made inquiries through Scotland Yard, and was informed today that a bag of precisely similar appearance had been cloak-roomed yesterday afternoon at Paddington, main line. I hurried round there, and was told by the clerk that just before the police warning came through the bag had been claimed by a man in motor-cycling kit. A porter said he saw the man leave the station, and a loiterer observed him riding off on a motor-bicycle. That was about an hour before. It seemed pretty hopeless, as, of course, nobody had noticed even the make of the bike, let alone the number. Fortunately, however, there was a smart little girl. The smart little girl had been dawdling round outside the station, and had heard a motor-cyclist ask a taxi-driver the quickest route to Finchley. I left the police hunting for the taxi-driver, and started off, and in Finchley I found an intelligent boy-scout. He had seen a motor-cyclist with a bag on the carrier, and had waved and shouted to him that the strap was loose. The cyclist had got off and tightened the strap, and gone straight on up the road towards Chipping Barnet. The boy hadn't been near enough to identify the machine—the only thing he knew for certain was that it wasn't a Douglas, his brother having one of that sort. At Barnet I got an odd little story of a man in a motor-coat who had staggered into a pub with a ghastly white face and drunk two double brandies and gone out and ridden off furiously. Number?—of course not. The barmaid told me. *She* didn't notice the number. After that it was a tale of furious driving all along the road. After Hatfield, I got the story of a road-race. And here were are."

"It seems to me, my lord," said the superintendent, "that the furious driving can't have been all on one side."

"I admit it," said the other, "though I do plead in extenuation that I spared the women and children and hit up the miles in the wide, open spaces. The point at the moment is—"

"Well, my lord," said the superintendent, "I've got your story, and, if it's all right, it can be verified by inquiry at Paddington and Finchley and so on. Now, as for these two gentlemen—"

"It's perfectly obvious," broke in Mr. Walters, "the bag dropped off this man's carrier, and, when he saw me coming after him with it, he thought it was a good opportunity to saddle me with the cursed thing. Nothing could be clearer."

"It's a lie," said Mr. Simpkins. "Here's this fellow has got hold of the bag—I don't say how, but I can guess—and he has the bright idea of shoving the blame on me. It's easy enough to *say* a thing's fallen off a man's carrier. Where's the proof? Where's the strap? If his story's true, you'd find the broken strap on my bus. The bag *was* on *his* machine—tied on, tight."

"Yes, with string," retorted the other. "If I'd gone and murdered someone and run off with their head, do you think I'd be such an ass as to tie it on with a bit of two-penny twine? The strap's worked loose and fallen off on the road somewhere; that's what happened to that."

"Well, look here," said the man addressed as "my lord," "I've got an idea for what it's worth. Suppose, superintendent, you turn out as many of your men as you think adequate to keep an eye on three desperate criminals, and we all tool down to Hatfield together. I can take two in my bus at a pinch, and no doubt you have a police car. If this thing *did* fall off the carrier, somebody beside Mr. Walters may have seen it fall."

"They didn't," said Mr. Simpkins.

"There wasn't a soul," said Mr. Walters, "but how do *you* know there wasn't, eh? I thought you didn't know anything about it."

"I mean, it didn't fall off, so nobody *could* have seen it," gasped the other.

"Well, my lord," said the superintendent, "I'm inclined to accept your suggestion, as it gives us a chance of inquiring into your story at the same time. Mind you, I'm not saying I doubt it, you being who you are. I've read about some of your detective work, my lord, and very smart I considered it. But, still, it wouldn't be my duty not to get corroborative evidence if possible."

"Good egg! Quite right," said his lordship. "Forward the light brigade. We can do it easily in — that is to say, at the legal rate of progress it needn't take us much over an hour and a half."

About three-quarters of an hour later, the racing car and the police car loped quietly side by side into Hatfield. Henceforward, the four-seater, in which Walters and Simpkins sat glaring at each other, took the lead, and presently Walters waved his hand and both cars came to a stop.

"It was just about here, as near as I can remember, that it fell off," he said. "Of course, there's no trace of it now."

"You're quite sure as there wasn't a strap fell off with it?" suggested the superintendent, "because, you see, there must 'a' been something holding it on."

"Of course there wasn't a strap," said Simpkins, white with passion. "You haven't any business to ask him leading questions like that."

"Wait a minute," said Walters slowly. "No, there was no strap. But I've got a sort of recollection of seeing something on the road about a quarter of a mile farther up."

"It's a lie!" screamed Simpkins. "He's inventing it."

"Just about where we passed that man with the side-car a minute or two ago," said his lordship. "I told you we ought to have stopped and asked if we could help him, superintendent. Courtesy of the road, you know, and all that."

"He couldn't have told us anything," said the superintendent. "He'd probably only just stopped."

"I'm not so sure," said the other. "Didn't you notice what he was doing? Oh, dear, dear, where were your eyes? Hullo! here he comes."

He sprang out into the road and waved to the rider, who, seeing four policemen, though it better to pull up.

"Excuse me," said his lordship. "Thought we'd just like to stop you and ask if you were all right, and all that sort of thing, you know. Wanted to stop in passing, throttle jammed open, couldn't shut the confounded thing. Little trouble, what?"

"Oh, yes, perfectly all right, thanks, except that I would be glad if you could spare a gallon of petrol. Tank came adrift. Beastly nuisance. Had a bit of a struggle. Happily, Providence placed a broken strap in my way and I've fixed it. Split a bit, though, where that bolt came off. Lucky not to have an explosion, but there's a special cherub for motor-cyclists."

"Strap, eh?" said the superintendent. "Afraid I'll have to trouble you to let me have a look at that."

"What?" said the other. "And just as I've got the damned thing fixed? What the — ? All right, dear, all right" — to his passenger. "Is it something serious, officer?"

"Afraid so, sir. Sorry to trouble you."

"Hi!" yelled one of the policemen, neatly fielding Mr. Simpkins as he was taking a dive over the back of the car. "No use doin' that. You're for it, my lad."

"No doubt about it," said the superintendent trimphantly, snatching at the strap which the side-car rider held out to him. "Here's his name on it, 'J. SIMPKINS,' written on in ink as large as life. Very much obliged to *you*, sir, I'm sure. You've helped us effect a very important capture."

"No! *Who* is it?" cried the girl in the side-car. "How frightfully thrilling! Is it a murder?"

"Look in your paper tomorrow, miss," said the superintendent, "and you may see something. Here, Briggs, better put the handcuffs on him."

"And how about my tank?" said the man mournfully. "It's all right for you to be excited, Babs, but you'll have to get out and help push."

"Oh, no," said his lordship. "Here's a strap. A *much* nicer strap. A really superior strap. And petrol. *And* a pocket-flask. Everything a young man ought to have. And, when you're in town, mind you both look me up. Lord Peter Wimsey, 110A Piccadilly. Delighted to see you any time. Chin, chin!"

"Cheerio!" said the other, wiping his lips and much mollified. "Only too charmed to be of use. Remember it in my favour, officer, next time you catch me speeding."

"Very fortunate we spotted him," said the superintendent complacently, as they continued their way into Hatfield. "Quite providential, as you might say."

"I'll come across with it," said the wretched Simpkins, sitting handcuffed in the Hatfield police-station. "I swear to God I know nothing whatever about it—about the murder, I mean. There's a man I know who has a jewellery business in Birmingham. I don't know him very well. In fact, I only met him at Southend last Easter, and we got pally. His name's Owen— Thomas Owen. He wrote me yesterday and said he'd accidentally left a bag in the cloakroom at Paddington and asked if I'd take it out—he enclosed the ticket—and bring it up next time I came that way. I'm in transport service, you see—you've got my card—and I'm always up and down the country. As it happened, I was just going up in that direction with this Norton, so I fetched the thing out at lunch-time and started off with it. I didn't notice the date on the cloakroom ticket. I know there wasn't anything to pay on it, so it can't have been there long. Well, it all went just as you said up to Finchley, and there that boy told me my strap was loose and I went to tighten it up. And then I noticed that the corner of the bag was split, and it was damp—and—well, I saw what you saw. That sort of turned me over, and I lost my head. The only thing I could think of was to get rid of it, quick. I remembered there were a lot of lonely stretches on the Great North Road, so I cut the strap nearly through—that was when I stopped for that drink at Barnet—and then, when I thought there wasn't anybody in sight, I just reached back and gave it a tug, and it went—strap and all; I hadn't put it through the slots. It fell off, just like a great weight dropping off my mind. I suppose Walters must have just come round into sight as it fell. I had to slow down

a mile or two farther on for some sheep going into a field, and
then I heard him hooting at me—and—oh, my God!"

He groaned, and buried his head in his hands.

"I see," said the Eaton Socon superintendent. "Well, that's
your statement. Now, about this Thomas Owen—"

"Oh," cried Lord Peter Wimsey, "never mind Thomas Owen.
He's not the man you want. You can't suppose that a bloke who'd
committed a murder would want a fellow tailin' after him to
Birmingham with the head. It stands to reason that was intended
to stay in Paddington cloakroom till the ingenious perpetrator
had skipped, or till it was unrecognizable, or both. Which, by the
way, is where we'll find those family heirlooms of mine, which
your engaging friend Mr. Owen lifted out of my car. Now, Mr.
Simpkins, just pull yourself together and tell us who was standing next to you at the cloakroom when you took out that bag. Try
hard to remember, because this jolly little island is no place for
him, and he'll be taking the next boat while we stand talking."

"I can't remember," moaned Simpkins. "I didn't notice.
My head's all in a whirl."

"Never mind. Go back. Think quietly. Make a picture of
yourself getting off your machine—leaning it up against something—"

"No, I put it on the stand."

"Good! That's the way. Now, think—you're taking the
cloakroom ticket out of your pocket and going up—trying to
attract the man's attention."

"I couldn't at first. There was an old lady trying to cloakroom a canary, and a very bustling man in a hurry with some
golf-clubs. He was quite rude to a quiet little man with a—by
Jove! yes, a hand-bag like that one. Yes, that's it. The timid
man had had it on the counter quite a long time, and the big
man pushed him aside. I don't know what happened, quite,
because mine was handed out to me just then. The big man
pushed his luggage in front of both of us and I had to reach
over it—and I suppose—yes, I must have taken the wrong
one. Good God! Do you mean to say that that timid little
insignificant-looking man was a murderer?"

"Lots of 'em like that," put in the Hatfield superintendent. "But what was he like—come!"

"He was only about five foot five, and he wore a soft hat and a long, dust-coloured coat. He was very ordinary, with rather weak, prominent eyes, I think, but I'm not sure I should know him again. Oh, wait a minute! I do remember one thing. He had an odd scar—crescent-shaped—under his left eye."

"That settles it," said Lord Peter. "I thought as much. Did you recognize the—the face when we took it out, superintendent? No? I did. It was Dahlia Dallmeyer, the actress, who is supposed to have sailed for America last week. And the short man with the crescent-shaped scar is her husband, Philip Storey. Sordid tale and all that. She ruined him, treated him like dirt, and was unfaithful to him, but it looks as though he had had the last word in the argument. And now, I imagine, the Law will have the last word with him. Get busy on the wires, superintendent, and you might ring up the Paddington people and tell 'em to let me have my bag, before Mr. Thomas Owen tumbles to it that there's been a slight mistake."

"Well, anyhow," said Mr. Walters, extending a magnanimous hand to the abashed Mr. Simpkins, "it was a top-hole race—well worth a summons. We must have a return match one of these days."

Early the following morning a little, insignificant-looking man stepped aboard the trans-Atlantic liner *Volucria*. At the head of the gangway two men blundered into him. The younger of the two, who carried a small bag, was turning to apologize, when a light of recognition flashed across his face.

"Why, if it isn't Mr. Storey!" he exclaimed loudly. "Where are you off to? I haven't seen you for an age."

"I'm afraid," said Philip Storey, "I haven't the pleasure—"

"Cut it out," said the other, laughing. "I'd know that scar of yours anywhere. Going out to the States?"

"Well, yes," said the other, seeing that his acquaintance's boisterous manner was attracting attention. "I beg your pardon. It's Lord Peter Wimsey, isn't it? Yes, I'm joining the wife out there."

"And how is she?" inquired Wimsey, steering the way into the bar and sitting down at a table. "Left this week didn't she? I saw it in the papers."

"Yes. She's just cabled me to join her. We're—er—taking a holiday in—er—the lakes. Very pleasant there in summer."

"Cabled you, did she? And so here we are on the same boat. Odd how things turn out, what? I only got my sailing orders at the last minute. Chasing criminals—my hobby, you know."

"Oh, really?" Mr. Storey licked his lips.

"Yes. This is Detective-Inspector Parker of Scotland Yard—great pal of mine. Yes. Very unpleasant matter, annoying and all that. Bag that ought to have been reposin' peacefully at Paddington Station turns up at Eaton Socon. No business there, what?"

He smacked the bag on the table so violently that the lock sprang open.

Storey leapt to his feet with a shriek, flinging his arms across the opening of the bag as though to hide its contents.

"How did you get that?" he screamed. "Eaton Socon? It— I never—"

"It's mine," said Wimsey quietly, as the wretched man sank back, realizing that he had betrayed himself. "Some jewellery of my mother's. What did you think it was?"

Detective Parker touched his charge gently on the shoulder.

"You needn't answer that," he said. "I arrest you, Philip Storey, for the murder of your wife. Anything that you say may be used against you."

THE UNPRINCIPLED AFFAIR OF
THE PRACTICAL JOKER

The *Zambesi*, they said, was expected to dock at six in the morning. Mrs. Ruyslaender booked a bedroom at the Magnifical, with despair in her heart. A bare nine hours and she would be greeting her husband. After that would begin the sickening period of waiting—it might be days, it might be weeks, possibly even months—for the inevitable discovery.

The reception-clerk twirled the register towards her. Mechanically, as she signed it, she glanced at the preceding entry:

"Lord Peter Wimsey and valet—London—Suite 24."

Mrs. Ruyslaender's heart seemed to stop for a second. Was it possible that, even now, God had left a loophole? She expected little from Him—all her life he had shown Himself a sufficiently stern creditor. It was fantastic to base the frailest hope on this signature of a man she had never even seen.

Yet the name remained in her mind while she dined in her own room. She dismissed her maid presently, and sat for a long time looking at her own haggard reflection in the mirror.

Twice she rose and went to the door—then turned back, calling herself a fool. The third time she turned the handle quickly and hurried down the corridor, without giving herself time to think.

A large golden arrow at the corner directed her to Suite 24. It was eleven o'clock, and nobody was within view. Mrs. Ruyslaender gave a sharp knock on Lord Peter Wimsey's door and stood back, waiting, with the sort of desperate relief one experiences after hearing a dangerous letter thump the bottom of the pillar-box. Whatever the adventure, she was committed to it.

The manservant was of the imperturbable sort. He neither invited or rejected, but stood respectfully upon the threshold.

"Lord Peter Wimsey?" murmured Mrs. Ruyslaender.

"Yes, madam."

"Could I speak to him for a moment?"

"His lordship has just retired, madam. If you will step in, I will inquire."

Mrs. Ruyslaender followed him into one of those palatial sitting-rooms which the Magnifical provides for the wealthy pilgrim.

"Will you take a seat, madam?"

The man stepped noiselessly to the bedroom door and passed, shutting it behind him. The lock, however, failed to catch, and Mrs. Ruyslaender caught the conversation.

"Pardon me, my lord, a lady has called. She mentioned no appointment, so I considered it better to acquaint your lordship."

"Excellent discretion," said a voice. It had a slow, sarcastic intonation, which brought a painful flush to Mrs. Ruyslaender's cheek. "I never make appointments. Do I know the lady?"

"No, my lord. But—hem—I know her by sight, my lord. It is Mrs. Ruyslaender."

"Oh, the diamond merchant's wife. Well, find out tactfully what it's all about, and, unless it's urgent, ask her to call tomorrow."

The valet's remark was inaudible, but the reply was:

"Don't be coarse, Bunter."

The valet returned.

"His lordship desires me to ask you, madam, in what way he can be of service to you?"

"Will you say to him that I have heard of him in connexion with the Attenbury diamond case, and am anxious to ask his advice."

"Certainly, madam. May I suggest that, as his lordship is greatly fatigued, he would be better able to assist you after he has slept."

"If tomorrow would have done, I would not have thought of disturbing him tonight. Tell him, I am aware of the trouble I am giving—"

"Excuse me one moment, madam."

This time the door shut properly. After a short interval Bunter returned to say, "His lordship will be with you immediately, madam," and to place a decanter of wine and a box of Sobranies beside her.

Mrs. Ruyslaender lit a cigarette, but had barely sampled its flavour when she was aware of a soft step beside her. Looking round, she perceived a young man, attired in a mauve dressing-gown of great splendour, from beneath the hem of which peeped coyly a pair of primrose silk pyjamas.

"You must think it very strange of me, thrusting myself on you at this hour," she said, with a nervous laugh.

Lord Peter put his head on one side.

"Don't know the answer to that," he said. "If I say, 'Not at all,' it sounds abandoned. If I say, 'Yes, very,' it's rude. Supposin' we give it a miss, what? and you tell me what I can do for you."

Mrs. Ruyslaender hesitated. Lord Peter was not what she had expected. She noted the sleek, straw-coloured hair, brushed flat back from a rather sloping forehead, the ugly, lean, arched nose, and the faintly foolish smile, and her heart sank within her.

"I—I'm afraid it's ridiculous of me to suppose you can help me," she began.

"Always my unfortunate appearance," moaned Lord Peter, with such alarming acumen as to double her discomfort. "Would it invite confidence more, d'you suppose, if I dyed my hair black an' grew a Newgate fringe? It's very tryin', you can't think, always to look as if one's name was Algy."

"I only meant," said Mrs. Ruyslaender, "that I don't think *anybody* could possibly help. But I saw your name in the hotel book, and it seemed just a chance."

Lord Peter filled the glasses and sat down.

"Carry on," he said cheerfully; "it sounds interestin'."

Mrs. Ruyslaender took the plunge.

"My husband," she explained, "is Henry Ruyslaender, the diamond merchant. We came over from Kimberley ten years ago, and settled in England. He spends several months in Africa every year on business, and I am expecting him back on the *Zambesi* tomorrow morning. Now, this is the trouble. Last year he gave me a magnificent diamond necklace of a hundred and fifteen stones—"

"The Light of Africa—I know," said Wimsey.

She looked a little surprised, but assented. "The necklace has been stolen from me, and I can't hope to conceal the loss from him. No duplicate would deceive him for an instant."

She paused, and Lord Peter prompted gently;

"You have come to me, I presume, because it is not to be a police matter. Will you tell me quite frankly why?"

"The police would be useless. I know who took it."

"Yes?"

"There is a man we both know slightly—a man called Paul Melville."

Lord Peter's eyes narrowed. "M'm, yes, I fancy I've seen him about the clubs. New Army, but transferred himself into the Regulars. Dark. Showy. Bit of an ampelopsis, what?"

"Ampelopsis?"

"Suburban plant that climbs by suction. *You* know—first year, tender little shoots—second year, fine show—next year, all over the shop. Now tell me I am rude."

Mrs. Ruyslaender giggled. "Now you mention it, he is *exactly* like an ampelopsis. What a relief to be able to think of him as that. . . . Well, he is some sort of distant relation of my husband's. He called one evening when I was alone. We talked about jewels, and I brought down my jewel-box and showed him the Light of Africa. He knows a good deal about stones. I was in and out of the room two or three times, but didn't think to lock up the box. After he left, I was putting the things away, and I opened the jeweller's case the diamonds were in—and they had gone!"

"H'm—pretty barefaced. Look here, Mrs. Ruyslaender, you agree he's an ampelopsis, but you won't call in the police. Honestly, now—forgive me; you're askin' my advice, you know—is he worth botherin' about?"

"It's not that," said the woman in a low tone. "Oh, no! But he took something else as well. He took—a portrait—a small painting set with diamonds."

"Oh!"

"Yes. It was in a secret drawer in the jewel-box. I can't imagine how he knew it was there, but the box was an old casket, belonging to my husband's family, and I fancy he must have known about the drawer and—well, thought that investigation might prove profitable. Anyway, the evening the diamonds went the portrait went too, and he knows I daren't try to get the necklace back because they'd both be found together."

"Was there something more than just the portrait, then? A portrait in itself isn't necessarily hopeless of explanation. It was given you to take care of, say."

"The names were on it—and—and an inscription which nothing, *nothing* could ever explain away. A—a passage from Petronius."

"Oh, dear!" said Lord Peter, "dear me, yes. Rather a lively author."

"I was married very young," said Mrs. Ruyslaender, "and my husband and I have never got on well. Then one year, when he was in Africa, it all happened. We were wonderful—and shameless. It came to an end. I was bitter. I wish I had not been. He left me, you see, and I couldn't forgive it. I prayed day and night for revenge. Only now—I don't want it to be through me!"

"Wait a moment," said Wimsey, "you mean that, if the diamonds are found and the portrait is found too, all this story is bound to come out."

"My husband would get a divorce. He would never forgive me—or him. It is not so much that I mind paying the price myself, but—"

She clenched her hands.

"I have cursed him again and again, and the clever girl who married him. She played her card so well. This would ruin them both."

"But if *you* were the instrument of vengeance," said Wimsey gently, "you would hate yourself. And it would be terrible to you because he would hate you. A woman like you couldn't stoop to get your own back. I see that. If God makes a thunderbolt, how awful and satisfying—if you help to make a beastly row, what a rotten business it would be."

"You seem to understand," said Mrs. Ruyslaender. "How unusual."

"I understand perfectly. Though let me tell you," said Wimsey, with a wry little twist of the lips, "that it's sheer foolishness for a woman to have a sense of honour in such matters. It only gives her excruciating pain, and nobody expects it, anyway. Look here, don't let's get all worked up. You certainly shan't have your vengeance thrust upon you by an ampelopsis. Why should you? Nasty fellow. We'll have him up—root, branch and little suckers. Don't worry. Let's see. My business here will only take a day. Then I've got to get to know Melville—say a week. Then I've got to get the doings—say another week, provided he hasn't sold them yet, which isn't likely. Can you hold your husband off 'em for a fortnight, d'you think?"

"Oh, yes. I'll say they're in the country, or being cleaned, or something. But do you really think you can—?"

"I'll have a jolly good try, anyhow, Mrs. Ruyslaender. Is the fellow hard up, to start stealing diamonds?"

"I fancy he has got into debt over horses lately. And possibly poker."

"Oh! Poker player, is he? That makes an excellent excuse for gettin' to know him. Well, cheer up—we'll get the goods, even if we have to buy 'em. But we won't, if we can help it. Bunter!"

"My lord?" The valet appeared from the inner room.

"Just go an' give the 'All Clear,' will you?"

Mr. Bunter accordingly stepped into the passage, and, having seen an old gentleman safely away to the bathroom and a young lady in a pink kimono pop her head out of an adjacent door and hurriedly pop it back on beholding him, blew his nose with a loud, trumpeting sound.

"Good night," said Mrs. Ruyslaender, "and thank you."

She slipped back to her room unobserved.

"Whatever has induced you, my dear boy," said Colonel Marchbanks, "to take up with that very objectionable fellow Melville?"

"Diamonds," said Lord Peter. "Do you find him so, really?"

"Perfectly dreadful man," said the Hon. Frederick Arbuthnot. "Hearts. What did you want to go and get him a room here for? This used to be quite a decent club."

"Two clubs?" said Sir Impey Biggs, who had been ordering a whisky, and had only caught the last word.

"No, no, one heart."

"I beg your pardon. Well, partner, how about spades? Perfectly good suit."

"Pass," said the Colonel. "I don't know what the Army's coming to nowadays."

"No trumps," said Wimsey. "It's all right, children. Trust your Uncle Pete. Come on, Freddy, how many of those hearts are you going to shout for?"

"None, the Colonel havin' let me down so 'orrid," said the Hon. Freddy.

"Cautious blighter. All content? Righty-ho! Bring out your dead, partner. Oh, very pretty indeed. We'll make it a slam this time. I'm rather glad to hear that expression of opinion from you, Colonel, because I particularly want you and Biggy to hang on this evening and take a hand with Melville and me."

"What happens to me?" inquired the Hon. Freddy.

"You have an engagement and go home early, dear old thing. I've specially invited friend Melville to meet the redoubtable Colonel Marchbanks and our greatest criminal lawyer. Which hand am I supposed to be playin' this from? Oh, yes. Come on, Colonel—you've got to hike that old king out some time, why not now?"

"It's a plot," said Mr. Arbuthnot, with an exaggerated expression of mystery. "Carry on, don't mind me."

"I take it you have your own reasons for cultivating the man," said Sir Impey.

"The rest are mine, I fancy. Well, yes, I have. You and the Colonel would really do me a favour by letting Melville cut in tonight."

"If you wish it," growled the Colonel, "but I hope the impudent young beggar won't presume on the acquaintance."

"I'll see to that," said his lordship. "Your cards, Freddy. Who had the ace of hearts? Oh! I had it myself, of course. Our honours. . . . Hullo! Evenin', Melville."

The ampelopsis was rather a good-looking creature in his own way. Tall and bronzed, with a fine row of very persuasive teeth. He greeted Wimsey and Arbuthnot heartily, the Colonel with a shade too much familiarity, and expressed himself delighted to be introduced to Sir Impey Biggs.

"You're just in time to hold Freddy's hand," said Wimsey; "he's got a date. Not his little paddy-paw, I don't mean—but the dam' rotten hand he generally gets dealt him. Joke."

"Oh, well," said the obedient Freddy, rising, "I s'pose I'd better make a noise like a hoop and roll away. Night, night, everybody."

Melville took his place, and the game continued with vary-
ing fortunes for two hours, at the end of which time Colonel
Marchbanks, who had suffered much under his partner's eloquent theory of the game, was beginning to wilt visibly.

Wimsey yawned.

"Gettin' a bit bored, Colonel? Wish they'd invent somethin' to liven this game up a bit."

"Oh, bridge is a one-horse show, anyway," said Melville.
"Why not have a little flutter at poker, Colonel? Do you all the
good in the world. What d'you say, Biggs?"

Sir Impey turned on Wimsey a thoughtful eye, accustomed to the sizing-up of witnesses. Then he replied:

"I'm quite willing, if the others are."

"Damn good idea," said Lord Peter. "Come now, Colonel,
be a sport. You'll find the chips in that drawer I think. I always lose money at poker, but what's the odds so long as
you're happy. Let's have a new pack."

"Any limit?"

"What do *you* say, Colonel?"

The Colonel proposed a twenty-shilling limit. Melville,
with a grimace, amended this to one-tenth of the pool. The
amendment was carried and the cards cut, the deal falling to
the Colonel.

Contrary to his own prophecy, Wimsey began by winning
considerably, and grew so garrulously imbecile in the process
that even the experienced Melville began to wonder whether
this indescribable fatuity was the cloak of ignorance or the
mask of the hardened poker-player. Soon, however, he was re-
assured. The luck came over to his side, and he found himself
winning hands down, steadily from Sir Impey and the
Colonel, who played cautiously and took little risk—heavily
from Wimsey, who appeared reckless and slightly drunk, and
was staking foolishly on quite impossible cards.

"I never knew such luck as yours, Melville," said Sir
Impey, when that young man had scooped in the proceeds
from a handsome straight-flush.

"My turn tonight, yours tomorrow," said Melville, push-ing the cards across to Biggs, whose deal it was.

Colonel Marchbanks required one card. Wimsey laughed vacantly and demanded an entirely fresh hand; Biggs asked for three; and Melville, after a pause for consideration, took one.

It seemed as though everybody had something respectable this time — though Wimsey was not to be depended upon, fre-quently going the limit upon a pair of jacks in order, as he ex-pressed it, to keep the pot a-boiling. He became peculiarly obstinate now, throwing his chips in with a flushed face, in spite of Melville's confident air.

The Colonel got out, and after a short time Biggs followed his example. Melville held on till the pool mounted to some-thing under a hundred pounds, when Wimsey suddenly turned restive and demanded to see him.

"Four kings," said Melville.

"Blast you!" said Lord Peter, laying down four queens. "No holdin' this feller tonight, is there? Here, take the ruddy cards, Melville, and give somebody else a look in, will you."

He shuffled them as he spoke, and handed them over. Melville dealt, satisfied the demands of the other three play-ers, and was in the act of taking three new cards for himself, when Wimsey gave a sudden exclamation, and shot a swift hand across the table.

"Hullo! Melville," he said, in a chill tone which bore no re-semblance to his ordinary speech, "what exactly does this mean?"

He lifted Melville's left arm clear of the table and, with a sharp gesture, shook it. From the sleeve something fluttered to the table and glided away to the floor. Colonel Marchbanks picked it up, and in a dreadful silence laid the joker on the table.

"Good God!" said Sir Impey.

"You young blackguard!" gasped the Colonel, recovering speech.

"What the hell do you mean by this?" gasped Melville,

with a face like chalk. "How dare you! This is a trick—a plant—" A horrible fury gripped him. "You dare to say that I have been cheating. You liar! You filthy sharper. You put it there. I tell you, gentlemen," he cried, looking desperately round the table, "he must have put it there."

"Come, come," said Colonel Marchbanks, "no good carryin' on that way, Melville. Dear me, no good at all. Only makes matters worse. We all saw it, you know. Dear, dear, I don't know what the Army's coming to."

"Do you mean you believe it?" shrieked Melville. "For God's sake, Wimsey, is this a joke or what? Biggs—you've got a head on your shoulders—are you going to believe this half-drunk fool and this doddering old idiot who ought to be in his grave?"

"That language won't do you any good, Melville," said Sir Impey. "I'm afraid we all saw it clearly enough."

"I've been suspectin' this some time, y'know," said Wimsey. "That's why I asked you two to stay tonight. We don't want to make a public row, but—"

"Gentlemen," said Melville more soberly, "I swear to you that I am absolutely innocent of this ghastly thing. Can't you believe me?"

"I can believe the evidence of my own eyes, sir," said the Colonel, with some heat.

"For the good of the club," said Wimsey, "this couldn't go on, but—also for the good of the club—I think we should all prefer the matter to be quietly arranged. In the face of what Sir Impey and the Colonel can witness, Melville, I'm afraid your protestations are not likely to be credited."

Melville looked from the soldier's face to that of the great criminal lawyer.

"I don't know what your game is," he said sullenly to Wimsey, "but I can see you've laid a trap and pulled it off all right."

"I think, gentlemen," said Wimsey, "that if I might have a word in private with Melville in his own room, I could get the thing settled satisfactorily, without undue fuss."

"He'll have to resign his commission," growled the Colonel.

"I'll put it to him in that light," said Peter. "May we go to your room for a minute, Melville?"

With a lowering brow, the young soldier led the way. Once alone with Wimsey, he turned furiously on him.

"What do you want? What do you mean by making this monstrous charge? I'll take action for libel!"

"Do," said Wimsey coolly, "if you think anybody is likely to believe your story."

He lit a cigarette, and smiled lazily at the angry young man.

"Well, what's the meaning of it, anyway?"

"The meaning," said Wimsey, "is simply that you, an officer and a member of this club, have been caught redhanded cheating at cards while playing for money, the witnesses being Sir Impey Biggs, Colonel Marchbanks, and myself. Now, I suggest to you, Captain Mellville, that your best plan is to let me take charge of Mrs. Ruyslaender's diamond necklace and portrait, and then just to trickle away quiet-like from these halls of dazzlin' light—without any questions asked."

Melville leapt to his feet.

"My God!" he cried. "I can see it now. It's blackmail."

"You may certainly call it blackmail, and theft too," said Lord Peter, with a shrug. "But why use ugly names? I hold five aces, you see. Better chuck in your hand."

"Suppose I say I never heard of the diamonds?"

"It's a bit late now, isn't it?" said Wimsey flatly. "But in that case, I'm beastly sorry and all that, of course, but we shall have to make tonight's business public."

"Damn you!" muttered Melville, "you sneering devil."

He showed all his white teeth, half springing, with crouched shoulders. Wimsey waited quietly, his hands in his pockets.

The rush did not come. With a furious gesture, Melville pulled out his keys and unlocked his dressing-case.

"Take them," he growled, flinging a small parcel on the table; "you've got me. Take 'em and go to hell."

"Eventually—why not now?" murmured his lordship. "Thanks frightfully. Man of peace myself, you know—hate unpleasantness and all that." He scrutinized his booty carefully, running the stones expertly between his fingers. Over the portrait he pursed up his lips. "Yes," he murmured, "that *would* have made a row." He replaced the wrapping and slipped the parcel into his pocket.

"Well, good night, Melville—and thanks for a pleasant game."

"I say, Biggs," said Wimsey, when he had returned to the card-room. "You've had a lot of experience. What tactics d'you think one's justified in usin' with a blackmailer?"

"Ah!" said the K.C. "There you've put your finger on Society's sore place, where the Law is helpless. Speaking as a man, I'd say nothing could be too bad for the brute. It's a crime crueller and infinitely worse in its results than murder. As a lawyer, I can only say that I have consistently refused to defend a blackmailer or to prosecute any poor devil who does away with his tormentor."

"H'm," replied Wimsey. "What do you say, Colonel?"

"A man like that's a filthy pest," said the little warrior stoutly. "Shootin's too good for him. I knew a man—close personal friend, in fact—hounded to death—blew his brains out—one of the best. Don't like to talk about it."

"I want to show you something," said Wimsey.

He picked up the pack which still lay scattered on the table, and shuffled it together.

"Catch hold of these, Colonel, and lay 'em out face downwards. That's right. First of all you cut 'em at the twentieth card—you'll see the seven of diamonds at the bottom. Correct? Now I'll call 'em. Ten of hearts, ace of spades, three of clubs, five of clubs, king of diamonds, nine, jack, two of hearts. Right? I could pick 'em all out, you see, except the ace of hearts, and that's here."

He leaned forward and produced it dexterously from Sir Impey's breast-pocket.

"I learnt it from a man who shared my dug-out near Ypres," he said. "You needn't mention tonight's business, you two. There are crimes which the Law cannot reach."

THE UNDIGNIFIED MELODRAMA

OF THE BONE OF CONTENTION

I am afraid you have brought shocking weather with you, Lord Peter," said Mrs. Frobisher-Pym, with playful reproof. "If it goes on like this they will have a bad day for the funeral."

Lord Peter Wimsey glanced out of the morning-room window to the soaked green lawn and the shrubbery, where the rain streamed down remorselessly over the laurel leaves, stiff and shiny like mackintoshes.

"Nasty exposed business, standing round at funerals," he agreed.

"Yes, I always think it's such a shame for the old people. In a tiny village like this it's about the only pleasure they get during the winter. It makes something for them to talk about for weeks."

"Is it anybody's funeral in particular?"

"My dear Wimsey," said his host, "it is plain that you, coming from your little village of London, are quite out of the

swim. There has never been a funeral like it in Little Doddering before. It's an event."

"Really?"

"Oh, dear, yes. You may possibly remember old Burdock?"

"Burdock? Let me see. Isn't he a sort of local squire, or
something?"

"He was," corrected Mr. Frobisher-Pym. "He's dead—died
in New York about three weeks ago, and they're sending him
over to be buried. The Burdocks have lived in the big house for
hundreds of years, and they're all buried in the churchyard,
except, of course, the one who was killed in the war. Burdock's
secretary cabled the news of his death across, and said the
body was following as soon as the embalmers had finished with
it. The boat gets in to Southampton this morning, I believe. At
any rate, the body will arrive here by the 6:30 from Town."

"Are you going down to meet it, Tom?"

"No, my dear. I don't think that is called for. There will be
a grand turn-out of the village, of course. Joliffe's people are
having the time of their lives; they borrowed an extra pair of
horses from young Mortimer for the occasion. I only hope
they don't kick over the traces and upset the hearse. Mortimer's horseflesh is generally on the spirited side."

"But, Tom, we must show some respect to the Burdocks."

"We're attending the funeral tomorrow, and that's quite
enough. We must do that, I suppose, out of consideration for
the family, though, as far as the old man himself goes, respect
is the very last thing anybody would think of paying him."

"Oh, Tom, he's dead."

"And quite time too. No, Agatha, it's no use pretending
that old Burdock was anything but a spiteful, bad-tempered,
dirty-living old blackguard that the world's well rid of. The
last scandal he stirred up made the place too hot to hold him.
He had to leave the country and go to the States, and, even so,
if he hadn't had the money to pay the people off, he'd probably have been put in gaol. That's why I'm so annoyed with
Hancock. I don't mind his calling himself a priest, though cler-

gyman was always good enough for dear old Weeks—who, after all, was a canon—and I don't mind his vestments. He can wrap himself up in a Union Jack if he likes—it doesn't worry *me*. But when it comes to having old Burdock put on trestles in the south aisle, with candles round him, and Hubbard from the 'Red Cow' and Duggins's boy praying over him half the night, I think it's time to draw the line. The people don't like it, you know—at least, the older generation don't. It's all right for the young ones, I dare say; they must have their amusement; but it gives offence to a lot of the farmers. After all, they knew Burdock a bit too well. Simpson—he's people's warden, you know—came up quite in distress to speak to me about it last night. You couldn't have a sounder man than Simpson. I said I would speak to Hancock. I did speak to him this morning, as a matter of fact, but you might as well talk to the west door of the church."

"Mr. Hancock is one of those young men who fancy they know everything," said his wife. "A sensible man would have listened to you, Tom. You're a magistrate and have lived here all your life, and it stands to reason you know considerably more about the parish than he does."

"He took up the ridiculous position," said Mr. Frobisher-Pym, "that the more sinful the old man had been the more he needed praying for. I said, 'I think it would need more praying than you or I could do to help old Burdock out of the place he's in now.' Ha, ha! So he said, 'I agree with you, Mr. Frobisher-Pym; that is why I am having eight watchers to pray all through the night for him.' I admit he had me there."

"Eight people?" exclaimed Mrs. Frobisher-Pym.

"Not all at once, I understand; in relays, two at a time. 'Well,' I said, 'I think you ought to consider that you will be giving a handle to the Nonconformists.' Of course, he couldn't deny that."

Wimsey helped himself to marmalade. Nonconformists, it seemed, were always searching for handles. Though what kind—whether door-handles, tea-pot handles, pump-handles, or starting-handles—was never explained, nor what the han-

dles were to be used for when found. However, having been
brought up in the odour of the Establishment, he was familiar
with this odd dissenting peculiarity, and merely said:

"Pity to be extreme in a small parish like this. Disturbs the
ideas of the simple fathers of the hamlet and the village blacksmith, with his daughter singin' in the choir and the Old Hun-
dredth and all the rest of it. Don't Burdock's family have
anything to say to it? There are some sons, aren't there?"

"Only the two, now. Aldine was the one that was killed, of
course, and Martin is somewhere abroad. He went off after
that row with his father, and I don't think he has been back in
England since."

"What was the row about?"

"Oh, that was a disgraceful business. Martin got a girl into
trouble—a film actress or a typist or somebody of that sort—
and insisted on marrying her."

"Oh?"

"Yes, so dreadful of him," said the lady, taking up the tale,
"when he was practically engaged to the Delaprime girl—the
one with glasses, you know. It made a terrible scandal. Some
horribly vulgar people came down and pushed their way into
the house and insisted on seeing old Mr. Burdock. I will say
for him he stood up to them—he wasn't the sort of person you
could intimidate. He told them the girl had only herself to
blame, and they could sue Martin if they liked—*he* wouldn't
be blackmailed on his son's account. The butler was listening
at the door, naturally, and told the whole village about it. And
then Martin Burdock came home and had a quarrel with his
father you could have heard for miles. He said that the whole
thing was a lie, and that he meant to marry the girl, anyway. I
cannot understand how anybody could marry into a blackmailing family like that."

"My dear," said Mr. Frobisher-Pym gently, "I don't think
you're being quite fair to Martin, or his wife's parents, either.
From what Martin told me, they were quite decent people,
only not his class, of course, and they came in a well-meaning
way to find out what Martin's 'intentions' were. You would

want to do the same yourself, if it were a daughter of ours. Old
Burdock, naturally, thought they meant blackmail. He was the
kind of man who thinks everything can be paid for; and he
considered a son of his had a perfect right to seduce a young
woman who worked for a living. I don't say Martin was altogether in the right—"

"Martin is a chip of the old block, I'm afraid," retorted the
lady. "He married the girl, anyway, and why should he do
that, unless he had to?"

"Well, they've never had any children, you know," said
Mr. Frobisher-Pym.

"That's as may be. I've no doubt the girl was in league with
her parents. And you know the Martin Burdocks have lived in
Paris ever since."

"That's true," admitted her husband. "It was an unfortunate affair altogether. They've had some difficulty in tracing
Martin's address, too, but no doubt he'll be coming back
shortly. He is engaged in producing some film play, they tell
me, so possibly he can't get away in time for the funeral."

"If he had any natural feeling, he would not let a film play
stand in his way," said Mrs. Frobisher-Pym.

"My dear, there are such things as contracts, with very
heavy monetary penalties for breaking them. And I don't suppose Martin could afford to lose a big sum of money. It's not
likely that his father will have left him anything."

"Martin is the younger son, then?" asked Wimsey, politely
showing more interest than he felt in the rather well-worn plot
of this village melodrama.

"No, he is the eldest of the lot. The house is entailed, of
course, and so is the estate, such as it is. But there's no money
in the land. Old Burdock made his fortune in rubber shares
during the boom, and the money will go as he leaves it—wherever that may be, for they haven't found any will yet. He's
probably left it all to Haviland."

"The younger son?"

"Yes. He's something in the City—a director of a company—connected with silk stockings, I believe. Nobody has

seen very much of him. He came down as soon as he heard of his father's death. He's staying with the Hancocks. The big house has been shut up since old Burdock went to the States four years ago. I suppose Haviland thought it wasn't worth while opening it up till they knew what Martin was going to do about it. That's why the body is being taken to the church."

"Much less trouble, certainly," said Wimsey.

"Oh, yes—though, mind you, I think Haviland ought to take a more neighbourly view of it. Considering the position the Burdocks have always held in the place, the people had a right to expect a proper reception after the funeral. It's usual. But these business people think less of tradition than we do down here. And, naturally, since the Hancocks are putting Haviland up, he can't raise much objection to the candles and the prayers and things."

"Perhaps not," said Mrs. Frobisher-Pym, "but it would have been more suitable if Haviland had come to us, rather than to the Hancocks, whom he doesn't even know."

"My dear, you forget that very unpleasant dispute I had with Haviland Burdock about shooting over my land. After the correspondence that passed between us, last time he was down here, I could scarcely offer him hospitality. His father took a perfectly proper view of it, I will say that for him, but Haviland was exceedingly discourteous to me, and things were said which I could not possibly overlook. However, we mustn't bore you, Lord Peter, with our local small-talk. If you've finished your breakfast, what do you say to a walk around the place? It's a pity it's raining so hard—and you don't see the garden at its best this time of year, of course— but I've got some cocker span'els you might like to have a look at."

Lord Peter expressed eager anxiety to see the spaniels, and in a few minutes' time found himself squelching down the gravel path which led to the kennels.

"Nothing like a healthy country life," said Mr. Frobisher-Pym. "I always think London is so depressing in the winter. Nothing to do with oneself. All right to run up for a day or two and see a theatre now and again, but how you people stick it week in and week out beats me. I must speak to Plunkett about this archway," he added. "It's getting out of trim."

He broke off a dangling branch of ivy as he spoke. The plant shuddered revengefully, tipping a small shower of water down Wimsey's neck.

The cocker spaniel and her family occupied a comfortable and airy stall in the stable buildings. A youngish man in breeches and leggings emerged to greet the visitors, and produced the little bundles of puppy-hood for their inspection. Wimsey sat down on an upturned bucket and examined them gravely one by one. The bitch, after cautiously reviewing his boots and grumbling a little, decided that he was trustworthy and slobbered genially over his knees.

"Let me see," said Mr. Frobisher-Pym, "how old are they?"

"Thirteen days, sir."

"Is she feeding them all right?"

"Fine, sir. She's having some of the malt food. Seems to suit her very well, sir."

"Ah, yes. Plunkett was a little doubtful about it, but I heard it spoken very well of. Plunkett doesn't care for experiments, and, in a general way, I agree with him. Where is Plunkett, by the way?"

"He's not very well this morning, sir."

"Sorry to hear that, Merridew. The rheumatics again?"

"No, sir. From what Mrs. Plunkett tells me, he's had a bit of a shock."

"A shock? What sort of a shock? Nothing wrong with Alf or Elsie, I hope?"

"No, sir. The fact is—I understand he's seen something, sir."

"What do you mean, seen something?"

"Well, sir—something in the nature of a warning, from what he says."

"A warning? Good heavens, Merridew, he mustn't get those sort of ideas in his head. I'm surprised at Plunkett; I always thought he was a very level-headed man. What sort of warning did he say it was?"

"I couldn't say, sir."

"Surely he mentioned what he thought he'd seen."

Merridew's face took on a slightly obstinate look.

"I can't say, I'm sure, sir."

"This will never do. I must go and see Plunkett. Is he at the cottage?"

"Yes, sir."

"We'll go down there at once. You don't mind, do you, Wimsey? I can't allow Plunkett to make himself ill. If he's had a shock he'd better see a doctor. Well, carry on, Merridew, and be sure you keep her warm and comfortable. The damp is apt to come up through these brick floors. I'm thinking of having the whole place re-set with concrete, but it takes money, of course. I can't imagine," he went on, as he led the way past the greenhouse towards a trim cottage set in its own square of kitchen-garden, "what can have happened to have upset Plunkett. I hope it's nothing serious. He's getting elderly, of course, but he ought to be above believing in warnings. You wouldn't believe the extra-ordinary ideas these people get hold of. Fact is, I expect he's been round at the Weary Traveller, and caught sight of somebody's washing hung out on the way home."

"Not washing," corrected Wimsey mechanically. He had a deductive turn of mind which exposed the folly of the suggestion even while irritably admitting that the matter was of no importance. "It poured with rain last night, and, besides, it's Thursday. But Tuesday and Wednesday were fine, so the drying would have all been done then. No washing."

"Well, well—something else then—a post, or old Mrs. Giddens's white donkey. Plunkett does occasionally take a drop too much, I'm sorry to say, but he's a very good kennel-man, so one overlooks it. They're superstitious round about these parts, and they can tell some queer tales if once you get into their confidence. You'd be surprised how far off the main track we are as regards civilization. Why, not here, but at Ab-

botts Bolton, fifteen miles off, it's as much as one's life's worth
to shoot a hare. Witches, you know, and that sort of thing."

"I shouldn't be a bit surprised. They'll still tell you about
werewolves in some parts of Germany."

"Yes, I dare say. Well, here we are." Mr. Frobisher-Pym
rapped loudly with his walking-stick on the door of the cottage and turned the handle without waiting for permission.

"You there, Mrs. Plunkett? May we come in? Ah! good
morning. Hope we're not disturbing you, but Merridew told
me Plunkett was not so well. This is Lord Peter Wimsey—a
very old friend of mine; that is to say, I'm a very old friend of
his; ha, ha!"

"Good morning, sir; good morning, your lordship. I'm
sure Plunkett will be very pleased to see you. Please step in.
Plunkett, here's Mr. Pym to see you."

The elderly man who sat crouching over the fire turned a
mournful face towards them, and half rose, touching his forehead.

"Well, now, Plunkett, what's the trouble?" inquired Mr.
Frobisher-Pym, with the hearty bedside manner adopted by
country gentlefolk visiting their dependants. "Sorry not to see
you out and about. Touch of the old complaint, eh?"

"No, sir; no, sir. Thank you, sir. I'm well enough in myself.
But I've had a warning, and I'm not long for this world."

"Not long for this world? Oh, nonsense, Plunkett. You
mustn't talk like that. A touch of indigestion, that's what
you've got, I expect. Gives one the blues, I know. I'm sure I
often feel like nothing on earth when I've got one of my bilious
attacks. Try a dose of castor-oil, or a good old-fashioned blue
pill and black draught. Nothing like it. Then you won't talk
about warnings and dying."

"No medicine won't do no good to *my* complaint, sir. Nobody as see what I've seed ever got the better of it. But as you
and the gentleman are here, sir, I'm wondering if you'll do me
a favour."

"Of course, Plunkett, anything you like. What is it?"

"Why, just to draw up my will, sir. Old Parson, he used to

do it. But I don't fancy this new young man, with his candles and bits of things. It don't seem as if he'd make it good and legal, sir, and I wouldn't like it if there was any dispute after I was gone. So as there ain't much time left me, I'd be grateful if you'd put it down clear for me in pen and ink that I wants my little bit all to go to Sarah here, and after her to Alf and Elsie, divided up equal."

"Of course I'll do that for you, Plunkett, any time you like. But it's all nonsense to be talking about wills. Bless my soul, I shouldn't be surprised if you were to see us all underground."

"No, sir. I've been a hale and hearty man, I'm not denying. But I've been called, sir, and I've got to go. It must come to all of us, I know that. But it's a fearful thing to see the death-coach come for one, and know that the dead are in it, that cannot rest in the grave."

"Come now, Plunkett, you don't mean to tell me you believe in that old foolishness about the death-coach. I thought you were an educated man. What would Alf say if he heard you talking such nonsense?"

"Ah, sir, young people don't know everything, and there's many more things in God's creation than what you'll find in the printed books."

"Oh, well," said Mr. Frobisher-Pym, finding this opening irresistible, "we know there are more things in heaven and earth, Horatio, than are dreamt of in your philosophy. Quite so. But that doesn't apply nowadays," he added contradictorily. "There are no ghosts in the twentieth century. Just you think the matter out quietly, and you'll find you've made a mistake. There's probably some quite simple explanation. Dear me! I remember Mrs. Frobisher-Pym waking up one night and having a terrible fright, because she thought somebody'd been and hanged himself on our bedroom door. Such a silly idea, because I was safe in bed beside her—snoring, *she* said, ha, ha!—and, if anybody was feeling like hanging himself, he wouldn't come into our bedroom to do it. Well, she clutched my arm in a great state of mind, and when I went to see what had alarmed her, what do you think it was? My trousers, which I'd hung up by the braces, with the socks still in the legs! My word! and didn't I get a wigging for not having put my things away tidy!"

Mr. Frobisher-Pym laughed, and Mrs. Plunkett said dutifully, "There now!" Her husband shook his head.

"That may be, sir, but I see the death-coach last night with my own eyes. Just striking midnight it was, by the church clock, and I see it come up the lane by the old priory wall."

"And what were you doing out of bed at midnight, eh?"

"Well, sir, I'd been round to my sister's, that's got her boy home on leaf of his ship."

"And you'd been drinking his health, I dare say, Plunkett," Mr. Frobisher-Pym wagged an admonitory forefinger.

"No, sir, I don't deny I'd had a glass or two of ale, but not to fuddle me. My wife can tell you I was sober enough when I got home."

"That's right, sir. Plunkett hadn't taken too much last night, that I'll swear to."

"Well, what was it you saw, Plunkett?"

"I see the death-coach, same as I'm telling you, sir. It come up the lane, all ghostly white, sir, and never making no more sound than the dead—which it were, sir."

"A wagon or something going through to Lymptree or Herriotting."

"No, sir—'tweren't a wagon. I counted the horses—four white horses, and they went by with never a sound of hoof or bridle. And that weren't—"

"Four horses! Come, Plunkett, you must have been seeing double. There's nobody about here would be driving four horses, unless it was Mr. Mortimer from Abbotts Bolton, and he wouldn't be taking his horseflesh out at midnight."

"Four horses they was, sir. I see them plain. And it weren't Mr. Mortimer, neither, for he drives a drag, and this were a big, heavy coach, with no lights on it, but shinin' all of itself, with a colour like moonshine."

"Oh, nonsense, man! You couldn't see the moon last night. It was pitch-dark."

"No, sir, but the coach shone all moony-like, all the same."

"And no lights? I wonder what the police would say to that."

"No mortal police could stop that coach," said Plunkett contemptuously, "nor no mortal man could abide the sight on it. I tell you, sir, that ain't the worst of it. The horses—"

"Was it going slowly?"

"No, sir. It were going at a gallop, only the hoofs didn't touch the ground. There weren't no sound, and I see the black road and the white hoofs half a foot off of it. And the horses had no heads."

"No heads?"

"No, sir."

Mr. Frobisher-Pym laughed.

"Come, come, Plunkett, you don't expect us to swallow that. No heads? How could even a ghost drive horses with no heads? How about the reins, eh?"

"You may laugh, sir, but we know that with God all things are possible. Four white horses they was. I see them clearly, but there was neither head nor neck beyond the collar, sir. I see the reins shining like silver, and they ran up to the rings of the hames, and they didn't go no further. If I was to drop down dead this minute, sir, that's what I see."

"Was there a driver to this wonderful turn-out?"

"Yes, sir, there was a driver."

"Headless too, I suppose?"

"Yes, sir, headless too. At least, I couldn't see nothing of him beyond his coat, which had them old-fashioned capes at the shoulders."

"Well, I must say, Plunkett, you're very circumstantial. How far off was this—er—apparition when you saw it?"

"I was passing by the War Memorial, sir, when I see it come up the lane. It wouldn't be above twenty or thirty yards from where I stood. It went by at a gallop, and turned off to the left round the churchyard wall."

"Well, well, it sounds odd, certainly, but it was a dark night, and at that distance your eyes may have deceived you. Now, if you'll take my advice you'll think no more about it."

"Ah, sir, it's all very well saying that, but everybody knows the man who sees the death-coach of the Burdocks is doomed to die within the week. There's no use rebelling against it, sir; it is so. And if you'll be so good as to oblige me over that matter of a will, I'd die happier for knowing as Sarah and the children was sure of their bit of money."

Mr. Frobisher-Pym obliged over the will, though much against the grain, exhorting and scolding as he wrote. Wimsey added his own signature as one of the witnesses, and contributed his own bit of comfort.

"I shouldn't worry too much about the coach, if I were you," he said. "Depend upon it, if it's the Burdock coach it'll just have come for the soul of the old squire. It couldn't be expected to go to New York for him, don't you see? It's just gettin' ready for the funeral tomorrow."

"That's likely enough," agreed Plunkett. "Often and often it's been seen in these parts when one of the Burdocks was taken. But it's terrible unlucky to see it."

The thought of the funeral seemed, however, to cheer him a little. The visitors again begged him not to think about it, and took their departure.

"Isn't it wonderful," said Mr. Frobisher-Pym, "what imagination will do with these people? And they're obstinate. You could argue with them till you were black in the face."

"Yes. I say, let's go down to the church and have a look at the place. I'd like to know how much he could really have seen from where he was standing."

The parish church of Little Doddering stands, like so many country churches, at some distance from the houses. The main road from Herriotting, Abbotts Bolton, and Frimpton runs past the west gate of the churchyard—a wide God's acre, crowded with ancient stones. On the south side is a narrow and gloomy lane, heavily overhung with old elm trees, dividing the church from the still more ancient ruins of Doddering Priory. On the main road, a little beyond the point

where Old Priory Lane enters, stands the War Memorial, and from here the road runs straight on into Little Doddering. Round the remaining two sides of the churchyard winds another lane, known to the village simply as the Back Lane. This branches out from the Herriotting road about a hundred yards north of the church, connects with the far end of Priory Lane, and thence proceeds deviously to Shootering Underwood, Hamsey, Thripsey, and Wyck.

"Whatever it was Plunkett thinks he saw," said Mr. Frobisher-Pym, "it must have come from Shootering. The Back Lane only leads round by some fields and a cottage or two, and it stands to reason anybody coming from Frimpton would have taken the main road, going and coming. The lane is in a very bad state with all this rain. I'm afraid even your detective ability, my dear Wimsey, would not avail to find wheelmarks on this modern tarmac."

"Hardly," said Wimsey, "especially in the case of a ghostly chariot which gets along without touching the ground. But your reasoning seems perfectly sound, sir."

"It was probably a couple of belated wagons going to market," pursued Mr. Frobisher-Pym, "and the rest of it is superstition and, I am afraid, the local beer. Plunkett couldn't have seen all those details about drivers and hames and so on at this distance. And, if it was making no noise, how did he come to notice it at all, since he'd got past the turn and was walking in the other direction? Depend upon it, he heard the wheels and imagined the rest."

"Probably," said Wimsey.

"Of course," went on his host, "if the wagons really were going about without lights, it ought to be looked into. It is a very dangerous thing, with all these motor vehicles about, and I've had to speak severely about it before now. I fined a man only the other day for the very same thing. Do you care to see the church while we're here?"

Knowing that in country places it is always considered proper to see the church, Lord Peter expressed his eagerness to do so.

"It's always open nowadays," said the magistrate, leading the way to the west entrance. "The vicar has an idea that churches should be always open for private prayer. He comes from a town living, of course. Round about here the people are always out on the land, and you can't expect them to come into church in their working clothes and muddy boots. They wouldn't think it respectful, and they've other things to do. Besides, I said to him, consider the opportunity it gives for undesirable conduct. But he's a young man, and he'll have to learn by experience."

He pushed the door open. A curious, stuffy waft of stale incense, damp, and stoves rushed out at them as they entered—a kind of concentrated extract of Church of England. The two altars, bright with flowers and gilding, and showing as garish splashes among the heavy shadows and oppressive architecture of the little Norman building, sounded the same note of contradiction; it was the warm and human that seemed exotic and unfamiliar; the cold and unwelcoming that seemed native to the place and people.

"This Lady-chapel, as Hancock calls it, in the south aisle, is new, of course," said Mr. Frobisher-Pym. "It aroused a good deal of opposition, but the Bishop is lenient with the High Church party—too lenient, some people think—but, after all, what does it matter? I'm sure I can say my prayers just as well with two communion-tables as with one. And, I will say for Hancock, he is very good with the young men and girls. In these days of motor-cycles, it's something to get them interested in religion at all. Those trestles in the chapel are for old Burdock's coffin, I suppose. Ah! Here is the vicar."

A thin man in a cassock emerged from a door beside the high altar and came down towards them, carrying a tall, oaken candlestick in his hand. He greeted them with a slightly professional smile of welcome. Wimsey diagnosed him promptly as earnest, nervous, and not highly intellectual.

"The candlesticks have only just come," he observed after the usual introductions had been made. "I was afraid they would not be here in time. However, all is now well."

He set the candlestick beside the coffin-trestles, and proceeded to decorate its brass spike with a long candle of unbleached wax, which he took from a parcel in a neighbouring pew.

Mr. Frobisher-Pym said nothing. Wimsey felt it incumbent on him to express his interest, and did so.

"It is very gratifying," said Mr. Hancock, thus encouraged, "to see the people beginning to take a real interest in their church. I have really had very little difficulty in finding watchers for tonight. We are having eight watchers, two by two, from ten o'clock this evening—till which time I shall be myself on duty—till six in the morning, when I come in to say Mass. The men will carry on till two o'clock, then my wife and daughter will relieve them, and Mr. Hubbard and Young Rawlinson have kindly consented to take the hours from four till six."

"What Rawlinson is that?" demanded Mr. Frobisher-Pym.

"Mr. Graham's clerk from Herriotting. It is true he is not a member of the parish, but he was born here, and was good enough to wish to take his turn in watching. He is coming over on his motor-cycle. After all, Mr. Graham has had charge of Burdock's family affairs for very many years, and no doubt they wished to show their respect in some way."

"Well, I only hope he'll be awake enough to do his work in the morning, after gadding about all night," said Mr. Frobisher-Pym gruffly. "As for Hubbard, that's his own lookout, though I must say it seems an odd occupation for a publican. Still, if he's pleased and you're pleased, there's no more to be said about it."

"You've got a very beautiful old church here, Mr. Hancock," said Wimsey, seeing that controversy seemed imminent.

"Very beautiful indeed," said the vicar. "Have you noticed that apse? It is rare for a village church to possess such a perfect Norman apse. Perhaps you would like to come and look at it." He genuflected as they passed a hanging lamp which burned before a niche. "You see, we are permitted Reservation. The Bishop—" He prattled cheerfully as they wandered up the chancel, digressing from time to time to draw attention to the handsome miserere seats ("Of course, this was the original Priory Church"), and a beautifully carved piscina and aumbry ("It is rare to find them so well preserved"). Wimsey assisted him to carry down the remaining candles from the vestry, and, when these had been put in position, joined Mr. Frobisher-Pym at the door.

"I think you said you were dining with the Lumsdens tonight," said the magistrate, as they sat smoking after lunch. "How are you going? Will you have the car?"

"I'd rather you'd lend me one of the saddle horses," said Wimsey. "I get few opportunities of riding in town."

"Certainly, my dear boy, certainly. Only I'm afraid you'll have rather a wet ride. Take Polly Flinders; it will do her good to get some exercise. You are quite sure you would prefer it? Have you got your kit with you?"

"Yes—I brought an old pair of bags down with me, and, with this raincoat, I shan't come to any harm. They won't expect me to dress. How far is it to Frimpton, by the way?"

"Nine miles by the main road, and tarmac all the way, I'm afraid, but there's a good wide piece of grass each side. And, of course, you can cut off a mile or so by going across the common. What time will you want to start?"

"Oh, about seven o'clock, I should think. And, I say, sir— will Mrs. Frobisher-Pym think it very rude if I'm rather late back? Old Lumsden and I went through the war together, and if we get yarning over old times we may go on into the small hours. I don't want to feel I'm treating your house like a hotel, but—"

"Of course not, of course not! That's absolutely all right. My wife won't mind in the very least. We want you to enjoy your visit and do exactly what you like. I'll give you the key, and I'll remember not to put the chain up. Perhaps you wouldn't mind doing that yourself when you come in?"

"Rather not. And how about the mare?"

"I'll tell Merridew to look out for you; he sleeps over the stables. I only wish it were going to be a better night for you. I'm afraid the glass is going back. Yes. Dear, dear! It's a bad lookout for tomorrow. By the way, you'll probably pass the funeral procession at the church. It should be along by about then, if the train is punctual."

The train, presumably, was punctual, for as Lord Peter cantered up to the west gate of the church he saw a hearse of great funereal pomp drawn up before it, surrounded by a little crowd of people. Two mourning coaches were in attendance; the driver of the second seemed to be having some difficulty with the horses, and Wimsey rightly inferred that this was the pair which had been borrowed from Mr. Mortimer. Restraining Polly Flinders as best he might, he sidled into a respectful position on the edge of the crowd, and watched the coffin taken from the hearse and carried through the gate, where it was met by Mr. Hancock, in full pontificals, attended by a thurifer and two torch-bearers. The effect was a little marred by the rain, which had extinguished the candles, but the village seemed to look upon it as an excellent show nevertheless. A massive man, dressed with great correctness in a black frock coat and tall hat, and accompanied by a woman in handsome mourning and furs, was sympathetically commented on. This was Haviland Burdock of silk-stocking fame, the younger son of the deceased. A vast number of white wreaths were then handed out, and greeted with murmurs of admiration and approval. The choir struck up a hymn, rather raggedly, and the procession filed away into the church. Polly Flinders shook her head vigorously, and Wimsey, taking this as a signal to be gone, replaced his hat and ambled gently away towards Frimpton.

He followed the main road for about four miles, winding up through finely wooded country to the edge of Frimpton Common. Here the road made a wide sweep, skirting the common and curving gently down into Frimpton village. Wimsey hesitated for a moment, considering that it was growing dark and that both the way and the animal he rode were strange to him. There seemed, however, to be a well-defined bridle-path across the common, and eventually he decided to take it. Polly Flinders seemed to know it well enough, and cantered along without hesitation. A ride of about a mile and a half brought them without adventure into the main road again. Here a fork in the road presented itself confusingly; an electric torch, however, and a signpost solved the problem; after which ten minutes' ride brought the traveller to his goal.

Major Lumsden was a large, cheerful man—none the less cheerful for having lost a leg in the War. He had a large, cheerful wife, a large, cheerful house, and a large, cheerful family. Wimsey soon found himself seated before a fire as large and cheerful as the rest of the establishment, exchanging gossip with his hosts over a whisky-and-soda. He described the Burdock funeral with irreverent gusto, and went on to tell the story of the phantom coach. Major Lumsden laughed.

"It's a quaint part of the country," he said. "The policeman is just as bad as the rest of them. Do you remember, dear, the time I had to go out and lay a ghost, down at Pogson's farm?"

"I do, indeed," said his wife emphatically. "The maids had a wonderful time. Trivett—that's our local constable—came rushing in here and fainted in the kitchen, and they all sat round howling and sustaining him with our best brandy, while Dan went down and investigated."

"Did you find the ghost?"

"Well, not the ghost, exactly, but we found a pair of boots and half a pork-pie in the empty house, so we put it all down to a tramp. Still, I must say odd things do happen about here. There were those fires on the common last year. They were never explained."

"Gipsies, Dan."

"Maybe; but nobody ever saw them, and the fires would start in the most unexpected way, sometimes in the pouring rain; and, before you could get near one, it would be out, and only a sodden wet black mark left behind it. And there's another bit of the common that animals don't like—near what they call the Dead Man's Post. My dogs won't go near it. Funny brutes.

I've never seen anything there, but even in broad daylight they don't seem to fancy it. The common's not got a good reputation. It used to be a great place for highwaymen."

"Is the Burdock coach anything to do with highwaymen?"

"No. I fancy it was some rakehelly dead-and-gone Burdock. Belonged to the Hell-fire Club or something. The usual sort of story. All the people round here believe in it, of course. It's rather a good thing. Keeps the servants indoors at night. Well, let's go and have some grub, shall we?"

"Do you remember," said Major Lumsden, "that damned old mill, and the three elms by the pig-sty?"

"Good Lord, yes! You very obligingly blew them out of the landscape for us, I remember. They made us a damned sight too conspicuous."

"We rather missed them when they were gone."

"Thank heaven you didn't miss them when they were there. I'll tell you what you did miss, though."

"What's that?"

"The old sow."

"By Jove, yes. Do you remember old Piper fetching her in?"

"I'll say I do. That reminds me. You knew Bunthorne . . ."

"I'll say good night," said Mrs. Lumsden, "and leave you people to it."

"Do you remember," said Lord Peter Wimsey, "that awkward moment when Popham went off his rocker?"

"No. I'd been sent back with a batch of prisoners. I heard about it though. I never knew what became of him."

"I got him sent home. He's married now and living in Lincolnshire."

"Is he? Well, he couldn't help himself, I suppose. He was only a kid. What's happened to Philpotts?"

"Oh, Philpotts . . ."

"Where's your glass, old man?"

"Oh, rot, old man. The night is still young . . ."

• • •

"Really? Well, but look here, why not stay the night? My wife will be delighted. I can fix you up in no time."

"No, thanks most awfully. I must be rolling off home. I said I'd be back; and I'm booked to put the chain on the door."

"As you like, of course, but it's still raining. Not a good night for a ride on an open horse."

"I'll bring a saloon next time. We shan't hurt. Rain's good for the complexion—makes the roses grow. Don't wake your man up. I can saddle her myself."

"My dear man, it's no trouble."

"No, really, old man."

"Well, I'll come along and lend you a hand."

A gust of rain and wind blew in through the hall door as they struggled out into the night. It was past one in the morning and pitch-dark. Major Lumsden again pressed Wimsey to stay.

"No, thanks, really. The old lady's feelings might be hurt. It's not so bad, really—wet, but not cold. Come up, Polly, stand over, old lady."

He put the saddle on and girthed it, while Lumsden held the lantern. The mare, fed and rested, came delicately dancing out of the warm loose-box, head well stretched forward, and nostrils snuffing at the rain.

"Well, so long, old lad. Come back and look us up again. It's been great."

"Rather! By Jove, yes. Best respects to madame. Is the gate open?"

"Yes."

"Well, cheerio!"

"Cheerio!"

Polly Flinders, with her nose turned homewards, settled down to make short work of the nine miles of high-road. Once outside the gates, the night seemed lighter, though the rain poured heavily. Somewhere buried behind the thronging clouds there was a moon, which now and again showed as a pale stain on the sky, a paler reflection on the black road.

Wimsey, with a mind full of memories and a skin full of whisky, hummed to himself as he rode.

As he passed the fork, he hesitated for a moment. Should he take the path over the common or stick to the road? On consideration, he decided to give the common a miss—not because of its sinister reputation, but because of ruts and rabbit-holes. He shook the reins, bestowed a word of encouragement on his mount, and continued by the road, having the common on his right hand, and, on the left, fields bounded by high hedges, which gave some shelter from the driving rain.

He had topped the rise, and passed the spot where the bridlepath again joined the high-road, when a slight start and stumble drew his attention unpleasantly to Polly Flinders.

"Hold up, mare," he said disapprovingly.

Polly shook her head, moved forward, tried to pick up her easy pace again. "Hullo!" said Wimsey, alarmed. He pulled her to a standstill.

"Lame in the near fore," he said, dismounting. "If you've been and gone and strained anything, my girl, four miles from home, father *will* be pleased." It occurred to him for the first time how curiously lonely the road was. He had not seen a single car. They might have been in the wilds of Africa.

He ran an exploratory hand down the near foreleg. The mare stood quietly enough, without shrinking or wincing. Wimsey was puzzled.

"If these had been the good old days," he said, "I'd have thought she'd picked up a stone. But what—"

He lifted the mare's foot, and explored it carefully with fingers and pocket-torch. His diagnosis had been right, after all. A steel nut, evidently dropped from a passing car, had wedged itself firmly between the shoe and the frog. He grunted and felt for his knife. Happily, it was one of that excellent old-fashioned kind which included, besides blades and corkscrews, an ingenious apparatus for removing foreign bodies from horses' feet.

The mare nuzzled him gently as he stooped over his task. It was a little awkward getting to work; he had to wedge the torch under his arm, so as to leave one hand free for the tool and the other to hold the hoof. He was swearing gently at these difficulties when, happening to glance down the road ahead, he fancied he caught the gleam of something moving. It was not easy to see, for at this point the tall trees stood up on both sides of the road, which dipped abruptly from the edge of the common. It was not a car; the light was too faint. A wagon, probably, with a dim lantern. Yet it seemed to move fast. He puzzled of a moment, then bent to work again.

The nut resisted his efforts, and the mare, touched in a tender spot, pulled away, trying to get her foot down. He soothed her with his voice and patted her neck. The torch slipped from his arm. He cursed it impatiently, set down the hoof, and picked up the torch from the edge of the grass, into which it had rolled. As he straightened himself again, he looked along the road and saw.

Up from under the dripping dark of the trees it came, shining with a thin, moony radiance. There was no clatter of hoofs, no rumble of wheels, no ringing of bit or bridle. He saw the white, sleek, shining shoulders with the collar that lay on each, like a faint fiery ring, enclosing nothing. He saw the gleaming reins, their cut ends slipping back and forward unsupported through the ring of the hames. The feet, that never touched earth, ran swiftly—four times four noiseless hoofs, bearing the pale bodies by like smoke. The driver leaned forward, brandishing his whip. He was faceless and headless, but his whole attitude bespoke desperate haste. The coach was barely visible through the driving rain, but Wimsey saw the dimly spinning wheels and a faint whiteness, still and stiff, at the window. It went past at a gallop—headless driver and headless horse and silent coach. Its passing left a stir, a sound that was less a sound than a vibration—and the wind roared suddenly after it, with a great sheer of water blown up out of the south.

"Good God!" said Wimsey. And then: "How many whiskies did we have?"

He turned and looked back along the road, straining his

eyes. Then suddenly he remembered the mare, and, without troubling further about the torch, picked up her foot and went to work by touch. The nut gave no more trouble, but dropped out into his hand almost immediately. Polly Flinders sighed gratefully and blew into his ear.

Wimsey led her forward a few steps. She put her feet down firmly and strongly. The nut, removed without delay, had left no tenderness. Wimsey mounted, let her go—then pulled her head round suddenly.

"I'm going to see," he said resolutely. "Come up, mare! We won't let any headless horses get the better of *us*. Perfectly indecent, goin' about without heads. Get on, old lady. Over the common with you. We'll catch 'em at the crossroads."

Without the slightest consideration for his host or his host's property, he put the mare to the bridle-path again, and urged her into a gallop.

At first he thought he could make out a pale, fluttering whiteness, moving away ahead of him on the road. Presently, as high-road and bridle-path diverged, he lost it altogether. But he knew there was no side-road. Bar any accident to his mount, he was bound to catch it before it came to the fork. Polly Flinders, answering easily to the touch of his heel, skimmed over the rough track with the indifference born of familiarity. In less than ten minutes her feet rang out again on the tarmac. He pulled her up, faced round in the direction of Little Doddering, and stared down the road. He could see nothing yet. Either he was well ahead of the coach, or it had already passed at unbelievable speed, or else—

He waited. Nothing. The violent rain had ceased, and the moon was struggling out again. The road appeared completely deserted. He glanced over his shoulder. A small beam of light near the ground moved, turned, flashed green, and red, and white again, and came towards him. Presently he made out that it was a policeman wheeling a bicycle.

"A bad night, sir," said the man civilly, but with a faint note of inquiry in his voice.

"Rotten," said Wimsey.

"Just had to mend a puncture, to make it all the pleasanter," added the policeman.

Wimsey expressed sympathy. "Have you been here long?"
he added.

"Best part o' twenty minutes."

"Did you see anything pass along this way from Little
Doddering?"

"Ain't been nothing along while I've been here. What sort
of thing did you mean, sir?"

"I thought I saw—" Wimsey hesitated. He did not care
about the idea of making a fool of himself. "A carriage with
four horses," he said hesitatingly. "It passed me on this road
not a quarter of an hour ago—down at the other end of the
common. I—I came back to see. It seemed unusual—" He became aware that his story sounded very lame.

The policeman spoke rather sharply and rapidly.

"There ain't been nothing past here."

"You're sure?"

"Yes, sir; and, if you don't mind me sayin' so, you'd best be
getting home. It's a lonesome bit o' road."

"Yes, isn't it?" said Wimsey. "Well, good night, sergeant."

He turned the mare's head back along the Little Doddering road, going very quietly. He saw nothing, heard nothing,
and passed nothing. The night was brighter now, and, as he
rode back, he verified the entire absence of side-roads. Whatever the thing was which he had seen, it had vanished somewhere along the edge of the common; it had not gone by the
main road, nor by any other.

Wimsey came down rather late for breakfast in the morning, to find his hosts in a state of some excitement.

"The most extraordinary thing has happened," said Mrs.
Frobisher-Pym.

"Outrageous!" added her husband. "I warned Hancock—
he can't say I didn't warn him. Still, however much one may
disapprove of his goings-on, there is no excuse whatever for

such abominable conduct. Once let me get hold of the beg-
gars, whoever they are—"

"What's up?" said Wimsey, helping himself to broiled kidneys at the sideboard.

"A most scandalous thing," said Mrs. Frobisher-Pym.
"The vicar came up to Tom at once—I hope we didn't disturb
you, by the way, with all the excitement. It appears that when
Mr. Hancock got to the church this morning at six o'clock to
take the early service—"

"No, no, my dear, you've got it wrong. Let *me* tell it. When
Joe Grinch—that's the sexton, you know, and he has to get
there first to ring the bell—when he arrived, he found the
south door wide open and nobody in the chapel, where they
should have been, beside the coffin. He was very much per-
plexed, of course, but he supposed that Hubbard and young
Rawlinson had got sick of it and gone off home. So he went on
to the vestry to get the vestments and things ready, and to his
amazement he heard women's voices, calling out to him from
inside. He was so astonished, didn't know where he was, but
he went on and unlocked the door—"

"With his own key?" put in Wimsey.

"The key was in the door. As a rule it's kept hanging up on
a nail under a curtain near the organ, but it was in the lock—
where it ought not to have been. And inside the vestry he
found Mrs. Hancock and her daughter, nearly dead with
fright and annoyance."

"Great Scott!"

"Yes, indeed. They had a most extraordinary story to tell.
They'd taken over at two o'clock from the other pair of watchers, and had knelt down by the coffin in the Lady-chapel, according to plan, to say the proper sort of prayers, whatever
they are. They'd been there, to the best of their calculation,
about ten minutes, when they heard a noise up by the High
Altar, as though somebody was creeping stealthily about. Miss
Hancock is a very plucky girl, and she got up and walked up
the aisle in the dark, with Mrs. Hancock following on behind

because, as she said, she didn't want to be left alone. When they'd got as far as the roodscreen, Miss Hancock called out aloud, 'Who's there?' At that they heard a sort of rustling sound, and a noise like something being knocked over. Miss Hancock most courageously snatched up one of the church-warden's staffs, which was clipped on to the choir-stalls, and ran forward, thinking, she says, that somebody was trying to steal the ornaments off the altar. There's a very fine fifteenth-century cross—"

"Never mind the cross, Tom. That hasn't been taken, at any rate."

"No, it hasn't, but she thought it might be. Anyhow, just as she got up to the sanctuary steps, with Mrs. Hancock coming close after her and begging her to be careful, somebody seemed to rush out of the choir-stalls, and caught her by the arms and frog's-marched her—that's her expression—into the vestry. And before she could get breath even to shriek, Mrs. Hancock was pushed in beside her, and the door locked on them."

"By Jove! You do have exciting times in your village."

"Well," said Mr. Frobisher-Pym, "of course they were dreadfully frightened, because they didn't know but what these wretches would come back and murder them, and, in any case, they thought the church was being robbed. But the vestry windows are very narrow and barred, and they couldn't do anything except wait. They tried to listen, but they couldn't hear much. Their only hope was that the four-o'clock watchers might come early and catch the thieves at work. But they waited and they waited, and they heard four strike, and five, and nobody came."

"What had happened to what's-his-name and Rawlinson then?"

"They couldn't make out, and nor could Grinch. However, they had a good look round the church, and nothing seemed to be taken or disturbed in any way. Just then the vicar came along, and they told him all about it. He was very much shocked, naturally, and his first thought—when he found the ornaments were safe and the poor-box all right—was that some Kensitite people had been stealing the wafers from the what d'you call it."

"The tabernacle," suggested Wimsey.

"Yes, that's his name for it. That worried him very much, and he unlocked it and had a look, but the wafers were all there all right, and, as there's only one key, and that was on his own watch-chain, it wasn't a case of anyone substituting unconsecrated wafers for consecrated ones, or any practical joke of that kind. So he sent Mrs. and Miss Hancock home, and had a look round the church outside, and the first thing he saw, lying in the bushes near the south door, was young Rawlinson's motor-cycle."

"Oho!"

"So his next idea was to hunt for Rawlinson and Hubbard. However, he didn't have to look far. He'd got round the church as far as the furnace-house on the north side, when he heard a terrific hullabaloo going on, and people shouting and thumping on the door. So he called Grinch, and they looked in through the little window, and there, if you please, were Hubbard and young Rawlinson, bawling and going on and using the most shocking language. It seems they were set on in exactly the same way, only before they got inside the church. Rawlinson had been passing the evening with Hubbard, I understand, and they had a bit of a sleep downstairs in the back bar, to avoid disturbing the house early—or so they say, though I dare say if the truth was known they were having drinks; and if that's Hancock's idea of a suitable preparation for going to church and saying prayers, all I can say is, it isn't mine. Anyway, they started off just before four, Hubbard going down on the carrier of Rawlinson's bicycle. They had to get off at the south gate, which was pushed to, and while Rawlinson was wheeling the machine up the path two or three men—they couldn't see exactly—jumped out from the trees. There was a bit of a scuffle, but what with the bicycle, and its being so unexpected, they couldn't put up a very good fight, and the men dropped blankets over their heads, or something. I don't know all the details. At any rate, they were bundled into the furnace-house and left there. They may be there still, for all I know, if they haven't found the key. There should be a spare key, but I don't know what's become of it. They sent up for it this morning, but I haven't seen it about for a long time."

"It wasn't left in the lock this time, then?"

"No, it wasn't. They've had to send for the locksmith. I'm going down now to see what's to be done about it. Like to come, if you're ready?"

Wimsey said he would. Anything in the nature of a problem always fascinated him.

"You were back pretty late, by the way," said Mr. Frobisher-Pym jovially, as they left the house. "Yarning over old times, I suppose."

"We were, indeed," said Wimsey.

"Hope the old girl carried you all right. Lonely bit of road, isn't it? I don't suppose you saw anybody worse than yourself, as the saying goes?"

"Only a policeman," said Wimsey thoughtfully. He had not yet quite decided about the phantom coach. No doubt Plunkett would be relieved to know that he was not the only person to whom the "warning" had come. But, then, had it really been the phantom coach, or merely a delusion, begotten by whisky upon reminiscence? Wimsey, in the cold light of day, was none too certain.

On arriving at the church, the magistrate and his guest found quite a little crowd collected, conspicuous among whom were the vicar, in cassock and biretta, gesticulating freely, and the local policeman, his tunic buttoned awry and his dignity much impaired by the small fry of the village, who clustered round his legs. He had just finished taking down the statements of the two men who had been released from the stoke-hole. The younger of these, a fresh-faced, impudent-looking fellow of twenty-five or so, was in the act of starting up his motor-cycle. He greeted Mr. Frobisher-Pym pleasantly. "Afraid they've made us look a bit small, sir. You'll excuse me, won't you? I'll have to be getting back to Herriotting. Mr. Graham won't be any too pleased if I'm late for the office. I think some of the bright lads have been having a joke with us." He grinned as he pushed the throttle-lever over and departed in a smother of unnecessary smoke that made Mr. Frobisher-Pym sneeze. His fellow-victim, a large, fat man, who looked the sporting publican that he was, grinned shamefacedly at the magistrate.

"Well, Hubbard," said the latter, "I hoped you've enjoyed your experience. I must say I'm surprised at a man of your size letting himself be shut up in a coal-hole like a naughty urchin."

"Yes, sir, I was surprised myself at the time," retorted the publican, good-humouredly enough. "When that there blanket came down on my head, I was the most surprised man in this here country. I gave 'em a hack or two on the shins, though, to remember me by," he added, with a reminiscent chuckle.

"How many of them were there?" asked Wimsey.

"Three or four, I should say, sir. But not 'avin' seen 'em, I can only tell from 'earin' 'em talk. There was two laid 'old of me, I'm pretty sure, and young Rawlinson thinks there was only one 'ad 'old of 'im, but 'e was a wonderful strong 'un."

"We must leave no stone unturned to find out who these people were," said the vicar excitedly. "Ah, Mrs. Frobisher-Pym, come and see what they have done in the church. It is as I thought—an anti-Catholic protest. We must be most thankful that they have done no more than they have."

He led the way in. Someone had lit two or three hanging lamps in the gloomy little chancel. By their light Wimsey was able to see that the neck of the eagle lectern was decorated with an enormous red-white-and-blue bow, and bore a large placard—obviously pinched from the local newspaper offices—"VATICAN BANS IMMODEST DRESS." In each of the choir-stalls a teddy-bear sat, lumpishly amiable, apparently absorbed in reading the choir-books upside-down, while on the ledge before them copies of the *Pink 'Un* were obtrusively displayed. In the pulpit, a waggish hand had set up a pantomime ass's head, elegantly arrayed in a nightgown, and crowned with a handsome nimbus, cut from gold paper.

"Disgraceful, isn't it?" said the vicar.

"Well, Hancock," replied Mr. Frobisher-Pym. "I must say I think you have brought it upon yourself—though I quite agree, of course, that this sort of thing cannot possibly be allowed, and the offenders must be discovered and severely punished. But you must see that many of your practices appear to these people to be papistical nonsense at best, and while that is no excuse . . ."

His reprimanding voice barked on.

". . . what I really can only look upon as this sacrilegious business with old Burdock—a man whose life . . ."

The policeman had by this time shoved away the attendant villagers and was standing beside Lord Peter at the entrance of the rood-screen.

"Was that you was out on the road this morning, sir? Ah! I thought I reckernized your voice. Did you get home all right, sir? Didn't meet nothing?"

There seemed to be a shade more than idle questioning in the tone of his voice. Wimsey turned quickly.

"No, I met nothing—more. Who is it drives a coach with four white horses about this village of a night, sergeant?"

"Not sergeant, sir—I ain't due for promotion yet awhile. Well, sir, as to white horses, I don't altogether like to say. Mr. Mortimer over at Abbotts Bolton has some nice greys, and he's the biggest horse-breeder about these parts—but, well, there, sir, he wouldn't be driving out in all that rain, sir, would he?"

"It doesn't seem a sensible thing to do, certainly."

"No, sir. And"—the constable leaned close to Wimsey and spoke into his ear—"and Mr. Mortimer is a man that's got a head on his shoulders—*and, what's more, so have his horses.*"

"Why," said Wimsey, a little startled by the aptness of this remark, "did you ever know a horse that hadn't?"

"No, sir," said the policeman, with emphasis. "I never knew no *livin'* horse that hadn't. But that's neether here nor there, as the sayin' goes. But as to this church business, that's just a bit of a lark got up among the boys, that's what that is. They don't mean no harm, you know, sir; they likes to be up to their tricks. It's all very well for the vicar to talk, sir, but this ain't no Kensitites nor anything of that, as you can see with half an eye. Just a bit of fun, that's all it is."

"I'd come to the same conclusion myself," said Wimsey, interested, "but I'd rather like to know what makes you think so."

"Lord bless you, sir, ain't it plain as the nose on your face? If it had a-bin these Kensitites, wouldn't they have gone for the crosses and the images and the lights and—that there?" He extended a horny finger in the direction of the tabernacle. "No, sir, these lads what did this ain't laid a finger on the things what you might call sacred images—and they ain't done no harm neether to the communion-table. So I says as it ain't a case of controvversy, but more a bit of fun, like. And they've treated Mr. Burdock's corpse respectful, sir, you see, too. That shows they wasn't meaning anything wrong at heart, don't you see?"

"I agree absolutely," said Wimsey. "In fact, they've taken particular care not to touch anything that a church-man holds really sacred. How long have you been on this job, officer?"

"Three years, sir, come February."

"Ever had any idea of going to town or taking up the detective side of the business?"

"Well, sir—I have—but it isn't just ask and have, as you might say."

Wimsey took a card from his note-case.

"If you ever think seriously about it," he said, "give this card to Chief Inspector Parker, and have a chat with him. Tell him I think you haven't got opportunities enough down here. He's a great friend of mind, and he'll give you a good chance, I know."

"I've heard of you, my lord," said the constable, gratified, "and I'm sure it's very kind of your lordship. Well, I suppose I'd best be getting along now. You leave it to me, Mr. Frobisher-Pym, sir; we'll soon get at the bottom of this here."

"I hope you do," said the magistrate. "Meanwhile, Mr. Hancock, I trust you will realize the inadvisability of leaving the church doors open at night. Well, come along, Wimsey; we'll leave them to get the church straight for the funeral. What have you found there?"

"Nothing," said Wimsey, who had been peering at the floor of the Lady-chapel. "I was afraid you'd got the worm in here, but I see it's only sawdust." He dusted his fingers as he spoke, and followed Mr. Frobisher-Pym out of the building.

When you are staying in a village, you are expected to take part in the interests and amusements of the community. Accordingly, Lord Peter duly attended the funeral of Squire Burdock, and beheld the coffin safely committed to the ground, in a drizzle, certainly, but not without the attendance of a large and reverent congregation. After this ceremony, he was formally introduced to Mr. and Mrs. Haviland Burdock, and was able to confirm his previous impression that the lady was well, not to say too well, dressed, as might be expected from one whose wardrobe was based upon silk stockings. She was a handsome woman, in a large, bold style, and the hand that clasped Wimsey's was quite painfully encrusted with diamonds. Haviland was disposed to be friendly—and, indeed, silk manufacturers have no reason to be otherwise to rich men of noble birth. He seemed to be aware of Wimsey's reputation as an antiquarian and book-collector, and extended a hearty invitation to him to come and see the old house.

"My brother Martin is still abroad," he said, "but I'm sure he would be delighted to have you come and look at the place. I'm told there are some very fine old books in the library. We shall be staying here till Monday—if Mrs. Hancock will be good enough to have us. Suppose you come along tomorrow afternoon."

Wimsey said he would be delighted.

Mrs. Hancock interposed and said, wouldn't Lord Peter come to tea at the vicarage first.

Wimsey said it was very good of her.

"Then that's settled," said Mrs. Burdock. "You and Mr. Pym come to tea, and then we'll all go over the house together. I've hardly seen it myself yet."

"It's very well worth seeing," said Mr. Frobisher-Pym. "Fine old place, but takes some money to keep up. Has nothing been seen of the will yet, Mr. Burdock?"

"Nothing whatever," said Haviland. "It's curious, because Mr. Graham—the solicitor, you know, Lord Peter—certainly drew one up, just after poor Martin's unfortunate difference with our father. He remembers it perfectly."

"Can't he remember what's in it?"

"He could, of course, but he doesn't think it etiquette to say. He's one of the crusted old type. Poor Martin always called him an old scoundrel—but then, of course, he never approved of Martin, so Martin was not altogether unprejudiced. Besides, as Mr. Graham says, all that was some years ago, and it's quite possible that the governor destroyed the will later, or made a new one in America."

" 'Poor Martin' doesn't seem to have been popular hereabouts," said Wimsey to Mr. Frobisher-Pym, as they parted from the Burdocks and turned homewards.

"N-no," said the magistrate. "Not with Graham, anyway. Personally, I rather liked the lad, though he was a bit harum-scarum. I dare say he's sobered up with time—and marriage. It's odd that they can't find the will. But, if it was made at the time of the rumpus, its bound to be in Haviland's favour."

"I think Haviland thinks so," said Wimsey. "His manner seemed to convey a chastened satisfaction. I expect the discreet Graham made it fairly clear that the advantage was not with the unspeakable Martin."

The following morning turned out fine, and Wimsey, who was supposed to be enjoying a rest-and-fresh-air cure in Little Doddering, petitioned for a further loan of Polly Flinders. His host consented with pleasure, and only regretted that he could not accompany his guest, being booked to attend a Board of Guardians' meeting in connexion with the workhouse.

"But you could go up and get a good blow on the common," he suggested. "Why not go round by Petering Friars, turn off across the common till you get to Dead Man's Post, and come back by the Frimpton road? It makes a very pleasant round—about nineteen miles. You'll be back in nice time for lunch if you take it easy."

Wimsey fell in with the plan—the more readily that it exactly coincided with his own inward purpose. He had a reason for wishing to ride over the Frimpton road by daylight.

"You'll be careful about Dead Man's Post," said Mrs. Frobisher-Pym a little anxiously. "The horses have a way of shying at it. I don't know why. People say, of course—"

"All nonsense," said her husband. "The villagers dislike the place and that makes the horses nervous. It's remarkable how a rider's feelings communicate themselves to his mount. I've never had any trouble at Dead Man's Post."

It was a quiet and pretty road, even on a November day, that led to Petering Friars. Jogging down the winding Essex lanes in the wintry sunshine, Wimsey felt soothed and happy. A good burst across the common raised his spirits to exhilaration pitch. He had entirely forgotten Dead Man's Post and its uncanny reputation, when a violent start and swerve, so sudden that it nearly unseated him, recalled him to what he was doing. With some difficulty, he controlled Polly Flinders, and brought her to a standstill.

He was at the highest point of the common, following a bridle-path which was bordered on each side by gorse and dead bracken. A little way ahead of him another bridle-path seemed to run into it, and at the junction of the two was something which he had vaguely imagined to be a decayed sign-post. Certainly it was short and thick for a sign-post, and had no arms. It appeared, however, to bear some sort of inscription on the face that was turned towards him.

He soothed the mare, and urged her gently towards the post. She took few hesitating steps, and plunged sideways, snorting and shivering.

"Queer!" said Wimsey. "If this is my state of mind communicating itself to my mount, I'd better see a doctor. My nerves must be in a rotten state. Come up, old lady! What's the matter with you!"

Polly Flinders, apologetic but determined, refused to budge. He urged her gently with his heel. She sidled away, with ears laid back, and he saw the white of a protesting eye. He slipped from the saddle, and, putting his hand through the bridle, endeavoured to lead her forward. After a little persuasion, the mare followed him, with stretched neck and treading as though on egg-shells. After a dozen hesitating paces, she stopped again, trembling in all her limbs. He put his hand on her neck and found it wet with sweat.

"Damn it all!" said Wimsey. "Look here, I'm jolly well going to read what's on that post. If you won't come, will you stand still?"

He dropped the bridle. The mare stood quietly with hanging head. He left her and went forward, glancing back from time to time to see that she showed no disposition to bolt. She stood quietly enough, however, only shifting her feet uneasily.

Wimsey walked up to the post. It was a stout pillar of ancient oak, newly painted white. The inscription, too, had been recently blacked in. It read:

ON THIS SPOT
GEORGE WINTER
WAS FOULLY MURTHERED
IN DEFENSE OF
HIS MASTER'S GOODS
BY BLACK RALPH
OF HERRIOTTING
WHO WAS AFTERWARD
HANGED IN CHAINS
ON THE PLACE OF HIS CRIME
9 NOVEMBER 1674

FEAR JUSTICE

"And very nice, too," said Wimsey. "Dead Man's Post without a doubt. Polly Flinders seems to share the local feeling about the place. Well, Polly, if them's your sentiments, I won't do violence to them. But may I ask why, if you're so sensitive about a mere post, you should swallow a death-coach and four headless horses with such hardened equanimity?"

The mare took the shoulder of his jacket gently between her lips and mumbled at it.

"Just so," said Wimsey. "I perfectly understand. You would if you could, but you really can't. But those horses, Polly—did they bring with them no brimstone blast from the nethermost pit? Can it be that they really exuded nothing but an honest and familiar smell of stables?"

He mounted, and, turning Polly's head to the right, guided her in a circle, so as to give Dead Man's Post a wide berth before striking the path again.

"The supernatural explanation is, I think, excluded. Not on *a priori* grounds, which would be unsound, but on the evidence of Polly's senses. There remain the alternatives of whisky and jiggery-pokery. Further investigation seems called for."

He continued to muse as the mare moved quietly forward.

"Supposing I wanted, for some reason, to scare the neighbourhood with the apparition of a coach and headless horses, I should choose a dark, rainy night. Good! It was that kind of night. Now, if I took black horses and painted their bodies white—poor devils! what a state they'd be in. No. How do they do these Maskelyne-and-Devant stunts where they cut off people's heads? White horses, of course—and black felt clothing over their heads. Right! And luminous paint on the harness, with a touch here and there on their bodies, to make good contrast and ensure that the whole show wasn't invisible. No difficulty about that. But they must go silently. Well, why not? Four stout black cloth bags filled with bran, drawn well up and tied round the fetlocks would make any horse go quietly enough, especially if there was a bit of a wind going. Rags round the bridle-rings to prevent clinking, and round the ends of the traces to keep from squeaking. Give 'em a coachman in a white coat and a black mask, hitch 'em to a rubber-tyred fly, picked out with phosphorus and well-oiled at the joints—and I swear I'd make something quite ghostly enough to startle a rather well-irrigated gentleman on a lonely road at half past two in the morning."

He was pleased with this thought, and tapped his boot cheerfully with his whip.

"But damn it all! They never passed me again. Where did they go to? A coach-and-horses can't vanish into thin air, you know. There must be a side-road after all—or else, Polly Flinders, you've been pulling my leg all the time."

The bridle-path eventually debouched upon the highway at the now familiar fork where Wimsey had met the policeman. As he slowly ambled homewards, his lordship scanned the left-hand hedgerow, looking for the lane which surely must exist. But nothing rewarded his search. Enclosed fields with pad-locked gates presented the only breaks in the hedge, till he again found himself looking down the avenue of trees up which the death-coach had come galloping two nights before.

"Damn!" said Wimsey.

It occurred to him for the first time that the coach might perhaps have turned round and gone back through Little Doddering. Certainly it had been seen by Little Doddering Church on Wednesday. But on that occasion, also, it had gal-loped off in the direction of Frimpton. In fact, thinking it over, Wimsey concluded that it had approached from Frimpton, gone round the church—widdershins, naturally—by the Back Lane, and returned by the high-road whence it came. But in that case—

"Turn again, Whittington," said Wimsey, and Polly Flinders rotated obediently in the road. "Through one of those fields it went, or I'm a Dutchman."

He pulled Polly into a slow walk, and passed along the strip of grass at the right-hand side, staring at the ground as though he were an Aberdonian who had lost a sixpence.

The first gate led into a ploughed field, harrowed smooth

and sown with autumn wheat. It was clear that no wheeled thing had been across it for many weeks. The second gate looked more promising. It gave upon fallow ground, and the entrance was seamed with innumerable wheel-ruts. On further examination, however, it was clear that this was the one and only gate. It seemed unlikely that the mysterious coach should have been taken into a field from which there was no way out. Wimsey decided to seek farther.

The third gate was in bad repair. It sagged heavily from its hinges; the hasp was gone, and gate and post had been secured with elaborate twists of wire. Wimsey dismounted and examined these, convincing himself that their rusty surface had not been recently disturbed.

There remained only two more gates before he came to the cross-roads. One led into plough again, where the dark ridge-and-furrow showed no sign of disturbance, but at sight of the last gate Wimsey's heart gave a leap.

There was plough-land here also, but round the edge of the field ran a wide, beaten path, rutted and water-logged. The gate was not locked, but opened simply with a spring catch. Wimsey examined the approach. Among the wide ruts made by farm-wagons was the track of four narrow wheels — the unmistakable prints of rubber tyres. He pushed the gate open and passed through.

The path skirted two sides of the plough; then came another gate and another field, containing a long barrow of mangold wurzels and a couple of barns. At the sound of Polly's hoofs, a man emerged from the nearest barn, with a paint-brush in his hand, and stood watching Wimsey's approach.

"Morning!" said the latter genially.

"Morning, sir."

"Fine day after the rain."

"Yes, it is, sir."

"I hope I'm not trespassing?"

"Where was you wanting to go, sir?"

"I thought, as a matter of fact — hullo!"

"Anything wrong, sir?"

Wimsey shifted in the saddle.

"I fancy this girth's slipped a bit. It's a new one." (This was a fact.) "Better have a look."

The man advanced to investigate, but Wimsey had dismounted and was tugging at the strap, with his head under the mare's belly.

"Yes, it wants taking up a trifle. Oh! Thanks most awfully. Is this a short cut to Abbotts Bolton, by the way?"

"Not to the village, sir, though you can get through this way. It comes out by Mr. Mortimer's stables."

"Ah, yes. This his land?"

"No, sir, it's Mr. Topham's land, but Mr. Mortimer rents this field and the next for fodder."

"Oh, yes." Wimsey peered across the hedge. "Lucerne, I suppose. Or clover."

"Clover, sir. And the mangolds is for the cattle."

"Oh—Mr. Mortimer keeps cattle as well as horses?"

"Yes, sir."

"Very jolly. Have a gasper?" Wimsey had sidled across to the barn in his interest, and was gazing absently into its dark interior. It contained a number of farm implements and a black fly of antique construction, which seemed to be undergoing renovation with black varnish. Wimsey pulled some vestas from his pocket. The box was apparently damp, for, after one or two vain attempts he abandoned it, and struck a match on the wall of the barn. The flame, lighting up the ancient fly, showed it to be incongruously fitted with rubber tyres.

"Very fine stud, Mr. Mortimer's, I understand," said Wimsey carelessly.

"Yes, sir, very fine indeed."

"I suppose he hasn't any greys, by any chance. My mother—queenly woman, Victorian ideas, and all that—is rather keen on greys. Sports a carriage and pay-ah, don't you know."

"Yes, sir? Well, Mr. Mortimer would be able to suit the lady, I think, sir. He has several greys."

"No? has he though? I must really go over and see him. Is it far?"

"Matter of five or six mile by the fields, sir."

Wimsey looked at his watch.

"Oh, dear! I'm really afraid it's too far for this morning. I absolutely promised to get back to lunch. I must come over another day. Thanks *so* much. Is that girth right now? Oh, really, I'm immensely obliged. Get yourself a drink, won't you—and tell Mr. Mortimer not to sell his greys till I've seen them. Well, *good* morning, and many thanks."

He set Polly Flinders on the homeward path and trotted gently away. Not till he was out of sight of the barn did he pull up and, stooping from the saddle, thoughtfully examine his boots. They were liberally plastered with bran.

"I must have picked it up in the barn," said Wimsey. "Curious, if true. Why should Mr. Mortimer be lashing the stuffing out of the greys in an old fly at dead of night—and with muffled hoofs and no heads to boot? It's not a kind thing to do. It frightened Plunkett very much. It made me think I was drunk—a thought I hate to think. Ought I to tell the police? Are Mr. Mortimer's jokes any business of mine? What do *you* think, Polly?"

The mare, hearing her name, energetically shook her head.

"You think not? Perhaps you are right. Let us say that Mr. Mortimer did it for a wager. Who am I to interfere with his amusements? All the same," added his lordship, "I'm glad to know it wasn't Lumsden's whisky."

"This is the library," said Haviland, ushering in his guests. "A fine room—and a fine collection of books, I'm told, though literature isn't much in my line. It wasn't much in the governor's line, either, I'm afraid. The place wants doing up, as you see. I don't know whether Martin will take it in hand. It's a job that'll cost money, of course."

Wimsey shivered a little as he gazed round—more from sympathy than from cold, though a white November fog lay curled against the tall windows and filtered damply through the frames.

A long, mouldering room, in the frigid neo-classical style, the library was melancholy enough in the sunless grey afternoon, even without the signs of neglect which wrung the book-collector's heart. The walls, panelled to half their height with bookcases, ran up in plaster to the moulded ceiling. Damp had blotched them into grotesque shapes, and here and there were ugly cracks and squamous patches, from which the plaster had fallen in yellowish flakes. A wet chill seemed to ooze from the books, from the calf bindings peeling and perishing, from the stains of greenish mildew which spread horridly from volume to volume. The curious musty odour of decayed leather and damp paper added to the general cheerlessness of the atmosphere.

"Oh, dear, dear!" said Wimsey, peering dismally into this sepulchre of forgotten learning. With his shoulders hunched like the neck-feathers of a chilly bird, with his long nose and half-shut eyes, he resembled a dilapidated heron, brooding over the stagnation of a wintry pool.

"What a freezing-cold place!" exclaimed Mrs. Hancock. "You really ought to scold Mrs. Lovall, Mr. Burdock. When she was put in here as caretaker, I said to my husband—didn't I, Philip?—that your father had chosen the laziest woman in Little Doddering. She ought to have kept up big fires here, *at least* twice a week! It's really shameful, the way she has let things go."

"Yes, isn't it?" agreed Haviland.

Wimsey said nothing. He was nosing along the shelves, every now and then taking a volume down and glancing at it.

"It was always rather a depressing room," went on Haviland. "I remember, when I was a kid, it used to overawe me rather. Martin and I used to browse about among the books, you know, but I think we were always afraid that something or somebody would stalk out upon us from the dark corners. What's that you've got there, Lord Peter? Oh, *Foxe's Book of Martyrs*. Dear me! How those pictures did terrify me in the old days! And there was a *Pilgrim's Progress*, with a most alarming picture of Apollyon straddling over the whole breadth of the way, which gave me many nightmares. Let me see. It used to live over in this bay, I think. Yes, here it is. How it does bring all back, to be sure! Is it valuable, by the way?"

"No, not really. But this first edition of Burton is worth money; badly spotted, though—you'd better send it to be cleaned. And this is an extremely fine Boccaccio; take care of it."

"John Boccace—*The Dance of Machabree*. It's a good title, anyhow. Is that the same Boccaccio that wrote the naughty stories?"

"Yes," said Wimsey, a little shortly. He resented this attitude towards Boccaccio.

"Never read them," said Haviland, with a wink at his wife, "but I've seen 'em in the windows of those surgical shops—so I suppose they're naughty, eh? The vicar's looking shocked."

"Oh, not at all," said Mr. Hancock, with a conscientious assumption of broad-mindedness. *"Et ego in Arcadia*—that is to say, one doesn't enter the Church without undergoing a classical education, and making the acquaintance of much more worldly authors even than Boccaccio. Those woodcuts are very fine, to my uninstructed eye."

"Very fine indeed," said Wimsey.

"There's another old book I remember, with jolly pictures," said Haviland. "A chronicle of some sort—what's 'is name—place in Germany—*you* know—where that hangman came from. They published his diary the other day. I read it, but it wasn't really exciting; not half as gruesome as old Harrison Ainsworth. What's the name of the place?"

"Nuremburg?" suggested Wimsey.

"That's it, of course—the *Nuremberg Chronicle*. I wonder if that's still in its old place. It was over here by the window, if I remember rightly."

He led the way to the end of one of the bays, which ran up close against a window. Here the damp seemed to have done its worst. A pane of glass was broken, and rain had blown in.

"Now where has it gone to? A big book, it was, with a stamped leather binding. I'd like to see the old *Chronicle* again. I haven't set eyes on it for donkey's years."

His glance roamed vaguely over the shelves. Wimsey, with the book-lover's instinct, was the first to spot the *Chronicle*, wedged at the extreme end of the shelf against the outer wall. He hitched his finger into the top edge of the spine, but finding that the rotting leather was ready to crumble at a touch, he dislodged a neighbouring book and drew the *Chronicle* gently out, using his whole hand.

"Here he is—in pretty bad condition, I'm afraid. Hullo!"

As he drew the book away from the wall, a piece of folded parchment came away with it, and fell at his feet. He stooped and picked it up.

"I say, Burdock—isn't this what you've been looking for?"

Haviland Burdock, who had been rooting about on one of the lower shelves, straightened himself quickly, his face red from stooping.

"By Jove!" he said, turning first redder and then pale with excitement. "Look at this, Winnie. It's the governor's will. What an extraordinary thing! Whoever would have thought of looking for it here, of all places?"

"Is it really the will?" cried Mrs. Hancock.

"No doubt about it, I should say," observed Wimsey coolly. "Last Will and Testament of Simon Burdock." He stood, turning the grimy document over and over in his hands, looking from the endorsement to the plain side of the folded parchment.

"Well, well!" said Mr. Hancock. "How strange! It seems almost providential that you should have taken that book down."

"What does the will say?" demanded Mrs. Burdock, in some excitement.

"I beg your pardon," said Wimsey, handing it over to her. "Yes, as you say, Mr. Hancock, it does almost seem as if I was meant to find it." He glanced down again at the *Chronicle*, mournfully tracing with his finger the outline of a damp stain which had rotted the cover and spread to the inner pages, almost obliterating the colophon.

Haviland Burdock meanwhile had spread the will out on the nearest table. His wife leaned over his shoulder. The Hancocks, barely controlling their curiosity, stood near, awaiting the result. Wimsey, with an elaborate pretence of non-interference in this family matter, examined the wall against which the *Chronicle* had stood, feeling its moist surface and examining the damp-stains. They had assumed the appearance of a grinning face. He compared them with the corresponding mark on the book, and shook his head desolately over the damage.

Mr. Frobisher-Pym, who had wandered away some time before and was absorbed in an ancient book of Farriery, now approached, and enquired what the excitement was about.

"Listen to this!" cried Haviland. His voice was quiet, but a suppressed triumph throbbed in it and glittered from his eyes.

" 'I bequeath everything of which I die possessed'—there's a lot of enumeration of properties here, which doesn't matter—'to my eldest son, Martin'—"

Mr. Frobisher-Pym whistled.

"Listen! 'To my eldest son Martin, for so long as my body shall remain above ground. But so soon as I am buried, I direct that the whole of this property shall revert to my younger son Haviland absolutely'—"

"Good God!" said Mr. Frobisher-Pym.

"There's a lot more," said Haviland, "but that's the gist of it."

"Let me see," said the magistrate.

He took the will from Haviland, and read it through with a frowning face.

"That's right," he said. "No possible doubt about it. Martin has had his property and lost it again. How very curious. Up till yesterday everything belonged to him, though nobody knew it. Now it is all yours, Burdock. This certainly is the strangest will I ever saw. Just fancy that. Martin the heir, up to the time of the funeral. And now—well, Burdock, I must congratulate you."

"Thank you," said Haviland. "It is very unexpected." He laughed unsteadily.

"But what a queer idea!" cried Mrs. Burdock. "Suppose Martin had been at home. It almost seems a mercy that he wasn't, doesn't it? I mean, it would all have been so awkward. What would have happened if he had tried to stop the funeral, for instance?"

"Yes," said Mrs. Hancock. "Could he have done anything? Who decides about funerals?"

"The executors, as a rule," said Mr. Frobisher-Pym.

"Who are the executors in this case?" enquired Wimsey.

"I don't know. Let me see." Mr. Frobisher-Pym examined the document again. "Ah, yes! Here we are. 'I appoint my two sons, Martin and Haviland, joint executors of this my will.' What an extraordinary arrangement."

"I call it a wicked, un-Christian arrangement," cried Mrs. Hancock. "It might have caused dreadful mischief if the will hadn't been—quite providentially—lost!"

"Hush, my dear!" said her husband.

"I'm afraid," said Haviland grimly, "that that was my father's idea. It's no use my pretending he wasn't spiteful; he was, and I believe he hated both Martin and me like poison."

"Don't say that," pleaded the vicar.

"I do say it. He made our lives a burden to us, and he obviously wanted to go on making them a burden after he was dead. If he'd seen us cutting each other's throats, he'd only have been too pleased. Come, vicar, it's no use pretending. He hated our mother and was jealous of us. Everybody knows that. It probably pleased his unpleasant sense of humour to think of us squabbling over his body. Fortunately, he overreached himself when he hid the will here. He's buried now, and the problem settles itself."

"Are you quite sure of that?" said Wimsey.

"Why, of course," said the magistrate. "The property goes

to Mr. Haviland Burdock as soon as his father's body is underground. Well, his father was buried yesterday."

"But are you sure of *that*?" repeated Wimsey. He looked from one to the other quizzically, his long lips curling into something like a grin.

"Sure of that?" exclaimed the vicar. "My dear Lord Peter, you were present at the funeral. You saw him buried yourself."

"I saw his coffin buried," said Wimsey mildly. "That the body was in it is merely an unverified inference."

"I think," said Mr. Frobisher-Pym, "this is rather an unseemly kind of jest. There is no reason to imagine that the body was not in the coffin."

"I saw it in the coffin," said Haviland, "and so did my wife."

"And so did I," said the vicar. "I was present when it was transferred from the temporary shell in which it crossed over from the States to a permanent lead-and-oak coffin provided by Joliffe. And, if further witnesses are necessary, you can easily get Joliffe himself and his men, who put the body in and screwed it down."

"Just so," said Wimsey. "I'm not denying that the body was in the coffin when the coffin was placed in the chapel. I only doubt whether it was there when it was put in the ground."

"That is a most unheard-of suggestion to make, Lord Peter," said Mr. Frobisher-Pym, with severity. "May I ask if you have anything to go upon? And, if the body is not in the grave, perhaps you wouldn't mind telling us where you imagine it to be?"

"Not at all," said Wimsey. He perched himself on the edge of the table and sat, swinging his legs and looking down at his own hands, as he ticked his points off on his fingers.

"I think," he said, "that this story begins with young Rawlinson. He is a clerk in the office of Mr. Graham, who drew up this will, and I fancy he knows something about its conditions. So, of course, does Mr. Graham, but I don't somehow suspect *him* of being mixed up in this. From what I can hear, he is not a man to take sides — or not Mr. Martin's side, at any rate.

"When the news of Mr. Burdock's death was cabled over from the States, I think young Rawlinson remembered the terms of the will, and considered that Mr. Martin — being abroad and all that — would be rather at a disadvantage. Rawlinson must be rather attached to your brother, by the way —"

"Martin always had a way of picking up good-for-nothing youths and wasting his time with them," agreed Haviland sulkily.

The vicar seemed to feel that this statement needed some amendment, and murmured that he had always heard how good Martin was with the village lads.

"Quite so," said Wimsey. "Well, I think young Rawlinson wanted to give Martin an equal chance of securing the legacy, don't you see. He didn't like to say anything about the will — which might or might not turn up — and possibly he thought that even if it did turn up there might be difficulties. Well, anyway, he decided that the best thing to do was to steal the body and keep it above-ground till Martin came home to see to things himself."

"This is an extraordinary accusation," began Mr. Frobisher Pym.

"I daresay I'm mistaken," said Wimsey, "but it's just my idea. It makes a damn good story, anyhow — you see! Well, then, young Rawlinson saw that this was too big a job to carry out alone, so he looked round for somebody to help him. And he pitched on Mr. Mortimer."

"Mortimer?"

"I don't know Mr. Mortimer personally, but he seems to be a sportin' sort of customer from what I can hear, with certain facilities which everybody hasn't got. Young Rawlinson and Mortimer put their heads together and worked out a plan of action. Of course, Mr. Hancock, you helped them enormously, with this lying-in-state idea of yours. Without that, I don't know if they could have worked it."

Mr. Hancock made an embarrassed clucking sound.

"The idea was this. Mortimer was to provide an antique fly and four white horses, made up with luminous paint and black cloth to represent the Burdock death-coach. The advantage of that idea was that nobody would feel inclined to inspect the turn-out too closely if they saw it hangin' round the churchyard at unearthly hours. Meanwhile, young Rawlinson had to get himself accepted as a watcher for the chapel, and to find a sporting companion to watch with him and take a hand in the game. He fixed things up with the publican-fellow, and spun a tale for Mr. Hancock, so as to get the vigil from four to six. Didn't it strike you as odd, Mr. Hancock, that he should be so keen to come all the way from Herriotting?"

"I am accustomed to find keenness in my congregation," said Mr. Hancock stiffly.

"Yes, but Rawlinson didn't belong to your congregation. Anyway it was all worked out, and there was a dress rehearsal on the Wednesday night, which frightened your man Plunkett into fits, sir."

"If I thought this was true—" said Mr. Frobisher-Pym.

"On Thursday night," pursued Wimsey, "the conspirators were ready, hidden in the chancel at two in the morning. They waited till Mrs. and Miss Hancock had taken their places, and then made a row to attract their attention. When the ladies courageously advanced to find out what was up, they popped out and bundled 'em into the vestry."

"Good gracious!" said Mrs. Hancock.

"That was when the death-coach affair was timed to drive up to the south door. It came round the Back Lane, I fancy, though I can't be sure. Then Mortimer and the other two took the embalmed body out of the coffin and filled its place up with bags of sawdust. I know it was sawdust, because I found the remains of it on the Lady-chapel floor in the morning. They put the body in the fly, and Mortimer drove off with it. They passed me on the Herriotting Road at half past two, so they can't have wasted much time over the job. Mortimer may have been alone, or possibly he had someone with him to see to the body while he himself did the headless coachman business in a black mask. I'm not certain about that. They drove through the last gate before you come to the fork at Frimpton, and went across the fields to Mortimer's barn. They left the fly there—I know that, because I saw it, and I saw the bran they used to muffle the horses' hoofs, too. I expect they took it on from there in a car, and fetched the horses up next day—but that's a detail. I don't know, either, where they took the body to, but I expect, if you went and asked Mortimer about it, he would be able to assure you that it was still above ground."

Wimsey paused. Mr. Frobisher-Pym and the Hancocks were looking only puzzled and angry, but Haviland's face was green. Mrs. Haviland showed a red, painted spot on each cheek, and her mouth was haggard. Wimsey picked up the *Nuremburg Chronicle* and caressed its covers thoughtfully as he went on.

"Meanwhile, of course, young Rawlinson and his companion were doing the camouflage in the church, to give the idea of a Protestant outrage. Having fixed everything up neat and pretty, all they had to do was to lock themselves up in the furnace-house and chuck the key through the window. You'll probably find it there, Mr. Hancock, if you care to look. Didn't you think that story of an assault by two or three men was a bit thin? Hubbard is a hefty great fellow, and Rawlinson's a sturdy lad—and yet, on their own showing, they were bundled into a coalhole like helpless infants, without a scratch on either of 'em. Look for the men in buckram, my dear sir, look for the men in buckram!"

"Look here, Wimsey, are you sure you're not romancing?" said Mr. Frobisher-Pym. "One would need some very clear proof before—"

"Certainly," said Wimsey. "Get a Home Office order. Open the grave. You'll soon see whether it's true or whether it's just my diseased imagination."

"I think this whole conversation is disgusting," cried Mrs. Burdock. "Don't listen to it, Haviland. Anything more heartless on the day after father's funeral than sitting here and inventing such a revolting story I simply can't imagine. It is not worth paying a moment's attention to. You will certainly not permit your father's body to be disturbed. It's horrible. It's a desecration."

"It is very unpleasant indeed," said Mr. Frobisher-Pym gravely, "but if Lord Peter is seriously putting forward this astonishing theory, which I can scarcely credit—"

Wimsey shrugged his shoulders.

"—then I feel bound to remind you, Mr. Burdock, that your brother, when he returns, may insist on having the matter investigated."

"But he can't, can he?" said Mrs. Burdock.

"Of course he can, Winnie," snapped her husband savagely. "He's an executor. He has as much right to have the governor dug up as I have to forbid it. Don't be a fool."

"If Martin had any decency, he would forbid it, too," said Mrs. Burdock.

"Oh, well!" said Mrs. Hancock, "shocking as it may seem, there's the money to be considered. Mr. Martin might think it a duty to his wife, and his family, if he should ever have any—"

"The whole thing is preposterous," said Haviland decidedly. "I don't believe a word of it. If I did, naturally I should be the first person to take action in the matter—not only in justice to Martin, but on my own account. But if you ask me to believe that a responsible man like Mortimer would purloin a corpse and desecrate a church—the thing only has to be put into plain words to show how absurd and unthinkable it is. I suppose Lord Peter Wimsey, who consorts, as I understand, with criminals and police officers, finds the idea conceivable. I can only say that I do not. I am sorry that his mind should have become so blunted to all decent feeling. That's all. Good afternoon."

Mr. Frobisher-Pym jumped up.

"Come, come, Burdock, don't take that attitude. I am sure Lord Peter intended no discourtesy. I must say I think he's all wrong, but, 'pon my soul, things have been so disturbed in the village these last few days, I'm not surprised anybody should think there was something behind it. Now, let's forget about it—and hadn't we better be moving out of this terribly cold room? It's nearly dinner-time. Bless me, what will Agatha think of us?"

Wimsey held out his hand to Burdock, who took it reluctantly.

"I'm sorry," said Wimsey. "I suffer from hypertrophy of the imagination, y'know. Over-stimulation of the thyroid probably. Don't mind me. I apologize, and all that."

"I don't think, Lord Peter," said Mrs. Burdock acidly, "you ought to exercise your imagination at the expense of good taste."

Wimsey followed her from the room in some confusion. Indeed, he was so disturbed that he carried away the *Nuremberg Chronicle* beneath his arm, which was an odd thing for him to do under the circumstances.

"I am gravely distressed," said Mr. Hancock.

He had come over, after Sunday evening service, to call upon the Frobisher-Pyms. He sat upright on his chair, his thin face flushed with anxiety.

"I could never have believed such a thing of Hubbard. It has been a grievous shock to me. It is not only the great wickedness of stealing a dead body from the very precincts of the church, though that is grave enough. It is the sad hypocrisy of his behaviour—the mockery of sacred things— the making use of the holy services of his religion to further worldly ends. He actually attended the funeral, Mr. Frobisher-Pym, and exhibited every sign of grief and respect. Even now he hardly seems to realize the sinfulness of his conduct. I feel it very much, as a priest and as a pastor—very much indeed."

"Oh, well, Hancock," said Mr. Frobisher-Pym, "you must make allowances, you know. Hubbard's not a bad fellow, but you can't expect refinement of feeling from a man of his class. The point is, what are we to do about it? Mr. Burdock must be told, of course. It's a most awkward situation. Dear me! Hubbard confessed the whole conspiracy, you say? How did he come to do that?"

"I taxed him with it," said the parson. "When I came to think over Lord Peter Wimsey's remarks, I was troubled in my mind. It seemed to me—I cannot say why—that there might be some truth in the story, wild as it appeared. I was so worried about it that I swept the floor of the Lady-chapel myself last night, and I found quite a quantity of sawdust among the sweepings. That led me to search for the key of the furnace-house, and I discovered it in some bushes at a little distance—in fact, within a stone's throw—of the furnace-house window. I sought guidance in prayer—and from my wife, whose judgement I greatly respect—and I made up my mind to speak to Hubbard after Mass. It was a great relief to me that he did not present himself at Early Celebration. Feeling as I did, I should have had scruples."

"Just so, just so," said the magistrate, a little impatiently. "Well, you taxed him with it, and he confessed?"

"He did. I am sorry to say he showed no remorse at all. He even laughed. It was a most painful interview."

"I am sure it must have been," said Mrs. Frobisher-Pym sympathetically.

"We must go and see Mr. Burdock," said the magistrate, rising. "Whatever old Burdock may or may not have intended by that iniquitous will of his, it's quite evident that Hubbard and Mortimer and Rawlinson were entirely in the wrong. Upon my word, I've no idea whether it's an indictable offence to steal a body. I must look it up. But I should say it was. If there is any property in a corpse, it must belong to the family or the executors. And in any case, it's sacrilege, to say nothing of the scandal in the parish. I must say, Hancock, it won't do us any good in the eyes of the Nonconformists. However, no doubt you realize that. Well, it's an unpleasant job, and the sooner we tackle it the better. I'll run over to the vicarage with you and help you to break it to the Burdocks. How about you, Wimsey? You were right, after all, and I think Burdock owes you an apology."

"Oh, I'll keep out of it," said Wimsey. "I shan't be exactly _persona grata_, don't you know. It's going to mean a deuce of a big financial loss to the Haviland Burdocks."

"So it is. Most unpleasant. Well, perhaps you're right. Come along, vicar."

Wimsey and his hostess sat discussing the matter by the fire for half an hour or so, when Mr. Frobisher-Pym suddenly put his head in and said:

"I say, Wimsey—we're all going over to Mortimer's. I wish you'd come and drive the car. Merridew always has the day off on Sunday, and I don't care about driving at night, particularly in this fog."

"Right you are," said Wimsey. He ran upstairs, and came down in a few moments wearing a heavy leather flying-coat, and with a parcel under his arm. He greeted the Burdocks briefly, climbed into the driving-seat, and was soon steering cautiously through the mist along the Herriotting Road.

He smiled a little grimly to himself as they came up under the trees to the spot where the phantom coach had passed him. As they passed the gate through which the ingenious apparition had vanished, he indulged himself by pointing it out, and was rewarded by hearing a snarl from Haviland. At the well-remembered fork, he took the right-hand turning into Frimpton and drove steadily for six miles or so, till a warning shout from Mr. Frobisher-Pym summoned him to look out for the turning up to Mortimer's.

Mr. Mortimer's house, with its extensive stabling and farm buildings, stood about two miles back from the main road. In the darkness Wimsey could see little of it; but he noticed that the ground-floor windows were all lit up, and, when the door opened to the magistrate's imperative ring, a loud burst of laughter from the interior gave evidence that Mr. Mortimer was not taking his misdoings too seriously.

"Is Mr. Mortimer at home?" demanded Mr. Frobisher-Pym, in the tone of a man not to be trifled with.

"Yes, sir. Will you come in, please?"

They stepped into a large, old-fashioned hall, brilliantly lit, and made cosy with a heavy oak screen across the door. As Wimsey advanced, blinking, from the darkness, he saw a large, thick-set man, with a ruddy face, advancing with hand outstretched in welcome.

"Frobisher-Pym! By Jove! how decent of you to come over! We've got some old friends of yours here. Oh!" (in a slightly altered tone) "Burdock! Well, well—"

"Damn you!" said Haviland Burdock, thrusting furiously past the magistrate, who was trying to hold him back. "Damn you, you swine! Chuck this bloody farce. What have you done with the body?"

"The body, eh?" said Mr. Mortimer, retreating in some confusion.

"Yes, curse you! Your friend Hubbard's split. It's no good denying it. What the devil do you mean by it? You've got the body here somewhere. Where is it? Hand it over!"

He strode threateningly round the screen into the lamp-light. A tall, thin man rose up unexpectedly from the depths of an armchair and confronted him.

"Hold hard, old man!"

"Good God!" said Haviland, stepping heavily back on Wimsey's toes. "Martin!"

"Sure," said the other. "Here I am. Come back like a bad half-penny. How are you?"

"So *you're* at the bottom of this!" stormed Haviland. "I might have known it. You damned, dirty hound! I suppose you think it's decent to drag your father out of his coffin and tote him about the country like a circus. It's degrading. It's disgusting. It's abominable. You must be perfectly dead to all decent feeling. You don't deny it, I suppose?"

"I say, Burdock!" expostulated Mortimer.

"Shut up, curse you!" said Haviland. "I'll deal with you in a minute. Now, look here, Martin, I'm not going to stand any more of this disgraceful behaviour. You'll give up that body, and—"

"Just a moment, just a moment," said Martin. He stood, smiling a little, his hands thrust into the pockets of his dinner-jacket. "This *éclaircissement* seems to be rather public. Who are all these people? Oh, it's the vicar. I see. I'm afraid we owe you a little explanation, vicar. And, er—"

"This is Lord Peter Wimsey," put in Mr. Frobisher-Pym, "who discovered your—I'm afraid, Burdock, I must agree with your brother in calling it your disgraceful plot."

"Oh, Lord!" said Martin. "I say, Mortimer, you didn't know you were up against Lord Peter Wimsey, did you? No wonder the cat got out of the bag. The man's known to be a perfect Sherlock. However, I seem to have got home at the crucial moment, so there's no harm done. Diana, this is Lord Peter Wimsey—my wife."

A young and pretty woman in a black evening dress greeted Wimsey with a shy smile, and turned deprecatingly to her brother-in-law.

"Haviland, we want to explain—"

He paid no attention to her.

"Now then, Martin, the game's up."

"I think it is, Haviland. But why make all this racket?"

"Racket! I like that. You take your own father's body out of its coffin—"

"No, no, Haviland. I knew nothing about it. I swear that. I only got the news of his death a few days ago. We were right out in the wilds, filming a show in the Pyrenees, and I came straight back as soon as I could get away. Mortimer here, with Rawlinson and Hubbard, staged the whole show by themselves. I never heard a word about it till yesterday morning in Paris, when I found his letter waiting at my old digs. Honestly, Haviland, I had nothing to do with it. Why should I? I didn't need to."

"What do you mean?"

"Well, if I'd been here, I should only have had to speak to stop the funeral altogether. Why on earth should I have gone to the trouble of stealing the body? Quite apart from the irreverence and all that. As it is, when Mortimer told me about it, I must say I was a bit revolted at the idea, though I appreciated the kindness and the trouble they'd been to on my account. I think Mr. Hancock has most cause for wrath, really. But Mortimer has been as careful as possible, sir—really he has. He has placed the old governor quite reverently and decently in what used to be the chapel, and put flowers round him and so on. You will be quite satisfied, I'm sure."

"Yes, yes," said Mortimer. "No disrespect intended, don't you know. Come and see him."

"This is dreadful," said the vicar helplessly.

"They had to do the best they could, don't you see, in my absence," said Martin. "As soon as I can, I'll make proper arrangement for a suitable tomb—above ground, of course. Or possibly cremation would fit the case."

"What!" gasped Haviland. "Do you mean to say you imagine I'm going to let my father stay unburied, simply because of your disgusting greed about money?"

"My dear chap, do you think I'm going to let you put him underground, simply to enable you to grab my property?"

"I'm the executor of his will, and I say he shall be buried, whether you like it or not!"

"And *I'm* an executor too—and I say he shan't be buried. He can be kept absolutely decently above ground, and he shall be."

"But hear me," said the vicar, distracted between these two disagreeable and angry young men.

"I'll see what Graham says about you," bawled Haviland.

"Oh, yes—the honest lawyer, Graham," sneered Martin. "*He* knew what was in the will, didn't he? I suppose he didn't mention it to *you* by any chance?"

"He did not," retorted Haviland. "He knew too well the sort of skunk *you* were to say anything about it. Not content with disgracing us with your miserable, blackmailing marriage—"

"Mr. Burdock, Mr. Burdock—"

"Take care, Haviland!"

"You have no more decency—"

"Stop it!"

"Than to steal your father's body and my money so that you and your damned wife can carry on your loose-living, beastly ways with a parcel of film-actors and chorus-girls—"

"Now then, Haviland. Keep your tongue off my wife and

my friends. How about your own? Somebody told me Winnie'd been going the pace pretty well—next door to bankruptcy, aren't you, with the gees and the tables and God knows what! No wonder you want to do your brother out of his money. I never thought much of you, Haviland, but by God—"

"One moment!"

Mr. Frobisher-Pym at last succeeded in asserting himself, partly through the habit of authority, and party because the brothers had shouted themselves breathless.

"One moment, Martin. I will call you so, because I have known you a long time, and your father too. I understand your anger at the things Haviland has said. They were unpardonable, as I am sure he will realize when he comes to his right mind. But you must remember that he has been greatly shocked and upset—as we all have been—by this very painful business. And it is not fair to say that Haviland has tried to 'do you out' of anything. He knew nothing about this iniquitous will, and he naturally saw to it that the funeral arrangements were carried out in the usual way. You must settle the future amicably between you, just as you would have done had the will not been accidentally mislaid. Now, Martin—and Haviland too—think it over. My dear boys, this scene is simply appalling. It really must not happen. Surely the estate can be divided up in a friendly manner between you. It is horrible that an old man's body should be a bone of contention between his own sons, just over a matter of money."

"I'm sorry," said Martin. "I forgot myself. You're quite right, sir. Look here, Haviland, forget it. I'll let you have half the money—"

"Half the money! But it's all mine. *You'll* let me have half? How damned generous! My own money!"

"No, old man. It's mine at the moment. The governor's not buried yet, you know. That's right, isn't it, Mr. Frobisher-Pym?"

"Yes; the money is yours, legally, at this moment. You must see that, Haviland. But your brother offers you half, and—"

"Half! I'm damned if I'll take half. The man's tried to swindle me out of it. I'll send for the police, and have him put in gaol for robbing the Church. You see if I don't. Give me the telephone."

"Excuse me," said Wimsey. "I don't want to butt in on your family affairs any more than I have already, but I really don't advise you to send for the police."

"*You* don't, eh? What the hell's it got to do with you?"

"Well," said Wimsey deprecatingly, "if this will business comes into court, I shall probably have to give evidence, because I was the bird who found the thing, don't you see?"

"Well, then?"

"Well, then. They might ask how long the will was supposed to have been where I found it."

Haviland appeared to swallow something which obstructed his speech.

"What about it, curse you!"

"Yes. Well, you see, it's rather odd when you come to think of it. I mean, your late father must have hidden that will in the bookcase before he went abroad. That was—how long ago? Three years? Five years?"

"About four years."

"Quite. And since then your bright caretaker has let the damp get into the library, hasn't she? No fires, and the window getting broken, and so on. Ruinous to the books. Very distressin' to anybody like myself, you know. Yes. Well, supposin' they asked that question about the will—and you said it had been there in the damp for four years. Wouldn't they think it a bit funny if I told 'em that there was a big stain like a grinning face on the end of the bookshelf, and a big, damp, grinning face on the jolly old *Nuremberg Chronicle* to correspond with it, and no stain on the will which had been sittin' for four years between the two?"

Mrs. Haviland screamed suddenly. "Haviland! You fool! You utter fool!"

"Shut up!"

Haviland snapped round at his wife with a cry of rage,

and she collapsed into a chair, with her hand snatched to her mouth.

"Thank you, Winnie," said Martin. "No, Haviland—don't trouble to explain. Winnie's given the show away. So you knew—you *knew* about the will, and you deliberately hid it away and let the funeral go on. I'm immensely obliged to you—nearly as obliged as I am to the discreet Graham. Is it fraud or conspiracy or what, to conceal wills? Mr. Frobisher-Pym will know."

"Dear, dear!" said the magistrate. "Are you certain of your facts, Wimsey?"

"Positive," said Wimsey, producing the *Nuremberg Chronicle* from under his arm. "Here's the stain—you can see it yourself. Forgive me for having borrowed your property, Mr. Burdock. I was rather afraid Mr. Haviland might think this little discrepancy over in the still watches of the night, and decide to sell the *Chronicle*, or give it away, or even think it looked better without its back pages and cover. Allow me to return it to you, Mr. Martin—intact. You will perhaps excuse my saying that I don't very much admire any of the roles in this melodrama. It throws, as Mr. Pecksniff would say, a sad light on human nature. But I resent extremely the way in which I was wangled up to that bookshelf and made to be the bright little independent witness who found the will. I may be an ass, Mr. Haviland Burdock, but I'm not a bloody ass. Good night. I will wait in the car till you are all ready."

Wimsey stalked out with some dignity.

Presently he was followed by the vicar and by Mr. Frobisher-Pym.

"Mortimer's taking Haviland and his wife to the station," said the magistrate. "They're going back to town at once. You can send their traps off in the morning, Hancock. We'd better make ourselves scarce."

Wimsey pressed the self-starter.

As he did so, a man ran hastily down the steps and came up to him. It was Martin.

"I say," he muttered. "You've done me a good turn—more

than I deserve, I'm afraid. You must think I'm a damned swine. But I'll see the old man decently put away, and I'll share with Haviland. You mustn't judge him too hardly, either. That wife of his is an awful woman. Run him over head and ears in debt. Bust up his business. I'll see it's all squared up. See? Don't want you to think us too awful."

"Oh, right-ho!" said Wimsey.

He slipped in the clutch, and faded away into the wet, white fog.

THE VINDICTIVE STORY OF THE
FOOTSTEPS THAT RAN

Mr. Bunter withdrew his head from beneath the focusing cloth.

"I fancy that will be quite adequate, sir," he said deferentially, "unless there are any further patients, if I may call them so, which you would wish put on record."

"Not today," replied the doctor. He took the last stricken rat gently from the table, and replaced it in its cage with an air of satisfaction. "Perhaps on Wednesday, if Lord Peter can kindly spare your services once again—"

"What's that?" murmured his lordship, withdrawing his long nose from the investigation of a number of unattractive-looking glass jars. "Nice old dog," he added vaguely. "Wags his tail when you mention his name, what? Are these monkey-glands, Hartman, or a south-west elevation of Cleopatra's duodenum?"

"You don't know anything, do you?" said the young physician, laughing. "No use playing your bally-fool-with-an-eyeglass tricks on me, Wimsey. I'm up to them. I was saying to Bunter that I'd be no end grateful if you'd let him turn up again three days hence to register the progress of the specimens—always supposing they do progress, that is."

"Why ask, dear old thing?" said his lordship. "Always a pleasure to assist a fellow-sleuth, don't you know. Trackin' down murderers—all in the same way of business and all that. All finished? Good egg! By the way, if you don't have that cage mended you'll lose one of your patients—Number 5. The last wire but one is workin' loose—assisted by the intelligent occupant. Jolly little beasts, aren't they? No need of dentists—wish I was a rat—wire much better for the nerves than that fizzlin' drill."

Dr. Hartman uttered a little exclamation.

"How in the world did you notice that, Wimsey? I didn't think you'd even looked at the cage."

"Built noticin'—improved by practice," said Lord Peter quietly. "Anythin' wrong leaves a kind of impression on the eye; brain trots along afterwards with the warnin'. I saw that when we came in. Only just grasped it. Can't say my mind was glued on the matter. Shows the victim's improvin', anyhow. All serene, Bunter?"

"Everything perfectly satisfactory, I trust, my lord," replied the manservant. He had packed up his camera and plates, and was quietly restoring order in the little laboratory, whose fittings—compact as those of an ocean liner—had been disarranged for the experiment.

"Well," said the doctor, "I am enormously obliged to you, Lord Peter, and to Bunter too. I am hoping for a great result from these experiments, and you cannot imagine how valuable an assistance it will be to me to have a really good series of photographs. I can't afford this sort of thing—yet," he added, his rather haggard young face wistful as he looked at the great camera, "and I can't do the work at the hospital. There's no time; I've got to be here. A struggling G.P. can't afford to let his practice go, even in Bloomsbury. There are times when even a half-crown visit makes all the difference between making both ends meet and having an ugly hiatus."

"As Mr. Micawber said," replied Wimsey, " 'Income twenty pounds, expenditure nineteen, nineteen, six—result: happiness; expenditure twenty pounds, ought, six—result: misery.' Don't prostrate yourself in gratitude, old bean; nothin' Bunter loves like messin' round with pyro and hyposulphite. Keeps his hand in. All kinds of practice welcome. Finger-prints and process plates spell seventh what-you-may-call-it of bliss, but focal-plane work on scurvy-ridden rodents (good phrase!) acceptable if no crime forthcoming. Crimes have been rather short lately. Been eatin' our heads off, haven't we, Bunter? Don't know what's come over London. I've taken to prying into my neighbour's affairs to keep from goin' stale. Frightened the postman into a fit the other day by askin' him how his young lady at Croydon was. He's a married man, livin' in Great Ormond Street."

"How did you know?"

"Well, I didn't really. But he lives just opposite to a friend of mine—Inspector Parker; and his wife—not Parker's, he's unmarried; the postman's, I mean—asked Parker the other day whether the flyin' shows at Croydon went on all night. Parker, bein' flummoxed, said 'No,' without thinkin'. Bit of a giveaway, what? Thought I'd give the poor devil a word in season, don't you know. Uncommonly thoughtless of Parker."

The doctor laughed. "You'll stay to lunch, won't you?" he said. "Only cold meat and salad, I'm afraid. My woman won't come Sundays. Have to answer my own door. Deuced unprofessional, I'm afraid, but it can't be helped."

"Pleasure," said Wimsey, as they emerged from the laboratory and entered the dark little flat by the back door. "Did you build this place on?"

"No," said Hartman; "the last tenant did that. He was an artist. That's why I took the place. It comes in very useful, ramshackle as it is, though this glass roof is a bit sweltering on a hot day like this. Still, I had to have something on the ground floor, cheap, and it'll do till times get better."

"Till your vitamin experiments make you famous, eh?" said Peter cheerfully. "You're goin' to be the comin' man, you know. Feel it in my bones. Uncommonly neat little kitchen you've got, anyhow."

"It does," said the doctor. "The lab makes it a bit gloomy, but the woman's only here in the daytime."

He led the way into a narrow little dining-room, where the table was laid for a cold lunch. The one window at the end farthest from the kitchen looked out into Great James Street. The room was little more than a passage, and full of doors—the kitchen door, a door in the adjacent wall leading into the entrance-hall, and a third on the opposite side, through which his visitor caught a glimpse of a moderate-sized consulting-room.

Lord Peter Wimsey and his host sat down to table, and the doctor expressed a hope that Mr. Bunter would sit down with them. That correct person, however, deprecated any such suggestion.

"If I might venture to indicate my own preference, sir," he said, "it would be to wait upon you and his lordship in the usual manner."

"It's no use," said Wimsey. "Bunter likes me to know my place. Terrorizin' sort of man, Bunter. Can't call my soul my own. Carry on, Bunter; we wouldn't presume for the world."

Mr. Bunter handed the salad, and poured out the water with a grave decency appropriate to a crusted old tawny port.

It was a Sunday afternoon in that halcyon summer of 1921. The sordid little street was almost empty. The ice-cream man alone seemed thriving and active. He leaned luxuriously on the green post at the corner, in the intervals of driving a busy trade. Bloomsbury's swarm of able-bodied and able-voiced infants was still; presumably within-doors, eating steamy Sunday dinners inappropriate to the tropical weather. The only disturbing sounds came from the flat above, where heavy footsteps passed rapidly to and fro.

"Who's the merry-and-bright bloke above?" inquired Lord Peter presently. "Not an early riser, I take it. Not that anybody is on a Sunday mornin'. Why an inscrutable Providence ever inflicted such a ghastly day on people livin' in town

I can't imagine. I ought to be in the country, but I've got to
meet a friend at Victoria this afternoon. Such a day to
choose . . . Who's the lady? Wife or accomplished friend?
Gather she takes a properly submissive view of woman's duties in the home, either way. That's the bedroom overhead, I
take it."

Hartman looked at Lord Peter in some surprise.

" 'Scuse my beastly inquisitiveness, old thing," said Wimsey. "Bad habit. Not my business."

"How did you — ?"

"Guesswork," said Lord Peter, with disarming frankness.
"I heard the squawk of an iron bedstead on the ceiling and a
heavy fellow get out with a bump, but it may quite well be a
couch or something. Anyway, he's been potterin' about in his
stocking feet over these few feet of floor for the last half-hour,
while the woman has been clatterin' to and fro, in and out of
the kitchen and away into the sittin'-room, with her high heels
on, ever since we've been here. Hence deduction as to domestic habits of the first-floor tenants."

"I thought," said the doctor, with an aggrieved expression,
"you'd been listening to my valuable exposition of the benefi-
cial effects of Vitamin B, and Lind's treatment of scurvy with
fresh lemons in 1755."

"I was listenin'," agreed Lord Peter hastily, "but I heard
the footsteps as well. Fellow's toddled into the kitchen — only
wanted the matches, though; he's gone off into the sittin'-room
and left her to carry on the good work. What was I sayin'?
Oh, yes! You see, as I was sayin' before, one hears a thing or
sees it without knowin' or thinkin' about it. Then afterwards
one starts meditatin', and it all comes back, and one sorts out
one's impressions. Like those plates of Bunter's. Picture's all
there, l —, la —, what's the word I want, Bunter?"

"Latent, my lord."

"That's it. My right-hand man, Bunter; couldn't do a thing
without him. The picture's latent till you put the developer on.
Same with the brain. No mystery. Little grey books all my respected grandmother! Little grey matter's all you want to re-

member things with. As a matter of curiosity, was I right about those people above?"

"Perfectly. The man's a gas-company's inspector. A bit surly, but devoted (after his own fashion) to his wife. I mean, he doesn't mind hulking in bed on a Sunday morning and letting her do the chores, but he spends all the money he can spare on giving her pretty hats and fur coats and what not. They've only been married about six months. I was called in to her when she had a touch of flu in the spring, and he was almost off his head with anxiety. She's a lovely little woman, I must say—Italian. He picked her up in some eating-place in Soho, I believe. Glorious dark hair and eyes: Venus sort of figure; proper contours in all the right places; good skin—all that sort of thing. She was a bit of a draw to that restaurant while she was there, I fancy. Lively. She had an old admirer round here one day—awkward little Italian fellow, with a knife—active as a monkey. Might have been unpleasant, but I happened to be on the spot, and her husband came along. People are always laying one another out in these streets. Good for business, of course, but one gets tired of tying up broken heads and slits in the jugular. Still, I suppose the girl can't help being attractive, though I don't say she's what you might call standoffish in her manner. She's sincerely fond of Brotherton, I think, though—that's his name."

Wimsey nodded inattentively. "I suppose life is a bit monotonous here," he said.

"Professionally, yes. Births and drunks and wife-beatings are pretty common. And all the usual ailments, of course. Just at present I'm living on infant diarrhoea chiefly—bound to, this hot weather, you know. With the autumn, flu and bronchitis set in. I may get an occasional pneumonia. Legs, of course, and varicose veins—God!" cried the doctor explosively, "if only I could get away, and do my experiments!"

"Ah!" said Peter, "where's that eccentric old millionaire with a mysterious disease, who always figures in the novels? A lightning diagnosis—a miraculous cure—'God bless you, doctor; here are five thousand pounds'—Harley Street—"

"That sort doesn't live in Bloomsbury," said the doctor.

"It must be fascinatin', diagnosin' things," said Peter thoughtfully. "How d'you do it? I mean, is there a regular set of symptoms for each disease, like callin' a club to show you want your partner to go no trumps? You don't just say: 'This fellow's got a pimple on his nose, therefore he has fatty degeneration of the heart—'"

"I hope not," said the doctor drily.

"Or is it more like getting' a clue to a crime?" went on Peter. "You see somethin'—a room, or a body, say, all knocked about anyhow, and there's a damn sight of symptoms of somethin' wrong, and you've got just to pick out the ones which tell the story?"

"That's more like it," said Dr. Hartman. "Some symptoms are significant in themselves—like the condition of the gums in scurvy, let us say—others in conjunction with—"

He broke off, and both sprang to their feet as a shrill scream sounded suddenly from the flat above, followed by a heavy thud. A man's voice cried out lamentably; feet ran violently to and fro; then, as the doctor and his guests stood frozen in consternation, came the man himself— falling down the stairs in his haste, hammering at Hartman's door.

"Help! Help! Let me in! My wife! He's murdered her!"

They ran hastily to the door and let him in. He was a big, fair man, in his shirt-sleeves and stockings. His hair stood up, and his face was set in bewildered misery.

"She is dead—dead. He was her lover," he groaned. "Come and look—take her away—Doctor! I have lost my wife! My Maddalena—" He paused, looked wildly for a moment, and then said hoarsely, "Someone's been in—somehow—stabbed her— murdered her. I'll have the law on him, doctor. Come quickly— she was cooking the chicken for my dinner—Ah-h-h!"

He gave a long, hysterical shriek, which ended in a hiccupping laugh. The doctor took him roughly by the arm and shook him. "Pull yourself together, Mr. Brotherton," he said sharply. "Perhaps she is only hurt. Stand out of the way!"

"Only hurt?" said the man, sitting heavily down on the nearest chair. "No—no—she is dead—little Maddalena—Oh, my God!"

Dr. Hartman snatched a roll of bandages and a few surgical appliances from the consulting-room, and he ran upstairs, followed closely by Lord Peter. Bunter remained for a few moments to combat hysterics with cold water. Then he stepped across to the dining-room window and shouted.

"Well, wot is it?" cried a voice from the street.

"Would you be so kind as to step in here a minute, officer?" said Mr. Bunter. "There's been murder done."

When Brotherton and Bunter arrived upstairs with the constable, they found Dr. Hartman and Lord Peter in the little kitchen. The doctor was kneeling beside the woman's body. At their entrance he looked up, and shook his head.

"Death instantaneous," he said. "Clean through the heart. Poor child. She cannot have suffered at all. Oh, constable, it is very fortunate you are here. Murder appears to have been done—though I'm afraid the man has escaped. Probably Mr. Brotherton can give us some help. He was in the flat at the time."

The man had sunk down on a chair, and was gazing at the body with a face from which all meaning seemed to have been struck out. The policeman produced a notebook.

"Now, sir," he said, "don't let's waste any time. Sooner we can get to work the more likely we are to catch our man. Now, you was 'ere at the time, was you?"

Brotherton stared a moment, then, making a violent effort, he answered steadily:

"I was in the sitting-room, smoking and reading the paper. My—*she*—was getting the dinner ready in here. I heard her give a scream, and I rushed in and found her lying on the floor. She didn't have time to say anything. When I found she was dead, I rushed to the window, and saw the fellow scrambling away over the glass roof there. I yelled at him, but he disappeared. Then I ran down—"

" 'Arf a mo'," said the policeman. "Now, see 'ere, sir, didn't you think to go after 'im at once?"

"My first thought was for her," said the man. "I thought maybe she wasn't dead. I tried to bring her round—" His speech ended in a groan.

"You say he came in through the window," said the policeman.

"I beg your pardon, officer," interrupted Lord Peter, who had been apparently making a mental inventory of the contents of the kitchen. "Mr. Brotherton suggested that the man went *out* through the window. It's better to be accurate."

"It's the same thing," said the doctor. "It's the only way he could have come in. These flats are all alike. The staircase door leads into the sitting-room, and Mr. Brotherton was there, so the man couldn't have come that way."

"And," said Peter, "he didn't get in through the bedroom window, or we should have seen him. We were in the room below. Unless, indeed, he let himself down from the roof. Was the door between the bedroom and the sitting-room open?" he asked suddenly, turning to Brotherton.

The man hesitated a moment. "Yes," he said finally. "Yes, I'm sure it was."

"Could you have seen the man if he had come through the bedroom window?"

"I couldn't have helped seeing him."

"Come, come, sir," said the policeman, with some irritation, "better let *me* ask the questions. Stands to reason the fellow wouldn't get in through the bedroom window in full view of the street."

"How clever of you to think of that," said Wimsey. "Of course not. Never occurred to me. Then it must have been this window, as you say."

"And what's more, here's his marks on the windowsill," said the constable triumphantly, pointing to some blurred traces among the London soot. "That's right. Down he goes by that drain-pipe, over the glass roof down there—what's that the roof of?"

"My laboratory," said the doctor. "Heavens! to think that while we were there at dinner this murdering villain—"

"Quite so, sir," agreed the constable. "Well, he'd get away over the wall into the court be'ind. 'E'll 'ave been seen there, no fear; you needn't anticipate much trouble in layin' 'ands on 'im, sir. I'll go round there in 'arf a tick. Now then, sir"—turning to Brotherton—" 'ave you any idea wot this party might have looked like?"

Brotherton lifted a wild face, and the doctor interposed.

"I think you ought to know, constable," he said, "that there was—well, not a murderous attack, but what might have been one, made on this woman before—about eight weeks ago—by a man named Marincetti—an Italian waiter—with a knife."

"Ah!" The policeman licked his pencil eagerly. "Do you know this party as 'as been mentioned?" he inquired of Brotherton.

"That's the man," said Brotherton, with concentrated fury. "Coming here after my wife—God curse him! I wish to God I had him dead here beside her!"

"Quite so," said the policeman. "Now, sir"—to the doctor—" 'ave you got the weapon wot the crime was committed with?"

"No," said Hartman, "there was no weapon in the body when I arrived."

"Did *you* take it out?" pursued the constable, to Brotherton.

"No," said Brotherton, "he took it with him."

"Took it with 'im," the constable entered the fact in his notes. "Phew! Wonderful 'ot it is in 'ere, ain't it, sir?" he added, mopping his brow.

"It's the gas-oven, I think," said Peter mildly. "Uncommon hot thing, a gas-oven, in the middle of July. D'you mind if I turn it out? There's the chicken inside, but I don't suppose you want—"

Brotherton groaned, and the constable said: "Quite right, sir. A man wouldn't 'ardly fancy 'is dinner after a thing like this. Thank you, sir. Well, now, doctor, wot kind of weapon do you take this to 'ave been?"

"It was a long, narrow weapon—something like an Italian stiletto, I imagine," said the doctor, "about six inches long. It was thrust in with great force under the fifth rib, and I should say it had pierced the heart centrally. As you see, there has been practically no bleeding. Such a wound would cause instant death. Was she lying just as she is now when you first saw her, Mr. Brotherton?"

"On her back, just as she is," replied the husband.

"Well, that seems clear enough," said the policeman. "This 'ere Marinetti, or wotever 'is name is, 'as a grudge against the poor young lady—"

"I believe he was an admirer," put in the doctor.

"Quite so," agreed the constable. "Of course, these foreigners are like that—even the decentest of 'em. Stabbin' and such-like seems to come nateral to them, as you might say. Well, this 'ere Marinetti climbs in 'ere, sees the poor young lady standin' 'ere by the table all alone, gettin' the dinner ready; 'e comes in be'ind, catches 'er round the waist, stabs 'er—easy job, you see; no corsets nor nothink—she shrieks out, 'e pulls 'is stiletty out of 'er an' makes tracks. Well, now we've got to find 'im, and by your leave, sir, I'll be gettin' along. We'll 'ave 'im by the 'eels before long, sir, don't you worry. I'll 'ave to put a man in charge 'ere, sir, to keep folks out, but that needn't worry you. Good mornin' gentlemen."

"May we move the poor girl now?" asked the doctor.

"Certainly. Like me to 'elp you, sir?"

"No. Don't lose any time. We can manage." Dr. Hartman turned to Peter as the constable clattered downstairs. "Will you help me, Lord Peter?"

"Bunter's better at that sort of thing," said Wimsey, with a hard mouth.

The doctor looked at him in some surprise, but said nothing, and he and Bunter carried the still form away. Brotherton did not follow them. He sat in a grief-stricken heap, with his head buried in his hands. Lord Peter walked about the little kitchen, turning over the various knives and kitchen utensils, peering into the sink bucket, and apparently taking an inventory of the bread, butter, condiments, vegetables, and so forth which lay about in preparation for the Sunday meal. There were potatoes in the sink, half peeled, a pathetic witness to the quiet domestic life which had been so horribly interrupted. The colander was filled with green peas. Lord Peter turned these things over with an inquisitive finger, gazed into the smooth surface of a bowl of dripping as though it were a divining-crystal, ran his hands several times right through a bowl of flour—then drew his pipe from his pocket and filled it slowly.

The doctor returned, and put his hand on Brotherton's shoulder.

"Come," he said gently, "we have laid her in the other bedroom. She looks very peaceful. You must remember that, except for that moment of terror when she saw the knife, she suffered nothing. It is terrible for you, but you must try not to give way. The police—"

"The police can't bring her back to life," said the man savagely. "She's dead. Leave me alone, curse you! Leave me alone, I say!"

He stood up, with a violent gesture.

"You must not sit here," said Hartman firmly. "I will give you something to take, and you must try to keep calm. Then we will leave you, but if you don't control yourself—"

After some further persuasion, Brotherton allowed himself to be led away.

"Bunter," said Lord Peter, as the kitchen door closed behind them, "do you know why I am doubtful about the success of those rat experiments?"

"Meaning Dr. Hartman's, my lord?"

"Yes. Dr. Hartman has a theory. In any investigations, my Bunter, it is most damnably dangerous to have a theory."

"I have heard you say so, my lord."

"Confound you—you know it as well as I do! What is wrong with the doctor's theories, Bunter?"

"You wish me to reply, my lord, that he only sees the facts which fit in with the theory."

"Thought-reader!" exclaimed Lord Peter bitterly.

"And that he supplies them to the police, my lord."

"Hush!" said Peter, as the doctor returned.

"I have got him to lie down," said Dr. Hartman, "and I think the best thing we can do is to leave him to himself."

"D'you know," said Wimsey, "I don't cotton to that idea, somehow."

"Why? Do you think he's likely to destroy himself?"

"That's as good a reason to give as any other, I suppose," said Wimsey, "when you haven't got any reason which can be put into words. But my advice is, don't leave him for a moment."

"But why? Frequently, with a deep grief like this, the presence of other people is merely an irritant. He begged me to leave him."

"Then for God's sake go back to him," said Peter.

"Really, Lord Peter," said the doctor, "I think I ought to know what is best for my patient."

"Doctor," said Wimsey, "this is not a question of your patient. A crime has been committed."

"But there is no mystery."

"There are twenty mysteries. For one thing, when was the window-cleaner here last?"

"The window-cleaner?"

"Who shall fathom the ebony-black enigma of the window-cleaner?" pursued Peter lightly, putting a match to his pipe. "You are quietly in your bath, in a state of more or less innocent nature, when an intrusive head appears at the window, like the ghost of Hamilton Tighe, and a gruff voice, suspended between earth and heaven, says 'Good morning, sir.' Where do window-cleaners go between visits? Do they hibernate, like busy bees? Do they—?"

"Really, Lord Peter," said the doctor, "don't you think you're going a bit beyond the limit?"

"Sorry you feel like that," said Peter, "but I really want to know about the window-cleaner. Look how clear these panes are."

"He came yesterday, if you want to know," said Dr. Hartman, rather stiffly.

"You are sure?"

"He did mine at the same time."

"I thought as much," said Lord Peter. "In the words of the song:

> *I thought as much,*
> *It was a little—window-cleaner.*

In that case," he added, "it is absolutely imperative that Brotherton should not be left alone for a moment. Bunter! Confound it all, where's that fellow got to?"

The door into the bedroom opened.

"My lord?" Mr. Bunter unobtrusively appeared, as he had unobtrusively stolen out to keep an unobtrusive eye upon the patient.

"Good," said Wimsey. "Stay where you are." His lackadaisical manner had gone, and he looked at the doctor as four years previously he might have looked at a refractory subaltern.

"Dr. Hartman," he said, "something is wrong. Cast your mind back. We were talking about symptoms. Then came the scream. Then came the sound of feet running. *Which direction did they run in?*"

"I'm sure I don't know."

"Don't you? Symptomatic, though, doctor. They have been troubling me all the time, subconsciously. Now I know why. They ran *from the kitchen.*"

"Well?"

"Well! And now the window-cleaner—"

"What about him?"

"Could you swear that it wasn't the window-cleaner who made those marks on the sill?"

"And the man Brotherton saw—?"

"Have we examined your laboratory roof for his foot-steps?"

"But the weapon? Wimsey, this is madness! Someone took the weapon."

"I know. But did you think the edge of the wound was clean enough to have been made by a smooth stiletto? It looked ragged to me."

"Wimsey, what are you driving at?"

"There's a clue here in the flat—and I'm damned if I can remember it. I've seen it—I know I've seen it. It'll come to me presently. Meanwhile, don't let Brotherton—"

"What?"

"Do whatever it is he's going to do."

"But what is it?"

"If I could tell you that I could show you the clue. Why couldn't he make up his mind whether the bedroom door was open or shut? Very good story, but not quite thought out. Anyhow—I say, doctor, make some excuse, and strip him, and bring me his clothes. And send Bunter to me."

The doctor stared at him, puzzled. Then he made a gesture of acquiescence and passed into the bedroom. Lord Peter followed him, casting a ruminating glance at Brotherton as he went. Once in the sitting-room, Lord Peter sat down on a red velvet armchair, fixed his eyes on a gilt-framed oleograph, and became wrapped in contemplation.

Presently Bunter came in, with his arms full of clothing. Wimsey took it, and began to search it, methodically enough, but listlessly. Suddenly he dropped the garments, and turned to the manservant.

"No," he said, "this is a precaution, Bunter mine, but I'm on the wrong track. It wasn't here I saw—whatever I did see. It was in the kitchen. Now, what was it?"

"I could not say, my lord, but I entertain a conviction that I was also, in a manner of speaking, conscious—not consciously conscious, my lord, if you understand me, but still conscious of an incongruity."

"Hurray!" said Wimsey suddenly. "Cheer-oh! for the subconscious what's-his-name! Now let's remember the kitchen. I cleared out of it because I was gettin' obfuscated. Now then. Begin at the door. Fryin'-pans and saucepans on the wall. Gas-stove—oven goin'—chicken inside. Rack of wooden spoons on the wall, gas-lighter, pan-lifter. Stop me when I'm gettin' hot. Mantelpiece. Spice-boxes and stuff. Anything wrong with them? No. Dresser. Plates. Knives and forks—all clean; flour dredger—milk-jug—sieve on the wall—nutmeg-grater. Three-tier steamer. Looked inside—no grisly secrets in the steamer."

"Did you look in all the dresser drawers, my lord?"

"No. That could be done. But the point is, I *did* notice somethin'. What did I notice? That's the point. Never mind. On with the dance—let joy be unconfined! Knife-board. Knife-powder. Kitchen table. Did you speak?"

"No," said Bunter, who had moved from his attitude of wooden deference.

"Table stirs a chord. Very good. On table. Choppin'-board. Remains of ham and herb stuffin'. Packet of suet. An-other sieve. Several plates. Butter in a glass dish. Bowl of drippin'—"

"Ah!"

"Drippin'—! Yes, there was—"

"Something unsatisfactory, my lord—"

"About the drippin'! Oh, my head! what's that they say in *Dear Brutus*, Bunter? 'Hold on to the workbox.' That's right. Hold on to the drippin'. Beastly slimy stuff to hold on to—Wait!"

There was a pause.

"When I was a kid," said Wimsey, "I used to love to go down into the kitchen and talk to old cookie. Good old soul she was, too. I can see her now, gettin' chicken ready, with me dan-glin' my legs on the table. *She* used to pluck an' draw 'em her-self. I revelled in it. Little beasts boys are, ain't they, Bunter? Pluck it, draw it, wash it, stuff it, tuck its little tail through its little what-you-may-call-it, truss it, grease the dish—Bunter?"

"My lord!"

"Hold on to the—"

"The bowl, my lord—"

"The bowl—visualize it—what was wrong?"

"It was full, my lord!"

"Got it—got it—*got* it! The bowl was full—smooth surface. Golly! I knew there was something queer about it. Now why shouldn't it be full? Hold on to the—"

"The bird was in the oven."

"Without dripping!"

"Very careless cookery, my lord."

"The bird—in the oven—no dripping. Bunter! Suppose it was never put in till after she was dead? Thrust in hurriedly by someone who had something to hide—horrible!"

"But with what object, my lord?"

"Yes, why? That's the point. One more mental association with the bird. It's just coming. Wait a moment. Pluck, draw, wash, stuff, tuck up, truss—By God!"

"My lord?"

"Come on, Bunter. Thank Heaven we turned off the gas!"

He dashed through the bedroom, disregarding the doctor and the patient, who sat up with a smothered shriek. He flung open the oven door and snatched out the baking-tin. The skin of the bird had just begun to discolour. With a little gasp of triumph, Wimsey caught the iron ring that protruded from the wing, and jerked out—the six-inch spiral skewer.

The doctor was struggling with the excited Brotherton in the door-way. Wimsey caught the man as he broke away, and shook him into the corner with a ju-jitsu twist.

"Here is the weapon," he said.

"Prove it, blast you!" said Brotherton savagely.

"I will," said Wimsey. "Bunter, call in the policeman whom you will find at the door. Doctor, we shall need your microscope."

In the laboratory the doctor bent over the microscope. A thin layer of blood from the skewer had been spread upon the slide.

"Well?" said Wimsey impatiently.

"It's all right," said Hartman. "The roasting didn't get anywhere near the middle. My God, Wimsey, yes, you're right—round corpuscles, diameter 1/3621—mammalian blood—probably human—"

"Her blood," said Wimsey.

"It was very clever, Bunter," said Lord Peter, as the taxi trundled along on the way to his flat in Piccadilly. "If that fowl had gone on roasting a bit longer the blood-corpuscles might easily have been destroyed beyond all hope of recognition. It all goes to show that the unpremeditated crime is usually the safest."

"And what does your lordship take the man's motive to have been?"

"In my youth," said Wimsey meditatively, "they used to make me read the Bible. Trouble was, the only books I ever took to naturally were the ones they weren't over and above keen on. But I got to know the Song of Songs pretty well by heart. Look it up, Bunter; at your age it won't hurt you; it talks sense about jealousy."

"I have perused the work in question, your lordship," replied Mr. Bunter, with a sallow blush. "It says, if I remember rightly: *Jealousy is cruel as the grave.*"

THE BIBULOUS BUSINESS OF A
MATTER OF TASTE

"**H**alte-là! . . . *Attention!* . . .
F—e!"

The young man in the grey suit pushed his way through
the protesting porters and leapt nimbly for the footboard of
the guard's van as the Paris-Évreux express steamed out of the
Invalides. The guard, with an eye to a tip, fielded him adroitly
from among the detaining hands.

"It is happy for monsieur that he is so agile," he remarked.
"Monsieur is in a hurry?"

"Somewhat. Thank you. I can get through by the corridor?"

"But certainly. The *premières* are two coaches away, beyond the luggage-van."

The young man rewarded his rescuer, and made his way
forward, mopping his face. As he passed the piled-up luggage,
something caught his eye, and he stopped to investigate. It
was a suitcase, nearly new, of expensive-looking leather, labelled conspicuously:

LORD PETER WIMSEY,
        Hôtel Saumon d'Or,
            Verneuil-sur-Eure

and bore witness to its itinerary thus:

London   Paris
(Waterloo)   (Gare Saint Lazare)
via Southhampton-Havre.

Paris — Verneuil
(Ch. De Fer de l'Ouest)

The young man whistled, and sat down on a trunk to think
it out.

Somewhere there had been a leakage, and they were on
his trail. Nor did they care who knew it. There were hundreds
of people in London and Paris who would know the name of
Wimsey, not counting the police of both countries. In addition
to belonging to one of the oldest ducal families in England,
Lord Peter had made himself conspicuous by his meddling
with crime detection. A label like this was a gratuitous advertisement.

But the amazing thing was that the pursuers were not
troubling to hide themselves from the pursued. That argued
very great confidence. That he should have got into the
guard's van was, of course, an accident, but, even so, he might
have seen it on the platform, or anywhere.

An accident? It occurred to him — not for the first time,
but definitely now, and without doubt — that it was indeed an
accident for them that he was here. The series of maddening
delays that had held him up between London and the Invalides presented itself to him with an air of pre-arrangement.
The preposterous accusation for instance, of the woman who
had accosted him in Piccadilly, and the slow process of extri-
cating himself at Marlborough Street. It was easy to hold a
man up on some trumped-up charge till an important plan had

matured. Then there was the lavatory door at Waterloo, which had so ludicrously locked itself upon him. Being athletic, he had climbéd over the partition, to find the attendant mysteriously absent. And, in Paris, was it by chance that he had had a deaf taxi-driver, who mistook the direction "Quai d'Orléans" for "Gare de Lyon," and drove a mile and a half in the wrong direction before the shouts of his fare attracted his attention? They were clever, the pursuers, and circumspect. They had accurate information; they would delay him, but without taking any overt step; they knew that, if only they could keep time on their side, they needed no other ally.

Did they know he was on the train? If not, he still kept the advantage, for they would travel in a false security, thinking him to be left, raging and helpless, in the Invalides. He decided to make a cautious reconnaissance.

The first step was to change his grey suit for another of inconspicuous navy-blue cloth, which he had in his small black bag. This he did in the privacy of the toilet, substituting for his grey soft hat a large travelling-cap, which pulled well down over his eyes.

There was little difficulty in locating the man he was in search of. He found him seated in the inner corner of a first-class compartment, facing the engine, so that the watcher could approach unseen from behind. On the rack was a handsome dressing-case, with the initials P. D. B. W. The young man was familiar with Wimsey's narrow, beaky face, flat yellow hair, and insolent dropped eyelids. He smiled a little grimly.

"He is confident," he thought, "and has regrettably made the mistake of underrating the enemy. Good! This is where I retire into a *seconde* and keep my eyes open. The next act of this melodrama will take place, I fancy, at Dreux."

It is a rule on the Chemin de Fer de l'Ouest that all Paris-Évreux trains, whether of Grande Vitesse or what Lord Peter Wimsey preferred to call Grande Paresse, shall halt for an interminable period at Dreux. The young man (now in navy-blue) watched his quarry safely into the refreshment-room, and slipped unobtrusively out of the station. In a quarter of an hour he was back—this time in a heavy motoring-coat, helmet, and goggles, at the wheel of a powerful hired Peugeot. Coming quietly on to the platform, he took up his station behind the wall of the *lampisterie*, whence he could keep an eye on the train and the buffet door. After fifteen minutes his patience was rewarded by the sight of his man again boarding the express, dressing-case in hand. The porters slammed the doors, crying: "Next stop Verneuil!" The engine panted and groaned; the long train of grey-green carriages clanked slowly away. The motorist drew a breath of satisfaction, and, hurrying past the barrier, started up the car. He knew that he had a good eighty miles an hour under his bonnet, and there is no speed-limit in France.

Mon Souci, the seat of that eccentric and eremitical genius the Comte de Rueil, is situated three kilometres from Verneuil. It is a sorrowful and decayed *château*, desolate at the termination of its neglected avenue of pines. The mournful state of a nobility without an allegiance surrounds it. The stone nymphs droop greenly over their dry and mouldering fountains. An occasional peasant creaks with a single wagon-load of wood along the ill-forested glades. It has the atmosphere of sunset at all hours of the day. The woodwork is dry and gaping for lack of paint. Through the *jalousies* one sees the prim *salon*, with its beautiful and faded furniture. Even the last of its ill-dressed, ill-favoured women has withered away from Mon Souci, with her inbred, exaggerated features and her long white gloves. But at the rear of the *château* a chimney smokes incessantly. It is the furnace of the laboratory, the only living and modern thing among the old and dying; the only place tended and loved, petted and spoiled, heir to the long solicitude which counts of a more light-hearted day had given to stable and kennel, portrait-gallery and ball-room. And below, in the cool cellar, lie row upon row the dusty bottles, each an enchanted glass coffin in which the Sleeping Beauty of the vine grows ever more ravishing in sleep.

As the Peugeot came to a standstill in the courtyard, the

driver observed with considerable surprise that he was not the count's only visitor. An immense super-Renault, like a *merveilleuse* of the Directoire, all bonnet and no body, had been drawn so ostentatiously across the entrance as to embarrass the approach of any newcomer. Its glittering panels were embellished with a coat of arms, and the count's elderly servant was at that moment staggering beneath the weight of two large and elaborate suit-cases bearing in silver letters that could be read a mile away the legend: "LORD PETER WIMSEY."

The Peugeot driver gazed with astonishment at this display, and grinned sardonically. "Lord Peter seems rather ubiquitous in this country," he observed to himself. Then, taking pen and paper from his bag, he busied himself with a little letter-writing. By the time that the suit-cases had been carried in, and the Renault had purred its smooth way to the out-buildings, the document was complete and enclosed in an envelope addressed to the Comte de Rueil. "The hoist with his own petard touch," said the young man, and stepping up to the door, presented the envelope to the manservant.

"I am the bearer of a letter of introduction to monsieur le comte," he said. "Will you have the obligingness to present it to him? My name is Bredon — Death Bredon."

The man bowed, and begged him to enter.

"If monsieur will have the goodness to seat himself in the hall for a few moments. Monsieur le comte is engaged with another gentleman, but I will lose no time in making monsieur's arrival known."

The young man sat down and waited. The windows of the hall looked out upon the entrance, and it was not long before the château's sleep was disturbed by the hooting of yet another motor-horn. A station taxi-cab came noisily up the avenue. The man from the first-class carriage and the luggage labelled P. D. B. W. were deposited upon the doorstep. Lord Peter Wimsey dismissed the driver and rang the bell.

"Now," said Mr. Bredon, "the fun is going to begin." He effaced himself as far as possible in the shadow of a tall *armoire normande*.

"Good evening," said the newcomer to the manservant, in admirable French, "I am Lord Peter Wimsey. I arrive upon the invitation of monsieur le comte de Rueil. Monsieur le comte is at liberty?"

"Milord Peter Wimsey? Pardon, monsieur, but I do not understand. Milord de Wimsey is already arrived and is with monsieur le comte at this moment."

"You surprise me," said the other, with complete imperturbability, "for certainly no one but myself has any right to that name. It seems as though some person more ingenious than honest has had the bright idea of impersonating me."

The servant was clearly at a loss.

"Perhaps," he suggested, "monsieur can show his *papiers d'identité.*"

"Although it is somewhat unusual to produce one's credentials on the doorstep when paying a private visit," replied his lordship, with unaltered good humour, "I have not the slightest objection. Here is my passport, here is a *permis de séjour* granted to me in Paris, here my visiting-card, and here a quantity of correspondence addressed to me at the Hôtel Meurice, Paris, at my flat in Piccadilly, London, at the Marlborough club, London, and at my brother's house at King's Denver. Is that sufficiently in order?"

The servant perused the documents carefully, appearing particularly impressed by the *permis de séjour.*

"It appears there is some mistake," he murmured dubiously; "if monsieur will follow me, I will acquaint monsieur le comte."

They disappeared through the folding doors at the back of the hall and Bredon was left alone.

"Quite a little boom in Richmonds today," he observed, "each of us more unscrupulous than the last. The occasion calls for a refined subtlety of method."

After what he judged to be a hectic ten minutes in the count's library, the servant reappeared, searching for him.

"Monsieur le comte's compliments, and would monsieur step this way?"

Bredon entered the room with a jaunty step. He had created for himself the mastery of this situation. The count, a thin, elderly man, his fingers deeply stained with chemicals, sat, with a perturbed expression, at his desk. In two armchairs sat the two Wimseys. Bredon noted that, while the Wimsey he had seen in the train (whom he mentally named Peter I) retained his unruffled smile, Peter II (he of the Renault) had the flushed and indignant air of an Englishman affronted. The two men were superficially alike, both fair, lean, and long-nosed, with the nondescript, inelastic face which predominates in any assembly of well-bred Anglo-Saxons.

"Mr. Bredon," said the count, "I am charmed to have the pleasure of making your acquaintance, and regret that I must at once call upon you for a service as singular as it is important. You have presented to me a letter of introduction from your cousin, Lord Peter Wimsey. Will you now be good enough to inform me which of these gentlemen he is?"

Bredon let his glance pass slowly from the one claimant to the other, meditating what answer would best serve his own ends. One, at any rate, of the men in this room was a formidable intellect, trained in the detection of imposture.

"Well?" said Peter II. "Are you going to acknowledge me, Bredon?"

Peter I extracted a cigarette from a silver case. "Your confederate does not seem very well up in his part," he remarked, with a quiet smile at Peter II.

"Monsieur le comte," said Bredon, "I regret extremely that I cannot assist you in the matter. My acquaintance with my cousin, like your own, has been made and maintained entirely through correspondence on a subject of common interest. My profession," he added, "has made me unpopular with my family."

There was a very slight sigh of relief somewhere. The false Wimsey—whichever he was—had gained a respite. Bredon smiled.

"An excellent move, Mr. Bredon," said Peter I, "but it will hardly explain—Allow me." He took the letter from the count's hesitating hand. "It will hardly explain the fact that the ink of this letter of recommendation, dated three weeks ago, is even now scarcely dry—though I congratulate you on the very plausible imitation of my handwriting."

"If *you* can forge my handwriting," said Peter II, "so can this Mr. Bredon." He read the letter aloud over his double's shoulder.

" 'Monsieur le comte—I have the honour to present to you my friend and cousin, Mr. Death Bredon, who, I understand, is to be travelling in your part of France next month. He is very anxious to view your interesting library. Although a journalist by profession, he really knows something about books.' I am delighted to learn for the first time that I have such a cousin. An interviewer's trick, I fancy, monsieur le comte. Fleet Street appears well informed about our family names. Possibly it is equally well informed about the object of my visit to Mon Souci?"

"If," said Bredon boldly, "you refer to the acquisition of the de Rueil formula for poison gas for the British Government, I can answer for my own knowledge, though possibly the rest of Fleet Street is less completely enlightened." He weighed his words carefully now, warned by his slip. The sharp eyes and detective ability of Peter I alarmed him far more than the caustic tongue of Peter II.

The count uttered an exclamation of dismay.

"Gentlemen," he said, "one thing is obvious—that there has been somewhere a disastrous leakage of information. Which of you is the Lord Peter Wimsey to whom I should entrust the formula I do not know. Both of you are supplied with papers of identity; both appear completely instructed in this matter; both of your handwritings correspond with the letters I have previously received from Lord Peter, and both of you have offered me the sum agreed upon in Bank of England notes. In addition, this third gentleman arrives endowed with an equal facility in handwritings, an introductory letter surrounded by most suspicious circumstances, and a degree of acquaintance with this whole matter which alarms me. I can see but one solution. All of you must remain here at the *château* while I send to England for some elucidation of this mystery.

To the genuine Lord Peter I offer my apologies, and assure him that I will endeavour to make his stay as agreeable as possible. Will this satisfy you? It will? I am delighted to hear it. My servants will show you to your bedrooms, and dinner will be at half past seven."

"It is delightful to think," said Mr. Bredon, as he finished his glass and passed it before his nostrils with the air of a connoisseur, "that whichever of these gentlemen has the right to the name which he assumes is assured tonight of a truly Olympian satisfaction." His impudence had returned to him, and he challenged the company with an air. "Your cellars, monsieur le comte, are as well known among men endowed with a palate as your talents among men of science. No eloquence could say more."

The two Lord Peters murmured assent.

"I am the more pleased by your commendation," said the count, "that it suggests to me a little test which, with your kind cooperation, will, I think, assist us very much in determining which of you gentlemen is Lord Peter Wimsey and which his talented impersonator. Is it not matter of common notoriety that Lord Peter has a palate for wine almost unequalled in Europe?"

"You flatter me, monsieur le comte," said Peter II modestly.

"I wouldn't like to say unequalled," said Peter I, chiming in like a well-trained duet; "let's call it fair to middling. Less liable to misconstruction and all that."

"Your lordship does yourself an injustice," said Bredon, addressing both men with impartial deference. "The bet which you won from Mr. Frederick Arbuthnot at the Egotists' Club when he challenged you to name the vintage years of seventeen wines blindfold, received its due prominence in the *Evening Wire*."

"I was in extra form that night," said Peter I.

"A fluke," laughed Peter II.

"The test I propose, gentlemen, is on similar lines," pursued the count, "though somewhat less strenuous. There are six courses ordered for dinner tonight. With each we shall drink a different wine, which my butler shall bring me with the label concealed. You shall each in turn give me your opinion upon the vintage. By this means we shall perhaps arrive at something, since the most brilliant forger—of whom I gather I have at least two at my table tonight—can scarcely forge a palate for wine. If too hazardous a mixture of wines should produce a temporary incommodity in the morning, you will, I feel sure, suffer it gladly for this once in the cause of truth."

The two Wimseys bowed.

"*In vino veritas,*" said Mr. Bredon, with a laugh. He at least was well seasoned, and foresaw opportunities for himself.

"Accident, and my butler, having placed you at my right hand, monsieur," went on the count, addressing Peter I, "I will ask you to begin by pronouncing, as accurately as may be, upon the wine which you have just drunk."

"That is scarcely a searching ordeal," said the other, with a smile. "I can say definitely that it is a very pleasant and well-matured Chablis Moutonne; and, since ten years is an excellent age for a Chablis—a real Chablis—I should vote for 1916, which was perhaps the best of the war vintages in that district."

"Have you anything to add to that opinion, monsieur?" inquired the count, deferentially, of Peter II.

"I wouldn't like to be dogmatic to a year or so," said that gentleman critically, "but if I must commit myself, don't you know, I should say 1915—decidedly 1915."

The count bowed, and turned to Bredon.

"Perhaps you, too, monsieur, would be interested to give an opinion," he suggested, with the exquisite courtesy always shown to the plain man in the society of experts.

"I'd rather not set a standard which I might not be able to live up to," replied Bredon, a little maliciously. "I know that it is 1915, for I happened to see the label."

Peter II looked a little disconcerted.

"We will arrange matters better in future," said the count.

"Pardon me." He stepped apart for a few moments' conference with the butler, who presently advanced to remove the oysters and bring in the soup.

The next candidate for attention arrived swathed to the lip in damask.

"It is your turn to speak first, monsieur," said the count to Peter II. "Permit me to offer you an olive to cleanse the palate. No haste, I beg. Even for the most excellent political ends, good wine must not be used with disrespect."

The rebuke was not unnecessary, for, after a preliminary sip, Peter II had taken a deep draught of the heady white richness. Under Peter I's quizzical eye he wilted quite visibly.

"It is—it is Sauterne," he began, and stopped. Then, gathering encouragement from Bredon's smile, he said, with more aplomb, "Château Yquem, 1911—ah! the queen of white wines, sir, as what's-his-name says." He drained his glass defiantly.

The count's face was a study as he slowly detached his fascinated gaze from Peter II to fix it on Peter I.

"If I had to be impersonated by somebody," murmured the latter gently, "it would have been more flattering to have had it undertaken by a person to whom all white wines were *not* alike. Well, now, sir, this admirable vintage is, of course, a Montrachet of—let me see"—he rolled the wine delicately upon his tongue—"of 1911. And a very attractive wine it is, though, with all due deference to yourself, monsieur le comte, I feel that it is perhaps slightly too sweet to occupy its present place in the menu. True, with this excellent *consommé marmite,* a sweetish wine is not altogether out of place, but, in my own humble opinion, it would have shown to better advantage with the *confitures.*"

"There, now," said Bredon innocently, "it just shows how one may be misled. Had not I had the advantage of Lord Peter's expert opinion—for certainly nobody who could mistake Montrachet for Sauterne has any claim to the name of Wimsey—I should have pronounced this to be, not the Montrachet-Aîné, but the Chevalier-Montrachet of the same year, which is a trifle sweeter. But no doubt, as your lordship says, drinking it with the soup has caused it to appear sweeter to me than it actually is."

The count looked sharply at him, but made no comment.

"Have another olive," said Peter I kindly. "You can't judge wine if your mind is on other flavours."

"Thanks frightfully," said Bredon. "And that reminds me—" He launched into a rather pointless story about olives, which lasted out the soup and bridged the interval to the entrance of an exquisitely cooked sole.

The count's eye followed the pale amber wine rather thoughtfully as it trilled into the glasses. Bredon raised his in the approved manner to his nostrils, and his face flushed a little. With the first sip he turned excitedly to his host.

"Good God, sir—" he began.

The lifted hand cautioned him to silence.

Peter I sipped, inhaled, sipped again, and his brows clouded. Peter II had by this time apparently abandoned his pretensions. He drank thirstily, with a beaming smile and a lessening hold upon reality.

"*Eh bien, monsieur?*" inquired the count gently.

"This," said Peter I, "is certainly hock, and the noblest hock I have ever tasted, but I must admit that for the moment I cannot precisely place it."

"No?" said Bredon. His voice was like bean-honey now, sweet and harsh together. "Nor the other gentleman? And yet I fancy I could place it within a couple of miles, though it is a wine I had hardly looked to find in a French cellar at this time. It is hock, as your lordship says, and at that it is Johannisberger. Not the plebeian cousin, but the *echter* Schloss Johannisberger from the castle vineyard itself. Your lordship must have missed it (to your great loss) during the war years. My father laid some down the year before he died, but it appears that the ducal cellars at Denver were less well furnished."

"I must set about remedying the omission," said the remaining Peter, with determination.

The *poulet* was served to the accompaniment of an argument over the Lafitte, his lordship placing it at 1878, Bredon maintaining it to be a relic of the glorious 'seventy-fives, slightly overmatured, but both agreeing as to its great age and noble pedigree.

As to the Clos-Vougeôt, on the other hand, there was complete agreement; after a tentative suggestion of 1915, it was pronounced finally by Peter I to belong to the equally admirable though slightly lighter 1911 crop. The *pré-salé* was removed amid general applause, and the dessert was brought in.

"Is it necessary," asked Peter I, with a slight smile in the direction of Peter II—now happily murmuring, "Damn good wine, damn good dinner, damn good show"—"is it necessary to prolong this farce any further?"

"Your lordship will not, surely, refuse to proceed with the discussion?" cried the count.

"The point is sufficiently made, I fancy."

"But no one will surely ever refuse to discuss wine," said Bredon, "least of all your lordship, who is so great an authority."

"Not on this," said the other. "Frankly, it is a wine I do not care about. It is sweet and coarse, qualities that would damn any wine in the eyes—the mouth, rather—of a connoisseur. Did your excellent father have this laid down also, Mr. Bredon?"

Bredon shook his head.

"No," he said, "no. Genuine Imperial Tokay is beyond the opportunities of Grub Street, I fear. Though I agree with you that it is horribly overrated—with all due deference to yourself, monsieur le comte."

"In that case," said the count, "we will pass at once to the liqueur. I admit that I had thought of puzzling these gentlemen with the local product, but, since one competitor seems to have scratched, it shall be brandy—the only fitting close to a good wine-list."

In a slightly embarrassing silence the huge, round-bellied balloon glasses were set upon the table, and the few precious drops poured gently into each and set lightly swinging to release the bouquet.

"This," said Peter I, charmed again into amiability, "is, indeed, a wonderful old French brandy. Half a century old, I suppose."

"Your lordship's praise lacks warmth," replied Bredon. "This is *the* brandy—the brandy of brandies—the superb—the incomparable—the true Napoleon. It should be honoured like the emperor it is."

He rose to his feet, his napkin in his hand.

"Sir," said the count, turning to him, "I have on my right a most admirable judge of wine, but you are unique." He motioned to Pierre, who solemnly brought forward the empty bottles, unswathed now, from the humble Chablis to the stately Napoleon, with the imperial seal blown in the glass. "Every time you have been correct as to the growth and year. There cannot be six men in the world with such a palate as yours, and I thought that but one of them was an Englishman. Will you not favour us, this time, with your real name?"

"It doesn't matter what his name is," said Peter I. He rose. "Put up your hands, all of you. Count, the formula!"

Bredon's hands came up with a jerk, still clutching the napkin. The white folds spurted flame as his shot struck the other's revolver cleanly between trigger and barrel, exploding the charge, to the extreme detriment of the glass chandelier. Peter I stood shaking his paralysed hand and cursing.

Bredon kept him covered while he cocked a wary eye at Peter II, who, his rosy visions scattered by the report, seemed struggling back to aggressiveness.

"Since the entertainment appears to be taking a lively turn," observed Bredon, "perhaps you would be so good, count, as to search these gentlemen for further firearms. Thank you. Now, why should we not all sit down again and pass the bottle round?"

"You—*you* are—" growled Peter I.

"Oh, my name is Bredon all right," said the young man cheerfully. "I loathe aliases. Like another fellow's clothes, you know—never seem quite to fit. Peter Death Bredon Wimsey—a bit lengthy and all that, but handy when taken in instalments. I've got a passport and all those things, too, but I didn't offer them, as their reputation here seems a little blown upon, so to speak. As regards the formula, I think I'd better give you my personal cheque for it—all sorts of people seem able to go about flourishing Bank of England notes. Personally, I think all this secret diplomacy work is a mistake, but that's the War Office's pigeon. I suppose we all brought similar credentials. Yes, I thought so. Some bright person seems to have sold himself very successfully in two places at once. But you two must have been having a lively time, each thinking the other was me."

"My lord," said the count heavily, "these two men are, or were, Englishmen, I suppose. I do not care to know what governments have purchased their treachery. But where they stand, I, alas! stand too. To our venal and corrupt Republic I, as a Royalist, acknowledge no allegiance. But it is in my heart that I have agreed to sell my country to England because of my poverty. Go back to your War Office and say I will not give you the formula. If war should come between our countries—which may God avert—I will be found on the side of France. That, my lord, is my last word."

Wimsey bowed.

"Sir," said he, "it appears that my mission has, after all, failed. I am glad of it. This trafficking in destruction is a dirty kind of business after all. Let us shut the door upon these two, who are neither flesh nor fowl, and finish the brandy in the library."

THE LEARNED ADVENTURE

OF THE DRAGON'S HEAD

U ncle Peter!"

"Half a jiff, Gherkins. No, I don't think I'll take a Catullus, Mr. Ffolliott. After all, thirteen guineas is a bit steep without either the title or the last folio, what? But you might send me round the Vitruvius and the Satyricon when they come in; I'd like to have a look at them, anyhow. Well, old man, what is it?"

"Do come and look at these pictures, Uncle Peter. I'm sure it's an awfully old book."

Lord Peter Wimsey sighed as he picked his way out of Mr. Ffolliott's dark back shop, strewn with the flotsam and jetsam of many libraries. An unexpected outbreak of measles at Mr. Bultridge's excellent preparatory school, coinciding with the absence of the Duke and Duchess of Denver on the Continent, had saddled his lordship with his ten-year-old nephew, Viscount St. George, more commonly known as Young Jerry, Jerrykins, or Pickled Gherkins. Lord Peter was not one of those born uncles who delight old nurses by their fascinating "way with" children. He succeeded, however, in earning tolerance on honourable terms by treating the young with the same scrupulous politeness which he extended to their elders. He therefore prepared to receive Gherkins's discovery with respect, though a child's taste was not to be trusted, and the book might quite well be some horror of woolly mezzotints or an inferior modern reprint adorned with leprous electros. Nothing much better was really to be expected from the "cheap shelf" exposed to the dust of the street.

"Uncle! there's such a funny man here, with a great long nose and ears and a tail and dogs' heads all over his body. *Monstrum hoc Cracoviae*—that's a monster, isn't it? I should jolly well think it was. What's *Cracoviae*, Uncle Peter?"

"Oh," said Lord Peter, greatly relieved, "the Cracow monster?" A portrait of that distressing infant certainly argued a respectable antiquity. "Let's have a look. Quite right, it's a very old book—Munster's *Cosmographia Universalis.* I'm glad you know good stuff when you see it, Gherkins. What's the *Cosmographia* doing out here, Mr. Ffolliott, at five bob?"

"Well, my lord," said the bookseller, who had followed his customers to the door, "it's in a very bad state, you see; covers loose and nearly all the doublepage maps missing. It came in a few weeks ago—dumped in with a collection we bought from a gentleman in Norfolk—you'll find his name in it—Dr. Conyers of Yelsall Manor. Of course, we might keep it and try to make up a complete copy when we get another example. But it's rather out of our line, as you know, classical authors being our specialty. So we just put it out to go for what it would fetch in the *status quo*, as you might say."

"Oh, look!" broke in Gherkins. "Here's a picture of a man being chopped up in little bits. What does it say about it?"

"I thought you could read Latin."

"Well, but it's all full of sort of pothooks. What do they mean?"

"They're just contractions," said Lord Peter patiently. " '*Solent quoque hujus insulae cultores*'—It is the custom of the dwellers in this island, when they see their parents stricken in years and of no further use, to take them down into the market-place and sell them to the cannibals, who kill them and eat them for food. This they do also with younger persons when they fall into any desperate sickness."

"Ha, ha!" said Mr. Ffolliott. "Rather sharp practice on the poor cannibals. They never got anything but tough old joints or diseased meat, eh?"

"The inhabitants seem to have had thoroughly advanced notions of business," agreed his lordship.

The viscount was enthralled.

"I *do* like this book," he said; "could I buy it out of my pocket-money, please?"

"Another problem for uncles," thought Lord Peter, rapidly ransacking his recollections of the *Cosmographia* to determine whether any of its illustrations were indelicate; for he knew the duchess to be straitlaced. On consideration, he could only remember one that was dubious, and there was a sporting chance that the duchess might fail to light upon it.

"Well," he said judicially, "in your place, Gherkins, I should be inclined to buy it. It's in a bad state, as Mr. Ffolliott has honourably told you—otherwise, of course, it would be exceedingly valuable; but, apart from the lost pages, it's a very nice clean copy, and certainly worth five shillings to you, if you think of starting a collection."

Till that moment, the viscount had obviously been more impressed by the cannibals than by the state of the margins, but the idea of figuring next term at Mr. Bultridge's as a collector of rare editions had undeniable charm.

"None of the other fellows collect books," he said; "they collect stamps, mostly. I think stamps are rather ordinary, don't you, Uncle Peter? I was rather thinking of giving up stamps. Mr. Porter, who takes us for history, has got a lot of books like yours, and he is a splendid man at footer."

Rightly interpreting this reference to Mr. Porter, Lord Peter gave it as his opinion that book-collecting could be a perfectly manly pursuit. Girls, he said, practically never took it up, because it meant so much learning about dates and typefaces and other technicalities which called for a masculine brain.

"Besides," he added, "it's a very interesting book in itself, you know. Well worth dipping into."

"I'll take it, please," said the viscount, blushing a little at transacting so important and expensive a piece of business; for the duchess did not encourage lavish spending by little boys, and was strict in the matter of allowances.

Mr. Ffolliott bowed, and took the *Cosmographia* away to wrap it up.

"Are you all right for cash?" inquired Lord Peter discreetly. "Or can I be of temporary assistance?"

"No, thank you, uncle; I've got Aunt Mary's half-crown and four shillings of my pocket-money, because, you see, with the measles happening, we didn't have our dormitory spread, and I was saving up for that."

The business being settled in this gentlemanly manner, and the budding bibliophile taking personal and immediate charge of the stout, square volume, a taxi was chartered which, in due course of traffic delays, brought the *Cosmographia* to 110A Piccadilly.

"And who, Bunter, is Mr. Wilberforce Pope?"

"I do not think we know the gentleman, my lord. He is asking to see your lordship for a few minutes on business."

"He probably wants me to find a lost dog for his maiden aunt. What it is to have acquired a reputation as a sleuth! Show him in. Gherkins, if this good gentleman's business turns out to be private, you'd better retire into the diningroom."

"Yes, Uncle Peter," said the viscount dutifully. He was extended on his stomach on the library hearthrug, laboriously picking his way through the more exciting-looking bits of the *Cosmographia*, with the aid of Messrs. Lewis & Short, whose monumental compilation he had hitherto looked upon as a barbarous invention for the annoyance of upper forms.

Mr. Wilberforce Pope turned out to be a rather plump,

fair gentleman in the late thirties, with a prematurely bald forehead, horn-rimmed spectacles, and an engaging manner.

"You will excuse my intrusion, won't you?" he began. "I'm sure you must think me a terrible nuisance. But I wormed your name and address out of Mr. Ffolliott. Not his fault, really. You won't blame him, will you? I positively badgered the poor man. Sat down on his doorstep and refused to go, though the boy was putting up the shutters. I'm afraid you will think me very silly when you know what it's all about. But you really mustn't hold poor Mr. Ffolliott responsible, now, will you?"

"Not at all," said his lordship. "I mean, I'm charmed and all that sort of thing. Something I can do for you about books? You're a collector, perhaps? Will you have a drink or anything?"

"Well, no," said Mr. Pope, with a faint giggle. "No, not exactly a collector. Thank you very much, just a spot—no, no, literally a spot. Thank you; no"—he glanced round the bookshelves, with their rows of rich old leather bindings— "certainly not a collector. But I happen to be er, interested— sentimentally interested—in a purchase you made yesterday. Really, such a very small matter. You will think it foolish. But I am told you are the present owner of a copy of Munster's *Cosmographia*, which used to belong to my uncle, Dr. Conyers."

Gherkins looked up suddenly, seeing that the conversation had a personal interest for him.

"Well, that's not quite correct," said Wimsey. "I was there at the time, but the actual purchaser is my nephew. Gerald, Mr. Pope is interested in your *Cosmographia*. My nephew, Lord St. George."

"How do you do, young man," said Mr. Pope affably. "I see that the collecting spirit runs in the family. A great Latin scholar, too, I expect, eh? Ready to decline *jusjurandum* with the best of us? Ha, ha! And what are you going to do when you grow up? Be Lord Chancellor, eh? Now, I bet you think you'd rather be an engine-driver, what, what?"

"No, thank you," said the viscount, with aloofness.

"What, not an engine-driver? Well, now, I want you to be a real business man this time. Put through a book deal, you know. Your uncle will see I offer you a fair price, what? Ha, ha! Now, you see, that picture-book of yours has a great value for me that it wouldn't have for anybody else. When *I* was a little boy of your age it was one of my very greatest joys. I used to have it to look at on Sundays. Ah, dear! the happy hours I used to spend with those quaint old engravings, and the funny old maps with the ships and salamanders and '*Hic dracones*' — you know what *that* means, I dare say. What does it mean?"

"Here are dragons," said the viscount, unwillingly but still politely.

"Quite right. I *knew* you were a scholar."

"It's a very attractive book," said Lord Peter. "My nephew was quite entranced by the famous Cracow monster."

"Ah yes — a glorious monster, isn't it?" agreed Mr. Pope, with enthusiasm. "Many's the time I've fancied myself as Sir Lancelot or somebody on a white war horse, charging that monster, lance in rest, with the captive princess cheering me on. Ah! childhood! You're living the happiest days of your life, young man. You won't believe me, but you are."

"Now what is it exactly you want my nephew to do?" inquired Lord Peter a little sharply.

"Quite right, quite right. Well now, you know, my uncle, Dr. Conyers, sold his library a few months ago. I was abroad at the time, and it was only yesterday, when I went down to Yelsall on a visit, that I learnt the dear old book had gone with the rest. I can't tell you how distressed I was. I know it's not valuable — a great many pages missing and all that — but I can't bear to think of its being gone. So, purely from sentimental reasons, as I said, I hurried off to Ffolliott's to see if I could get it back. I was quite upset to find I was too late, and gave poor Mr. Ffolliott no peace till he told me the name of the purchaser. Now, you see, Lord St. George, I'm here to make you an offer for the book. Come, now, double what you gave for it. That's a good offer, isn't it, Lord Peter? Ha, ha! And you will be doing me a very great kindness as well."

Viscount St. George looked rather distressed, and turned appealingly to his uncle.

"Well, Gerald," said Lord Peter, "it's your affair, you know. What do you say?"

The viscount stood first on one leg and then on the other. The career of a book collector evidently had its problems, like other careers.

"If you please, Uncle Peter," he said, with embarrassment, "may I whisper?"

"It's not usually considered the thing to whisper, Gherkins, but you could ask Mr. Pope for time to consider his offer. Or you could say you would prefer to consult me first. That would be quite in order."

"Then, if you don't mind, Mr. Pope, I should like to consult my uncle first."

"Certainly, certainly; ha, ha!" said Mr. Pope. "Very prudent to consult a collector of greater experience, what? Ah! the younger generation, eh, Lord Peter? Regular little business men already."

"Excuse us, then, for one moment," said Lord Peter, and drew his nephew into the dining-room.

"I say, Uncle Peter," said the collector breathlessly, when the door was shut, "*need* I give him my book? I don't think he's a very nice man. I *hate* people who ask you to decline nouns for them."

"Certainly you needn't, Gherkins, if you don't want to. The book is yours, and you've a right to it."

"What would *you* do, uncle?"

Before replying, Lord Peter, in the most surprising manner, tiptoed gently to the door which communicated with the library and flung it suddenly open, in time to catch Mr. Pope kneeling on the hearthrug intently turning over the pages of the coveted volume, which lay as the owner had left it. He started to his feet in a flurried manner as the door opened.

"Do help yourself, Mr. Pope, won't you?" cried Lord Peter hospitably, and closed the door again.

"What is it, Uncle Peter?"

"If you want my advice, Gherkins, I should be rather careful how you had any dealings with Mr. Pope. I don't think he's telling the truth. He called those wood-cuts engravings — though, of course, that may be just his ignorance. But I can't believe that he spent all his childhood's Sunday afternoons studying those maps and picking out the dragons in them, because, as you may have noticed for yourself, old Munster put very few dragons into his maps. They're mostly just plain maps — a bit queer to our ideas of geography, but perfectly straightforward. That was why I brought in the Cracow monster, and, you see, he thought it was some sort of dragon."

"Oh, I say, uncle! So you said that on purpose!"

"If Mr. Pope wants the *Cosmographia,* it's for some reason he doesn't want to tell us about. And, that being so, I wouldn't be in too big a hurry to sell, if the book were mine. See?"

"Do you mean there's something frightfully valuable about the book, which we don't know?"

"Possibly."

"How exciting! It's just like a story in the *Boys' Friend Library.* What am I to say to him, uncle?"

"Well, in your place I wouldn't be dramatic or anything. I'd just say you've considered the matter, and you've taken a fancy to the book and have decided not to sell. You thank him for his offer, of course."

"Yes — er, won't you say it for me, uncle?"

"I think it would look better if you did it yourself."

"Yes, perhaps it would. Will he be very cross?"

"Possibly," said Lord Peter, "but if he is, he won't let on. Ready?"

The consulting committee accordingly returned to the library. Mr. Pope had prudently retired from the hearthrug and was examining a distant bookcase.

"Thank you very much for your offer, Mr. Pope," said the viscount, striding stoutly up to him, "but I have considered it, and I have taken a-a-a fancy for the book and decided not to sell."

"Sorry and all that," put in Lord Peter, "but my nephew's adamant about it. No, it isn't the price; he wants the book. Wish I could oblige you, but it isn't in my hands. Won't you take something else before you go? Really? Ring the bell, Gherkins. My man will see you to the lift. Good evening."

When the visitor had gone, Lord Peter returned and thoughtfully picked up the book.

"We were awful idiots to leave him with it, Gherkins, even for a moment. Luckily, there's no harm done."

"You don't think he found out anything while we were away, do you, uncle?" gasped Gherkins, open-eyed.

"I'm sure he didn't."

"Why?"

"He offered me fifty pounds for it on the way to the door. Gave the game away. H'm! Bunter."

"My lord?"

"Put this book in the safe and bring me back the keys. And you'd better set all the burglar alarms when you lock up."

"Oo-er!" said Viscount St. George.

On the third morning after the visit of Mr. Wilberforce Pope, the viscount was seated at a very late breakfast in his uncle's flat, after the most glorious and soul-satisfying night that ever boy experienced. He was almost too excited to eat the kidneys and bacon placed before him by Bunter, whose usual impeccable manner was not in the least impaired by a rapidly swelling and blackening eye.

It was about two in the morning that Gherkins — who had not slept very well, owing to too lavish and grown-up a dinner and theatre the evening before — became aware of a stealthy sound somewhere in the direction of the fire-escape. He had got out of bed and crept very softly into Lord Peter's room and woken him up. He had said: "Uncle Peter, I'm sure there's burglars on the fire-escape." And Uncle Peter, instead of saying, "Nonsense, Gherkins, hurry up and get back to bed," had sat up and listened and said: "By Jove, Gherkins, I believe you're right." And had sent Gherkins to call Bunter. And on his return, Gherkins, who had always regarded his uncle as a very top-hatted sort of person, actually saw him take from his handkerchief-drawer an undeniable automatic pistol.

It was at this point that Lord Peter was apotheosed from the state of Quite Decent Uncle to that of Glorified Uncle. He said:

"Look here, Gherkins, we don't know how many of these blighters there'll be, so you must be jolly smart and do anything I say sharp, on the word of command — even if I have to say 'Scoot.' Promise?"

Gherkins promised, with his heart thumping, and they sat waiting in the dark, till suddenly a little electric bell rang sharply just over the head of Lord Peter's bed and a green light shone out.

"The library window," said his lordship, promptly silencing the bell by turning a switch. "If they heard, they may think better of it. We'll give them a few minutes."

They gave them five minutes, and then crept very quietly down the passage.

"Go round by the dining-room, Bunter," said his lordship; "they may bolt that way."

With infinite precaution, he unlocked and opened the library door, and Gherkins noticed how silently the locks moved.

A circle of light from an electric torch was moving slowly along the bookshelves. The burglars had obviously heard nothing of the counter-attack. Indeed, they seemed to have troubles enough of their own to keep their attention occupied. As his eyes grew accustomed to the dim light, Gherkins made out that one man was standing holding the torch, while the other took down and examined the books. It was fascinating to watch his apparently disembodied hands move along the shelves in the torch-light.

The men muttered discontentedly. Obviously the job was proving a harder one than they had bargained for. The habit of ancient authors of abbreviating the titles on the backs of their volumes, or leaving them completely untitled, made things extremely awkward. From time to time the man with the torch extended his hand into the light. It held a piece of paper, which they anxiously compared with the title-page of a book. Then the volume was replaced and the tedious search went on.

Suddenly some slight noise — Gherkins was sure *he* did not make it; it may have been Bunter in the dining-room — seemed to catch the ear of the kneeling man.

"Wot's that?" he gasped, and his startled face swung round into view.

"Hands up!" said Lord Peter, and switched the light on.

The second man made one leap for the dining-room door, where a smash and an oath proclaimed that he had encountered Bunter. The kneeling man shot his hands up like a marionette.

"Gherkins," said Lord Peter, "do you think you can go across to that gentleman by the bookcase and relieve him of the article which is so inelegantly distending the right-hand pocket of his coat? Wait a minute. Don't on any account get between him and my pistol, and mind you take the thing out *very* carefully. There's no hurry. That's splendid. Just point it at the floor while you bring it across, would you? Thanks. Bunter has managed for himself, I see. Now run into my bedroom, and in the bottom of my wardrobe you will find a bundle of stout cord. Oh! I beg your pardon; yes, put your hands down by all means. It must be very tiring exercise."

The arms of the intruders being secured behind their backs with a neatness which Gherkins felt to be worthy of the best traditions of Sexton Blake, Lord Peter motioned his captives to sit down and despatched Bunter for whisky-and-soda.

"Before we send for the police," said Lord Peter, "you would do me a great personal favour by telling me what you were looking for, and who sent you. Ah! thanks, Bunter. As our guests are not at liberty to use their hands, perhaps you would be kind enough to assist them to a drink. Now then, say when."

"Well, you're a gentleman, guv'nor," said the First Burglar, wiping his mouth politely on his shoulder, the back of his hand not being available. "If we'd a known wot a job this wos goin' ter be, blow me if we'd a touched it. The bloke said, ses 'e, 'It's takin' candy from a baby,' 'e ses. 'The gentleman's a reg'lar softie,' 'e ses, 'one o' these 'ere sersiety toffs wiv a maggot fer old books,' that's wot 'e ses, 'an' ef yer can find this 'ere old book fer me,' 'e ses, 'there's a pony fer yer.' Well! Sech a job! 'E didn't mention as 'ow there'd be five 'undred fousand bleedin' ole books all as alike as a regiment o' bleedin' dragoons. Nor as 'ow yer kept a nice little machine-gun like that 'andy by the bedside, *nor* yet as 'ow yer was so bleedin' good at tyin' knots in a bit o' string. No—'e didn't think ter mention them things."

"Deuced unsporting of him," said his lordship. "Do you happen to know the gentleman's name?"

"No—that was another o' them things wot 'e didn't mention. 'E's a stout, fair party, wiv 'orn rims to 'is goggles and a bald 'ead. One o' these 'ere philanthropists, I reckon. A friend o' mine, wot got inter trouble onct, got work froo 'im, and the gentleman comes round and ses to 'im, 'e ses, 'Could yer find me a couple o' lads ter do a little job?' 'e ses, an' my friend finkin' no 'arm, you see, guv'nor, but wot it might be a bit of a joke like, 'e gets 'old of my pal an' me, an' we meets the gentleman in a pub dahn Whitechapel way. W'ich we was ter meet 'im there again Friday night, us 'avin' allowed that time fer ter git 'old of the book."

"The book being, if I may hazard a guess, the *Cosmographia Universalis?*"

"Sumfink like that, guv'nor. I got its jaw-breakin' name wrote down on a bit o' paper, wot my pal 'ad in 'is 'and. Wot did yer do wiv that 'ere bit o' paper, Bill?"

"Well, look here," said Lord Peter, "I'm afraid I must send for the police, but I think it likely, if you give us your assistance to get hold of your gentleman, whose name I strongly suspect to be Wilberforce Pope, that you will get off pretty easily. Telephone the police, Bunter, and then go and put something on that eye of yours. Gherkins, we'll give these gentlemen another drink, and then I think perhaps you'd better hop back to bed; the fun's over. No? Well, put a good thick coat on, there's a good fellow, because what your mother will say to me if you catch a cold I don't like to think."

So the police had come and taken the burglars away, and now Detective-Inspector Parker, of Scotland Yard, a great personal friend of Lord Peter's, sat toying with a cup of coffee and listening to the story.

"But what's the matter with the jolly old book, anyhow, to make it so popular?" he demanded.

"I don't know," replied Wimsey; "but after Mr. Pope's little visit the other day I got kind of intrigued about it and had a look through it. I've got a hunch it may turn out rather valuable, after all. Unsuspected beauties and all that sort of thing. If only Mr. Pope had been a trifle more accurate in his facts, he might have got away with something to which I feel pretty sure he isn't entitled. Anyway, when I'd seen—what I saw, I wrote off to Dr. Conyers of Yelsall Manor, the late owner—"

"Conyers, the cancer man?"

"Yes. He's done some pretty important research in his time, I fancy. Getting on now, though; about seventy-eight, I fancy. I hope he's more honest than his nephew, with one foot in the grave like that. Anyway, I wrote (with Gherkins' permission, naturally) to say we had the book and had been specially interested by something we found there, and would he be so obliging as to tell us something of its history. I also—"

"But what did you find in it?"

"I don't think we'll tell him yet, Gherkins, shall we? I like to keep policemen guessing. As I was saying, when you so rudely interrupted me, I also asked him whether he knew anything about his good nephew's offer to buy it back. His answer has just arrived. He says he knows of nothing specially interesting about the book. It has been in the library untold years, and the tearing out of the maps must have been done a long time ago by some family vandal. He can't think why his nephew should be so keen on it, as he certainly never pored over it as a boy. In fact, the old man declares the engaging

Wilberforce has never even set foot in Yelsall Manor to his knowledge. So much for the fire-breathing monsters and the pleasant Sunday afternoons."

"Naughty Wilberforce!"

"M'm. Yes. So, after last night's little dust-up, I wired the old boy we were tooling down to Yelsall to have a heart-to-heart talk with him about his picture-book and his nephew."

"Are you taking the book down with you?" asked Parker. "I can give you a police escort for it if you like."

"That's not a bad idea," said Wimsey. "We don't know where the insinuating Mr. Pope may be hanging out, and I wouldn't put it past him to make another attempt."

"Better be on the safe side," said Parker. "I can't come myself, but I'll send down a couple of men with you."

"Good egg," said Lord Peter. "Call up your myrmidons. We'll get a car round at once. You're coming, Gherkins, I suppose? God knows what your mother would say. Don't ever be an uncle, Charles; it's frightfully difficult to be fair to all parties."

Yelsall Manor was one of those large, decaying country mansions which speak eloquently of times more spacious than our own. The original late Tudor construction had been masked by the addition of a wide frontage in the Italian manner, with a kind of classical portico surmounted by a pediment and approached by a semi-circular flight of steps. The grounds had originally been laid out in that formal manner in which grove nods to grove and each half duly reflects the other. A late owner, however, had burst out into the more eccentric sort of landscape gardening which is associated with the name of Capability Brown. A Chinese pagoda, somewhat resembling Sir William Chambers's erection in Kew Gardens, but smaller, rose out of a grove of laurustinus towards the eastern extremity of the house, while at the rear appeared a large artificial lake, dotted with numerous islands, on which odd little temples, grottos, tea-houses, and bridges peeped out from among clumps of shrubs, once ornamental, but now sadly overgrown. A boat-house, with wide eves like the designs on a willow-pattern plate, stood at one corner, its landing-stage fallen into decay and wreathed with melancholy weeds.

"My disreputable old ancestor, Cuthbert Conyers, settled down here when he retired from the sea in 1732," said Dr. Conyers, smiling faintly. "His elder brother died childless, so the black sheep returned to the fold with the determination to become respectable and found a family. I fear he did not succeed altogether. There were very queer tales as to where his money came from. He is said to have been a pirate, and to have sailed with the notorious Captain Blackbeard. In the village, to this day, he is remembered and spoken of as Cutthroat Conyers. It used to make the old man very angry, and there is an unpleasant story of his slicing the ears off a groom who had been heard to call him 'Old Cut-throat.' He was not an uncultivated person, though. It was he who did the landscape-gardening round at the back, and he built the pagoda for his telescope. He was reputed to study the Black Art, and there were certainly a number of astrological works in the library with his name on the fly-leaf, but probably the telescope was only a remembrance of his seafaring days.

"Anyhow, towards the end of his life he became more and more odd and morose. He quarrelled with his family, and turned his younger son out of doors with his wife and children. An unpleasant old fellow.

"On his deathbed he was attended by the parson—a good earnest, God-fearing sort of man, who must have put up with a deal of insult in carrying out what he firmly believed to be the sacred duty of reconciling the old man to this shamefully treated son. Eventually, 'Old Cut-throat' relented so far as to make a will, leaving to the younger son 'My treasure which I have buried in Munster.' The parson represented to him that it was useless to bequeath a treasure unless he also bequeathed the information where to find it, but the horrid old pirate only chuckled spitefully, and said that, as he had been at the pains to collect the treasure, his son might well be at the pains of looking for it. Further than that he would not go, and so he died, and I dare say went to a very bad place.

"Since then the family has died out, and I am the sole representative of the Conyers, and heir to the treasure, whatever and wherever it is, for it was never discovered. I do not suppose it was very honestly come by, but, since it would be useless now to try and find the original owners, I imagine I have a better right to it than anybody living.

"You may think it very unseemly, Lord Peter, that an old, lonely man like myself should be greedy for a hoard of pirate's gold. But my whole life has been devoted to studying the disease of cancer, and I believe myself to be very close to a solution of one part at least of the terrible problem. Research costs money, and my limited means are very nearly exhausted. The property is mortgaged up to the hilt, and I do most urgently desire to complete my experiments before I die, and to leave a sufficient sum to found a clinic where the work can be carried on.

"During the last year I have made very great efforts to solve the mystery of 'Old Cut-throat's' treasure. I have been able to leave much of my experimental work in the most capable hands of my assistant, Dr. Forbes, while I pursued my researches with the very slender clue I had to go upon. It was the more expensive and difficult that Cuthbert had left no indication in his will whether Münster in Germany or Munster in Ireland was the hiding-place of the treasure. My journeys and my search in other places cost money and brought me no further on my quest. I returned, disheartened, in August, and found myself obliged to sell my library, in order to defray my expenses and obtain a little money with which to struggle on with my sadly delayed experiments."

"Ah!" said Lord Peter. "I begin to see light."

The old physician looked at him inquiringly. They had finished tea, and were seated around the great fireplace in the study. Lord Peter's interested questions about the beautiful, dilapidated old house and estate had led the conversation naturally to Dr. Conyers's family, shelving for the time the problem of the *Cosmographia*, which lay on a table beside them.

"Everything you say fits into the puzzle," went on Wimsey, "and I think there's not the smallest doubt what Mr.

Wilberforce Pope was after, though how he knew that you had the *Cosmographia* here I couldn't say."

"When I disposed of the library, I sent him a catalogue," said Dr. Conyers. "As a relative, I thought he ought to have the right to buy anything he fancied. I can't think why he didn't secure the book then, instead of behaving in this most shocking fashion."

Lord Peter hooted with laughter.

"Why, because he never tumbled to it till afterwards," he said. "And oh, dear, how wild he must have been! I forgive him everything. Although," he added, "I don't want to raise your hopes too high, sir, for, even when we've solved old Cuthbert's riddle, I don't know that we're very much nearer to the treasure."

"To the *treasure?*"

"Well, now, sir. I want you first to look at this page, where there's a name scrawled in the margin. Our ancestors had an untidy way of signing their possessions higgledy-piggledy in margins instead of in a decent, Christian way in the fly-leaf. This is a handwriting of somewhere about Charles I's reign: 'Jac: Coniers.' I take it that goes to prove that the book was in the possession of your family at any rate as early as the first half of the seventeenth century, and has remained there ever since. Right, now we turn to page 1099, where we find a description of the discoveries of Christopher Columbus. It's headed, you see, by a kind of map, with some of Mr. Pope's monsters swimming about in it, and apparently representing the Canaries, or, as they used to be called, the Fortunate Isles. It doesn't look much more accurate than old maps usually are, but I take it the big island on the right is meant for Lanzarote, and the two nearest to it may be Teneriffe and Gran Canaria."

"But what's that writing in the middle?"

"That's just the point. The writing is later than 'Jac: Coniers's' signature; I should put it about 1700—but, of course, it may have been written a good deal later still. I mean, a man who was elderly in 1730 would still use the style of writing he adopted as a young man, especially if, like your ancestor the pirate, he had spent the early part of his life in outdoor pursuits and hadn't done much writing."

"Do you mean to say, Uncle Peter," broke in the viscount excitedly, "that that's 'Old Cut-throat's' writing?"

"I'd be ready to lay a sporting bet it is. Look here, sir, you've been scouring round Münster in Germany and Munster in Ireland—but how about good old Sebastian Munster here in the library at home?"

"God bless my soul! Is it possible?"

"It's pretty nearly certain, sir. Here's what he says, written, you see, round the head of that sort of sea-dragon:

> *Hic in capite draconis ardet perpetuo Sol.*
> *Here the sun shines perpetually upon the Dragon's Head.*

Rather doggy Latin—sea-dog Latin, you might say, in fact."

"I'm afraid," said Dr. Conyers, "I must be very stupid, but I can't see where that leads us."

"No: 'Old Cut-throat' was rather clever. No doubt he thought that, if anybody read it, they'd think it was just an allusion to where it says, further down, that 'the islands were called *Fortunatae* because of the wonderful temperature of the air and the clemency of the skies.' But the cunning old astrologer up in his pagoda had a meaning of his own. Here's a little book published in 1678—Middleton's *Practical Astrology*—just the sort of popular handbook an amateur like 'Old Cut-throat' would use. Here you are: 'If in your figure you find Jupiter or Venus or *Dragon's Head*, you may be confident there is Treasure in the place supposed. . . . If you find *Sol* to be the significator of the hidden Treasure, you may conclude there is Gold, or some jewels.' You know, sir, I think we may conclude it."

"Dear me!" said Dr. Conyers. "I believe, indeed, you must be right. And I am ashamed to think that if anybody had suggested to me that it could ever be profitable to me to learn the terms of astrology, I should have replied in my vanity that my

THE DRAGON'S HEAD

Liber V. 1099
DE NOVIS INSVLIS,
quomodo, quando, & per quem
illæ inuentæ sint.

Hriſtophorus Columbus natione Genuenſis, cùm diu in ſula regis Hiſpanⁱ
rùm deuerſatus fuiſſet, animum induxit, ut hactenus inacceſſas orbis partes p
ærarer Pernt reſanterea à rege ſtutxto ſuo qoadceſſes ſuxtuti ſihi & touſ Hiſ⸗

time was too valuable to waste on such foolishness. I am
deeply indebted to you."

"Yes," said Gherkins, "but where *is* the treasure, uncle?"

"That's just it," said Lord Peter. "The map is very vague;
there is no latitude or longitude given; and the directions, such
as they are, seem not even to refer to any spot on the islands,
but to some place in the middle of the sea. Besides, it is nearly
two hundred years since the treasure was hidden, and it may
already have been found by somebody or other."

Dr. Conyers stood up.

"I am an old man," he said, "but I still have some strength.
If I can by any means get together the money for an expedition, I will not rest till I have made every possible effort to find
the treasure and to endow my clinic."

"Then, sir, I hope you'll let me give a hand to the good
work," said Lord Peter.

•   •   •

Dr. Conyers had invited his guests to stay the night, and, after the excited viscount had been packed off to bed, Wimsey and the old man sat late, consulting maps and diligently reading Munster's chapter "De Novis Insulis," in the hope of discovering some further clue. At length, however, they separated, and Lord Peter went upstairs, the book under his arm. He was restless, however, and, instead of going to bed, sat for a long time at his window, which looked out upon the lake. The moon, a few days past the full, was riding high among small, windy clouds, and picked out the sharp eaves of the Chinese tea-houses and the straggling tops of the unpruned shrubs. "Old Cut-throat" and his landscape gardening! Wimsey could have fancied that the old pirate was sitting now beside his telescope in the preposterous pagoda, chuckling over his riddling testament and counting the craters of the moon. "If *Luna*, there is silver." The waters of the lake was silver enough; there was a great smooth path across it, broken by the sinister wedge of the boat-house, the black shadows of the islands, and, almost in the middle of the lake, a decayed fountain, a writhing Celestial dragon-shape, spiny-backed and ridiculous.

Wimsey rubbed his eyes. There was something strangely familiar about the lake; from moment to moment it assumed the queer unreality of a place which one recognizes without having ever known it. It was like one's first sight of the Leaning Tower of Pisa—too like its picture to be quite believable. Surely, thought Wimsey, he knew that elongated island on the right, shaped rather like a winged monster, with its two little clumps of buildings. And the island to the left of it, like the British Isles, but warped out of shape. And the third island, between the others, and nearer. The three formed a triangle, with the Chinese fountain in the centre, the moon shining steadily upon its dragon head. *Hic in capite draconis ardet perpetuo—*

Lord Peter sprang up with a loud exclamation, and flung open the door into the dressing-room. A small figure wrapped in an eiderdown hurriedly uncoiled itself from the window-seat.

"I'm sorry, Uncle Peter," said Gherkins. "I was so *dread-fully* wide awake, it wasn't any good staying in bed."

"Come here," said Lord Peter, "and tell me if I'm mad or dreaming. Look out of the window and compare it with the map—Old Cut-throat's 'New Islands.' He made 'em, Gherkins; he put 'em here. Aren't they laid out just like the Canaries? Those three islands in a triangle, and the fourth down here in the corner? And the boat-house where the big ship is in the picture? And the dragon fountain where the dragon's head is? Well, my son, that's where your hidden treasure's gone to. Get your things on, Gherkins, and damn the time when all good little boys should be in bed! We're going for a row on the lake, if there's a tub in that boat-house that'll float."

"Oh, Uncle Peter! This is a *real* adventure!"

"All right," said Wimsey. "Fifteen men on the dead man's chest, and all that! Yo-ho-ho, and a bottle of Johnny Walker! Pirate expedition fitted out in dead of night to seek hidden treasure and explore the Fortunate Isles! Come on, crew!"

Lord Peter hitched the leaky dinghy to the dragon's knobbly tail and climbed out carefully, for the base of the fountain was green and weedy.

"I'm afraid it's your job to sit there and bail, Gherkins," he said. "All the best captains bag the really interesting jobs for themselves. We'd better start with the head. If the old blighter said head, he probably meant it." He passed an arm affectionately round the creature's neck for support, while he methodically pressed and pulled the various knobs and bumps of its anatomy. "It seems beastly solid, but I'm sure there's a spring somewhere. You won't forget to bail, will you? I'd simply hate to turn round and find the boat gone. Pirate chief marooned on island and all that. Well, it isn't its back hair, anyhow. We'll try its eyes. I say, Gherkins, I'm sure I felt something move, only it's frightfully stiff. We might have thought to bring some oil. Never mind; it's dogged as does it. It's coming. It's coming. Booh! Pah!"

A fierce effort thrust the rusted knob inwards, releasing a

huge spout of water into his face from the dragon's gaping throat. The fountain, dry for many years, soared rejoicingly heavenwards, drenching the treasure-hunters, and making rainbows in the moonlight.

"I suppose this is 'Old Cut-throat's' idea of humour," grumbled Wimsey, retreating cautiously round the dragon's neck. "And now I can't turn it off again. Well, dash it all, let's try the other eye."

He pressed for a few moments in vain. Then, with a grinding clang, the bronze wings of the monster clapped down to its sides, revealing a deep square hole, and the fountain ceased to play.

"Gherkins!" said Lord Peter, "we've done it. (But don't neglect bailing on that account!) There's a box here. And it's beastly heavy. No; all right, I can manage. Gimme the boat-hook. Now I do hope the old sinner really did have a treasure. What a bore if it's only one of his little jokes. Never mind — hold the boat steady. There. Always remember, Gherkins, that you can make quite an effective crane with a boat-hook and a stout pair of braces. Got it? That's right. Now for home and beauty . . . Hullo! what's all that?"

As he paddled the boat round, it was evident that something was happening down by the boat-house. Lights were moving about, and a sound of voices came across the lake.

"They think we're burglars, Gherkins. Always misunderstood. Give way, my hearties —

> "A-roving, a-roving, since roving's been my ru-i-in,
> I'll go no more a-roving with you, fair maid."

"Is that you, my lord?" said a man's voice as they drew in to the boat-house.

"Why, it's our faithful sleuths!" cried his lordship. "What's the excitement?"

"We found this fellow sneaking round the boat-house," said the man from Scotland Yard. "He says he's the old gentleman's nephew. Do you know him, my lord?"

"I rather fancy I do," said Wimsey. "Mr. Pope, I think. Good evening. Were you looking for anything? Not a treasure, by any chance? Because we've just found one. Oh! don't say that. *Maxima reverentia,* you know. Lord St. George is of tender years. And, by the way, thank you so much for sending your delightful friends to call on me last night. Oh, yes, Thompson, I'll charge him all right. You there, doctor? Splendid. Now, if anybody's got a spanner or anything handy, we'll have a look at Great-grandpapa Cuthbert. And if he turns out to be old iron, Mr. Pope, you'll have had an uncommonly good joke for your money."

An iron bar was produced from the boat-house and thrust under the hasp of the chest. It creaked and burst. Dr. Conyers knelt down tremulously and threw open the lid.

There was a little pause.

"The drinks are on you, Mr. Pope," said Lord Peter. "I think, doctor, it ought to be a jolly good hospital when it's finished."

THE PISCATORIAL FARCE OF THE
STOLEN STOMACH

What in the world," said Lord Peter Wimsey, "is that?"

Thomas Macpherson disengaged the tall jar from its final swathings of paper and straw and set it tenderly upright beside the coffee-pot.

"That," he said, "is Great-Uncle Joseph's legacy."

"And who is Great-Uncle Joseph?"

"He was my mother's uncle. Name of Ferguson. Eccentric old boy. I was rather a favourite of his."

"It looks like it. Was that all he left you?"

"Imph'm. He said a good digestion was the most precious thing a man could have."

"Well, he was right there. Is this his? Was it a good one?"

"Good enough. He lived to be ninety-five, and never had a day's illness."

Wimsey looked at the jar with increased respect.

"What did he die of?"

"Chucked himself out of a sixth-storey window. He had a

stroke, and the doctors told him—or he guessed for himself—
that it was the beginning of the end. He left a letter. Said he
had never been ill in his life and wasn't going to begin now.
They brought in temporary insanity, of course, but I think he
was thoroughly sensible."

"I should say so. What was he when he was functioning?"

"He used to be in business—something to do with ship-
building, I believe, but he retired long ago. He was what the
papers call a recluse. Lived all by himself in a little top flat in
Glasgow, and saw nobody. Used to go off by himself for days
at a time, nobody knew where or why. I used to look him up
about once a year and take him a bottle of whisky."

"Had he any money?"

"Nobody knew. He ought to have had—he was a rich man
when he retired. But, when we came to look into it, it turned out
he only had a balance of about five hundred pounds in the Glasgow Bank. Apparently he drew out almost everything he had
about twenty years ago. There were one or two big bank fail-
ures round about that time, and they thought he must have got
the wind up. But what he did with it, goodness only knows."

"Kept it in an old stocking, I expect."

"I should think Cousin Robert devoutly hopes so."

"Cousin Robert?"

"He's the residuary legatee. Distant connexion of mine,
and the only remaining Ferguson. He was awfully wild when
he found he'd only got five hundred. He's rather a bright lad,
is Robert, and a few thousands would have come in handy."

"I see. Well, how about a bit of brekker? You might stick
Great-Uncle Joseph out of the way somewhere. I don't care
about the looks of him."

"I thought you were rather partial to anatomical specimens."

"So I am, but not on the breakfast-table. 'A place for everything and everything in its place,' as my grandmother used to
say. Besides, it would give Maggie a shock if she saw it."

Macpherson laughed, and transferred the jar to a cupboard.

"Maggie's shock-proof. I brought a few odd bones and things with me, by way of a holiday task. I'm getting near my final, you know. She'll just think this is another of them. Ring the bell, old man, would you? We'll see what the trout's like."

The door opened to admit the housekeeper, with a dish of grilled trout and a plate of fried scones.

"These look good, Maggie," said Wimsey, drawing his chair up and sniffing appreciatively.

"Aye, sir, they're gude, but they're awfu' wee fish."

"Don't grumble at them," said Macpherson. "They're the sole result of a day's purgatory upon Loch Whyneon. What with the sun fit to roast you and an east wind, I'm pretty well flayed alive. I very nearly didn't shave at all this morning." He passed a reminiscent hand over his red and excoriated face. "Ugh! It's a stiff pull up the hill, and the boat was going wallop, wallop all the time, like being in the Bay of Biscay."

"Damnable, I should think. But there's a change coming. The glass is going back. We'll be having some rain before we're many days older."

"Time, too," said Macpherson. "The burns are nearly dry, and there's not much water in the Fleet." He glanced out of the window to where the little river ran tinkling and skinkling over the stones at the bottom of the garden. "If only we get a few days' rain now, there'll be some grand fishing."

"It *would* come just as I've got to go, naturally," remarked Wimsey.

"Yes; can't you stay a bit longer? I want to have a try for some sea-trout."

"Sorry, old man, can't be done. I must be in Town on Wednesday. Never mind. I've had a fine time in the fresh air and got in some good rounds of golf."

"You must come up another time. I'm here for a month — getting my strength up for the exams and all that. If you can't get away before I go, we'll put it off till August and have a shot at the grouse. The cottage is always at your service, you know, Wimsey."

"Many thanks. I may get my business over quicker than I

think, and, if I do, I'll turn up here again. When did you say your great-uncle died?"

Macpherson stared at him.

"Some time in April, as far as I can remember. Why?"

"Oh, nothing—I just wondered. You were a favourite of his, didn't you say?"

"In a sense. I think the old boy liked my remembering him from time to time. Old people are pleased by little attentions, you know."

"M'm. Well, it's a queer world. What did you say his name was?"

"Ferguson—Joseph Alexander Ferguson, to be exact. You seem extraordinarily interested in Great-Uncle Joseph."

"I thought, while I was about it, I might look up a man I know in the ship-building line, and see if he knows anything about where the money went to."

"If you can do that, Cousin Robert will give you a medal. But, if you really want to exercise your detective powers on the problem, you'd better have a hunt through the flat in Glasgow."

"Yes—what is the address, by the way?"

Macpherson told him the address.

"I'll make a note of it, and, if anything occurs to me, I'll communicate with Cousin Robert. Where does he hang out?"

"Oh, he's in London, in a solicitor's office. Crosbie & Plump, somewhere in Bloomsbury. Robert was studying for the Scottish Bar, you know, but he made rather a mess of things, so they pushed him off among the Sassenachs. His father died a couple of years ago—he was a Writer to the Signet in Edinburgh—and I fancy Robert has rather gone to the bow-wows since then. Got among a cheerful crowd down there, don't you know, and wasted his substance somewhat."

"Terrible! Scotsmen shouldn't be allowed to leave home. What are you going to do with Great-Uncle?"

"Oh, I don't know. Keep him for a bit, I think. I liked the old fellow, and I don't want to throw him away. He'll look rather well in my consulting-room, don't you think, when I'm qualified and set up my brass plate. I'll say he was presented by a grateful patient on whom I performed a marvellous operation."

"That's a good idea. Stomach-grafting. Miracle of surgery never before attempted. He'll bring sufferers to your door in flocks."

"Good old Great-Uncle — he may be worth a fortune to me after all."

"So he may. I don't suppose you've got such a thing as a photograph of him, have you?"

"A photograph?" Macpherson stared again. "Great-Uncle seems to be becoming a passion with you. I don't suppose the old man had a photograph taken these thirty years. There was one done then — when he retired from business. I expect Robert's got that."

"Och aye," said Wimsey, in the language of the country.

Wimsey left Scotland that evening, and drove down through the night towards London, thinking hard as he went. He handled the wheel mechanically, swerving now and again to avoid the green eyes of rabbits as they bolted from the roadside to squat fascinated in the glare of his head-lamps. He was accustomed to say that his brain worked better when his immediate attention was occupied by the incidents of the road.

Monday morning found him in town with his business finished and his thinking done. A consultation with his shipbuilding friend had put him in possession of some facts about Great-Uncle Joseph's money, together with a copy of Great-Uncle Joseph's photograph, supplied by the London representative of the Glasgow firm to which he had belonged. It appeared that old Ferguson had been a man of mark in his day. The portrait showed a fine, dour old face, long-lipped and high in the cheek-bones — one of those faces which alter little in a lifetime. Wimsey looked at the photograph with satisfaction as he slipped it into his pocket and made a bee-line for Somerset House.

Here he wandered timidly about the wills department, till

a uniformed official took pity on him and inquired what he wanted.

"Oh, thank you," said Wimsey effusively, "thank you so much. Always feel nervous in these places. All these big desks and things, don't you know, so awe-inspiring and business-like. Yes, I just wanted to have a squint at a will. I'm told you can see anybody's will for a shilling. Is that really so?"

"Yes, sir, certainly. Anybody's will in particular, sir?"

"Oh, yes, of course—how silly of me. Yes. Curious, isn't it, that when you're dead any stranger can come and snoop round your private affairs—see how much you cut up for and who your lady friends were, and all that. Yes. Not at all nice. Horrid lack of privacy, what?"

The attendant laughed.

"I expect it's all one when you're dead, sir."

"That's awfully true. Yes, naturally, you're dead by then and it doesn't matter. May be a bit trying for your relations, of course, to learn what a bad boy you've been. Great fun annoyin' one's relations. Always do it myself. Now, what were we sayin'? Ah! yes—the will. (I'm always so absentminded.) Whose will, you said? Well, it's an old Scots gentleman called Joseph Ferguson that died at Glasgow—you know Glasgow, where the accent's so strong that even Scotsmen faint when they hear it—in April, this last April as ever was. If it's not troubling you too much, may I have a bob's-worth of Joseph Alexander Ferguson?"

The attendant assured him that he might, adding the caution that he must memorize the contents of the will and not on any account take notes. Thus warned, Wimsey was conducted into a retired corner, where in a short time the will was placed before him.

It was a commendably brief document, written in holograph, and was dated the previous January. After the usual preamble and the bequest of a few small sums and articles of personal ornament to friends, it proceeded somewhat as follows:

And I direct that, after my death, the alimentary organs be removed entire with their contents from my body, commencing with the oesophagus and ending with the anal canal, and that they be properly secured at both ends with a suitable ligature, and be enclosed in a proper preservative medium in a glass vessel and given to my great-nephew Thomas Macpherson of the Stone Cottage, Gatehouse-of-the-Fleet, in Kirkcudbrightshire, now studying medicine in Aberdeen. And I bequeath him these my alimentary organs with their contents for his study and edification, they having served me for ninety-five years without failure or defect, because I wish him to understand that no riches in the world are comparable to the riches of a good digestion. And I desire of him that he will, in the exercise of his medical profession, use his best endeavours to preserve to his patients the blessing of good digestion unimpaired, not needlessly filling their stomachs with drugs out of concern for his own pocket, but exhorting them to a sober and temperate life agreeably to the design of Almighty Providence.

After this remarkable passage, the document went on to make Robert Ferguson residuary legatee without particular specification of any property, and to appoint a firm of lawyers in Glasgow executors of the will.

Wimsey considered the bequest for some time. From the phraseology he concluded that old Mr. Ferguson had drawn up his own will without legal aid, and he was glad of it, for its wording thus afforded a valuable clue to the testator's mood and intention. He mentally noted three points: the "alimentary organs with their contents" were mentioned twice over, with a certain emphasis; they were to be ligatured top and bottom; and the legacy was accompanied by the expression of a wish that the legatee should not allow his financial necessities to interfere with the conscientious exercise of his professional duties. Wimsey chuckled. He felt he rather liked Great-Uncle Joseph.

He got up, collected his hat, gloves and stick, and advanced with the will in his hand to return it to the attendant. The latter was engaged in conversation with a young man, who seemed to be expostulating about something.

"I'm sorry, sir," said the attendant, "but I don't suppose the other gentleman will be very long. Ah!" He turned and saw Wimsey. "Here is the gentleman."

The young man, whose reddish hair, long nose, and slightly sodden eyes gave him the appearance of a dissipated fox, greeted Wimsey with a disagreeable stare.

"What's up? Want me?" asked his lordship airily.

"Yes, sir. Very curious thing, sir; here's a gentleman inquiring for that very same document as you've been studying, sir. I've been in this department fifteen yeas, and I don't know as I ever remember such a thing happening before."

"No," said Wimsey, "I don't suppose there's much of a run on any of your lines as a rule."

"It's a very curious thing indeed," said the stranger, with marked displeasure in his voice.

"Member of the family?" suggested Wimsey.

"I *am* a member of the family," said the foxy-faced man. "May I ask whether *you* have any connexion with us?"

"By all means," replied Wimsey graciously.

"I don't believe it. I don't know you."

"No, no—I meant you might ask, by all means."

The young man positively showed his teeth.

"Do you mind telling me who you are, anyhow, and why you're so damned inquisitive about my great-uncle's will?"

Wimsey extracted a card from his case and presented it with a smile. Mr. Robert Ferguson changed colour.

"If you would like a reference as to my respectability," went on Wimsey affably, "Mr. Thomas Macpherson will, I am sure, be happy to tell you about me. I am inquisitive," said his lordship—"a student of humanity. Your cousin mentioned to me the curious clause relating to your esteemed great-uncle's—er—stomach and appurtenances. Curious clauses are a passion with me. I came to look it up and add it to my collection of curious wills. I am engaged in writing a book on the subject—*Clauses and Consequences*. My publishers tell me it should enjoy a ready sale. I regret that my random jottings should have encroached upon your doubtless far more serious studies. I wish you a very good morning."

As he beamed his way out, Wimsey, who had quick ears, heard the attendant informing the indignant Mr. Ferguson that he was "a very funny gentleman—not quite all there, sir." It seemed that his criminological fame had not penetrated to the quiet recesses of Somerset House. "But," said Wimsey to himself, "I am sadly afraid that Cousin Robert has been given food for thought."

Under the spur of this alarming idea, Wimsey wasted no time, but took a taxi down to Hatton Garden, to call upon a friend of his. This gentleman, rather curly in the nose and fleshy about the eyelids, nevertheless came under Mr. Chesterton's definition of a nice Jew, for his name was neither Montagu nor McDonald, but Nathan Abrahams, and he greeted Lord Peter with a hospitality amounting to enthusiasm.

"So pleased to see you. Sit down and have a drink. You have come at last to select the diamonds for the future Lady Peter, eh?"

"Not yet," said Wimsey.

"No? That's too bad. You should make haste and settle down. It is time you became a family man. Years ago we arranged I should have the privilege of decking the bride for the happy day. That is a promise, you know. I think of it when the fine stones pass through my hands. I say, 'That would be the very thing for my friend Lord Peter.' But I hear nothing, and I sell them to stupid Americans who think only of the price and not of the beauty."

"Time enough to think of the diamonds when I've found the lady."

Mr. Abrahams threw up his hands.

"Oh, yes! And then everything will be done in a hurry!

'Quick, Mr. Abrahams! I have fallen in love yesterday and I am being married tomorrow.' But it may take months — years — to find and match perfect stones. It can't be done between today and tomorrow. Your bride will be married in something ready-made from the jeweller's."

"If three days are enough to choose a wife," said Wimsey, laughing, "one day should surely be enough for a necklace."

"That is the way with Christians," replied the diamond-merchant resignedly. "You are so casual. You do not think of the future. Three days to choose a wife! No wonder the divorce-courts are busy. My son Moses is being married next week. It has been arranged in the family these ten years. Rachel Goldstein, it is. A good girl, and her father is in a very good position. We are all very pleased, I can tell you. Moses is a good son, a very good son, and I am taking him into partnership."

"I congratulate you," said Wimsey heartily. "I hope they will be very happy."

"Thank you, Lord Peter. They will be happy, I am sure. Rachel is a sweet girl and very fond of children. And she is pretty, too. Prettiness is not everything, but it is an advantage for a young man in these days. It is easier for him to behave well to a pretty wife."

"True," said Wimsey. "I will bear it in mind when my time comes. To the health of the happy pair, and may you soon be an ancestor. Talking of ancestors, I've got an old bird here that you may be able to tell me something about."

"Ah, yes! Always delighted to help you in any way, Lord Peter."

"This photograph was taken some thirty years ago, but you may possibly recognize it."

Mr. Abrahams put on a pair of horn-rimmed spectacles, and examined the portrait of Great-Uncle Joseph with serious attention.

"Oh, yes, I know him quite well. What do you want to know about him, eh?" He shot a swift and cautious glance at Wimsey.

"Nothing to his disadvantage. He's dead, anyhow. I thought it just possible he had been buying precious stones lately."

"It is not exactly business to give information about a customer," said Mr. Abrahams.

"I'll tell you what I want it for," said Wimsey. He lightly sketched the career of Great-Uncle Joseph, and went on: "You see, I looked at it this way. When a man gets a distrust of banks, what does he do with his money? He puts it into property of some kind. It may be land, it may be houses—but that means rent, and more money to put into banks. He is more likely to keep it in gold or notes, or to be put into precious stones. Gold and notes are comparatively bulky; stones are small. Circumstances in this case led me to think he might have chosen stones. Unless we can discover what he did with the money, there will be a great loss to his heirs."

"I see. Well, if it is as you say, there is no harm in telling you. I know you to be an honourable man, and I will break my rule for you. This gentleman, Mr. Wallace—"

"Wallace, did he call himself?"

"That was not his name? They are funny, these secretive old gentlemen. But that is nothing unusual. Often, when they buy stones, they are afraid of being robbed, so they give another name. Yes, yes. Well, this Mr. Wallace used to come to see me from time to time, and I had instructions to find diamonds for him. He was looking for twelve big stones, all matching perfectly and of superb quality. It took a long time to find them, you know."

"Of course."

"Yes. I supplied him with seven altogether, over a period of twenty years or so. And other dealers supplied him also. He is well known in this street. I found the last one for him—let me see—in last December, I think. A beautiful stone—beautiful! He paid seven thousand pounds for it."

"Some stone. If they were all as good as that, the collection must be worth something."

"Worth anything. It is difficult to tell how much. As you

know, the twelve stones, all matched together, would be worth far more than the sum of the twelve separate prices paid for the individual diamonds."

"Naturally they would. Do you mind telling me how he was accustomed to pay for them?"

"In Bank of England notes — always — cash on the nail. He insisted on discount for cash," added Mr. Abrahams, with a chuckle.

"He was a Scotsman," replied Wimsey. "Well, that's clear enough. He had a safe-deposit somewhere, no doubt. And, having collected the stones, he made his will. That's clear as daylight, too."

"But what has become of the stones?" inquired Mr. Abrahams, with professional anxiety.

"I think I know that too," said Wimsey. "I'm enormously obliged to you, and so, I fancy, will his heir be."

"If they should come into the market again —" suggested Mr. Abrahams.

"I'll see you have the handling of them," said Wimsey promptly.

"That is kind of you," said Mr. Abrahams. "Business is business. Always delighted to oblige you. Beautiful stones — beautiful. If you thought of being the purchaser, I would charge you a special commission, as my friend."

"Thank you," said Wimsey, "but as yet I have no occasion for diamonds, you know."

"Pity, pity," said Mr. Abrahams. "Well, very glad to have been of service to you. You are not interested in rubies? No? Because I have something very pretty here."

He thrust his hand casually into a pocket, and brought out a little pool of crimson fire like a miniature sunset.

"Look nice in a ring, now, wouldn't it?" said Mr. Abrahams. "An engagement ring, eh?"

Wimsey laughed, and made his escape.

He was strongly tempted to return to Scotland and attend personally to the matter of Great-Uncle Joseph, but the thought of an important book sale next day deterred him.

There was a manuscript of Catullus which he was passionately anxious to secure, and he never entrusted his interests to dealers. He contented himself with sending a wire to Thomas Macpherson:

Advise opening up Greatuncle Joseph immediately.

The girl at the post-office repeated the message aloud and rather doubtfully. "Quite right," said Wimsey, and dismissed the affair from his mind.

He had great fun at the sale next day. He found a ring of dealers in possession, happily engaged in conducting a knockout. Having lain low for an hour in a retired position behind a large piece of statuary, he emerged, just as the hammer was falling upon the Catullus for a price representing the tenth part of its value, with an overbid so large, prompt, and sonorous that the ring gasped with a sense of outrage. Skrymes—a dealer who had sworn an eternal enmity to Wimsey on account of a previous little encounter over a Justinian—pulled himself together and offered a fifty-pound advance. Wimsey promptly doubled his bid. Skrymes overbid him fifty again. Wimsey instantly jumped another hundred, in the tone of a man prepared to go on till Doomsday. Skrymes scowled and was silent. Somebody raised it fifty more; Wimsey made it guineas and the hammer fell. Encouraged by this success, Wimsey, feeling that his hand was in, romped happily into the bidding for the next lot, a *Hypnerotomachia* which he already possessed, and for which he felt no desire whatever. Skrymes, annoyed by his defeat, set his teeth, determining that, if Wimsey was in the bidding mood, he should pay through the nose for his rashness. Wimsey, entering into the spirit of the thing, skied the bidding with enthusiasm. The dealers, knowing his reputation as a collector, and fancying that there must be some special excellence about the book that they had failed to observe, joined in wholeheartedly, and the fun became fast and furious. Eventually they all dropped out again, leaving Skrymes and Wimsey in together. At which point Wimsey, observing a note of hesitation in the dealer's voice, neatly extricated himself and left Mr. Skrymes with the baby. After this disaster, the ring became sulky and demoralized and refused to bid at all, and a timid little outsider, suddenly flinging himself into the arena, became the owner of a fine fourteenth-century missal at bargain price. Crimson with excitement and surprise, he paid for his purchase and ran out of the room like a rabbit, hugging the missal as though he expected to have it snatched from him. Wimsey thereupon set himself seriously to acquire a few fine early printed books, and, having accomplished this, retired, covered with laurels and hatred.

After this delightful and satisfying day, he felt vaguely hurt at receiving no ecstatic telegram from Macpherson. He refused to imagine that his deductions had been wrong, and supposed rather that the rapture of Macpherson would come the next day by post. However, at eleven next morning the telegram arrived. It said:

> Just got your wire what does it mean greatuncle stolen last night burglar escaped please write fully.

Wimsey committed himself to a brief comment in language usually confined to soldiery. Robert had undoubtedly got Great-Uncle Joseph, and, even if they could trace the burglary to him, the legacy was by this time gone for ever. He had never felt so furiously helpless. He even cursed the Catullus, which had kept him from going north and dealing with the matter personally.

While he was meditating what to do, a second telegram was brought in. It ran:

> Greatuncle's bottle found broken in fleet dropped by burglar in flight contents gone what next.

Wimsey pondered this.

•   •   •

"Of course," he said, "if the thief simply emptied the bottle and put Great-Uncle in his pocket, we're done. Or if he's simply emptied Great-Uncle and put the contents in his pocket, we're done. But 'dropped in flight' sounds rather as though Great-Uncle had gone overboard lock, stock, and barrel. Why can't the fool of a Scotsman put a few more details into his wires? It'd only cost him a penny or two. I suppose I'd better go up myself. Meanwhile a little healthy occupation won't hurt him."

He took a telegraph form from the desk and despatched a further message:

> Was greatuncle in bottle when dropped if so drag river if not pursue burglar probably Robert Ferguson spare no pains starting for Scotland tonight hope arrive early tomorrow urgent important put your back into it will explain.

The night express decanted Lord Peter Wimsey at Dumfries early the following morning, and a hired car deposited him at the Stone Cottage in time for breakfast. The door was opened to him by Maggie, who greeted him with hearty cordiality:

"Come awa' in, sir. All's ready for ye, and Mr. Macpherson will be back in a few minutes, I'm thinkin'. Ye'll be tired with your long journey, and hungry, maybe? Aye. Will ye tak' a bit parritch to your eggs and bacon? There's nae troot the day, though yesterday was a gran' day for the fush. Mr. Macpherson has been up and doun, up and doun the river wi' my Jock, lookin' for ane of his specimens, as he ca's them, that was dropped by the thief that cam' in. I dinna ken what the thing may be—my Jock says it's like a calf's pluck to look at, by what Mr. Macpherson tells him."

"Dear me!" said Wimsey. "And how did the burglary happen, Maggie?"

"Indeed, sir, it was a vera' remarkable circumstance. Mr.

Macpherson was awa' all day Monday and Tuesday, up at the big loch by the viaduct, fishin'. There was a big rain Saturday and Sunday, ye may remember, and Mr. Macpherson says, 'There'll be grand fishin' the morn, Jock,' says he. 'We'll go up to the viaduct if it stops rainin' and we'll spend the nicht at the keeper's lodge.' So on Monday it stoppit rainin' and was a grand warm, soft day, so aff they went together. There was a telegram come for him Tuesday mornin', and I set it up on the mantelpiece, where he'd see it when he cam' in, but it's been in my mind since that maybe that telegram had something to do wi' the burglary."

"I wouldn't say but you might be right, Maggie," replied Wimsey gravely.

"Aye, sir, that wadna surprise me." Maggie set down a generous dish of eggs and bacon before the guest and took up her tale again.

"Well, I was sittin' in my kitchen the Tuesday nicht, waitin' for Mr. Macpherson and Jock to come hame, and sair I pitied them, the puir souls, for the rain was peltin' down again, and the nicht was sae dark I was afraid they micht ha' tummelt into a bog-pool. Weel, I was listenin' for the sound o' the door-sneck when I heard something movin' in the front room. The door wasna lockit, ye ken, because Mr. Macpherson was expectit back. So I up from my chair and I thocht they had mebbe came in and I not heard them. I waited a meenute to set the kettle on the fire, and then I heard a crackin' sound. So I cam' out and I called. 'Is't you, Mr. Macpherson?' And there was nae answer, only anither big crackin' noise, so I ran forrit, and a man cam' quickly oot o' the front room, brushin' past me an puttin' me aside wi' his hand, so, and oot o' the front door like a flash o' lightnin'. So, wi' that, I let oot a skelloch, an' Jock's voice answered me fra' the gairden gate. 'Och!' I says, 'Jock! here's a burglar been i' the hoose!' An' I heerd him runnin' across the gairden, doun tae the river, tramplin' doun a' the young kail and the stra'berry beds, the blackguard!"

Wimsey expressed his sympathy.

"Aye, that was a bad business. An' the next thing, there was Mr. Macpherson and Jock helter-skelter after him. If Davie Murray's cattle had broken in, they couldna ha' done mair deevastation. An' then there was a big splashin' an' crashin', an', after a bit, back comes Mr. Macpherson an' he says, 'He's jumpit intil the Fleet,' he says, 'an' he's awa'. What has he taken?' he says. 'I dinna ken,' says I, 'for it all happened sae quickly I couldna see onything.' 'Come awa' ben,' says he, 'an' we'll see what's missin'.' So we lookit high and low, an' all we could find was the cupboard door in the front room broken open, and naething taken but this bottle wi' the specimen."

"Aha!" said Wimsey.

"Ah! an' they baith went oot tegither wi' lichts, but naething could they see of the thief. Sae Mr. Macpherson comes back, and 'I'm gaun to ma bed,' says he, 'for I'm that tired I can dae nae mair the nicht,' says he. 'Oh!' I said, 'I daurna gae tae bed; I'm frichtened.' An' Jock said, 'Hoots, wumman, dinna fash yersel'. There'll be nae mair burglars the nicht, wi' the fricht we've gied 'em.' So we lockit up a' the doors an' windies an' gaed to oor beds, but I couldna sleep a wink."

"Very natural," said Wimsey.

"It wasna till the next mornin'," said Maggie, "that Mr. Macpherson opened yon telegram. Eh! but he was in a taking. An' then the telegrams startit. Back an' forrit, back an' forrit atween the hoose an' the post-office. An' then they found the bits o' the bottle that the specimen was in, stuck between twa stanes i' the river. And aff goes Mr. Macpherson an' Jock wi' their waders on an' a couple o' gaffs, huntin' in a' the pools an' under the stanes to find the specimen. An' they're still at it."

At this point three heavy thumps sounded on the ceiling.

"Gude save us!" ejaculated Maggie, "I was forgettin' the puir gentleman."

"What gentleman?" enquired Wimsey.

"Him that was feshed oot o' the Fleet," replied Maggie. "Excuse me just a moment, sir."

She fled swiftly upstairs. Wimsey poured himself out a third cup of coffee and lit a pipe.

Presently a thought occurred to him. He finished the coffee—not being a man to deprive himself of his pleasures—and walked quietly upstairs in Maggie's wake. Facing him stood a bedroom door, half open—the room which he had occupied during his stay at the cottage. He pushed it open. In the bed lay a red-headed gentleman, whose long, foxy countenance was in no way beautified by a white bandage, tilted rakishly across the left temple. A breakfast-try stood on a table by the bed. Wimsey stepped forward with extended hand.

"Good morning, Mr. Ferguson," said he. "This is an unexpected pleasure."

"Good morning," said Mr. Ferguson snappishly.

"I had no idea, when we last met," pursued Wimsey, advancing to the bed and sitting down upon it, "that you were thinking of visiting my friend Macpherson."

"Get off my leg," growled the invalid. "I've broken my kneecap."

"What a nuisance! Frightfully painful, isn't it? And they say it takes years to get right—if it ever does get right. Is it what they call a Potts fracture? I don't know who Potts was, but it sounds impressive. How did you get it? Fishing?"

"Yes. A slip in that damned river."

"Beastly. Sort of thing that might happen to anybody. A keen fisher, Mr. Ferguson?"

"So-so."

"So am I, when I get the opportunity. What kind of fly do you fancy for this part of the country. I rather like a Greenaway's Gadget myself. Ever tried it?"

"No," said Mr. Ferguson briefly.

"Some people find a Pink Sisket better, so they tell me. Do you use one? Have you got your fly-book here?"

"Yes—no," said Mr. Ferguson. "I dropped it."

"Pity. But do give me your opinion of the Pink Sisket."

"Not so bad," said Mr. Ferguson. "I've sometimes caught trout with it."

"You surprise me," said Wimsey, not unnaturally, since he had invented the Pink Sisket on the spur of the moment, and had hardly expected his improvisation to pass muster. "Well, I suppose this unlucky accident has put a stop to your sport for the season. Damned bad luck. Otherwise, you might have helped us to have a go at the Patriarch."

"What's that? A trout?"

Yes—a frightfully wily old fish. Lurks about in the Fleet. You never know where to find him. Any moment he may turn up in some pool or other. I'm going out with Mac to try for him today. He's a jewel of a fellow. We've nicknamed him Great-Uncle Joseph. Hi! don't joggle about like that—you'll hurt that knee of yours. Is there anything I can get for you?"

He grinned amiably, and turned to answer a shout from the stairs.

"Hullo! Wimsey! is that you?"

"It is. How's sport?"

Macpherson came up the stairs four steps at a time, and met Wimsey on the landing as he emerged from the bedroom.

"I say, d'you know who that is? It's Robert."

"I know. I saw him in town. Never mind him. Have you found Great-Uncle?"

"No, we haven't. What's all this mystery about? And what's Robert doing here? What did you mean by saying he was the burglar? And why is Great-Uncle Joseph so important?"

"One thing at a time. Let's find the old boy first. What have you been doing?"

"Well, when I got your extraordinary messages I thought, of course, you were off your rocker." (Wimsey groaned with impatience.) "But then I considered what a funny thing it was that somebody should have thought Great-Uncle worth stealing, and thought there might be some sense in what you said, after all." ("Dashed good of you," said Wimsey.) "So I went out and poked about a bit, you know. Not that I think there's the faintest chance of finding anything, with the river coming down like this. Well, I hadn't got very far—by the way, I took

Jock with me. I'm sure he thinks I'm mad, too. Not that he says anything; these people here never commit themselves—"

"Confound Jock! Get on with it."

"Oh—well, before we'd got very far, we saw a fellow wading about in the river with a rod and a creel. I didn't pay much attention, because, you see, I was wondering what you—Yes. Well! Jock noticed him and said to me, 'Yon's a queer kind of fisherman, I'm thinkin'.' So I had a look, and there he was, staggering about among the stones with his fly floating away down the stream in front of him; and he was peering into all the pools he came to, and poking about with a gaff. So I hailed him, and he turned round, and then he put the gaff away in a bit of a hurry and started to reel in his line. He made an awful mess of it," added Macpherson appreciatively.

"I can believe it," said Wimsey. "A man who admits to catching trout with a Pink Sisket would make a mess of anything."

"A pink what?'

"Never mind. I only meant that Robert was no fisher. Get on."

"Well, he got the line hooked round something, and he was pulling and hauling, you know, and splashing about, and then it came out all of a sudden, and he waved it all over the place and got my hat. That made me pretty wild, and I made after him, and he looked round again, and I yelled out, 'Good God, it's Robert!' And he dropped his rod and took to his heels. And of course he slipped on the stones and came down an awful crack. We rushed forward and scooped him up and brought him home. He's got a nasty bang on the head and a fractured patella. Very interesting. I should have liked to have a shot at setting it myself, but it wouldn't do, you know, so I sent for Strachan. He's a good man."

"You've had extraordinary luck about this business so far," said Wimsey. "Now the only thing left is to find Great-Uncle. How far down have you got?"

"Not very far. You see, what with getting Robert home and setting his knee and so on, we couldn't do much yesterday."

"Damn Robert! Great-Uncle may be away out to sea by this time. Let's get down to it."

He took up a gaff from the umbrella-stand ("Robert's," interjected Macpherson), and led the way out. The little river was foaming down in a brown spate, rattling stones and small boulders along in its passage. Every hole, every eddy might be a lurking-place for Great-Uncle Joseph. Wimsey peered irresolutely here and there—then turned suddenly to Jock.

"Where's the nearest spit of land where things usually get washed up?" he demanded.

"Eh, well! there's the Battery Pool, about a mile doon the river. Ye'll whiles find things washed up there. Aye. Imph'm. There's a pool and a bit sand, where the river mak's a bend. Ye'll mebbe find it there, I'm thinkin'. Mebbe no. I couldna say."

"Let's have a look, anyway."

Macpherson, to whom the prospect of searching the stream in detail appeared rather a dreary one, brightened a little at this.

"That's a good idea. If we take the car down to just above Gatehouse, we've only got two fields to cross."

The car was still at the door; the hired driver was enjoying the hospitality of the cottage. They pried him loose from Maggie's scones and slipped down the road to Gatehouse.

"Those gulls seem rather active about something," said Wimsey, as they crossed the second field. The white wings swooped backwards and forwards in narrowing circles over the yellow shoal. Raucous cries rose on the wind. Wimsey pointed silently with his hand. A long, unseemly object, like a drab purse, lay on the shore. The gulls, indignant, rose higher, squawking at the intruders. Wimsey ran forward, stooped, rose again with the long bag dangling from his fingers.

"Great-Uncle Joseph, I presume," he said, and raised his hat with old-fashioned courtesy.

"The gulls have had a wee peck at it here and there," said Jock. "It'll be tough for them. Aye. They havena done so vera much with it."

"Aren't you going to open it?" said Macpherson impatiently.

"Not here," said Wimsey. "We might lose something." He dropped it into Jock's creel. "We'll take it home first and show it to Robert."

Robert greeted them with ill-disguised irritation.

"We've been fishing," said Wimsey cheerfully. "Look at our bonny wee fush." He weighed the catch in his hand. "What's inside this wee fush, Mr. Ferguson?"

"I haven't the faintest idea," said Robert.

"Then why did you go fishing for it?" asked Wimsey pleasantly. "Have you got a surgical knife there, Mac?"

"Yes—here. Hurry up."

"I'll leave it to you. Be careful. I should begin with the stomach."

Macpherson laid Great-Uncle Joseph on the table, and slit him open with a practised hand.

"Gude be gracious to us!" cried Maggie, peering over his shoulder. "What'll that be?"

Wimsey inserted a delicate finger and thumb into the cavities of Uncle Joseph. "One—two— three—" The stones glittered like fire as he laid them on the table. "Seven—eight—nine. That seems to be all. Try a little farther down, Mac."

Speechless with astonishment, Mr. Macpherson dissected his legacy.

"Ten—eleven," said Wimsey. "I'm afraid the sea-gulls have got number twelve. I'm sorry, Mac."

"But how did they get there?" demanded Robert foolishly.

"Simple as shelling peas. Great-Uncle Joseph makes his will, swallows his diamonds—"

"He must ha' been a grand man for a pill," said Maggie, with respect.

"—and jumps out of the window. It was as clear as crystal to anybody who read the will. He told you, Mac, that the stomach was given you to study."

Robert Ferguson gave a deep groan.

"I knew there was something in it," he said. "That's why I

went to look up the will. And when I saw *you* there, I knew I was right. (Curse this leg of mine!) But I never imagined for a moment—"

His eyes appraised the diamonds greedily.

"And what will the value of these same stones be?" inquired Jock.

"About seven thousand pounds apiece, taken separately. More than that, taken together."

"The old man was mad," said Robert angrily. "I shall dispute the will."

"I think not," said Wimsey. "There's such an offence as entering and stealing, you know."

"My God!" said Macpherson, handling the diamonds like a man in a dream. "My God!"

"Seven thousan' pund," said Jock. "Did I unnerstan' ye richtly to say that one o' they gulls is gaun aboot noo wi' seven thousan' punds' worth o' diamonds in his wame? Ech! it's just awfu' to think of. Guid day to you, sirs. I'll be gaun round to Jimmy McTaggart to ask will he send me the loan o' a gun."

THE UNSOLVED PUZZLE OF THE

MAN WITH NO FACE

And what would *you* say, sir,"
said the stout man, "to this here business of the bloke what's
been found down on the beach at East Felpham?"

The rush of travellers after the Bank Holiday had caused
an overflow of third-class passengers into the firsts, and the
stout man was anxious to seem at ease in his surroundings.
The youngish gentleman whom he addressed had obviously
paid full fare for a seclusion which he was fated to forgo. He
took the matter amiably enough, however, and replied in a
courteous tone:

"I'm afraid I haven't read more than the headlines. Murdered, I suppose, wasn't he?"

"It's murder, right enough," said the stout man, with rel-
ish. "Cut about he was, something shocking."

"More like as if a wild beast had done it," chimed in the
thin, elderly man opposite. "No face at all he hadn't got, by
what my paper says. It'll be one of these maniacs, I shouldn't
be surprised, what goes about killing children."

"I wish you wouldn't talk about such things," said his wife, with a shudder. "I lays awake at nights thinking what might 'appen to Lizzie's girls, till my head feels regular in a fever, and I has such a sinking in my inside I has to get up and eat biscuits. They didn't ought to put such dreadful things in the papers."

"It's better they should, ma'am," said the stout man, "then we're warned, so to speak, and can take our measures accordingly. Now, from what I can make out, this unfortunate gentleman had gone bathing all by himself in a lonely spot. Now, quite apart from cramps, as is a thing that might 'appen to the best of us, that's a very foolish thing to do."

"Just what I'm always telling my husband," said the young wife. The young husband frowned and fidgeted. "Well, dear, it really isn't safe, and you with your heart not strong—" Her hand sought his under the newspaper. He drew away, self-consciously, saying, "That'll do, Kitty."

"The way I look at it is this," pursued the stout man. "Here we've been and had a war, what has left 'undreds o' men in what you might call a state of unstable ekilibrium. They've seen all their friends blown up or shot to pieces. They've been through five years of 'orrors and bloodshed, and it's given 'em what you might call a twist in the mind towards 'orrors. They may seem to forget it and go along as peaceable as anybody to all outward appearance, but it's all artificial, if you get my meaning. Then, one day something 'appens to upset them— they 'as words with the wife, or the weather's extra hot, as it is today—and something goes pop inside their brains and makes raving monsters of them. It's all in the books. I do a good bit of reading myself of an evening, being a bachelor without encumbrances."

"That's all very true," said a prim little man, looking up from his magazine, "very true indeed—too true. But do you think it applies in the present case? I've studied the literature of crime a good deal—I may say I make it my hobby—and it's my opinion there's more in this than meets the eye. If you will compare this murder with some of the most mysterious crimes of late years—crimes which, mind you, have never been solved, and, in my opinion, never will be—what do you find?" He paused and looked round. "You will find many features in common with this case. But especially you will find that the face—and the face only, mark you—has been disfigured, as though to prevent recognition. As though to blot out the victim's personality from the world. And you will find that, in spite of the most thorough investigation, the criminal is never discovered. Now what does all that point to? To organization. Organization. To an immensely powerful influence at work behind the scenes. In this very magazine that I'm reading now"—he tapped the page impressively—"there's an account—not a faked-up story, but an account extracted from the annals of the police—of the organization of one of these secret societies, which mark down men against whom they bear a grudge, and destroy them. And, when they do this, they disfigure their faces with the mark of the Secret Society, and they cover up the track of the assassin so completely—having money and resources at their disposal—that nobody is ever able to get at them."

"I've read of such things, of course," admitted the stout man, "but I thought as they mostly belonged to the medeevial days. They had a thing like that in Italy once. What did they call it now? A Gomorrah, was it? Are there any Gomorrahs nowadays?"

"You spoke a true word, sir, when you said Italy," replied the prim man "The Italian mind is made for intrigue. There's the Fascisti. That's come to the surface now, of course, but it started by being a secret society. And, if you were to look below the surface, you would be amazed at the way in which that country is honeycombed with hidden organizations of all sorts. Don't you agree with me, sir?" he added, addressing the first-class passenger.

"Ah!" said the stout man, "no doubt this gentleman has been in Italy and knows all about it. Should you say this murder was the work of a Gomorrah, sir?"

"I hope not, I'm sure," said the first-class passenger. "I mean, it rather destroys the interest, don't you think? I like a nice, quiet, domestic murder myself, with the millionaire found dead in the library. The minute I open a detective story and find a Camorra in it, my interest seems to dry up and turn to dust and ashes—a sort of Sodom and Camorra, as you might say."

"I agree with you there," said the young husband, "from what you might call the artistic standpoint. But in this particular case I think there may be something to be said for this gentleman's point of view."

"Well," admitted the first-class passenger, "not having read the details—"

"The details are clear enough," said the prim man. "This poor creature was found lying dead on the beach at East Felpham early this morning, with his face cut about in the most dreadful manner. He had nothing on him but his bathing-dress—"

"Stop a minute. Who was he, to begin with?"

"They haven't identified him yet. His clothes had been taken—"

"That looks more like robbery, doesn't it?" suggested Kitty.

"If it was just robbery," retorted the prim man, "why should his face have been cut up in that way? No—the clothes were taken away, as I said, to prevent identification. That's what these societies always try to do."

"Was he stabbed?" demanded the first-class passenger.

"No," said the stout man. "He wasn't. He was strangled."

"Not a characteristically Italian method of killing," observed the first-class passenger.

"No more it is," said the stout man. The prim man seemed a little disconcerted.

"And if he went down there to bathe," said the thin, elderly man, "how did he get there? Surely somebody must have missed him before now, if he was staying at Felpham. It's a busy spot for visitors in the holiday season."

"No," said the stout man, "not East Felpham. You're thinking of West Felpham, where the yacht-club is. East Felpham is one of the loneliest spots on the coast. There's no house near except a little pub all by itself at the end of a long road, and after that you have to go through three fields to get to the sea. There's no real road, only a cart-track, but you can take a car through. I've been there."

"He came in a car," said the prim man. "They found the track of the wheels. But it had been driven away again."

"It looks as though the two men had come there together," suggested Kitty.

"I think they did," said the prim man. "The victim was probably gagged and bound and taken along in the car to the place, and then he was taken out and strangled and—"

"But why should they have troubled to put on his bathing-dress?" said the first-class passenger.

"Because," said the prim man, "as I said, they didn't want to leave any clothes to reveal his identity."

"Quite; but why not leave him naked? A bathing-dress seems to indicate an almost excessive regard for decorum, under the circumstances."

"Yes, yes," said the stout man impatiently, "but you 'aven't read the paper carefully. The two men couldn't have come there in company, and for why? There was only one set of footprints found, and they belonged to the murdered man."

He looked round triumphantly.

"Only one set of footprints, eh?" said the first-class passenger quickly. "This looks interesting. Are you sure?"

"It says so in the paper. A single set of footprints, it says, made by bare feet, which by a careful comparison 'ave been shown to be those of the murdered man, lead from the position occupied by the car to the place where the body was found. What do you make of that?"

"Why," said the first-class passenger, "that tells one quite a lot, don't you know. It gives one a sort of bird's eye view of the place, and it tells one the time of the murder, besides castin' quite a good bit of light on the character and circumstances of the murderer—or murderers."

"How do you make that out, sir?" demanded the elderly man.

"Well, to begin with—though I've never been near the place, there is obviously a sandy beach from which one can bathe."

"That's right," said the stout man.

"There is also, I fancy, in the neighbourhood, a spur of rock running out into the sea, quite possibly with a handy diving-pool. It must run out pretty far; at any rate, one can bathe there before it is high water on the beach."

"I don't know how you know that, sir, but it's a fact. There's rocks and a bathing-pool, exactly as you describe, about a hundred yards farther along. Many's the time I've had a dip off the end of them."

"And the rocks run right back inland, where they are covered with short grass."

"That's right."

"The murder took place shortly before high tide, I fancy, and the body lay just about at high-tide mark."

"Why so?"

"Well, you say there were footsteps leading right up to the body. That means that the water hadn't been up beyond the body. But there were no other marks. Therefore the murderer's footprints must have been washed away by the tide. The only explanation is that the two men were standing together just below the tide-mark. The murderer came up out of the sea. He attacked the other man—maybe he forced him back a little on his own tracks—and there he killed him. Then the water came up and washed out any marks the murderer may have left. One can imagine him squatting there, wondering if the sea was going to come up high enough."

"Ow!" said Kitty, "you make me creep all over."

"Now, as to these marks on the face," pursued the first-class passenger. "The murderer, according to the idea I get of the thing, was already in the sea when the victim came along. You see the idea?"

"I get you," said the stout man. "You think as he went in off them rocks that we was speaking of, and came up through the water, and that's why there weren't no footprints."

"Exactly. And since the water is deep round those rocks, as you say, he was presumably in a bathing-dress too."

"Looks like it."

"Quite so. Well, now—what was the face-slashing done with? People don't usually take knives out with them when they go for a morning dip."

"That's a puzzle," said the stout man.

"Not altogether. Let's say, either the murderer had a knife with him or he had not. If he had—"

"If he had," put in the prim man eagerly, "he must have laid wait for the deceased on purpose. And, to my mind, that bears out my idea of a deep and cunning plot."

"Yes. But, if he was waiting there with the knife, why didn't he stab the man and have done with it? Why strangle him, when he had a perfectly good weapon there to hand? No—I think he came unprovided, and, when he saw his enemy there, he made for him with his hands in the characteristic British way."

"But the slashing?"

"Well, I think that when he had got his man down, dead before him, he was filled with a pretty grim sort of fury and wanted to do more damage. He caught up something that was lying near him on the sand—it might be a bit of old iron, or even one of those sharp shells you sometimes see about, or a bit of glass—and he went for him with that in a desperate rage of jealousy or hatred."

"Dreadful, dreadful!" said the elderly woman.

"Of course, one can only guess in the dark, not having seen the wounds. It's quite possible that the murderer dropped his knife in the struggle and had to do the actual killing with his hands, picking the knife up afterwards. If the wounds were clean knife-wounds, that is probably what happened, and the murder was premeditated. But if they were rough, jagged gashes, made by an impromptu weapon, then I should say it was a chance encounter, and that the murderer was either mad or—"

"Or?"

"Or had suddenly come upon somebody whom he hated very much."

"What do you think happened afterwards?"

"That's pretty clear. The murderer, having waited, as I said, to see that all his footprints were cleaned up by the tide, waded or swam back to the rock where he had left his clothes, taking the weapon with him. The sea would wash away any blood from his bathing-dress or body. He then climbed out upon the rocks, walked, with bare feet, so as to leave no tracks on any seaweed or anything, to the short grass of the shore, dressed, went along to the murdered man's car, and drove it away."

"Why did he do that?"

"Yes, why? He may have wanted to get somewhere in a hurry. Or he may have been afraid that if the murdered man were identified too soon it would cast suspicion on him. Or it may have been a mixture of motives. The point is, where did he come from? How did he come to be bathing at that remote spot, early in the morning? He didn't get there by car, or there would be a second car to be accounted for. He may have been camping near the spot; but it would have taken him a long time to strike camp and pack all his belongings into the car, and he might have been seen. I am rather inclined to think he had bicycled there, and that he hoisted the bicycle into the back of the car and took it away with him."

"But, in that case, why take the car?"

"Because he had been down at East Felpham longer than he expected, and he was afraid of being late. Either he had to get back to breakfast at some house where his absence would be noticed, or else he lived some distance off, and had only just time enough for the journey home. I think, though, he had to be back to breakfast."

"Why?'

"Because, if it was merely a question of making up time on the road, all he had to do was to put himself and his bicycle on the train for part of the way. No; I fancy he was staying in a smallish hotel somewhere. Not a large hotel, because there nobody would notice whether he came in or not. And not, I think, in lodgings, or somebody would have mentioned before now that they had had a lodger who went bathing at East Felpham. Either he lives in the neighbourhood, in which case he should be easy to trace, or was staying with friends who have an interest in concealing his movements. Or else—which I think is more likely—he was in a smallish hotel, where he would be missed from the breakfast-table, but where his favourite bathing-place was not a matter of common knowledge."

"That seems feasible," said the stout man.

"In any case," went on the first-class passenger, "he must have been staying within easy bicycling distance of East Felpham, so it shouldn't be too hard to trace him. And then there is the car."

"Yes. Where is the car, on your theory?" demanded the prim man, who obviously still had hankerings after the Camorra theory.

"In a garage, waiting to be called for," said the first-class passenger promptly.

"Where?" persisted the prim man.

"Oh! somewhere on the other side of wherever it was the murderer was staying. If you have a particular reason for not wanting it to be known that you were in a certain place at a specified time, it's not a bad idea to come back from the opposite direction. I rather think I should look for the car at West Felpham, and the hotel in the nearest town on the main road beyond where the two roads to East and West Felpham join. When you've found the car, you've found the name of the victim, naturally. As for the murderer, you will have to look for an active man, a good swimmer and ardent bicyclist—probably not very well off, since he cannot afford to have a car— who has been taking a holiday in the neighbourhood of the Felphams, and who has a good reason for disliking the victim, whoever he may be."

"Well, I never," said the elderly woman admiringly. "How beautiful you do put it all together. Like Sherlock Holmes, I do declare."

"It's a very pretty theory," said the prim man, "but, all the same, you'll find it's a secret society. Mark my words. Dear me! We're just running in. Only twenty minutes late. I call that very good for holiday-time. Will you excuse me? My bag is just under your feet."

There was an eighth person in the compartment, who had remained throughout the conversation apparently buried in a newspaper. As the passengers decanted themselves upon the platform, this man touched the first-class passenger upon the arm.

"Excuse me, sir," he said. "That was a very interesting suggestion of yours. My name is Winterbottom, and I am investigating this case. Do you mind giving me your name? I might wish to communicate with you later on."

"Certainly," said the first-class passenger. "Always delighted to have a finger in any pie, don't you know. Here is my card. Look me up any time you like."

Detective-Inspector Winterbottom took the card and read the name:

LORD PETER WIMSEY
110A PICCADILLY

The *Evening Views* vendor outside Piccadilly Tube Station arranged his placard with some care. It looked very well, he thought.

MAN WITH
NO FACE
IDENTIFIED

It was, in his opinion, considerably more striking than that displayed by a rival organ, which announced, unimaginatively:

BEACH MURDER
VICTIM
IDENTIFIED

A youngish gentleman in a grey suit who emerged at that moment from the Criterion Bar appeared to think so too, for he exchanged a copper for the *Evening Views*, and at once plunged into its perusal with such concentrated interest that he bumped into a hurried man outside the station and had to apologize.

The *Evening Views*, grateful to murderer and victim alike for providing so useful a sensation in the dead days after the Bank Holiday, had torn Messrs Negretti & Zambra's rocketing thermometrical statistics from the "banner" position which they had occupied in the lunch edition, and substituted:

FACELESS VICTIM OF BEACH OUTRAGE
IDENTIFIED

MURDER OF PROMINENT
PUBLICITY ARTIST

POLICE CLUES

The body of a middle-aged man who was discovered, attired only in a bathing-costume and with his face horribly disfigured by some jagged instrument, on the beach at East Felpham last Monday morning has been identified as that of Mr. Coreggio Plant, studio manager of Messrs Crichton Ltd, the well-known publicity experts of Holborn.

Mr. Plant, who was forty-five years of age and a bachelor, was spending his annual holiday in making a motoring tour along the West Coast. He had no companion with him and had left no address for the forwarding of letters, so that, without the smart work of Detective-Inspector Winterbottom of the Westshire police, his disappearance might not in the ordinary way have been noticed until he became due to return to his place of business in three weeks' time. The murderer had no doubt counted on this, and had removed the motor-car, containing the belongings of his victim, in the hope of covering up all traces of this dastardly outrage so as to gain time for escape.

A rigorous search for the missing car, however, eventuated in its discovery in a garage at West Felpham, where it had been left for decarbonization and repairs to the magneto. Mr. Spiller, the garage proprietor, himself saw the man who left the car, and has furnished a description of him to the police. He is said to be a small, dark man of foreign appearance. The police hold a clue to his identity, and an arrest is confidently expected in the near future.

Mr. Plant was for fifteen years in the employment of Messrs Crichton, being appointed Studio Manager in the latter years of the war. He was greatly liked by all his colleagues, and his skill in the lay-out and designing of advertisements did much to justify the truth of Messrs Crichton's well-known slogan: "Crichton's for Admirable Advertising."

The funeral of the victim will take place tomorrow at Golders Green Cemetery.

(Pictures on Back Page.)

Lord Peter Wimsey turned to the back page. The portrait of the victim did not detain him long; it was one of those characterless studio photographs which establish nothing except that the sitter has a tolerable set of features. He noted that Mr. Plant had been thin rather than fat, commercial in appearance rather than artistic, and that the photographer had chosen to show him serious rather than smiling. A picture of East Felpham beach, marked with a cross where the body was found, seemed to arouse in him rather more than a casual interest. He studied it intently for some time, making little surprised noises. There was no obvious reason why he should have been surprised, for the photograph bore out in every detail the deductions he had made in the train. There was the curved line of sand, with a long spur of rock stretching out behind it into deep water, and running back till it mingled with the short, dry turf. Nevertheless, he looked at it for several minutes with close attention, before folding the newspaper and hailing a taxi; and when he was in the taxi he unfolded the paper and looked at it again.

"Your lordship having been kind enough," said Inspector Winterbottom, emptying his glass rather too rapidly for true connoisseurship, "to suggest I should look you up in Town, I made bold to give you a call in passing. Thank you, I won't say no. Well, as you've seen in the papers by now, we found that car all right."

Wimsey expressed his gratification at this result.

"And very much obliged I was to your lordship for the hint," went on the Inspector generously, "not but what I wouldn't say but I should have come to the same conclusion myself, given a little more time. And, what's more, we're on the track of the man."

"I see he's supposed to be foreign-looking. Don't say he's going to turn out to be a Camorrist after all!"

"No, my lord." The Inspector winked. "Our friend in the corner had got his magazine stories a bit on the brain, if you ask me. And *you* were a bit out too, my lord, with your bicyclist idea."

"Was I? That's a blow."

"Well, my lord, these here theories *sound* all right, but half the time they're too fine-spun altogether. Go for the facts — that's our motto in the Force — facts and motive, and you won't go far wrong."

"Oh! you've discovered the motive, then?"

The Inspector winked again.

"There's not many motives for doing a man in," said he. "Women or money — or women *and* money — it mostly comes down to one or the other. This fellow Plant went in for being a bit of a lad, you see. He kept a little cottage down Felpham way, with a nice little skirt to furnish it and keep the love-nest warm for him — see?"

"Oh! I thought he was doing a motor-tour."

"Motor-tour your foot!" said the Inspector, with more energy than politeness. "That's what the old [epithet] told 'em at the office. Handy reason, don't you see, for leaving no address behind him. No, no. There was a lady in it all right. I've seen her. A very taking piece too, if you like 'em skinny, which I don't. I prefer 'em better upholstered myself."

"That chair is really more comfortable with a cushion," put in Wimsey, with anxious solicitude. "Allow me."

"Thanks, my lord, thanks. I'm doing very well. It seems that his woman—by the way, we're speaking in confidence, you understand. I don't want this to go further till I've got my man under lock and key."

Wimsey promised discretion.

"That's all right, my lord, that's all right. I know I can rely on you. Well, the long and the short is, this young woman had another fancy man—a sort of an Italiano, whom she'd chucked for Plant, and this same dago got wind of the business and came down to East Felpham on the Sunday night, looking for her. He's one of these professional partners in a Palais de Danse up Cricklewood way, and that's where the girl comes from, too. I suppose she thought Plant was a cut above him. Anyway, down he comes, and busts in upon them Sunday night when they were having a bit of supper—and that's when the row started."

"Didn't you know about this cottage and the goings-on there?"

"Well, you know, there's such a lot of these week-enders nowadays. We can't keep tabs on all of them, so long as they behave themselves and don't make a disturbance. The woman's been there—so they tell me—since last June, with him coming down Saturday to Monday; but it's a lonely spot, and the constable didn't take much notice. He came in the evenings, so there wasn't anybody much to recognize him, except the old girl who did the slops and things, and she's half-blind. And of course, when they found him, he hadn't any face to recognize. It'd be thought he'd just gone off in the ordinary way. I dare say the dago fellow reckoned on that. As I was saying, there was a big row, and the dago was kicked out. He must have lain wait for Plant down by the bathing-place, and done him in."

"By strangling?"

"Well, he *was* strangled."

"Was his face cut up with a knife, then?"

"Well, no—I don't think it was a knife. More like a broken bottle, I should say, if you ask me. There's plenty of them come in with the tide."

"But then we're brought back to our old problem. If this Italian was lying in wait to murder Plant, why didn't he take a weapon with him, instead of trusting to the chance of his hands and a broken bottle?"

The Inspector shook his head.

"Flighty," he said. "All these foreigners are flighty. No headpiece. But there's our man and there's our motive, plain as a pikestaff. You don't want more."

"And where is the Italian fellow now?"

"Run away. That's pretty good proof of guilt in itself. But we'll have him before long. That's what I've come to Town about. He can't get out of the country. I've had an all-stations call sent out to stop him. The dance-hall people were able to supply us with a photo and a good description. I'm expecting a report in now any minute. In fact, I'd best be getting along. Thank you very much for your hospitality, my lord."

"The pleasure is mine," said Wimsey, ringing the bell to have the visitor shown out. "I have enjoyed our little chat immensely."

Sauntering into the Falstaff at twelve o'clock the following morning, Wimsey, as he had expected, found Salcombe Hardy supporting his rather plump contours against the bar. The reporter greeted his arrival with a heartiness amounting almost to enthusiasm, and called for two large Scotches immediately. When the usual skirmish as to who should pay had been honourably settled by the prompt disposal of the drinks and the standing of two more, Wimsey pulled from his pocket the copy of last night's *Evening Views*.

"I wish you'd ask the people over at your place to get hold of a decent print of this for me," he said, indicating the picture of East Felpham beach.

Salcombe Hardy gazed limpid inquiry at him from eyes like drowned violets.

"See here, you old sleuth," he said, "does this mean you've got a theory about the thing? I'm wanting a story badly. Must keep up the excitement, you know. The police don't seem to have got any further since last night."

"No; I'm interested in this from another point of view altogether. I did have a theory—of sorts—but it seems it's all wrong. Bally old Homer nodding, I suppose. But I'd like a copy of the thing."

"I'll get Warren to get you one when we come back. I'm just taking him down with me to Crichton's. We're going to have a look at a picture. I say, I wish you'd come too. Tell me what to say about the damned thing."

"Good God! I don't know anything about commercial art."

" 'Tisn't commercial art. It's supposed to be a portrait of this blighter Plant. Done by one of the chaps in his studio or something. Kid who told me about it says it's clever. I don't know. Don't suppose she knows, either. You go in for being artistic, don't you?"

"I wish you wouldn't use such filthy expressions, Sally. Artistic! Who is this girl?"

"Typist in the copy department."

"Oh, Sally!"

"Nothing of that sort. I've never met her. Name's Gladys Twitterton. I'm sure that's beastly enough to put anybody off. Rang us up last night and told us there was a bloke there who'd done old Plant in oils and was it any use to us? Drummer thought it might be worth looking into. Make a change from that everlasting syndicated photograph."

"I see. If you haven't got an exclusive story, an exclusive picture's better than nothing. The girl seems to have her wits about her. Friend of the artist's?"

"No—said he'd probably be frightfully annoyed at her having told me. But I can wangle that. Only I wish you'd come and have a look at it. Tell me whether I ought to say it's an unknown masterpiece or merely a striking likeness."

"How the devil can I say if it's a striking likeness of a bloke I've never seen?"

"I'll say it's that, in any case. But I want to know if it's well painted."

"Curse it, Sally, what's it matter whether it is or not? I've got other things to do. Who's the artist, by the way? Anybody one's ever heard of?"

"Dunno. I've got the name here somewhere." Sally rooted in his hip-pocket and produced a mass of dirty correspondence, its angles blunted by constant attrition. "Some comic name like Buggle or Snagtooth—wait a bit—here it is. Crowder. Thomas Crowder. I knew it was something out of the way."

"Singularly like Buggle or Snagtooth. All right, Sally. I'll make a martyr of myself. Lead me to it."

"We'll have another quick one. Here's Warren. This is Lord Peter Wimsey. This is on me."

"On me," corrected the photographer, a jaded young man with a disillusioned manner. "Three large White Labels, please. Well, here's all the best. Are you fit, Sally? Because we'd better make tracks. I've got to be up at Golders Green by two for the funeral."

Mr. Crowder of Crichton's appeared to have had the news broken to him already by Miss Twitterton, for he received the embassy in a spirit of gloomy acquiescence.

"The directors won't like it," he said, "but they've had to put up with such a lot that I suppose one irregularity more or less won't give 'em apoplexy." He had a small, anxious, yellow face like a monkey. Wimsey put him down as being in his late thirties. He noticed his fine, capable hands, one of which was disfigured by a strip of sticking-plaster.

"Damaged yourself?" said Wimsey pleasantly, as they made their way upstairs to the studio. "Mustn't make a practice of that, what? An artist's hands are his livelihood—except, of course, for Armless Wonders and people of that kind! Awkward job, painting with your toes."

"Oh, it's nothing much," said Crowder, "but it's best to

keep the paint out of surface scratches. There's such a thing as lead-poisoning. Well, here's this dud portrait, such as it is. I don't mind telling you that it didn't please the sitter. In fact he wouldn't have it at any price."

"Not flattering enough?" asked Hardy.

"As you say." The painter pulled out a four by three canvas from its hiding-place behind a stack of poster cartoons, and heaved it up on to the easel.

"Oh!" said Hardy, a little surprised. Not that there was any reason for surprise as far as the painting itself was concerned. It was a straight-forward handling enough; the skill and originality of the brushwork being of the kind that interests the painter without shocking the ignorant.

"Oh!" said Hardy. "Was he really like that?"

He moved closer to the canvas, peering into it as he might have peered into the face of the living man, hoping to get something out of him. Under this microscopic scrutiny, the portrait, as is the way of portraits, dislimned, and became no more than a conglomeration of painted spots and streaks. He made the discovery that, to the painter's eye, the human face is full of green and purple patches.

He moved back again, and altered the form of his question:

"So that's what he was like, was he?"

He pulled out the photograph of Plant from his pocket, and compared it with the portrait. The portrait seemed to sneer at his surprise.

"Of course, they touch these things up at these fashionable photographers," he said. "Anyway, that's not my business. This thing will make a jolly good eye-catcher, don't you think so, Wimsey? Wonder if they'd give us a two-column spread on the front page? Well, Warren, you'd better get down to it."

The photographer, bleakly unmoved by artistic or journalistic considerations, took silent charge of the canvas, mentally resolving it into a question of panchromatic plates and coloured screens. Crowder gave him a hand in shifting the easel into a better light. Two or three people from other de-

partments, passing through the studio on their lawful occasions, stopped and lingered in the neighbourhood of the disturbance, as though it were a street accident. A melancholy,
grey-haired man, temporary head of the studio, vice Coreggio
Plant, deceased, took Crowder aside, with a muttered apology,
to give him some instructions about adapting a whole quad to
an eleven-inch treble. Hardy turned to Lord Peter.

"It's damned ugly," he said. "Is it good?"

"Brilliant," said Wimsey. "You can go all out. Say what
you like about it."

"Oh, splendid! Could we discover one of our neglected
British masters?"

"Yes; why not? You'll probably make the man the fashion
and ruin him as an artist, but that's his pigeon."

"But, I say—do you think it's a good likeness? He's made
him look a most sinister sort of fellow. After all, Plant thought
it was so bad he wouldn't have it."

"The more fool he. Ever heard of the portrait of a certain
statesman that was so revealing of his inner emptiness that he
hurriedly bought it up and hid it to prevent people like you
from getting hold of it?"

Crowder came back.

"I say," said Wimsey, "whom does that picture belong to?
You? Or the heirs of the deceased, or what?"

"I suppose it's back on my hands," said the painter.
"Plant—well, he more or less commissioned it, you see, but—"

"How more or less?"

"Well, he kept on hinting, don't you know, that he would
like me to do him, and, as he was my boss, I thought I'd better. No price actually mentioned. When he saw it, he didn't
like it, and told me to alter it."

"But you didn't."

"Oh—well, I put it aside and said I'd see what I could do
with it. I thought he'd perhaps forget about it."

"I see. Then presumably it's yours to dispose of."

"I should think so. Why?"

"You have a very individual technique, haven't you?" pursued Wimsey. "Do you exhibit much?"

"Here and there. I've never had a show in London."

"I fancy I once saw a couple of small seascapes of yours somewhere. Manchester, was it? or Liverpool? I wasn't sure of your name, but I recognized the technique immediately."

"I dare say. I did send a few things to Manchester about two years ago."

"Yes—I felt sure I couldn't be mistaken. I want to buy the portrait. Here's my card, by the way. I'm not a journalist; I collect things."

Crowder looked from the card to Wimsey and from Wimsey to the card, a little reluctantly.

"If you want to exhibit it, of course," said Lord Peter, "I should be delighted to leave it with you as long as you liked."

"Oh, it's not that," said Crowder. "The fact is, I'm not altogether keen on the thing. I should like to—that is to say, it's not really finished."

"My dear man, it's a bally masterpiece."

"Oh, the painting's all right. But it's not altogether satisfactory as a likeness."

"What the devil does the likeness matter? I don't know what the late Plant looked like and I don't care. As I look at the thing it's a damn fine bit of brush-work, and if you tinker about with it you'll spoil it. You know that as well as I do. What's biting you? It isn't the price, is it? You know I shan't boggle about that. I can afford my modest pleasures, even in these thin and piping times. You don't want me to have it? Come now—what's the real reason?"

"There's no reason at all why you shouldn't have it if you really want it, I suppose," said the painter, still a little sullenly. "If it's really the painting that interests you."

"What do you suppose it is? The notoriety? I can have all I want of *that* commodity, you know, for the asking—or even without asking. Well, anyhow, think it over, and when you've decided, send me a line and name your price."

Crowder nodded without speaking, and the photographer having by this time finished his job, the party took their leave.

As they left the building, they became involved in the stream of Crichton's staff going out to lunch. A girl, who seemed to have been loitering in a semi-intentional way in the lower hall, caught them as the lift descended.

"Are you the *Evening Views* people? Did you get your picture all right?"

"Miss Twitterton?" said Hardy interrogatively. "Yes, rather—thank you so much for giving us the tip. You'll see it on the front page this evening."

"Oh! that's splendid! I'm frightfully thrilled. It has made an excitement here—all this business. Do they know anything yet about who murdered Mr. Plant? Or am I being horribly indiscreet?"

"We're expecting news of an arrest any minute now," said Hardy. "As a matter of fact, I shall have to buzz back to the office as fast as I can, to sit with one ear glued to the telephone. You will excuse me, won't you? And, look here—will you let me come round another day, when things aren't so busy, and take you out to lunch?"

"Of course. I should love to," Miss Twitterton giggled. "I do so want to hear about all the murder cases."

"Then here's the man to tell you about them, Miss Twitterton," said Hardy, with mischief in his eye. "Allow me to introduce Lord Peter Wimsey."

Miss Twitterton offered her hand in an ecstasy of excitement which almost robbed her of speech.

"How do you do?" said Wimsey. "As this blighter is in such a hurry to get back to his gossip-shop, what do you say to having a spot of lunch with me?"

"Well, really—" began Miss Twitterton.

"He's all right," said Hardy; "he won't lure you into any gilded dens of infamy. If you look at him, you will see he has a kind, innocent face."

"I'm sure I never thought of such a thing," said Miss Twitterton. "But you know—really—I've only got my old things on. It's no good wearing anything decent in this dusty old place."

"Oh, nonsense!" said Wimsey. "You couldn't possibly look nicer. It isn't the frock that matters—it's the person who wears it. *That's* all right, then. See you later, Sally! Taxi! Where shall we go? What time do you have to be back, by the way?"

"Two o'clock," said Miss Twitterton regretfully.

"Then we'll make the Savoy do," said Wimsey; "it's reasonably handy."

Miss Twitterton hopped into the waiting taxi with a little squeak of agitation.

"Did you see Mr. Crichton?" she said. "He went by just as we were talking. However, I dare say he doesn't really know me by sight. I hope not—or he'll think I'm getting too grand to need a salary." She rooted in her hand-bag. "I'm sure my face is getting all shiny with excitement. What a silly taxi. It hasn't got a mirror—and I've bust mine."

Wimsey solemnly produced a small looking-glass from his pocket.

"How wonderfully competent of you!" exclaimed Miss Twitterton. "I'm afraid, Lord Peter, you are used to taking girls about."

"Moderately so," said Wimsey. He did not think it necessary to mention that the last time he had used that mirror it had been to examine the back teeth of a murdered man.

"Of course," said Miss Twitterton, "they had to say he was popular with his colleagues. Haven't you noticed that murdered people are always well dressed and popular?"

"They have to be," said Wimsey. "It makes it more mysterious and pathetic. Just as girls who disappear are always bright and home-loving and have no men friends."

"Silly, isn't it?" said Miss Twitterton, with her mouth full of roast duck and green peas. "I should think everybody was only too glad to get rid of Plant—nasty, rude creature. So mean, too, always taking credit for other people's work. All those poor things in the studio, with all the spirit squashed out of them. I always say, Lord Peter, you can tell if a head of a department's fitted for his job by noticing the atmosphere of the place as you go into it. Take the copy-room, now. We're all as cheerful and friendly as you like, though I must say the language that goes on there is something awful, but these writing fellows are like that, and they don't mean anything by it. But then, Mr. Ormerod is a real gentleman—that's our copy-chief, you know—and he makes them all take an interest in the work, for all they grumble about the cheese-bills and the department-store bilge, they have to turn out. But it's quite different in the studio. A sort of dead-and-alive feeling about it, if you under-stand what I mean. We girls notice things like that more than some of the high-up people think. Of course, I'm very sensitive to these feelings—almost psychic, I've been told."

Lord Peter said there was nobody like a woman for sizing up character at a glance. Women, he thought, were remark-ably intuitive.

"That's a fact," said Miss Twitterton. "I've often said, if I could have a few frank words with Mr. Crichton, I could tell him a thing or two. There are wheels within wheels beneath the surface of a place like this that these brass-hats have no idea of."

Lord Peter said he felt sure of it.

"The way Mr. Plant treated people he thought were be-neath him," went on Miss Twitterton, "I'm sure it was enough to make your blood boil. I'm sure, if Mr. Ormerod sent me with a message to him, I was glad to get out of the room again. Humiliating, it was, the way he'd speak to you. I don't care if he's dead or not; being dead doesn't make a person's past be-haviour any better, Lord Peter. It wasn't so much the rude things he said. There's Mr. Birkett, for example; *he's* rude enough, but nobody minds him. He's just like a big, blunder-ing puppy—rather a lamb, really. It was Mr. Plant's nasty sneering way we all hated so. And he was always running peo-ple down."

"How about this portrait?" asked Wimsey. "Was it like him at all?"

"It was a lot too like him," said Miss Twitterton emphatically. "That's why he hated it so. He didn't like Crowder, ether. But, of course, he knew he could paint, and he made him do it, because he thought he'd be getting a valuable thing cheap. And Crowder couldn't very well refuse, or Plant would have got him sacked."

"I shouldn't have thought that would have mattered much to a man of Crowder's ability."

"Poor Mr. Crowder! I don't think he's ever had much luck. Good artists don't always seem able to sell their pictures. And I know he wanted to get married—otherwise he'd never have taken up this commercial work. He's told me a good bit about himself. I don't know why—but I'm one of the people men seem to tell things to."

Lord Peter filled Miss Twitterton's glass.

"Oh, please! No, really! Not a drop more! I'm talking a lot too much as it is. I don't know what Mr. Ormerod will say when I go in to take his letters. I shall be writing down all kinds of funny things. Ooh! I really must be getting back. Just look at the time!"

"It's not really late. Have a black coffee—just as a corrective." Wimsey smiled. "You haven't been talking at all too much. I've enjoyed your picture of office life enormously. You have a very vivid way of putting things, you know. I see now why Mr. Plant was not altogether a popular character."

"Not in the office, anyway—whatever he may have been elsewhere," said Miss Twitterton darkly.

"Oh?"

"Oh! he was a one," said Miss Twitterton. "He certainly was a one. Some friends of mine met him one evening up in the West End, and they came back with some nice stories. It was quite a joke in the office—old Plant and his rosebuds, you know. Mr. Cowley—he's *the* Cowley, you know, who rides in the motorcycle races—he always said he knew what to think of Mr. Plant and his motor-tours. That time Mr. Plant pretended he'd gone touring in Wales, Mr. Cowley was asking him about the roads, and he didn't know a thing about them.

Because Mr. Cowley really had been touring there, and he knew quite well Mr. Plant hadn't been where he said he had; and, as a matter of fact, Mr. Cowley knew he'd been staying the whole time in a hotel at Aberystwyth, in very attractive company."

Miss Twitterton finished her coffee and slapped the cup down defiantly.

"And now I really *must* run away, or I shall be most dreadfully late. And thank you ever so much."

"Hullo!" said Inspector Winterbottom, "you've bought that portrait, then?"

"Yes," said Wimsey. "It's a fine bit of work." He gazed thoughtfully at the canvas. "Sit down, inspector; I want to tell you a story."

"And I want to tell *you* a story," replied the inspector.

"Let's have yours first," said Wimsey, with an air of flattering eagerness.

"No, no, my lord. You take precedence. Go ahead."

He snuggled down with a chuckle into his arm-chair.

"Well!" said Wimsey. "Mine's a sort of a fairy-story. And, mind you, I haven't verified it."

"Go ahead, my lord, go ahead."

"Once upon a time—" said Wimsey, sighing.

"That's the good old-fashioned way to begin a fairy-story," said Inspector Winterbottom.

"Once upon a time," repeated Wimsey, "there was a painter. He was a good painter, but the bad fairy of Financial Success had not been asked to his christening—what?"

"That's often the way with painters," agreed the inspector.

"So he had to take up a job as a commercial artist, because nobody would buy his pictures, and, like so many people in fairy-tales, he wanted to marry a goose-girl."

"There's many people want to do the same," said the inspector.

"The head of his department," went on Wimsey, "was a man with a mean, sneering soul. He wasn't even really good at his job, but he had been pushed into authority during the war, when better men went to the Front. Mind you, I'm rather sorry for the man. He suffered from an inferiority complex" — the inspector snorted — "and he thought the only way to keep his end up was to keep other people's end down. So he became a little tin tyrant and a bully. He took all the credit for the work of the men under his charge, and he sneered and harassed them till they got inferiority complexes even worse than his own."

"I've known that sort," said the inspector, "and the marvel to me is how they get away with it."

"Just so," said Wimsey. "Well, I dare say this man would have gone on getting away with it all right, if he hadn't thought of getting this painter to paint his portrait."

"Damn silly thing to do," said the inspector. "It was only making the painter-fellow conceited with himself."

"True. But, you see, this tin tyrant person had a fascinating female in tow, and he wanted the portrait for the lady. He thought that, by making the painter do it, he would get a good portrait at starvation price. But unhappily he'd forgotten that, however much an artist will put up with in the ordinary way, he is bound to be sincere with his art. That's the one thing a genuine artist won't muck about with."

"I dare say," said the inspector. "I don't know much about artists."

"Well, you can take it from me. So the painter painted the portrait as he saw it, and he put the man's whole creeping, sneering, paltry soul on the canvas for everybody to see."

Inspector Winterbottom stared at the portrait, and the portrait sneered back at him.

"It's not what you'd call a flattering picture, certainly," he admitted.

"Now, when a painter paints a portrait of anybody," went on Wimsey, "that person's face is never the same to him again. It's like — what shall I say? Well, it's like the way a gunner, say, looks at a landscape where he happens to be posted. He doesn't see it as a landscape. He doesn't see it as a thing of

magic beauty, full of sweeping lines and lovely colour. He sees
it as so much cover, so many landmarks to aim by, so many
gun-emplacements. And when the war is over and he goes
back to it, he will still see it as cover and landmarks and gun-
emplacements. It isn't a landscape any more. It's a war map."

"I know that," said Inspector Winterbottom. "I was a
gunner myself."

"A painter gets just the same feeling of deadly familiarity
with every line of a face he's once painted," pursued Wimsey.
"And if it's a face he hates, he hates it with a new and more ir-
ritable hatred. It's like a defective barrel-organ, everlastingly
grinding out the same old maddening tune, and making the
same damned awful wrong note every time the barrel goes
round."

"Lord! how you can talk!" ejaculated the inspector.

"That was the way the painter felt about this man's hateful face. All day and every day he had to see it. He couldn't get
away because he was tied to his job, you see."

"He ought to have cut loose," said the inspector. "It's no
good going on like that, trying to work with uncongenial people."

"Well, anyway, he said to himself, he could escape for a bit
during his holidays. There was a beautiful little quiet spot he
knew on the West Coast, where nobody ever came. He'd been
there before and painted it. Oh! by the way, that reminds
me — I've got another picture to show you."

He went to a bureau and extracted a small panel in oils
from a drawer.

"I saw that two yeas ago at a show in Manchester, and I
happened to remember the name of the dealer who bought it."

Inspector Winterbottom gaped at the panel.

"But that's East Felpham!" he exclaimed.

"Yes. It's only signed T.C., but the technique is rather unmistakable, don't you think?"

The inspector knew little about technique, but initials he
understood. He looked from the portrait to the panel and back
at Lord Peter.

"The painter—"

"Crowder?"

"If it's all the same to you, I'd rather go on calling him the painter. He packed up his traps on his push-bike carrier, and took his tormented nerves down to this beloved and secret spot for a quiet week-end. He stayed at a quiet little hotel in the neighbourhood, and each morning he cycled off to this lovely little beach to bathe. He never told anybody at the hotel where he went, because it was *his* place, and he didn't want other people to find it out."

Inspector Winterbottom set the panel down on the table, and helped himself to whisky.

"One morning—it happened to be the Monday morning"—Wimsey's voice became slower and more reluctant—"he went down as usual. The tide was not yet fully in, but he ran out over the rocks to where he knew there was a deep bathing-pool. He plunged in and swam about, and let the small noise of his jangling troubles be swallowed up in the innumerable laughter of the sea."

"Eh?"

"κυμάτων ἀνήριθμον γέλασμα—quotation from the classics. Some people say it means the dimpled surface of the waves in the sunlight—but how could Prometheus, bound upon his rock, have seen it? Surely it was the chuckle of the incoming tide among the stones that came up to his ears on the lonely peak where the vulture fretted at his heart. I remember arguing about it with old Philpotts in class, and getting rapped over the knuckles for contradicting him. I didn't know at the time that he was engaged in producing a translation on his own account, or doubtless I should have contradicted him more rudely and been told to take my trousers down. Dear old Philpotts!"

"I don't know anything about that," said the inspector.

"I beg your pardon. Shocking way I have of wandering. The painter—well! he swam round the end of the rocks, for the tide was nearly in by that time; and, as he came up from the sea, he saw a man standing on the beach—that beloved beach, remember, which he thought was his own sacred haven

of peace. He came wading towards it, cursing the Bank Holiday rabble who must needs swarm about everywhere with
their cigarette-packets and their kodaks and their gramo-
phones—and then he saw that it was a face he knew. He knew
every hated line in it, on that clear sunny morning. And, early
as it was, the heat was coming up over the sea like a haze."

"It was a hot week-end," said the Inspector.

"And then the man hailed him, in his smug, mincing voice.
'Hullo!' he said, 'you here? How did you find my little
bathing-place?' And that was too much for the painter. He felt
as if his last sanctuary had been invaded. He leapt at the lean
throat—it's rather a stringy one, you may notice, with a prominent Adam's apple—an irritating throat. The water chuckled
round their feet as they swayed to and fro. He felt his thumbs
sink into the flesh he had painted. He saw, and laughed to see,
the hateful familiarity of the features change and swell into an
unrecognizable purple. He watched the sunken eyes bulge out
and the thin mouth distort itself as the blackened tongue
thrust through it—I am not unnerving you, I hope?"

The inspector laughed.

"Not a bit. It's wonderful, the way you describe things.
You ought to write a book."

"I sing but as the throstle sings,
    Amid the branches dwelling,"

replied his lordship negligently, and went on without further
comment.

"The painter throttled him. He flung him back on the
sand. He looked at him, and his heart crowed within him. He
stretched out his hand, and found a broken bottle, with a good
jagged edge. He went to work with a will, stamping and tearing away every trace of the face he knew and loathed. He blot-
ted it out and destroyed it utterly.

"He sat beside the thing he had made. He began to be
frightened. They had staggered back beyond the edge of the
water, and there were the marks of his feet on the sand. He

had blood on his face and on his bathing-suit, and he had cut his hand with the bottle. But the blessed sea was still coming in. He watched it pass over the bloodstains and the footprints and wipe the story of his madness away. He remembered that this man had gone from his place, leaving no address behind him. He went back, step by step, into the water, and, as it came up to his breast, he saw the red stains smoke away like a faint mist in the brown-blueness of the tide. He went—wading and swimming and plunging his face and arms deep in the water, looking back from time to time to see what he had left behind him. I think that when he got back to the point and drew himself out, clean and cool, upon the rocks, he remembered that he ought to have taken the body back with him and let the tide carry it away, but it was too late. He was clean, and he could not bear to go back for the thing. Besides, he was late, and they would wonder at the hotel if he was not back in time for breakfast. He ran lightly over the bare rocks and the grass that showed no footprint. He dressed himself, taking care to leave no trace of his presence. He took the car, which would have told a story. He put his bicycle in the back seat, under the rugs, and he went—but you know as well as I do where he went."

Lord Peter got up with an impatient movement, and went over to the picture, rubbing his thumb meditatively over the texture of the painting.

"You may say, if he hated the face so much, why didn't he destroy the picture? He couldn't. It was the best thing he'd ever done. He took a hundred guineas for it. It was cheap at a hundred guineas. But then—I think he was afraid to refuse me. My name is rather well known. I was a sort of blackmail, I suppose. But I wanted that picture."

Inspector Winterbottom laughed again.

"Did you take any steps, my lord, to find out if Crowder has really been staying at East Felpham?"

"No." Wimsey swung round abruptly. "I have taken no steps at all. That's your business. I have told you the story, and, on my soul, I'd rather have stood by and said nothing."

"You needn't worry." The inspector laughed for the third time. "It's a good story, my lord, and you told it well. But you're right when you say it's a fairy-story. We've found this Italian fellow— Francesco, he called himself, and he's the man all right."

"How do you know? Has he confessed?"

"Practically. He's dead. Killed himself. He left a letter to the woman, begging her forgiveness, and saying that when he saw her with Plant he felt murder come into his heart. 'I have revenged myself,' he says, 'on him who dared to love you.' I suppose he got the wind up when he saw we were after him— I wish these newspapers wouldn't be always putting these criminals on their guard—so he did away with himself to cheat the gallows. I may say it's been a disappointment to me."

"It must have been," said Wimsey. "Very unsatisfactory, of course. But I'm glad my story turned out to be only a fairy-tale after all. You're not going?"

"Got to get back to my duty," said the inspector, heaving himself to his feet. "Very pleased to have met you, my lord. And I mean what I say—you ought to take to literature."

Wimsey remained after he had gone, still looking at the portrait.

" 'What is Truth?' said jesting Pilate. No wonder, since it is so completely unbelievable. . . . I could prove it . . . if I liked . . . but the man had a villainous face, and there are few good painters in the world."

THE ADVENTUROUS EXPLOIT OF
THE CAVE OF ALI BABA

In the front room of a grim and narrow house in Lambeth a man sat eating kippers and glancing through the *Morning Post*. He was smallish and spare, with brown hair rather too regularly waved and a strong, brown beard, cut to a point. His double-breasted suit of navy-blue and his socks, tie, and handkerchief, all scrupulously matched, were a trifle more point-device than the best taste approves, and his boots were slightly too bright a brown. He did not look a gentleman, not even a gentleman's gentleman, yet there was something about his appearance which suggested that he was accustomed to the manner of life in good families. The breakfast-table, which he had set with his own hands, was arrayed with the attention to detail which is exacted of good-class servants. His action, as he walked over to a little side-table and carved himself a plate of ham, was the action of a superior butler; yet he was not old enough to be a retired butler; a footman, perhaps, who had come into a legacy.

He finished the ham with good appetite, and, as he sipped his coffee, read through attentively a paragraph which he had already noticed and put aside for consideration:

LORD PETER WIMSEY'S WILL
BEQUEST TO VALET
£10,000 TO CHARITIES

The will of Lord Peter Wimsey, who was killed last December while shooting big game in Tanganyika, was proved yesterday at £500,000. A sum of £10,000 was left to various charities, including [here followed a list of bequests]. To his valet, Mervyn Bunter, was left an annuity of £500 and the lease of the testator's flat in Piccadilly. [Then followed a number of personal bequests.] The remainder of the estate, including the valuable collection of books and pictures at 110A Piccadilly, was left to the testator's mother, the Dowager Duchess of Denver.

Lord Peter Wimsey was thirty-seven at the time of his death. He was the younger brother of the present Duke of Denver, who is the wealthiest peer in the United Kingdom. Lord Peter was distinguished as a criminologist and took an active part in the solution of several famous mysteries. He was a well-known book collector and man-about-town.

The man gave a sigh of relief.

"No doubt about that," he said aloud. "People don't give their money away if they're going to come back again. The blighter's dead and buried right enough. I'm free."

He finished his coffee, cleared the table, and washed up the crockery, took his bowler hat from the hall-stand, and went out.

A bus took him to Bermondsey. He alighted, and plunged into a network of gloomy streets, arriving after a quarter of an hour's walk at a seedy-looking public-house in a low quarter. He entered and called for a double whisky.

The house had only just opened, but a number of customers, who had apparently been waiting on the doorstep for this desirable event, were already clustered about the bar. The man who might have been a footman reached for his glass, and in doing so jostled the elbow of a flash person in a check suit and regrettable tie.

"Here!" expostulated the flash person, "what d'yer mean by it? We don't want your sort here. Get out!"

He emphasized his remarks with a few highly coloured words, and a violent push in the chest.

"Bar's free to everybody, isn't it?" said the other, returning the shove with interest.

"Now then!" said the barmaid, "none o' that. The gentleman didn't do it intentional, Mr. Jukes."

"Didn't he?" said Mr. Jukes. "Well, I *did*."

"And you ought to be ashamed of yourself," retorted the young lady, with a toss of the head. "I'll have no quarrelling in my bar—not this time in the morning."

"It was quite an accident," said the man from Lambeth. "I'm not one to make a disturbance, having always been used to the best houses. But if any gentleman *wants* to make trouble—"

"All right, all right," said Mr. Jukes, more pacifically. "I'm not keen to give you a new face. Not but what any alteration wouldn't be for the better. Mind your manners another time, that's all. What'll you have?"

"No, no," protested the other, "this one must be on me. Sorry I pushed you. I didn't mean it. But I didn't like to be taken up so short."

"Say no more about it," said Mr. Jukes generously. "I'm standing this. Another double whisky, miss, and one of the usual. Come over here where there isn't so much of a crowd, or you'll be getting yourself into trouble again."

He led the way to a small table in the corner of the room.

"That's all right," said Mr. Jukes. "Very nicely done. I

don't think there's any danger here, but you can't be too careful. Now, what about it, Rogers? Have you made up your mind to come in with us?"

"Yes," said Rogers, with a glance over his shoulder, "yes, I have. That is, mind you, if everything seems all right. I'm not looking for trouble, and I don't want to get let in for any dangerous games. I don't mind giving you information, but it's understood as I take no active part in whatever goes on. Is that straight?"

"You wouldn't be allowed to take an active part if you wanted to," said Mr. Jukes. "Why, you poor fish. Number One wouldn't have anybody but experts on his jobs. All you have to do is to let us know where the stuff is and how to get it. The Society does the rest. It's some organization, I can tell you. You won't even know who's doing it, or how it's done. You won't know anybody, and nobody will know you—except Number One, of course. He knows everybody."

"And you," said Rogers.

"And me, of course. But I shall be transferred to another district. We shan't meet again after today, except at the general meetings, and then we shall all be masked."

"Go on!" said Rogers incredulously.

"Fact. You'll be taken to Number One—he'll see you, but you won't see him. Then, if he thinks you're any good, you'll be put on the roll, and after that you'll be told where to make your reports to. There is a divisional meeting called once a fortnight, and every three months there's a general meeting and share-out. Each member is called up by number and has his whack handed over to him. That's all."

"Well, but suppose two members are put on the same job together?"

"It it's a daylight job, they'll be so disguised their mothers wouldn't know 'em. But it's mostly night work."

"I see. But, look here—what's to prevent somebody following me home and giving me away to the police?"

"Nothing, of course. Only I wouldn't advise him to try it, that's all. The last man who had that bright idea was fished out of the river down Rotherhithe way, before he had time to get his precious report in. Number One knows everybody, you see."

"Oh!—and who is this Number One?"

"There's lots of people would give a good bit to know that."

"Does nobody know?"

"Nobody. He's a fair marvel, is Number One. He's a gentleman, I can tell you that, and a pretty high-up one, from his ways. *And* he's got eyes all round his head. *And* he's got an arm as long as from here to Australia. *But* nobody knows anything about him, unless it's Number Two, and I'm not even sure about her."

"There are women in it, then?"

"You can bet your boots there are. You can't do a job without 'em nowadays. But that needn't worry you. The women are safe enough. They don't want to come to a sticky end, no more than you and me."

"But, look here, Jukes—how about the money? It's a big risk to take. Is it worth it?"

"Worth it?" Jukes leant across the little marble-topped table and whispered.

"Coo!" gasped Rogers. "And how much of that would I get, now?"

"You'd share and share alike with the rest, whether you'd been in that particular job or not. There's fifty members and you'd get one-fiftieth, same as Number One and same as me."

"Really? No kidding?"

"See that wet, see that dry!" Jukes laughed. "Say, can you beat it? There's never been anything like it. It's the biggest thing ever been known. He's a great man, is Number One."

"And do you pull off many jobs?"

"Many? Listen. You remember the Carruthers necklace, and the Gorleston Bank robbery? And the Faversham burglary? And the big Rubens that disappeared from the National Gallery? And the Frensham pearls? All done by the Society. And never one of them cleared up."

Rogers licked his lips.

"But now, look here," he said cautiously. "Supposing I was

a spy, as you might say, and supposing I was to go straight off and tell the police about what you've been saying?"

"Ah!" said Jukes, "suppose you did, eh? Well, supposing something nasty didn't happen to you on the way there — which I wouldn't answer for, mind —"

"Do you mean to say you've got me watched?"

"You can bet your sweet life we have. Yes. Well, *supposing* nothing happened on the way there, and you was to bring the slops to this pub, looking for yours truly —"

"Yes?"

"You wouldn't find me, that's all. I should have gone to Number Five."

"Who's Number Five?"

"Ah! I don't know. But he's the man that makes you a new face while you wait. Plastic surgery, they call it. And new fingerprints. New everything. We go in for up-to-date methods in our show."

Rogers whistled.

"Well, how about it?" asked Jukes, eyeing his acquaintance over the rim of his tumbler.

"Look here — you've told me a lot of things. Shall I be safe if I say 'no?' "

"Oh, yes — if you behave yourself and don't make trouble for us."

"H'm, I see. And if I say 'yes?' "

"Then you'll be a rich man in less than no time, with money in your pocket to live like a gentleman. And nothing to do for it, except to tell us what you know about the houses you've been to when you were in service. It's money for jam if you act straight by the Society."

Rogers was silent, thinking it over.

"I'll do it!" he said at last.

"Good for you. Miss! The same again, please. Here's to it, Rogers! I knew you were one of the right sort the minute I set eyes on you. Here's to money for jam, and take care of Number One! Talking of Number One, you'd better come round and see him tonight. No time like the present."

"Right you are. Where'll I come to? Here?"

"Nix. No more of this little pub for us. It's a pity because it's nice and comfortable, but it can't be helped. Now, what you've got to do is this. At ten o'clock tonight exactly, you walk north across Lambeth Bridge" (Rogers winced at this intimation that his abode was known), "and you'll see a yellow taxi standing there, with the driver doing something to his engine. You'll say to him, 'Is your bus fit to go?' and he'll say, 'Depends where you want to go to.' And you'll say, 'Take me to Number One, London.' There's a shop called that, by the way, but he won't take you there. You won't know where he is taking you, because the taxi-windows will be covered up, but you mustn't mind that. It's the rule for the first visit. Afterwards, when you're regularly one of us, you'll be told the name of the place. And when you get there, do as you're told and speak the truth, because, if you don't, Number One will deal with you. See?"

"I see."

"Are you game? You're not afraid?"

"Of course I'm not afraid."

"Good man! Well, we'd better be moving now. And I'll say good-bye, because we shan't see each other again. Good-bye—and good luck!"

"Good-bye."

They passed through the swing-doors, and out into the mean and dirty street.

The two years subsequent to the enrolment of the ex-footman Rogers in a crook society were marked by a number of startling and successful raids on the houses of distinguished people. There was the theft of the great diamond tiara from the Dowager Duchess of Denver; the burglary at the flat formerly occupied by the late Lord Peter Wimsey, resulting in the disappearance of £7,000 worth of silver and gold plate; the burglary at the country mansion of Theodore Winthrop, the millionaire—which, incidentally, exposed that thriving gentleman as a confirmed Society blackmailer and

caused a reverberating scandal in Mayfair; and the snatching
of the famous eight-string necklace of pearls from the Marchioness of Dinglewood during the singing of the Jewel
Song in *Faust* at Covent Garden. It is true that the pearls
turned out to be imitation, the original string having been
pawned by the noble lady under circumstances highly
painful to the Marquis, but the coup was nevertheless a sensational one.

On a Saturday afternoon in January, Rogers was sitting
in his room in Lambeth, when a slight noise at the front door
caught his ear. He sprang up almost before it had ceased,
dashed through the small hallway, and flung the door open.
The street was deserted. Nevertheless, as he turned back to
the sitting-room, he saw an envelope lying on the hat-stand. It
was addressed briefly to "Number Twenty-one." Accustomed
by this time to the somewhat dramatic methods used by the
Society to deliver its correspondence, he merely shrugged his
shoulders, and opened the note.

It was written in cipher, and, when transcribed, ran thus:

> Number Twenty-one, An Extraordinary General
> Meeting will be held tonight at the house of Number One
> at 11:30. You will be absent at your peril. The word is
> FINALITY.

Rogers stood for a little time considering this. Then he
made his way to a room at the back of the house, in which
there was a tall safe, built into the wall. He manipulated the
combination and walked into the safe, which ran back for
some distance, forming, indeed, a small strong-room. He
pulled out a drawer marked "Correspondence," and added the
paper he had just received to the contents.

After a few moments he emerged, re-set the lock to a new
combination, and returned to the sitting-room.

"Finality," he said. "Yes — I think so." He stretched out his
hand to the telephone — then appeared to alter his mind.

He went upstairs to an attic, and thence climbed into a loft close under the roof. Crawling among the rafters, he made his way into the farthest corner; then carefully pressed a knot on the timber-work. A concealed trap-door swung open. He crept through it, and found himself in the corresponding loft of the next house. A soft cooing noise greeted him as he entered. Under the skylight stood three cages, each containing a carrier pigeon.

He glanced cautiously out of the skylight, which looked out upon a high blank wall at the back of some factory or other. There was nobody in the dim little courtyard, and no window within sight. He drew his head in again, and, taking a small fragment of thin paper from his pocket-book, wrote a few letters and numbers upon it. Going to the nearest cage, he took out the pigeon and attached the message to its wing. Then he carefully set the bird on the window-ledge. It hesitated a moment, shifted its pink feet a few times, lifted its wings, and was gone. He saw it tower up into the already darkening sky over the factory roof and vanish into the distance.

He glanced at his watch and returned downstairs. An hour later he released the second pigeon, and in another hour the third. Then he sat down to wait.

At half past nine he went up to the attic again. It was dark, but a few frosty stars were shining, and a cold air blew through the open window. Something pale gleamed faintly on the floor. He picked it up—it was warm and feathery. The answer had come.

He ruffled the soft plumes and found the paper. Before reading it, he fed the pigeon and put it into one of the cages. As he was about to fasten the door, he checked himself.

"If anything happens to me," he said, "there's no need for you to starve to death, my child."

He pushed the window a little wider open and went downstairs again. The paper in his hand bore only the two letters, "O.K." It seemed to have been written hurriedly, for there was a long smear of ink in the upper left-hand corner. He noted this with a smile, put the paper in the fire, and, going out into the kitchen, prepared and ate a hearty meal of eggs and corned beef from a new tin. He ate it without bread, though there was a loaf on the shelf near at hand, and washed it down with water from the tap, which he let run for some time before venturing to drink it. Even then he carefully wiped the tap, both inside and outside, before drinking.

When he had finished, he took a revolver from a locked drawer, inspecting the mechanism with attention to see that it was in working order, and loaded it with new cartridges from an unbroken packet. Then he sat down to wait again.

At a quarter before eleven, he rose and went out into the street. He walked briskly, keeping well away from the wall, till he came out into a well-lighted thoroughfare. Here he took a bus, securing the corner seat next the conductor, from which he could see everybody who got on and off. A succession of buses eventually brought him to a respectable residential quarter of Hampstead. Here he alighted and, still keeping well away from the walls, made his way up to the Heath.

The night was moonless, but not altogether black, and, as he crossed a deserted part of the Heath, he observed one or two other dark forms closing in upon him from various directions. He paused in the shelter of a large tree, and adjusted to his face a black velvet mask, which covered him from brow to chin. At its base the number 21 was clearly embroidered in white thread.

At length a slight dip in the ground disclosed one of those agreeable villas which stand, somewhat isolated, among the rural surroundings of the Heath. One of the windows was lighted. As he made his way to the door, other dark figures, masked like himself, pressed forward and surrounded him. He counted six of them.

The foremost man knocked on the door of the solitary house. After a moment, it was opened slightly. The man advanced his head to the opening; there was a murmur, and the door opened wide. The man stepped in, and the door was shut.

When three of the men had entered, Rogers found himself to be the next in turn. He knocked, three times loudly, then twice faintly. The door opened to the extent of two or three inches, and an ear was presented to the chink. Rogers whispered "Finality." The ear was withdrawn, the door opened, and he passed in.

Without any further word of greeting, Number Twenty-one passed into a small room on the left, which was furnished like an office, with a desk, a safe, and a couple of chairs. At the desk sat a massive man in evening dress, with a ledger before him. The new arrival shut the door carefully after him; it clicked to, on a spring lock. Advancing to the desk, he announced, "Number Twenty-one, sir," and stood respectfully waiting. The big man looked up, showing the number 1 startlingly white on his velvet mask. His eyes, of a curious hard blue, scanned Rogers attentively. At a sign from him, Rogers removed his mask. Having verified his identity with care, the President said, "Very well, Number Twenty-one," and made an entry in the ledger. The voice was hard and metallic, like his eyes. The close scrutiny from behind the immovable black mask seemed to make Rogers uneasy; he shifted his feet, and his eyes fell. Number One made a sign of dismissal, and Rogers, with a faint sigh as though of relief, replaced his mask and left the room. As he came out, the next comer passed in in his place.

The room in which the Society met was a large one, made by knocking the two largest of the first-floor rooms into one. It was furnished in the standardized taste of twentieth-century suburbia and brilliantly lighted. A gramophone in one corner blared out a jazz tune, to which about ten couples of masked men and women were dancing, some in evening dress and others in tweeds and jumpers.

In one corner of the room was an American bar. Rogers went up and asked the masked man in charge for a double whisky. He consumed it slowly, leaning on the bar. The room filled. Presently somebody moved across to the gramophone and stopped it. He looked round. Number One had appeared on the threshold. A tall women in black stood beside him. The mask, embroidered with a white 2, covered hair and face completely; only her fine bearing and her white arms and bosom and the dark eyes shining through the eye-slits proclaimed her a woman of power and physical attraction.

"Ladies and gentlemen." Number One was standing at the upper end of the room. The woman sat beside him; her eyes were cast down and betrayed nothing, but her hands were clenched on the arms of the chair and her whole figure seemed tensely aware.

"Ladies and gentlemen. Our numbers are two short tonight." The masks moved; eyes were turned, seeking and counting. "I need not inform you of the disastrous failure of our plan for securing the plans of the Court-Windlesham helicopter. Our courageous and devoted comrades, Number Fifteen and Number Forty-eight, were betrayed and taken by the police."

An uneasy murmur rose among the company.

"It may have occurred to some of you that even the well-known steadfastness of these comrades might give way under examination. There is no cause for alarm. The usual orders have been issued, and I have this evening received the report that their tongues have been effectually silenced. You will, I am sure, be glad to know that these two brave men have been spared the ordeal of so great a temptation to dishonour, and that they will not be called upon to face a public trial and the rigours of a long imprisonment."

A hiss of intaken breath moved across the assembled members like the wind over a barley-field.

"Their dependants will be discreetly compensated in the usual manner. I call upon Numbers Twelve and Thirty-four to undertake this agreeable task. They will attend me in my office for their instructions after the meeting. Will the numbers I have named kindly signify that they are able and willing to perform this duty?"

Two hands were raised in salute. The President continued, looking at his watch:

"Ladies and gentlemen, please take your partners for the next dance."

The gramophone struck up again. Rogers turned to a girl

near him and a red dress. She nodded, and they slipped into the movement of a fox-trot. The couples gyrated solemnly and in silence. Their shadows were flung against the blinds as they turned and stepped to and fro.

"What has happened?" breathed the girl in a whisper, scarcely moving her lips. "I'm frightened, aren't you? I feel as if something awful was going to happen."

"It does take one a bit short, the President's way of doing things," agreed Rogers, "but it's safer like that."

"Those poor men —"

A dancer, turning and following on their heels, touched Rogers on the shoulder.

"No talking, please," he said. His eyes gleamed sternly; he twirled his partner into the middle of the crowd and was gone. The girl shuddered.

The gramophone stopped. There was a burst of clapping. The dancers again clustered before the President's seat.

"Ladies and gentlemen. You may wonder why this extraordinary meeting has been called. The reason is a serious one. The failure of our recent attempt was no accident. The police were not on the premises that night by chance. We have a traitor among us."

Partners who had been standing close together fell distrustfully apart. Each member seemed to shrink, as a snail shrinks from the touch of a finger.

"You will remember the disappointing outcome of the Dinglewood affair," went on the President, in his harsh voice. "You may recall other smaller matters which have not turned out satisfactorily. All these troubles have been traced to their origin. I am happy to say that our minds can now be easy. The offender has been discovered and will be removed. There will be no more mistakes. The misguided member who introduced the traitor to our Society will be placed in a position where his lack of caution will have no further ill-effects. There is no cause for alarm."

Every eye roved about the company, searching for the traitor and his unfortunate sponsor. Somewhere beneath the black masks a face must have turned white; somewhere under the stifling velvet there must have been a brow sweating, not with the heat of the dance. But the masks hid everything.

"Ladies and gentlemen, please take your partners for the next dance."

The gramophone struck into an old and half-forgotten tune: "There ain't nobody loves me." The girl in red was claimed by a tall mask in evening dress. A hand laid on Rogers's arm made him start. A small, plump woman in a green jumper slipped a cold hand into his. The dance went on.

When it stopped, amid the usual applause, everyone stood, detached, stiffened in expectation. The President's voice was raised again.

"Ladies and gentlemen, please behave naturally. This is a dance, not a public meeting."

Rogers led his partner to a chair and fetched her an ice. As he stooped over her, he noticed the hurried rise and fall of her bosom.

"Ladies and gentlemen." The endless interval was over. "You will no doubt wish to be immediately relieved from suspense. I will name the persons involved. Number Thirty-seven!"

A man sprang up with a fearful, strangled cry.

"Silence!"

The wretch choked and gasped.

"I never—I swear I never—I'm innocent."

"Silence. You have failed in discretion. You will be dealt with. If you have anything to say in defence of your folly, I will hear it later. Sit down."

Number Thirty-seven sank down upon a chair. He pushed his handkerchief under the mask to wipe his face. Two tall men closed in upon him. The rest fell back, feeling the recoil of humanity from one stricken by mortal disease.

The gramophone struck up.

"Ladies and gentlemen, I will now name the traitor. Number Twenty-one, stand forward."

Rogers stepped forward. The concentrated fear and

loathing of forty-eight pairs of eyes burned upon him. The miserable Jukes set up a fresh wail.

"Oh, my God! Oh, my God!"

"Silence! Number Twenty-one, take off your mask."

The traitor pulled the thick covering from his face. The intense hatred of the eyes devoured him.

"Number Thirty-seven, this man was introduced here by you, under the name of Joseph Rogers, formerly second footman in the service of the Duke of Denver, dismissed for pilfering. Did you take steps to verify that statement?"

"I did—I did! As God's my witness, it was all straight. I had him identified by two of the servants. I made inquiries. The tale was straight—I'll swear it was."

The President consulted a paper before him, then he looked at his watch again.

"Ladies and gentlemen, please take your partners . . ."

Number Twenty-one, his arms twisted behind him and bound, and his wrists handcuffed, stood motionless, while the dance of doom circled about him. The clapping, as it ended, sounded like the clapping of the men and women who sat, thirsty-lipped, beneath the guillotine.

"Number Twenty-one, your name has been given as Joseph Rogers, footman, dismissed for theft. Is that your real name?"

"No."

"What is your name?"

"Peter Death Bredon Wimsey."

"We thought you were dead."

"Naturally. You were intended to think so."

"What has become of the genuine Joseph Rogers?"

"He died abroad. I took his place. I may say that no real blame attaches to your people for not having realized who I was. I not only took Rogers's place; I *was* Rogers. Even when I was alone, I walked like Rogers, I sat like Rogers, I read Rogers's books, and wore Rogers's clothes. In the end, I almost thought Rogers's thoughts. The only way to keep up a successful impersonation is never to relax."

"I see. The robbery of your own flat was arranged?"

"Obviously."

"The robbery of the Dowager Duchess, your mother, was connived at by you?"

"It was. It was a very ugly tiara—no real loss to anybody with decent taste. May I smoke, by the way?"

"You may not. Ladies and gentlemen . . ."

The dance was like the mechanical jigging of puppets. Limbs jerked, feet faltered. The prisoner watched with an air of critical detachment.

"Numbers Fifteen, Twenty-two, and Forty-nine. You have watched the prisoner. Has he made any attempts to communicate with anybody?"

"None." Number Twenty-two was the spokesman. "His letters and parcels have been opened, his telephone tapped, and his movements followed. His water-pipes have been under observation for Morse signals."

"You are sure of what you say?"

"Absolutely."

"Prisoner, have you been alone in this adventure? Speak the truth, or things will be made somewhat more unpleasant for you than they might otherwise be."

"I have been alone. I have taken no unnecessary risks."

"It may be so. It will, however, be as well that steps should be taken to silence the man at Scotland Yard—what is his name?—Parker. Also the prisoner's manservant, Mervyn Bunter, and possibly also his mother and sister. The brother is a stupid oaf, and not, I think, likely to have been taken into the prisoner's confidence. A precautionary watch will, I think, meet the necessities of his case."

The prisoner appeared, for the first time, to be moved.

"Sir, I assure you that my mother and sister know nothing which could possibly bring danger on the Society."

"You should have thought of their situation earlier. Ladies and gentlemen, please take—"

"No—!" Flesh and blood could endure the mockery no longer.

"No! Finish with him. Get it over. Break up the meeting. It's dangerous. The police —"

"Silence!"

The President glanced round at the crowd. It had a dangerous look about it. He gave way.

"Very well. Take the prisoner away and silence him. He will receive Number 4 treatment. And be sure you explain it to him carefully first."

"Ah!"

The eyes expressed a wolfish satisfaction. Strong hands gripped Wimsey's arms.

"One moment — for God's sake let me die decently."

"You should have thought this over earlier. Take him away. Ladies and gentlemen, be satisfied — he will not die quickly."

"Stop! Wait!" cried Wimsey desperately. "I have something to say. I don't ask for life — only for a quick death. I-I have something to sell."

"To sell?"

"Yes."

"We make no bargains with traitors."

"No — but listen! Do you think I have not thought of this? I am not so mad. I have left a letter."

"Ah! now it is coming. A letter. To whom?"

"To the police. If I do not return tomorrow —"

"Well?"

"The letter will be opened."

"Sir," broke in Number Fifteen. "This is bluff. The prisoner has not sent any letter. He has been strictly watched for many months."

"Ah! but listen. I left the letter before I came to Lambeth."

"Then it can contain no information of value."

"Oh, but it does."

"What?"

"The combination of my safe."

"Indeed? Has this man's safe been searched?"

"Yes, sir."

"What did it contain?"

"No information of importance, sir. An outline of our organization—the name of this house—nothing that cannot be altered and covered before morning."

Wimsey smiled.

"Did you investigate the inner compartment of the safe?"

There was a pause.

"You hear what he says," snapped the President sharply. "Did you find this inner compartment?"

"There was no inner compartment, sir. He is trying to bluff."

"I hate to contradict you," said Wimsey, with an effort at his ordinary pleasant tone, "but I really think you must have overlooked the inner compartment."

"Well," said the President, "and what do you say is in this inner compartment, if it does exist?"

"The names of every member of this Society, with their addresses, photographs, and finger-prints."

"What?"

The eyes round him now were ugly with fear. Wimsey kept his face steadily turned towards the President.

"How do you say you have contrived to get this information?"

"Well, I have been doing a little detective work on my own, you know."

"But you have been watched."

"True. The finger-prints of my watchers adorn the first page of the collection."

"This statement can be proved?"

"Certainly. I will prove it. The name of Number Fifty, for example—"

"Stop!"

A fierce muttering arose. The President silenced it with a gesture.

"If you mention names here, you will certainly have no hope of mercy. There is a fifth treatment—kept specially for people who mention names. Bring the prisoner to my office. Keep the dance going."

The President took an automatic from his hip-pocket and faced his tightly fettered prisoner across the desk.

"Now speak!" he said.

"I should put that thing away, if I were you," said Wimsey contemptuously. "It would be a much pleasanter form of death than treatment Number Five, and I might be tempted to ask for it."

"Ingenious," said the President, "but a little too ingenious. Now, be quick; tell me what you know."

"Will you spare me if I tell you?"

"I make no promises. Be quick."

Wimsey shrugged his bound and aching shoulders.

"Certainly. I will tell you what I know. Stop me when you have heard enough."

He leaned forward and spoke low. Overhead the noise of the gramophone and the shuffling of feet bore witness that the dance was going on. Stray passers-by crossing the Heath noted that the people in the lonely house were making a night of it again.

"Well," said Wimsey, "am I to go on?"

From beneath the mask the President's voice sounded as though he were grimly smiling.

"My lord," he said, "your story fills me with regret that you are not, in fact, a member of our Society. Wit, courage, and industry are valuable to an association like ours. I fear I cannot persuade you? No—I supposed not."

He touched a bell on his desk.

"Ask the members kindly to proceed to the supper-room," he said to the mask who entered.

The "supper-room" was on the ground-floor, shuttered and curtained. Down its centre ran a long, bare table, with chairs set about it.

"A Barmecide feast, I see," said Wimsey pleasantly. It was the first time he had seen this room. At the far end, a trap-door in the floor gaped ominously.

The President took the head of the table.

"Ladies and gentlemen," he began, as usual — and the foolish courtesy had never sounded so sinister — "I will not conceal from you the seriousness of the situation. The prisoner has recited to me more than twenty names and addresses which were thought to be unknown, except to their owners and to me. There has been great carelessness" — his voice rang harshly — "which will have to be looked into. Finger-prints have been obtained — he has shown me the photographs of some of them. How our investigators came to overlook the inner door of this safe is a matter which calls for inquiry."

"Don't blame them," put in Wimsey. "It was meant to be overlooked, you know. I made it like that on purpose."

The President went on, without seeming to notice the interruption.

"The prisoner informs me that the book with the names and addresses is to be found in this inner compartment, together with certain letters and papers stolen from the houses of members, and numerous objects bearing authentic finger-prints. I believe him to be telling the truth. He offers the combination of the safe in exchange for a quick death. I think the offer should be accepted. What is your opinion, ladies and gentlemen?"

"The combination is known already," said Number Twenty-two.

"Imbecile! This man has told us, and has proved to me, that he is Lord Peter Wimsey. Do you think he will have forgotten to alter the combination? And then there is the secret of the inner door. If he disappears tonight and the police enter his house — "

"I say," said a woman's rich voice, "that the promise should be given and the information used — and quickly. Time is getting short."

A murmur of agreement went round the table.

"You hear," said the President, addressing Wimsey. "The Society offers you the privilege of a quick death in return for the combination of the safe and the secret of the inner door."

"I have your word for it?"

"You have."

"Thank you. And my mother and sister?"

"If you in your turn will give us your word—you are a man of honour—that these women know nothing that could harm us, they shall be spared."

"Thank you, sir. You may rest assured, upon my honour, that they know nothing. I should not think of burdening any woman with such dangerous secrets—particularly those who are dear to me."

"Very well. It is agreed—yes?"

The murmur of assent was given, though with less readiness than before.

"Then I am willing to give you the information you want. The word of the combination is UNRELIABILITY."

"And the inner door?"

"In anticipation of the visit of the police, the inner door— which might have presented difficulties—is open."

"Good! You understand that if the police interfere with our messenger—"

"That would not help me, would it?"

"It is a risk," said the President thoughtfully, "but a risk which I think we must take. Carry the prisoner down to the cellar. He can amuse himself by contemplating apparatus Number Five. In the meantime, Numbers Twelve and Forty-six—"

"No, no!"

A sullen mutter of dissent arose and swelled threateningly.

"No," said a tall man with a voice like treacle. "No—why should any members be put in possession of this evidence? We have found one traitor among us tonight and more than one fool. How are we to know that Numbers Twelve and Forty-six are not fools and traitors also?"

The two men turned savagely upon the speaker, but a girl's voice struck into the discussion, high and agitated.

"Hear, hear! That's right, I say. How about us? We ain't going to have our names read by somebody we don't know nothing about. I've had enough of this. They might sell the 'ole lot of us to the narks."

"I agree," said another member. "Nobody ought to be trusted, nobody at all."

The President shrugged his shoulders.

"Then what, ladies and gentlemen, do you suggest?"

There was a pause. Then the same girl shrilled out again:

"I say Mr. President oughter go himself. He's the only one as knows all the names. It won't be no cop to him. Why should we take all the risk and trouble and him sit at home and collar the money? Let him go himself, that's what I say."

A long rustle of approbation went round the table.

"I second that motion," said a stout man who wore a bunch of gold seals at his fob. Wimsey smiled as he looked at the seals; it was that trifling vanity which had led him directly to the name and address of the stout man, and he felt a certain affection for the trinkets on that account.

The President looked round.

"It is the wish of the meeting, then, that I should go?" he said, in an ominous voice.

Forty-five hands were raised in approbation. Only the woman known as Number Two remained motionless and silent, her strong white hands clenched on the arm of the chair.

The President rolled his eyes slowly round the threatening ring till they rested upon her.

"Am I to take it that this vote is unanimous?" he enquired.

The woman raised her head.

"Don't go," she gasped faintly.

"You hear," said the President, in a faintly derisive tone. "This lady says, don't go."

"I submit that what Number Two says is neither here nor there," said the man with the treacly voice. "Our own ladies might not like us to be going, if they were in madam's privileged position." His voice was an insult.

"Hear, hear!" cried another man. "This is a democratic society, this is. We don't want no privileged classes."

"Very well," said the President. "You hear, Number Two. The feeling of the meeting is against you. Have you any reasons to put forward in favour of your opinion?"

"A hundred. The President is the head and soul of our Society. If anything should happen to him—where should we
be? You"—she swept the company magnificently with her
eyes—"you have all blundered. We have your carelessness to
thank for all this. Do you think we should be safe for five minutes if the President were not here to repair your follies?"

"Something in that," said a man who had not hitherto
spoken.

"Pardon my suggesting," said Wimsey maliciously, "that,
as the lady appears to be in a position peculiarly favourable for
the reception of the President's confidences, the contents of
my modest volume will probably be no news to her. Why
should not Number Two go herself?"

"Because I say she must not," said the President sternly,
checking the quick reply that rose to his companion's lips. "If
it is the will of the meeting, I will go. Give me the key of the
house."

One of the men extracted it from Wimsey's jacket-pocket
and handed it over.

"Is the house watched?" he demanded of Wimsey.

"No."

"That is the truth?"

"It is the truth."

The President turned at the door.

"If I have not returned in two hours' time," he said, "act
for the best to save yourselves, and do what you like with the
prisoner. Number Two will give orders in my absence."

He left the room. Number Two rose from her seat with a
gesture of command.

"Ladies and gentlemen. Supper is now considered over.
Start the dancing again."

Down in the cellar the time passed slowly, in the contemplation of apparatus Number Five. The miserable Jukes, alternately wailing and raving, at length shrieked himself into
exhaustion. The four members guarding the prisoners whispered together from time to time.

"An hour and a half since the President left," said one.

Wimsey glanced up. Then he returned to his examination of the room. There were many curious things in it, which he wanted to memorize.

Presently the trap-door was flung open. "Bring him up!" cried a voice. Wimsey rose immediately, and his face was rather pale.

The members of the gang were again seated round the table. Number Two occupied the President's chair, and her eyes fastened on Wimsey's face with a tigerish fury, but when she spoke it was with a self-control which roused his admiration.

"The President has been two hours gone," she said. "What has happened to him? Traitor twice over—what has happened to him?"

"How should I know?" said Wimsey. "Perhaps he has looked after Number One and gone while the going was good!"

She sprang up with a little cry of rage, and came close to him.

"Beast! liar!" she said, and struck him on the mouth. "You know he would never do that. He is faithful to his friends. What have you done with him? Speak—or I will make you speak. You two, there—bring the irons. He *shall* speak!"

"I can only form a guess, madame," replied Wimsey, "and I shall not guess any the better for being stimulated with hot irons, like Pantaloon at the circus. Calm yourself, and I will tell you what I think. I think—indeed, I greatly fear—that Monsieur le Président in his hurry to examine the interesting exhibits in my safe may, quite inadvertently, no doubt, have let the door of the inner compartment close behind him. In which case—"

He raised his eyebrows, his shoulders being too sore for shrugging, and gazed at her with a limpid and innocent regret.

"What do you mean?"

Wimsey glanced round the circle.

"I think," he said, "I had better begin from the beginning

by explaining to you the mechanism of my safe. It is rather a nice safe," he added plaintively. "I invented the idea myself—not the principle of its working, of course; that is a matter for scientists—but just the idea of the thing.

"The combination I gave you is perfectly correct as far as it goes. It is a three-alphabet thirteen-letter lock by Bunn & Fishett—a very good one of its kind. It opens the outer door, leading into the ordinary strong-room, where I keep my cash and my Froth Blower's cuff-links and all that. But there is an inner compartment with two doors, which open in quite a different manner. The outermost of these two inner doors is merely a thin steel skin, painted to look like the back of the safe and fitting closely, so as not to betray any join. It lies in the same plane as the wall of the room, you understand, so that if you were to measure the outside and the inside of the safe you would discover no discrepancy. It opens outwards with an ordinary key, and, as I truly assured the President, it was left open when I quitted my flat."

"Do you think," said the woman sneeringly, "that the President is so simple as to be caught in a so obvious trap? He will have wedged open that inner door, undoubtedly."

"Undoubtedly, madame. But the sole purpose of that outer inner door, if I may so express myself, is to appear to be the only inner door. But hidden behind the hinge of that door is another door, a sliding panel, set so closely in the thickness of the wall that you would hardly see it unless you knew it was there. This door was also left open. Our revered Number One had nothing to do but to walk straight through into the inner compartment of the safe, which, by the way, is built into the chimney of the old basement kitchen, which runs up the house at that point. I hope I make myself clear?"

"Yes, yes—get on. Make your story short."

Wimsey bowed, and, speaking with even greater deliberation than ever, resumed:

"Now, this interesting list of the Society's activities, which I have had the honour of compiling, is written in a very large book—bigger, even, than Monsieur le Président's

ledger which he uses downstairs. (I trust, by the way, madame, that you have borne in mind the necessity of putting
that ledger in a safe place. Apart from the risk of investigation by some officious policeman, it would be inadvisable
that any junior member of the Society should get hold of it.
The feeling of the meeting would, I fancy, be opposed to such
an occurrence.)"

"It is secure," she answered hastily. "*Mon dieu!* get on with
you story."

"Thank you—you have relieved my mind. Very good. This
big book lies on a steel shelf at the back of the inner compartment. Just a moment. I have not described this inner compartment to you. It is six feet high, three feet wide, and three
feet deep. One can stand up in it quite comfortably, unless one
is very tall. It suits me nicely—as you may see, I am not more
than five feet eight and a half. The President has the advantage of me in height; he might be a little cramped, but there
would be room for him to squat if he grew tired of standing.
By the way, I don't know if you know it, but you have tied me
up rather tightly."

"I would have you tied till your bones were locked together. Beat him, you! He is trying to gain time."

"If you beat me," said Wimsey, "I'm damned if I'll speak at
all. Control yourself, madame; it does not do to move hastily
when your king is in check."

"Get on!" she cried again, stamping with rage.

"Where was I? Ah! The inner compartment. As I say, it is
a little snug—the more so that it is not ventilated in any way.
Did I mention that the book lay on a steel shelf?"

"You did."

"Yes. The steel shelf is balanced on a very delicate concealed spring. When the weight of the book—a heavy one, as
I said—is lifted, the shelf rises almost imperceptibly. In rising
it makes an electrical contact. Imagine to yourself madame;
our revered President steps in—propping the false door open
behind him—he sees the book—quickly he snatches it up. To
make sure that it is the right one, he opens it—he studies the

pages. He looks about for the other objects I have mentioned, which bear the marks of fingerprints. And silently, but very, very quickly—you can imagine it, can you not?—the secret panel, released by the rising of the shelf, leaps across like a panther behind him. Rather a trite simile, but apt, don't you think?"

"My God! oh, my God!" Her hand went up as though to tear the choking mask from her face. "You—you devil—devil! What is the word that opens the inner door? Quick! I will have it torn out of you—the word!"

"It is not a hard word to remember, madame—though it has been forgotten before now. Do you recollect, when you were a child, being told the tale of 'Ali Baba and the Forty Thieves?' When I had that door made, my mind reverted, with rather a pretty touch of sentimentality, in my opinion, to the happy hours of my childhood. The words that open the door are—'Open Sesame.' "

"Ah! How long can a man live in this devil's trap of yours?"

"Oh," said Wimsey cheerfully, "I should think he might hold out a few hours if he kept cool and didn't use up the available oxygen by shouting and hammering. If we went there at once, I dare say we should find him fairly all right."

"I shall go myself. Take this man and—do your worst with him. Don't finish him till I come back. I want to see him die!"

"One moment," said Wimsey, unmoved by this amiable wish. "I think you had better take me with you."

"Why—why?"

"Because, you see, I'm the only person who can open the door."

"But you have given me the word. Was that a lie?"

"No—the word's all right. But, you see, it's one of these new-style electric doors. In fact, it's really the very latest thing in doors. I'm rather proud of it. It opens to the words 'Open Sesame' all right—*but to my voice only.*"

"Your voice? I will choke your voice with my own hands. What do you mean—your voice only?"

"Just what I say. Don't clutch my throat like that, or you

may alter my voice so that the door won't recognize it. That's better. It's apt to be rather pernickety about voices. It got stuck up for a week once, when I had a cold and could only implore it in a hoarse whisper. Even in the ordinary way, I sometimes have to try several times before I hit on the exact right intonation."

She turned and appealed to a short, thick-set man standing beside her.

"Is this true? Is it possible?"

"Perfectly, ma'am, I'm afraid," said the man civilly. From his voice Wimsey took him to be a superior workman of some kind—probably an engineer.

"Is it an electrical device? Do you understand it?"

"Yes, ma'am. It will have a microphone arrangement somewhere which converts the sound into a series of vibrations controlling an electric needle. When the needle has traced the correct pattern, the circuit is completed and the door opens. The same thing can be done by light vibrations equally easily."

"Couldn't you open it with tools?"

"In time, yes, ma'am. But only by smashing the mechanism, which is probably well protected."

"You may take that for granted," interjected Wimsey reassuringly.

She put her hands to her head.

"I'm afraid we're done in," said the engineer, with a kind of respect in his tone for a good job of work.

"No—wait! Somebody must know—the workmen who made this thing?"

"In Germany," said Wimsey briefly.

"Or—yes, yes, I have it—a gramophone. This—this—*he*—shall be made to say the word for us. Quick—how can it be done?"

"Not possible, ma'am. Where would we get the apparatus at half past three on a Sunday morning? The poor gentleman would be dead long before—"

There was a silence, during which the sounds of the wakening day came through the shuttered windows. A motor-horn sounded distantly.

"I give in," she said. "We must let him go. Take the ropes off him. You will free him, won't you?" she went on, turning piteously to Wimsey. "Devil as you are, you are not such a devil as that! You will go straight back and save him!"

"Let him go, nothing!" broke in one of the men. "He doesn't go to peach to the police, my lady, don't you think it. The President's done in, that's all, and we'd all better make tracks while we can. It's all up, boys. Chuck this fellow down the cellar and fasten him in, so he can't make a row and wake the place up. I'm going to destroy the ledgers. You can see it done if you don't trust me. And you, Thirty, you know where the switch is. Give us a quarter of an hour to clear, and then you can blow the place to glory."

"No! You can't go—you can't leave him to die—your President—your leader—my—I won't let it happen. Set this devil free. Help me, one of you, with the ropes—"

"None of that, now," said the man who had spoken before. He caught her by the wrists, and she twisted, shrieking, in his arms, biting and struggling to get free.

"Think, think," said the man with the treacly voice. "It's getting on to morning. It'll be light in an hour or two. The police may be here any minute."

"The police!" She seemed to control herself by a violent effort. "Yes, yes, you are right. We must not imperil the safety of all for the sake of one man. *He* himself would not wish it. That is so. We will put this carrion in the cellar where it cannot harm us, and depart, every one to his own place, while there is time."

"And the other prisoner?"

"He? Poor fool—he can do no harm. He knows nothing. Let him go," she answered contemptuously.

In a few minutes' time Wimsey found himself bundled unceremoniously into the depths of the cellar. He was a little puzzled. That they should refuse to let him go, even at the price of Number One's life, he could understand. He had

taken the risk with his eyes open. But that they should leave
him as a witness against them seemed incredible.

The men who had taken him down strapped his ankles together and departed, switching the lights out as they went.

"Hi! Kamerad!" said Wimsey. "It's a bit lonely sitting
here. You might leave the light on."

"It's all right, my friend," was the reply. "You will not be
in the dark long. They have set the time-fuse."

The other man laughed with rich enjoyment, and they went
out together. So that was it. He was to be blown up with the
house. In that case the President would certainly be dead before
he was extricated. This worried Wimsey; he would rather have
been able to bring the big crook to justice. After all, Scotland
Yard had been waiting six years to break up this gang.

He waited, straining his ears. It seemed to him that he
heard footsteps over his head. The gang had all crept out by
this time. . . .

There was certainly a creak. The trap-door had opened;
he felt, rather than heard, somebody creeping into the cellar.

"Hush!" said a voice in his ear. Soft hands passed over his
face, and went fumbling about his body. There came the cold
touch of steel on his wrists. The ropes slackened and dropped
off. A key clicked in the handcuffs. The strap about his ankles
was unbuckled.

"Quick! Quick! they have set the time-switch. The house
is mined. Follow me as fast as you can. I stole back—I said I
had left my jewellery. It was true. I left it on purpose. *He* must
be saved—only you can do it. Make haste!"

Wimsey, staggering with pain, as the blood rushed back
into his bound and numbed arms, crawled after her into the
room above. A moment, and she had flung back the shutters
and thrown the window open.

"Now go! Release him! You promise?"

"I promise. And I warn you, madame, that this house is
surrounded. When my safe-door closed it gave a signal which
sent my servant to Scotland Yard. Your friends are all
taken—"

"'Ah! But you go—never mind me—quick! The time is almost up."

"Come away from this!"

He caught her by the arm, and they went running and stumbling across the little garden. An electric torch shone suddenly in the bushes.

"That you, Parker?" cried Wimsey. "Get your fellows away. Quick! the house is going up in a minute."

The garden seemed suddenly full of shouting, hurrying men. Wimsey, floundering in the darkness, was brought up violently against the wall. He made a leap at the coping, caught it, and hoisted himself up. His hands groped for the woman; he swung her up beside him. They jumped; everyone was jumping; the woman caught her foot and fell with a gasping cry. Wimsey tried to stop himself, tripped over a stone, and came down headlong. Then, with a flash and a roar, the night went up in fire.

Wimsey picked himself painfully out from among the débris of the garden wall. A faint moaning near him proclaimed that his companion was still alive. A lantern was turned suddenly upon them.

"Here you are!" said a cheerful voice. "Are you all right, old thing? Good lord! what a hairy monster!"

"All right," said Wimsey. "Only a bit winded. Is the lady safe? H'm—arm broken, apparently—otherwise sound. What's happened?"

"About half a dozen of 'em got blown up; the rest we've bagged." Wimsey became aware of a circle of dark forms in the wintry dawn. "Good Lord, what a day! What a come-back for a public character! You old stinker—to let us go on for two years thinking you were dead! I bought a bit of black for an arm-band. I did, really. Did anybody know, besides Bunter?"

"Only my mother and sister. I put it in a secret trust—you know, the thing you send to executors and people. We shall have an awful time with the lawyers, I'm afraid, proving I'm me. Hullo! Is that friend Sugg?"

"Yes, my lord," said Inspector Sugg, grinning and nearly weeping with excitement. "Damned glad to see your lordship again. Fine piece of work, your lordship. They're all wanting to shake hands with you, sir."

"Oh, Lord! I wish I could get washed and shaved first. Awfully glad to see you all again, after two years' exile in Lambeth. Been a good little show, hasn't it?"

"Is he safe?"

Wimsey started at the agonized cry.

"Good Lord!" he cried. "I forgot the gentleman in the safe. Here, fetch a car, quickly. I've got the great big top Moriarty of the whole bunch quietly asphyxiating at home. Here—hop in, and put the lady in too. I promised we'd get back and save him—though" (he finished the sentence in Parker's ear) "there may be murder charges too, and I wouldn't give much for his chance at the Old Bailey. Whack her up. He can't last much longer shut up there. He's the bloke you've been wanting, the man at the back of the Morrison case and the Hope-Wilmington case, and hundreds of others."

The cold morning had turned the streets grey when they drew up before the door of the house in Lambeth. Wimsey took the woman by the arm and helped her out. The mask was off now, and showed her face, haggard and desperate, and white with fear and pain.

"Russian, eh?" whispered Parker in Wimsey's ear.

"Something of the sort. Damn! the front door's blown shut, and the blighter's got the key with him in the safe. Hop through the window, will you?"

Parker bundled obligingly in, and in a few seconds threw open the door to them. The house seemed very still. Wimsey led the way to the back room, where the strong-room stood. The outer door and the second door stood propped open with chairs. The inner door faced them like a blank green wall.

"Only hope he hasn't upset the adjustment with thumping at it," muttered Wimsey. The anxious hand on his arm clutched feverishly. He pulled himself together, forcing his tone to one of cheerful commonplace.

"Come on, old thing," he said, addressing himself conversationally to the door. "Show us your paces. Open Sesame, confound you. Open Sesame!"

The green door slid suddenly away into the wall. The woman sprang forward and caught in her arms the humped and senseless thing that rolled out from the safe. Its clothes were torn to ribbons and its battered hands dripped blood.

"It's all right," said Wimsey, "it's all right! He'll live—to stand his trial."

The Solution
of the Crossword Puzzle in
"Uncle Meleager's Will"

Notes to the Solution

I.1　　VIRGO: The sign of the zodiac between LEO (strength) and LIBRA (justice). Allusion to parable of The Ten Virgins.

I.3　　R.S.: Royal Society, whose "Fellows" are addicted to studies usually considered dry-as-dust.

IV.3　　TESTAMENT (or will); search is to be directed to the Old Testament. Ref. to parable of New Cloth and Old Garment.

XIV.3　HI:　　He would answer to Hi!
　　　　　　Or to any loud cry.
　　　　　　　　　　　　The Hunting of the Snark

I.5　　TRANS: Abbreviation of Translation; ref. to building of Babel.

XI.5　　SCENT: Even the scent of roses
　　　　　　Is not what they supposes,
　　　　　　But more than mind discloses
　　　　　　And more than men believe.
　　　　　　G. K. Chesterton: *The Song of Quoodle*

VI.7　　ICTUS: Blow; add v (five) and you get VICTUS (vanquished); the ictus is the stress in a foot of verse; if the stress be misplaced the line goes lamely.

I.8　　SPINOZA: He wrote on the properties of optical glasses; also on metaphysics.

IV.13　THIRTY-ONE: Seven (months) out of the twelve of the sun's course through the heavens have thirty-one days.

XIV.13 ET: Conjunction. In astrology an aspect of the heavenly bodies. That Cicero was the master of this word indicates that it is a Latin one.

X.14.　BEZOAR: The bezoar stone was supposed to be a prophylactic against poison.

11.I　　PLAUD: If you would laud, then plaud (var. of applaud); Plaud-it also means "cheer."

10.II   ALIENA: *As You Like It,* II, 1, 130.

1.III   R.D.: "Refer to Drawer."

4.III   CANTICLES: The *Magnificent* and *Nunc Dimittis* are known as the Canticles, but the Book of Canticles (the Vulgate name for the Song of Songs, in which the solution is found) occurs earlier in the Bible.

2.VI   EST: ὁν και μη ὁν = *est* and *non est* — the problem of being and not-being. Ref. Marlowe: *Doctor Faustus* I, 1.

12.X   TOB: Add IT to get Tobit; the tale of Tobit and the Fish is in the Apocrypha (the book of hidden things).

1.XI   MANES: *"Un lion est une mâchoire et non pas une crinière:"* Émile Faguet: *Lit. du XVIIe siècle.* Manes: benevolent spirits of the dead.

1.XV   SAINT: Evidence of miraculous power is required for canonization.

THE IMAGE IN THE MIRROR

The little man with the cow-lick seemed so absorbed in the book that Wimsey had not the heart to claim his property, but, drawing up the other arm-chair and placing his drink within easy reach, did his best to entertain himself with the Dunlop Book, which graced, as usual, one of the tables in the lounge.

The little man read on, his elbows squared upon the arms of his chair, his ruffled red head bent anxiously over the text. He breathed heavily, and when he came to the turn of the page, he set the thick volume down on his knee and used both hands for his task. Not what is called "a great reader," Wimsey decided.

When he reached the end of the story, he turned laboriously back, and read one passage over again with attention. Then he laid the book, still open, upon the table, and in so doing caught Wimsey's eye.

"I beg your pardon, sir," he said in his rather thin Cockney voice, "is this your book?"

"It doesn't matter at all," said Wimsey graciously, "I know it by heart. I only brought it along with me because it's handy for reading a few pages when you're stuck in a place like this for the night. You can always take it up and find something entertaining."

"This chap Wells," pursued the red-haired man, "he's what you'd call a very clever writer, isn't he? It's wonderful how he makes it all so real, and yet some of the things he says, you wouldn't hardly think they could be really possible. Take this story now; would you say, sir, a thing like that could actually happen to a person, as it might be you—or me?"

Wimsey twisted his head round so as to get a view of the page.

"*The Plattner Experiment,*" he said, "that's the one about the schoolmaster who was blown into the fourth dimension and came back with his right and left sides reversed. Well, no, I don't suppose such a thing would really occur in real life, though of course it's very fascinating to play with the idea of a fourth dimension."

"Well—" He paused and looked up shyly at Wimsey. "I don't rightly understand about this fourth dimension. I didn't know there was such a place, but he makes it all very clear no doubt to them that know science. But this right-and-left business, now, I know that's a fact. By experience, if you'll believe me."

Wimsey extended his cigarette-case. The little man made an instinctive motion towards it with his left hand and then seemed to check himself and stretched his right across.

"There, you see. I'm always left-handed when I don't think about it. Same as this Plattner. I fight against it, but it doesn't seem any use. But I wouldn't mind that—it's a small thing and plenty of people are left-handed and think nothing of it. No. It's the dretful anxiety of not knowing what I mayn't be doing when I'm in this fourth dimension or whatever it is."

He sighed deeply.

"I'm worried, that's what I am, worried to death."

"Suppose you tell me about it," said Wimsey.

"I don't like telling people about it, because they might

think I had a slate loose. But it's fairly getting on my nerves. Every morning when I wake up I wonder what I've been doing in the night and whether it's the day of the month it ought to be. I can't get any peace till I see the morning paper, and even then I can't be sure. . . .

"Well, I'll tell you, if you won't take it as a bore or a liberty. It all began — " He broke off and glanced nervously about the room. "There's nobody to see. If you wouldn't mind, sir, putting your hand just here a minute — "

He unbuttoned his rather regrettable double-breasted waist-coat, and laid a hand on the part of his anatomy usually considered to indicate the site of the heart.

"By all means," said Wimsey, doing as he was requested.

"Do you feel anything?"

"I don't know that I do," said Wimsey. "What ought I to feel? A swelling or anything? If you mean your pulse, the wrist is a better place."

"Oh, you can feel it *there*, all right," said the little man. "Just try the other side of the chest, sir."

Wimsey obediently moved his hand across.

"I seem to detect a little flutter," he said after a pause.

"You do? Well, you wouldn't expect to find it that side and not the other, would you? Well, that's where it is. I've got my heart on the right side, that's what I wanted you to feel for yourself."

"Did it get displaced in an illness?" asked Wimsey sympathetically.

"In a manner of speaking. But that's not all. My liver's got round the wrong side, too, and my organs. I've had a doctor see it, and he told me I was all reversed. I've got my appendix on my left side — that is, I had till they took it away. If we was private, now, I could show you the scar. It was a great surprise to the surgeon when they told him about me. He said afterwards it made it quite awkward for him, coming left-handed to the operation, as you might say."

"It's unusual, certainly," said Wimsey, "but I believe such cases do occur sometimes."

"Not the way it occurred to me. It happened in an air-raid."

"In an air-raid?" said Wimsey, aghast.

"Yes—and if that was all it had done to me I'd put up with it and be thankful. Eighteen I was then, and I'd just been called up. Previous to that I'd been working in the packing department at Crichton's—you've heard of them, I expect—Crichton's for Admirable Advertising, with offices in Holborn. My mother was living in Brixton, and I'd come up to town on leave from the training-camp. I'd been seeing one or two of my old pals, and I thought I'd finish the evening by going to see a film at the Stoll. It was after supper—I had just time to get in to the last house, so I cut across from Leicester Square through Covent Garden Market. Well, I was getting along when wallop! A bomb came down it seemed to me right under my feet, and everything went black for a bit."

"That was the raid that blew up Oldham's, I suppose."

"Yes, it was January 28th, 1918. Well, as I say, everything went right out. Next thing as I knew, I was walking in some place in broad daylight, with green grass all round me, and trees, and water to the side of me, and knowing no more about how I got there than the man in the moon."

"Good Lord!" said Wimsey. "And was it the fourth dimension, do you think?"

"Well, no, it wasn't. It was Hyde Park, as I come to see when I had my wits about me. I was along the bank of the Serpentine and there was a seat with some women sitting on it, and children playing about."

"Had the explosion damaged you?"

"Nothing to see or feel, except that I had a big bruise on one hip and shoulder as if I'd been chucked up against something. I was fairly staggered. The air-raid had gone right out of my mind, don't you see, and I couldn't imagine how I came there, and why I wasn't at Crichton's. I looked at my watch, but that had stopped. I was feeling hungry. I felt in my pocket and found some money there, but it wasn't as much as I should have had—not by a long way. But I felt I must have a bit of something, so I got out of the Park by the Marble Arch gate, and went into a Lyons. I ordered two poached on toast and a pot of tea, and while I was waiting I took up a paper that somebody had left on the seat. Well, that finished me. The last thing I remembered was starting off to see that film on the 28th — and here was the date on the paper — January 30th! I'd lost a whole day and two nights somewhere!"

"Shock," suggested Wimsey. The little man took the suggestion and put his own meaning on it.

"Shock? I should think it was. I was scared out of my life. The girl who brought my eggs must have thought I was barmy. I asked her what day of the week it was, and she said 'Friday.' There wasn't any mistake.

"Well, I don't want to make this bit too long, because that's not the end by a long chalk. I got my meal down somehow, and went to see a doctor. He asked me what I remembered doing last, and I told him about the film, and he asked whether I was out in the air-raid. Well, then it came back to me, and I remembered the bomb falling, but nothing more. He said I'd had a nervous shock and lost my memory a bit, and that it often happened and I wasn't to worry. And then he said he'd look me over to see if I'd got hurt at all. So he started in with his stethoscope, and all of a sudden he said to me:

" 'Why, you keep your heart on the wrong side, my lad!'

" 'Do I?" said I. 'That's the first I've heard of it.'

"Well, he looked me over pretty thoroughly, and then he told me what I've told you, that I was all reversed inside, and he asked a lot of questions about my family. I told him I was an only child and my father was dead — killed by a motor-lorry, he was, when I was a kid of ten — and I lived with my mother in Brixton and all that. And he said I was an unusual case, but there was nothing to worry about. Bar being wrong side round I was sound as a bell, and he told me to go home and take things quietly for a day or two.

"Well, I did, and I felt all right, and I thought that was the end of it, though I'd overstayed my leave and had a bit of a job explaining myself to the R.T.O. It wasn't till several months afterwards the draft was called up, and I went along for my farewell leave. I was having a cup of coffee in the Mirror Hall at the Strand Corner House—you know it, down the steps?"

Wimsey nodded.

"All the big looking-glasses all round. I happened to look into the one near me, and I saw a young lady smiling at me as if she knew me. I saw her reflection, that is, if you understand me. Well, I couldn't make it out, for I had never seen her before, and I didn't take any notice, thinking she'd mistook me for somebody else. Besides, though I wasn't so very old then, I thought I knew her sort, and my mother had always brought me up strict. I looked away and went on with my coffee, and all of a sudden a voice said quite close to me:

" 'Hullo, Ginger—aren't you going to say good evening?'

"I looked up and there she was. Pretty, too, if she hadn't been painted up so much.

" 'I'm afraid,' I said, rather stiff, 'you have the advantage of me, miss.'

" 'Oh, Ginger,' says she, 'Mr. Duckworthy, and after Wednesday night!' A kind of mocking way she had of speaking.

"I hadn't thought so much of her calling me Ginger, because that's what any girl would say to a fellow with my sort of hair, but when she got my name off so pat, I tell you it did give me a turn.

" 'You seem to think we're acquainted, miss,' said I.

" 'Well, I should rather say so, shouldn't you?' said she.

"There! I needn't go into it all. From what she said I found out she thought she'd met me one night and taken me home with her. And what frightened me most of all, she said it had happened on the night of the big raid.

" 'It *was* you,' she said, staring into my face a little puzzled-like. 'Of course it was you. I knew you in a minute when I saw your face in the glass.'

"Of course, I couldn't say that it hadn't been. I knew no more of what I'd been and done that night than the babe unborn. But it upset me cruelly, because I was an innocent sort of lad in those days and hadn't ever gone with girls, and it seemed to me if I'd done a thing like that I ought know about it. It seemed to me I'd been doing wrong and not getting full value for my money either.

"I made some excuse to get rid of her, and I wondered what else I'd been doing. She couldn't tell me farther than the morning of the 29th, and it worried me a bit wondering if I'd done any other queer things."

"It must have," said Wimsey, and put his finger on the bell. When the waiter arrived, he ordered drinks for two and disposed himself to listen to the rest of Mr. Duckworthy's adventures.

"I didn't think much about it, though," went on the little man; "we went abroad, and I saw my first corpse and dodged my first shell and had my first dose of the trenches, and I hadn't much time for what they call introspection.

"The next queer thing that happened was in the C.C.S. at Ypres. I'd got a blighty one near Caudry in September during the advance from Cambrai—half buried, I was, in a mine explosion and laid out unconscious near twenty-four hours it must have been. When I came to, I was wandering about somewhere behind the lines with a nasty hole in my shoulder. Somebody had bandaged it up for me, but I hadn't any recollection of that. I walked a long way, not knowing where I was, till at last I fetched up in an aid-post. They fixed me up and sent me down the line to a base hospital. I was pretty feverish, and the next thing I knew, I was in bed, with a nurse looking after me. The bloke in the next bed to mine was asleep. I got talking to a chap in the next bed beyond him, and he told me where I was, when all of a sudden the other man woke up and says:

"'My God,' he says, 'you dirty ginger-haired swine, it's you, is it? What have you done with them vallables?'

"I tell you, I was struck all of a heap. Never seen the man in my life. But he went on at me and made such a row, the nurse came running in to see what was up. All the men were sitting up in bed listening—you never saw anything like it.

"The upshot was, as soon as I could understand what this

fellow was driving at, that he'd been sharing a shell-hole with a chap that he said was me, and that this chap and he had talked together a bit and then, when he was weak and helpless, the chap had looted his money and watch and revolver and what not and gone off with them. A nasty, dirty trick, and I couldn't blame him for making a row about it, if true. But I said and stood to it, it wasn't me, but some other fellow of the same name. He said he recognized me — said he and this other chap had been together a whole day, and he knew every feature in his face and couldn't be mistaken. However, it seemed this bloke had said he belonged to the Blankshires, and I was able to show my papers and prove I belonged to the Buffs, and eventually the bloke apologized and said he must have made a mistake. He died, anyhow, a few days after, and we all agreed he must have been wandering a bit. The two divisions were fighting side by side in that dust-up and it was possible for them to get mixed up. I tried afterwards to find out whether by any chance I had a double in the Blankshires, but they sent me back home, and before I was fit again the Armistice was signed, and I didn't take any more trouble.

"I went back to my old job after the war, and things seemed to settle down a bit. I got engaged when I was twenty-one to a regular good girl, and I thought everything in the garden was lovely. And then, one day — up it all went! My mother was dead then, and I was living by myself in lodgings. Well, one day I got a letter from my intended, saying that she had seen me down at Southend on the Sunday, and that was enough for her. All was over between us.

'Now, it was unfortunate that I'd had to put off seeing her that week-end, owing to an attack of influenza. It's a cruel thing to be ill all alone in lodgings, and nobody to look after you. You might die there all on your own and nobody the wiser. Just an unfurnished room I had, you see, and no attendance, and not a soul came near me, though I was pretty bad. But my young lady she said as she had seen me down at Southend with another young woman, and she would take no excuse. Of course, I said, what was *she* doing down at

Southend without me, anyhow, and that tore it. She sent me
back the ring, and the episode, as they say, was closed.

"But the thing that troubled me was, I was getting that
shaky in my mind, how did I know I hadn't been to Southend
without knowing it? I thought I'd been half sick and half
asleep in my lodgings, but it was misty-like to me. And knowing the things I had done other times—well, there! I hadn't
any clear recollection one way or another, except fever-
dreams. I had a vague recollection of wandering and walking
somewhere for hours together. Delirious, I thought I was, but
it might have been sleep-walking for all I knew. I hadn't a leg
to stand on by way of evidence. I felt it very hard, losing my
intended like that, but I could have got over that if it hadn't
been for the fear of myself and my brain giving way or something.

"You may think this is all foolishness and I was just being
mixed up with some other fellow of the same name that happened to be very like me. But now I'll tell you something.

"Terrible dreams I got to having about that time. There
was one thing as always haunted me—a thing that had frightened me as a little chap. My mother, though she was a good,
strict woman, liked to go to a cinema now and again. Of
course, in those days they weren't like what they are now, and
I expect we should think those old pictures pretty crude if we
was to see them, but we thought a lot of them at that time.
When I was about seven or eight I should think, she took me
with her to see a thing—I remember the name now—*The Student of Prague*, it was called. I've forgotten the story, but it was
a costume piece, about a young fellow at the university who
sold himself to the devil, and one day his reflection came stalk-
ing out of the mirror on its own, and went about committing
dreadful crimes, so that everybody thought it was him. At
least, I think it was that, but I forget the details, it's so long
ago. But what I shan't forget in a hurry is the fright it gave me
to see that dretful figure come out of the mirror. It was that
ghastly to see it, I cried and yelled, and after a time mother
had to take me out. For months and years after that I used to

dream of it. I'd dream I was looking in a great long glass, same as the student in the picture, and after a bit I'd see my reflection smiling at me and I'd walk up to the mirror holding out my left hand, it might be, and seeing myself walking to meet me with its right hand out. And just as it came up to me, it would suddenly—that was the awful moment—turn its back on me and walk away into the mirror again, grinning over its shoulder, and suddenly I'd know that *it* was the real person and *I* was only the reflection, and I'd make a dash after it into the mirror, and then everything would go grey and misty round me and with the horror of it I'd wake up all of a perspiration."

"Uncommonly disagreeable," said Wimsey. "That legend of the *Doppelgänger,* it's one of the oldest and the most widespread and never fails to terrify me. When *I* was a kid, my nurse had a trick that frightened me. If we'd been out, and she was asked if we'd met anybody, she used to say, 'Oh, no—we saw nobody nicer than ourselves.' I used to toddle after her in terror of coming round a corner and seeing a horrid and similar pair pouncing out at us. Of course I'd have rather died than tell a soul how the thing terrified me. Rum little beasts, kids."

The little man nodded thoughtfully.

"Well," he went on, "about that time the nightmare came back. At first it was only at intervals, you know, but it grew on me. At last it started coming every night. I hadn't hardly closed my eyes before there was the long mirror and the thing coming grinning along, always with its hand out as if it meant to catch hold of me and pull me through the glass. Sometimes I'd wake up with the shock, but sometimes the dream went on, and I'd be stumbling for hours through a queer sort of world—all mist and half-lights, and the walls would be all crooked like they are in that picture of *Dr. Caligari.* Lunatic, that's what it was. Many's the time I've sat up all night for fear of going to sleep. I didn't know, you see. I used to lock the bedroom door and hide the key for fear—you see, I didn't know what I might be doing. But then I read in a book that sleep-walkers can remember the places where they've hidden things when they were awake. So that was no use."

"Why didn't you get someone to share the room with you?"

"Well, I did." He hesitated. "I got a woman—she was a good kid. The dream went away then. I had blessed peace for three years. I was fond of that girl. Damned fond of her. Then she died."

He gulped down the last of his whisky and blinked.

"Influenza, it was. Pneumonia. It kind of broke me up. Pretty she was, too. . . .

"After that, I was alone again. I felt bad about it. I couldn't—I didn't like—but the dreams came back. Worse. I dreamed about doing things—well! That doesn't matter now.

"And one day it came in broad daylight . . .

"I was going along Holborn at lunch-time. I was still at Crichton's. Head of the packing department I was then, and doing pretty well. It was a wet beast of a day, I remember—dark and drizzling. I wanted a hair-cut. There's a barber's shop on the south side, about half-way along—one of those places where you go down a passage and there's a door at the end with a mirror and the name written across it in gold letters. You know what I mean.

"I went in there. There was a light in the passage, so I could see quite plainly. As I got up to the mirror I could see my reflection coming to meet me, and all of a sudden the awful dream-feeling came over me. I told myself it was all nonsense and put my hand out to the doorhandle—my left hand, because the handle was that side and I was still apt to be left-handed when I didn't think about it.

"The reflection, of course, put out its right hand—that was all right, of course—and I saw my own figure in my old squash hat and Burberry—but the face—oh, my God! It was grinning at me—and then just like in the dream, it suddenly turned its back and walked away from me, looking over its shoulder—

"I had my hand on the door, and it opened, and I felt myself stumbling and falling over the threshold.

"After that, I don't remember anything more. I woke up in my own bed and there was a doctor with me. He told me I had fainted in the street, and they'd found some letters on me with my address and taken me home.

"I told the doctor all about it, and he said I was in a highly nervous condition and ought to find a change of work and get out in the open air more.

"They were very decent to me at Crichton's. They put me on to inspecting their outdoor publicity. You know. One goes round from town to town inspecting the hoardings and seeing what posters are damaged or badly placed and reporting on them. They gave me a Morgan to run about in. I'm on that job now.

"The dreams are better. But I still have them. Only a few nights ago it came to me. One of the worst I've ever had. Fighting and strangling in a black, misty place. I'd tracked the devil—my other self—and got him down. I can feel my fingers on his throat now—killing myself.

"That was in London. I'm always worse in London. Then I came up here . . .

"You see why that book interested me. The fourth dimension . . . it's not a thing I ever heard of, but this man Wells seems to know all about it. You're educated now. Daresay you've been to college and all that. What do you think about it, eh?"

"I should think, you know," said Wimsey, "it was more likely your doctor was right. Nerves and all that."

"Yes, but that doesn't account for me having got twisted round the way I am, now, does it? Legends, you talked of. Well, there's some people think those medeeval johnnies knew quite a lot. I don't say I believe in devils and all that. But maybe some of them may have been afflicted, same as me. It stands to reason they wouldn't talk such a lot about it if they hadn't felt it, if you see what I mean. But what I'd like to know is, can't I get back any way? I tell you, it's a weight on my mind. I never know, you see."

"I shouldn't worry too much, if I were you," said Wimsey. "I'd stick to the fresh-air life. And I'd get married. Then you'd have a check on your movements, don't you see. And the dreams might go again."

"Yes. Yes. I've thought of that. But—did you read about that man the other day? Strangled his wife in his sleep, that's what he did. Now, supposing I—that would be a terrible thing to happen to a man, wouldn't it? Those dreams. . . ."

He shook his head and stared thoughtfully into the fire. Wimsey, after a short interval of silence, got up and went out into the bar. The landlady and the waiter and the barmaid were there, their heads close together over the evening paper. They were talking animatedly, but stopped abruptly at the sound of Wimsey's footsteps.

Ten minutes later, Wimsey returned to the lounge. The little man had gone. Taking up his motoring-coat, which he had flung on a chair, Wimsey went upstairs to his bedroom. He undressed slowly and thoughtfully, put on his pyjamas and dressing-gown, and then, pulling a copy of the *Evening News* from his motoring-coat pocket, he studied a front-page item attentively for some time. Presently he appeared to come to some decision, for he got up and opened his door cautiously. The passage was empty and dark. Wimsey switched on a torch and walked quietly along, watching the floor. Opposite one of the doors he stopped, contemplating a pair of shoes which stood waiting to be cleaned. Then he softly tried the door. It was locked. He tapped cautiously.

A red head emerged.

"May I come in a moment?" said Wimsey, in a whisper.

The little man stepped back, and Wimsey followed him in.

"What's up?" said Mr. Duckworthy.

"I want to talk to you," said Wimsey. "Get back into bed, because it may take some time."

The little man looked at him, scared, but did as he was told. Wimsey gathered the folds of his dressing-gown closely about him, screwed his monocle more firmly into his eye, and sat down on the edge of the bed. He looked at Mr. Duckworthy a few minutes without speaking, and then said:

"Look here. You've told me a queerish story tonight. For

some reason I believe you. Possibly it only shows what a silly ass I am, but I was born like that, so it's past praying for. Nice, trusting nature and so on. Have you seen the paper this evening?"

He pushed the *Evening News* into Mr. Duckworthy's hand and bent the monocle on him more glassily than ever.

On the front page was a photograph. Underneath was a panel in bold type, boxed for greater emphasis:

> The police at Scotland Yard are anxious to get into touch with the original of this photograph, which was found in the handbag of Miss Jessie Haynes, whose dead body was found strangled on Barnes Common last Thursday morning. The photograph bears on the back the words "J. H. with love from R. D." Anybody recognizing the photograph is asked to communicate immediately with Scotland Yard or any police station.

Mr. Duckworthy looked, and grew so white that Wimsey thought he was going to faint.

"Well?" said Wimsey.

"Oh, God, sir! Oh, God! It's come at last." He whimpered and pushed the paper away, shuddering. "I've always known something of this would happen. But as sure as I'm born I knew nothing about it."

"It's you all right, I suppose?"

"The photograph's me all right. Though how it came there I *don't* know. I haven't had one taken for donkey's years, on my oath I haven't—except once in a staff group at Crichton's. But I tell you, sir, honest-to-God, there's times when I don't know what I'm doing, and that's a fact."

Wimsey examined the portrait feature by feature.

"Your nose, now—it has a slight twist—if you'll excuse my referring to it—to the right, and so it has in the photograph. The left eyelid droops a little. That's correct, too. The forehead here seems to have a distinct bulge on the left side—unless that's an accident in the printing."

"No!" Mr. Duckworthy swept his tousled cowlick aside. "It's very conspicuous—unsightly, I always think, so I wear the hair over it."

With the ginger lock pushed back, his resemblance to the photograph was more startling than before.

"My mouth's crooked, too."

"So it is. Slants up to the left. Very attractive, a one-sided smile, I always think—on a face of your type, that is. I have known such things to look positively sinister."

Mr. Duckworthy smiled a faint, crooked smile.

"Do you know this girl, Jessie Haynes?"

"Not in my right senses, I don't, sir. Never heard of her— except, of course, that I read about the murder in the papers. Strangled—oh, my God!" He pushed his hands out in front of him and stared woefully at them.

"What can I do? If I was to get away—"

"You can't. They've recognized you down in the bar. The police will probably be here in a few minutes. No"—as Duckworthy made an attempt to get out of bed—"don't do that. It's no good, and it would only get you into worse trouble. Keep quiet and answer one or two questions. First of all, do you know who I am? No, how should you? My name's Wimsey— Lord Peter Wimsey—"

"The detective?"

"If you like to call it that. Now, listen. Where was it you lived at Brixton?"

The little man gave the address.

"Your mother's dead. Any other relatives?"

"There was an aunt. She came from somewhere in Surrey, I think. Aunt Susan, I used to call her. I haven't seen her since I was a kid."

"Married?"

"Yes—oh, yes—Mrs. Susan Brown."

"Right. Were you left-handed as a child?"

"Well, yes, I was, at first. But mother broke me of it."

"And the tendency came back after the air-raid. And were you ever ill as a child? To have the doctor, I mean?"

"I had measles once, when I was about four."

"Remember the doctor's name?"

"They took me to the hospital."

"Oh, of course. Do you remember the name of the barber in Holborn?"

This question came so unexpectedly as to stagger the wits of Mr. Duckworthy, but after a while he said he thought it was Biggs or Briggs.

Wimsey sat thoughtfully for a moment, and then said:

"I think that's all. Except—oh, yes! What is your Christian name?"

"Robert."

"And you assure me that, so far as you know, you had no hand in this business?"

"That," said the little man, "that I swear to. As far as I know, you know. Oh, my Lord! If only it was possible to prove an alibi! That's my only chance. But I'm so afraid, you see, that I *may* have done it. Do you think—do you think they would hang me for that?"

"Not if you could prove you knew nothing about it," said Wimsey. He did not add that, even so, his acquaintance might probably pass the rest of his life at Broadmoor.

"And you know," said Mr. Duckworthy, "if I'm to go about all my life killing people without knowing it, it would be much better that they should hang me and done with it. It's a terrible thing to think of."

"Yes, but you may not have done it, you know."

"I hope not, I'm sure," said Mr. Duckworthy. "I say—what's that?"

"The police, I fancy," said Wimsey lightly. He stood up as a knock came at the door, and said heartily, "Come in!"

The landlord, who entered first, seemed rather taken aback by Wimsey's presence.

"Come right in," said Wimsey hospitably. "Come in, sergeant; come in, officer. What can we do for you?"

"Don't," said the landlord, "don't make a row if you can help it."

The police sergeant paid no attention to either of them, but stalked across to the bed and confronted the shrinking Mr. Duckworthy.

"It's the man all right," said he. "Now, Mr. Duckworthy, you'll excuse this late visit, but as you may have seen by the papers, we've been looking for a person answering your description, and there's no time like the present. We want—"

"I didn't do it," cried Mr. Duckworthy wildly. "I know nothing about it—"

The officer pulled out his note-book and wrote: "He said before any question was asked him, 'I didn't do it.'"

"You seem to know all about it," said the sergeant.

"Of course he does," said Wimsey; "we've been having a little informal chat about it."

"You have, have you? And who might you be—sir?" The last word appeared to be screwed out of the sergeant forcibly by the action of the monocle.

"I'm so sorry," said Wimsey, "I haven't a card on me at the moment. I am Lord Peter Wimsey."

"Oh, indeed," said the sergeant. "And may I ask, my lord, what you know about this here?"

"You may, and I may answer if I like, you know. I know nothing at all about the murder. About Mr. Duckworthy I know what he has told me and no more. I dare say he will tell you, too, if you ask him nicely. But no third degree, you know, sergeant. No Savidgery."

Baulked by this painful reminder, the sergeant said, in a voice of annoyance:

"It's my duty to ask him what he knows about this."

"I quite agree," said Wimsey. "As a good citizen, it's his duty to answer you. But it's a gloomy time of night, don't you think? Why not wait till the morning? Mr. Duckworthy won't run away."

"I'm not so sure of that."

"Oh, but I am. I will undertake to produce him whenever you want him. Won't that do? You're not charging him with anything, I suppose?"

"Not yet," said the sergeant.

"Splendid. Then it's all quite friendly and pleasant, isn't it? How about a drink?"

The sergeant refused this kindly offer with some gruffness in his manner.

"On the waggon?" inquired Wimsey sympathetically. "Bad luck. Kidneys? Or liver, eh?"

The sergeant made no reply.

"Well, we are charmed to have had the pleasure of seeing you," pursued Wimsey. "You'll look us up in the morning, won't you? I've got to get back to town fairly early, but I'll drop in at the police-station on my way. You will find Mr. Duckworthy in the lounge, here. It will be more comfortable for you than at your place. Must you be going? Well, good night, all."

Later, Wimsey returned to Mr. Duckworthy, after seeing the police off the premises.

"Listen," he said, "I'm going up to town to do what I can. I'll send you up a solicitor first thing in the morning. Tell him what you've told me, and tell the police what he tells you to tell them and no more. Remember, they can't force you to say anything or to go down to the police-station unless they charge you. If they do charge you, go quietly and say nothing. And whatever you do, don't run away, because if you do, you're done for."

Wimsey arrived in town the following afternoon, and walked down Holborn, looking for a barber's shop. He found it without much difficulty. It lay, as Mr. Duckworthy had described it, at the end of a narrow passage, and it had a long mirror in the door, with the name Briggs scrawled across it in gold letters. Wimsey stared at his own reflection distastefully.

"Check number one," said he, mechanically setting his tie to rights. "Have I been led up the garden? Or is it a case of fourth dimensional mystery? 'The animals went in four by four, *vive la compagnie*! The camel he got stuck in the door.' There is something intensely unpleasant about making a camel of one's self. It goes for days without a drink and its table-manners are objectionable. But there is no doubt that this door is made of looking-glass. Was it always so, I wonder? On, Wimsey, on. I cannot bear to be shaved again. Perhaps a hair-cut might be managed."

He pushed the door open, keeping a stern eye on his reflection to see that it played him no trick.

Of his conversation with the barber, which was lively and varied, only one passage is deserving of record.

"It's some time since I was in here," said Wimsey. "Keep it short behind the ears. Been re-decorated, haven't you?"

"Yes, sir. Looks quite smart, doesn't it?"

"The mirror on the outside of the door—that's new, too, isn't it?"

"Oh, no, sir. That's been there ever since we took over."

"Has it! Then it's longer ago than I thought. Was it there three years ago?"

"Oh, yes, sir. Ten years Mr. Briggs has been here, sir."

"And the mirror too?"

"Oh, yes, sir."

"Then it's my memory that's wrong. Senile decay setting in. 'All, all are gone, the old familiar landmarks.' No, thanks, if I go grey I'll go grey decently. I don't want any hair-tonics today, thank you. No, nor even an electric comb. I've had shocks enough."

It worried him, though. So much so that when he emerged, he walked back a few yards along the street, and was suddenly struck by seeing the glass door of a tea-shop. It also lay at the end of a dark passage and had a gold name written across it. The name was "The Bridget Tea-shop," but the door was of plain glass. Wimsey looked at it for a few moments and then went in. He did not approach the tea-tables, but accosted the cashier, who sat at a little glass desk inside the door.

Here he went straight to the point and asked whether the young lady remembered the circumstance of a man's having fainted in the doorway some years previously.

The cashier could not say; she had only been there three months, but she thought one of the waitresses might remember. The waitress was produced, and after some consideration, thought she did recollect something of the sort. Wimsey thanked her, said he was a journalist—which seemed to be accepted as an excuse for eccentric questions—parted with half a crown, and withdrew.

His next visit was to Carmelite House. Wimsey had friends in every newspaper office in Fleet Street, and made his way without difficulty to the room where photographs are filed for reference. The original of the "J.D." portrait was produced for his inspection.

"One of yours?" he asked.

"Oh, no. Sent out by Scotland Yard. Why? Anything wrong with it?"

"Nothing. I wanted the name of the original photographer, that's all."

"Oh! Well, you'll have to ask them there. Nothing more I can do for you?"

"Nothing, thanks."

Scotland Yard was easy. Chief-Inspector Parker was Wimsey's closest friend. An inquiry of him soon furnished the photographer's name, which was inscribed at the foot of the print. Wimsey voyaged off at once in search of the establishment, where his name readily secured an interview with the proprietor.

As he had expected, Scotland Yard had been there before him. All information at the disposal of the firm had already been given. It amounted to very little. The photograph had been taken a couple of years previously, and nothing particular was remembered about the sitter. It was a small establishment, doing a rapid business in cheap portraits, and with no pretensions to artistic refinements.

Wimsey asked to see the original negative, which, after some search, was produced.

Wimsey looked it over, laid it down, and pulled from his

pocket the copy of the *Evening News* in which the print had appeared.

"Look at this," he said.

The proprietor looked, then looked back at the negative.

"Well, I'm dashed," he said. "That's funny."

"It was done in the enlarging lantern, I take it," said Wimsey.

"Yes. It must have been put in the wrong way round. Now, fancy that happening. You know, sir, we often have to work against time, and I suppose—but it's very careless. I shall have to inquire into it."

"Get me a print of it right way round," said Wimsey.

"Yes, sir, certainly, sir. At once."

"And send one to Scotland Yard."

"Yes, sir. Queer it should have been just this particular one, isn't it, sir? I wonder the party didn't notice. But we generally take three or four positions, and he might not remember, you know."

"You'd better see if you've got any other positions and let me have them too."

"I've done that already, sir, but there are none. No doubt this one was selected and the others destroyed. We don't keep all the rejected negatives, you know, sir. We haven't the space to file them. But I'll get three prints off at once."

"Do," said Wimsey. "The sooner the better. Quick-dry them. And don't do any work on the prints."

"No, sir. You shall have them in an hour or two, sir. But it's astonishing to me that the party didn't complain."

"It's not astonishing," said Wimsey. "He probably thought it the best likeness of the lot. And so it would be—to him. Don't you see—that's the only view he could ever take of his own face. That photograph, with the left and right sides reversed, is the face he sees in the mirror every day—the only face he can really recognize as his. 'Wad the gods the giftie gie us,' and all that."

"Well, that's quite true, sir. And I'm much obliged to you for pointing the mistake out."

Wimsey reiterated the need for haste, and departed. A brief visit to Somerset House followed; after which he called it a day and went home.

Inquiry in Brixton, in and about the address mentioned by Mr. Duckworthy, eventually put Wimsey on to the track of persons who had known him and his mother. An aged lady who had kept a small green-grocery in the same street for the last forty years remembered all about them. She had the encyclopaedic memory of the almost illiterate, and was positive as to the date of their arrival.

"Thirty-two years ago, if we lives another month," she said. "Michaelmas it was they come. She was a nice-looking young woman, too, and my daughter, as was expecting her first, took a lot of interest in the sweet little boy."

"The boy was not born here?"

"Why, no, sir. Born somewheres on the south side, he was, but I remember she never rightly said where—only that it was round about the New Cut. She was one of the quiet sort and kep' herself to herself. Never one to talk, she wasn't. Why even to my daughter, as might 'ave good reason for bein' interested, she wouldn't say much about 'ow she got through 'er bad time. Chlorryform she said she 'ad, I know, and she disremembered about it, but it's my belief it 'ad gone 'ard with 'er and she didn't care to think overmuch about it. 'Er 'usband—. a nice man 'e was, too—'e says to me, 'Don't remind 'er of it, Mrs. 'Arbottle, don't remind 'er of it.' Whether she was frightened or whether she was 'urt by it I don't know, but she didn't 'ave no more children. 'Lor!' I says to 'er time and again, 'you'll get used to it, my dear, when you've 'ad nine of 'em same as me,' and she smiled, but she never 'ad no more, none the more for that."

"I suppose it does take some getting used to," said Wimsey, "but nine of them don't seem to have hurt *you*, Mrs. Harbottle, if I may say so. You look extremely flourishing."

"I keeps my 'ealth, sir, I am glad to say, though stouter than I used to be. Nine of them does 'ave a kind of spreading action on the figure. You wouldn't believe it, sir, to look at me now, as I 'ad a eighteen-inch waist when I was a girl. Many's the time me pore mother broke the laces on me, with 'er knee in me back and me 'oldin' on to the bedpost."

"One must suffer to be beautiful," said Wimsey politely. "How old was the baby, then, when Mrs. Duckworthy came to live in Brixton?"

"Three weeks old, 'e was, sir — a darling dear — and a lot of 'air on 'is 'ead. Black 'air it was then, but it turned into the brightest red you ever see — like them carrots there. It wasn't so pretty as 'is ma's, though much the same colour. He didn't favour 'er in the face, neither, nor yet 'is dad. She said 'e took after some of 'er side of the family."

"Did you ever see any of the rest of the family?"

"Only 'er sister, Mrs. Susan Brown. A big, stern, 'ard-faced woman she was — not like 'er sister. Lived at Evesham she did, as well I remembers, for I was getting' my grass from there at the time. I never sees a bunch o' grass now but what I think of Mrs. Susan Brown. Stiff, she was, with a small 'ead, very like a stick o' grass."

Wimsey thanked Mrs. Harbottle in a suitable manner and took the next train to Evesham. He was beginning to wonder where the chase might lead him, but discovered, much to his relief, that Mrs. Susan Brown was well known in the town, being a pillar of the Methodist Chapel and a person well respected.

She was upright still, with smooth, dark hair parted in the middle and drawn tightly back — a woman broad in the base and narrow in the shoulder — not, indeed, unlike the stick of asparagus to which Mrs. Harbottle had compared her. She received Wimsey with stern civility, but disclaimed all knowledge of her nephew's movements. The hint that he was in a position of some embarrassment, and even danger, did not appear to surprise her.

"There was bad blood in him," she said. "My sister Hetty was softer by half than she ought to have been."

"Ah!" said Wimsey. "Well, we can't all be people of strong

character, though it must be a source of great satisfaction to those that are. I don't want to be a trouble to you, madam, and I know I'm given to twaddling rather, being a trifle on the soft side myself—so I'll get to the point. I see by the register at Somerset House that your nephew, Robert Duckworthy, was born in Southwark, the son of Alfred and Hester Duckworthy. Wonderful system they have there. But of course—being only human—it breaks down now and again—doesn't it?"

She folded her wrinkled hands over one another on the edge of the table, and he saw a kind of shadow flicker over her sharp dark eyes.

"If I'm not bothering you too much—in what name was the other registered?"

The hands trembled a little, but she said steadily:

"I do not understand you."

"I'm frightfully sorry. Never was good at explaining myself. There were twin boys born, weren't there? Under what name did they register the other? I'm so sorry to be a nuisance, but it's really rather important."

"What makes you suppose that there were twins?"

"Oh, I don't suppose it. I wouldn't have bothered you for a supposition. I know there was a twin brother. What became—at least, I do know more or less what became of him—"

"It died," she said hurriedly.

"I hate to seem contradictory," said Wimsey. "Most unattractive behaviour. But it didn't die, you know. In fact, it's alive now. It's only the name I want to know, you know."

"And why should I tell you anything, young man?"

"Because," said Wimsey, "if you will pardon the mention of anything so disagreeable to a refined taste, there's been a murder committed and your nephew Robert is suspected. As a matter of fact, I happen to know that the murder was done by the brother. That's why I want to get hold of him, don't you see. It would be such a relief to my mind—I am naturally nice-minded—if you would help me to find him. Because, if not, I shall have to go to the police, and then you might be subpoena'd as a witness, and I shouldn't like—I really shouldn't

like—to see you in the witness-box at a murder trial. So much
unpleasant publicity, don't you know. Whereas, if we can lay
hands on the brother quickly, you and Robert need never
come into it at all."

Mrs. Brown sat in grim thought for a few minutes.

"Very well," she said, "I will tell you."

"Of course," said Wimsey to Chief-Inspector Parker a few
days later, "the whole thing was quite obvious when one had
heard about the reversal of friend Duckworthy's interior
economy."

"No doubt, no doubt," said Parker. "Nothing could be
simpler. But all the same, you are aching to tell me how you
deduced it and I am willing to be instructed. Are all twins
wrong-sided? And are all wrong-sided people twins?"

"Yes. No. Or rather, no, yes. Dissimilar twins and some
kinds of similar twins may both be quite normal. But the kind
of similar twins that result from the splitting of a single cell
may come out as looking-glass twins. It depends on the line of
fission in the original cell. You can do it artificially with tadpoles and a bit of horsehair."

"I will make a note to do it at once," said Parker gravely.

"In fact, I've read somewhere that a person with a reversed inside practically always turns out to be one of a pair
of similar twins. So you see, while poor old R. D. was burbling
on about the *Student of Prague* and the fourth dimension, I was
expecting the twin-brother.

"Apparently what happened was this. There were three
sisters of the name of Dart—Susan, Hester, and Emily. Susan
married a man called Brown; Hester married a man called
Duckworthy; Emily was unmarried. By one of those cheery
little ironies of which life is so full, the only sister who had a
baby, or who was apparently capable of having babies, was
the unmarried Emily. By way of compensation, she overdid it
and had twins.

"When this catastrophe was about to occur, Emily (deserted, of course, by the father) confided in her sisters, the

parents being dead. Susan was a tartar — besides, she had married above her station and was climbing steadily on a ladder of good works. She delivered herself of a few texts and washed her hands of the business. Hester was a kind-hearted soul. She offered to adopt the infant, when produced, and bring it up as her own. Well, the baby came, and, as I said before, it was twins.

"That was a bit too much for Duckworthy. He had agreed to one baby, but twins were more than he had bargained for. Hester was allowed to pick her twin, and, being a kindly soul, she picked the weaklier-looking one, which was our Robert — the mirror-image twin. Emily had to keep the other, and, as soon as she was strong enough, decamped with him to Australia, after which she was no more heard of.

"Emily's twin was registered in her own name of Dart and baptized Richard. Robert and Richard were two pretty men. Robert was registered as Hester Duckworthy's own child — there were no tiresome rules in those days requiring notification of births by doctors and midwives, and so one could do as one liked about these matters. The Duckworthys, complete with baby, moved to Brixton, where Robert was looked upon as being a perfectly genuine little Duckworthy.

"Apparently Emily died in Australia, and Richard, then a boy of fifteen, worked his passage home to London. He does not seem to have been a nice little boy. Two years afterwards, his path crossed that of Brother Robert and produced the episode of the air-raid night.

"Hester may have known about the wrong-sidedness of Robert, or she may not. Anyway, he wasn't told. I imagine that the shock of the explosion caused him to revert more strongly to his natural left-handed tendency. It also seems to have induced a new tendency to amnesia under similar shock-conditions. The whole thing preyed on his mind, and he became more and more vague and somnambulant.

"I rather think that Richard may have discovered the existence of his double and turned it to account. That explains the central incident of the mirror. I think Robert must have mistaken the glass door of the tea-shop for the door of the barber's shop. It really was Richard who came to meet him, and who retired again so hurriedly for fear of being seen and noted. Circumstances played into his hands, of course—but these meetings do take place, and the fact that they were both wearing soft hats and Burberrys is not astonishing on a dark, wet day.

"And then there is the photograph. No doubt the original mistake was the photographer's, but I shouldn't be surprised if Richard welcomed it and chose that particular print on that account. Though that would mean, of course, that he knew about the wrong-sidedness of Robert. I don't know how he could have done that, but he may have had opportunities for inquiry. It was known in the Army, and rumours may have got round. But I won't press that point.

"There's one rather queer thing, and that is that Robert should have had that dream about strangling, on the very night, as far as one could make out, that Richard was engaged in doing away with Jessie Haynes. They say that similar twins are always in close sympathy with one another—that each knows what the other is thinking about, for instance, and contracts the same illness on the same day and all that. Richard was the stronger twin of the two, and perhaps he dominated Robert more than Robert did him. I'm sure I don't know. Daresay it's all bosh. The point is that you've found him all right."

"Yes. Once we'd got the clue there was no difficulty."

"Well, let's toddle round to the Cri and have one."

Wimsey got up and set his tie to rights before the glass."

"All the same," he said, "there's something queer about mirrors. Uncanny, a bit, don't you think so?"

THE INCREDIBLE ELOPEMENT OF
LORD PETER WIMSEY

That house, señor?" said the landlord of the little *posada*. "That is the house of the American physician, whose wife, may the blessed saints preserve us, is bewitched." He crossed himself, and so did his wife and daughter.

"Bewitched, is she?" said Langley sympathetically. He was a professor of ethnology, and this was not his first visit to the Pyrenees. He had, however, never before penetrated to any place quite so remote as this tiny hamlet, clinging, like a rock-plant, high up the scarred granite shoulders of the mountain. He scented material here for his book on Basque folk-lore. With tact, he might persuade the old man to tell his story.

"And in what manner," he asked, "is the lady bespelled?"

"Who knows?" replied the landlord, shrugging his shoulders. " 'The man that asked questions on Friday was buried on Saturday.' Will your honour consent to take his supper?"

Langley took the hint. To press the question would be to

encounter obstinate silence. Later, when they knew him better, perhaps—

His dinner was served to him at the family table—the
oily, pepper-flavoured stew to which he was so well accustomed, and the harsh red wine of the country. His hosts chattered to him freely enough in that strange Basque language
which has no fellow in the world, and is said by some to be
the very speech of our first fathers in Paradise. They spoke
of the bad winter, and young Esteban Arramandy, so strong
and swift at the pelota, who had been lamed by a falling rock
and now halted on two sticks; of three valuable goats carried
off by a bear; of the torrential rains that, after a dry summer,
had scoured the bare ribs of the mountains. It was raining
now, and the wind was howling unpleasantly. This did not
trouble Langley; he knew and loved this haunted and im-
penetrable country at all times and seasons. Sitting in that
rude peasant inn, he thought of the oak-panelled hall of his
Cambridge college and smiled, and his eyes gleamed happily
behind his scholarly pince-nez. He was a young man, in spite
of his professorship and the string of letters after his name.
To his university colleagues it seemed strange that this man,
so trim, so prim, so early old, should spend his vacations eating garlic, and scrambling on mule-back along precipitous
mountain-tracks. You would never think it, they said, to look
at him.

There was a knock at the door.

"That is Martha," said the wife.

She drew back the latch, letting in a rush of wind and rain
which made the candle gutter. A small, aged woman was
blown in out of the night, her grey hair straggling in wisps
from beneath her shawl.

"Come in, Martha, and rest yourself. It is a bad night. The
parcel is ready—oh, yes. Dominique brought it from the town
this morning. You must take a cup of wine or milk before you
go back."

The old woman thanked her and sat down, panting.

"And how goes all at the house? The doctor is well?"

"He is well."

"And *she*?"

The daughter put the question in a whisper, and the land-lord shook his head at her with a frown.

"As always at this time of the year. It is but a month now to the Day of the Dead. Jesu-Maria! it is a grievous affliction for the poor gentleman, but he is patient, patient."

"He is a good man," said Dominique, "and a skilful doctor, but an evil like that is beyond his power to cure. You are not afraid, Martha?"

"Why should I be afraid? The Evil One cannot harm *me*. I have no beauty, no wits, no strength for him to envy. And the Holy Relic will protect me."

Her wrinkled fingers touched something in the bosom of her dress.

"You come from the house yonder?" asked Langley.

She eyed him suspiciously.

"The señor is not of our country?"

"The gentleman is a guest, Martha," said the landlord hurriedly. "A learned English gentleman. He knows our country and speaks our language as you hear. He is a great traveller, like the American doctor, your master."

"What is your master's name?" asked Langley. It occurred to him that an American doctor who had buried himself in this remote corner of Europe must have something unusual about him. Perhaps he also was an ethnologist. If so, they might find something in common.

"He is called Wetherall." She pronounced the name several times before he was sure of it.

"Wetherall? Not Standish Wetherall?"

He was filled with extraordinary excitement.

The landlord came to his assistance.

"This parcel is for him," he said. "No doubt the name will be written there."

It was a small package, neatly sealed, bearing the label of a firm of London chemists and addressed to "Standish Wetherall Esq., M.D."

"Good heavens!" exclaimed Langley. "But this is strange. Almost a miracle. I know this man. I knew his wife, too—"

He stopped. Again the company made the sign of the cross.

"Tell me," he said in great agitation, and forgetting his caution, "you say his wife is bewitched—afflicted—how is this? Is she the same woman I know? Describe her. She was tall, beautiful, with gold hair and blue eyes like the Madonna. Is this she?"

There was a silence. The old woman shook her head and muttered something inaudible, but the daughter whispered:

"True—it is true. Once we saw her thus, as the gentleman says—"

"Be quiet," said her father.

"Sir," said Martha, "we are in the hand of God."

She rose, and wrapped her shawl about her.

"One moment," said Langley. He pulled out his notebook and scribbled a few lines. "Will you take this letter to your master the doctor? It is to say that I am here, his friend whom he once knew, and to ask if I may come and visit him. That is all."

"You would not go to that house, excellence?" whispered the old man fearfully.

"If he will not have me, maybe he will come to me here." He added a word or two and drew a piece of money from his pocket. "You will carry my note for me?"

"Willingly, willingly. But the señor will be careful? Perhaps, though a foreigner, you are of the Faith?"

"I am a Christian," said Langley.

This seemed to satisfy her. She took the letter and the money, and secured them, together with the parcel, in a remote pocket. Then she walked to the door, strongly and rapidly for all her bent shoulders and appearance of great age.

Langley remained lost in thought. Nothing could have astonished him more than to meet the name of Standish Wetherall in this place. he had thought that episode finished and done with over three years ago. Of all people! The brilliant surgeon in the prime of his life and reputation, and Alice Wetherall, that delicate piece of golden womanhood — exiled in this forlorn corner of the world! His heart beat a little faster at the thought of seeing her again. Three years ago, he had decided that it would be wiser if he did not see too much of that porcelain loveliness. That folly was past now — but still he could not visualize her except against the background of the great white house in Riverside Drive, with the peacocks and the swimming-pool and the gilded tower with the roof-garden. Wetherall was a rich man, the son of old Hiram Wetherall the automobile magnate. What was Wetherall doing here?

He tried to remember. Hiram Wetherall, he knew, was dead, and all the money belonged to Standish, for there were no other children. There had been trouble when the only son had married a girl without parents or history. He had brought her from "somewhere out west." There had been some story of his having found her, years before, as a ne-glected orphan, and saved her from something or cured her of something and paid for her education, when he was still scarcely more than a student. Then, when he was a man over forty and she a girl of seventeen, he had brought her home and married her.

And now he had left his house and his money and one of the finest specialist practices in New York to come to live in the Basque country — in a spot so out of the way that men still believed in Black Magic, and could barely splutter more than a few words of bastard French or Spanish — a spot that was uncivilized even by comparison with the primitive civilization surrounding it. Langley began to be sorry that he had written to Wetherall. It might be resented.

The landlord and his wife had gone out to see to their cat-tle. The daughter sat close to the fire, mending a garment. She did not look at him, but he had the feeling that she would be glad to speak.

"Tell me, child," he said gently, "what is the trouble which afflicts these people who may be friends of mine?"

"Oh!" She glanced up quickly and leaned across to him, her arms stretched out over the sewing in her lap. "Sir, be advised. Do not go up there. No one will stay in that house at this time of the year, except Tomaso, who has not all his wits, and old Martha, who is—"

"What?"

"A saint—or something else," she said hurriedly.

"Child," said Langley again, "this lady when I knew—"

"I will tell you," she said, "but my father must not know. The good doctor brought her here three years ago last June, and then she was as you say. She was beautiful. She laughed and talked in her own speech—for she knew no Spanish or Basque. But on the Night of the Dead—"

She crossed herself.

"All-Hallows Eve," said Langley softly.

"Indeed, I do not know what happened. But she fell into the power of the darkness. She changed. There were terrible cries—I cannot tell. But little by little she became what she is now. Nobody sees her but Martha and she will not talk. But the people say it is not a woman at all that lives there now."

"Mad?" said Langley.

"It is not madness. It is—enchantment. Listen. Two years since on Easter Day—is that my father?"

"No, no."

"The sun had shone and the wind came up from the valley. We heard the blessed church bells all day long. That night there came a knock at the door. My father opened and one stood there like Our Blessed Lady herself, very pale like the image in the church and with a blue cloak over her head. She spoke, but we could not tell what she said. She wept and wrung her hands and pointed down the valley path, and my father went to the stable and saddled the mule. I thought of the flight from bad King Herod. But then—the American doctor came. He had run fast and was out of breath. And she shrieked at sight of him."

A great wave of indignation swept over Langley. If the

man was brutal to his wife, something must be done quickly. The girl hurried on.

"He said—Jesus-Maria—he said that his wife was bewitched. At Easter-tide the power of the Evil One was broken and she would try to flee. But as soon as the Holy Season was over, the spell would fall on her again, and therefore it was not safe to let her go. My parents were afraid to have touched the evil thing. They brought out the Holy Water and sprinkled the mule, but the wickedness had entered into the poor beast and she kicked my father so that he was lame for a month. The American took his wife away with him and we never saw her again. Even old Martha does not always see her. But every year the power waxes and wanes—heaviest at Hallow-tide and lifted again at Easter. Do not go to that house, señor, if you value your soul! Hush! they are coming back."

Langley would have liked to ask more, but his host glanced quickly and suspiciously at the girl. Taking up his candle, Langley went to bed. He dreamed of wolves, long, lean and black, running on the scent of blood.

Next day brought an answer to his letter:

DEAR LANGLEY, Yes, this is myself, and of course I remember you well. Only too delighted to have you come and cheer our exile. You will find Alice somewhat changed, I fear, but I will explain our misfortunes when we meet. Our household is limited, owing to some kind of superstitious avoidance of the afflicted, but if you will come along about half past seven, we can give you a meal of sorts. Martha will show you the way.

CORDIALLY,
STANDISH WETHERALL

The doctor's house was small and old, stuck halfway up the mountain-side on a kind of ledge in the rock-wall. A stream, unseen but clamorous, fell echoing down close at hand. Langley followed his guide into a dim, square room with a great hearth at one end and, drawn close before the fire, an armchair with wide, sheltering ears. Martha, muttering some sort of apology, hobbled away and left him standing there in the half-light. The flames of the wood fire, leaping and falling, made here a gleam and there a gleam, and, as his eyes grew familiar with the room, he saw that in the centre was a table laid for a meal, and that there were pictures on the walls. One of these struck a familiar note. He went close to it and recognized a portrait of Alice Wetherall that he had last seen in New York. It was painted by Sargent in his happiest mood, and the lovely wildflower face seemed to lean down to him with the sparkling smile of life.

A log suddenly broke and fell in the hearth, flaring. As though the little noise and light had disturbed something, he heard, or thought he heard, a movement from the big chair before the fire. He stepped forward, and then stopped. There was nothing to be seen, but a noise had begun; a kind of low, animal muttering, extremely disagreeable to listen to. It was not made by a dog or a cat, he felt sure. It was a sucking, slobbering sound that affected him in a curiously sickening way. It ended in a series of little grunts or squeals, and then there was silence.

Langley stepped backwards towards the door. He was positive that something was in the room with him that he did not care about meeting. An absurd impulse seized him to run away. He was prevented by the arrival of Martha, carrying a big, old-fashioned lamp, and behind her, Wetherall, who greeted him cheerfully.

The familiar American accents dispelled the atmosphere of discomfort that had been gathering about Langley. He held out a cordial hand.

"Fancy meeting *you* here," said he.

"The world is very small," replied Wetherall. "I am afraid that is a hardy bromide, but I certainly am pleased to see you," he added, with some emphasis.

The old woman had put the lamp on the table, and now asked if she should bring in the dinner. Wetherall replied in the affirmative, using a mixture of Spanish and Basque which she seemed to understand well enough.

"I didn't know you were a Basque scholar," said Langley.

"Oh, one picks it up. These people speak nothing else. But of course Basque is your specialty, isn't it?"

"Oh, yes."

"I daresay they have told you some queer things about us. But we'll go into that later. I've managed to make the place reasonably comfortable, though. I could do with a few more modern conveniences. However, it suits us."

Langley took the opportunity to mumble some sort of inquiry about Mrs. Wetherall.

"Alice? Ah, yes, I forgot—you have not seen her yet." Wetherall looked hard at him with a kind of half-smile. "I should have warned you. You were—rather an admirer of my wife in the old days."

"Like everyone else," said Langley.

"No doubt. Nothing specially surprising about it, was there? Here comes dinner. Put it down, Martha, and we will ring when we are ready."

The old woman set down a dish upon the table, which was handsomely furnished with glass and silver, and went out. Wetherall moved over to the fireplace, stepping sideways and keeping his eyes oddly fixed on Langley. Then he addressed the armchair.

"Alice! Get up, my dear, and welcome an old admirer of yours. Come along. You will both enjoy it. Get up."

Something shuffled and whimpered among the cushions. Wetherall stooped, with an air of almost exaggerated courtesy, and lifted it to its feet. A moment, and it faced Langley in the lamplight.

It was dressed in a rich gown of gold satin and lace, that hung rucked and crumpled upon the thick and slouching body. The face was white and puffy, the eyes vacant, the mouth drooled open, with little trickles of saliva running from the loose corners. A dry fringe of rusty hair clung to the half-bald scalp, like the dead wisps on the head of a mummy.

"Come, my love," said Wetherall. "Say how do you do to Mr. Langley."

The creature blinked and mouthed out some inhuman sounds. Wetherall put his hand under its forearm, and it slowly extended a lifeless paw.

"There, she recognized you all right. I thought she would. Shake hands with him, my dear."

With a sensation of nausea, Langley took the inert hand. It was clammy and coarse to the touch and made no attempt to return his pressure. He let it go; it pawed vaguely in the air for a moment and then dropped.

"I was afraid you might be upset," said Wetherall, watching him. "I have grown used to it, of course, and it doesn't affect me as it would an outsider. Not that you are an outsider—anything but that—eh? Premature senility is the lay name for it, I suppose. Shocking, of course, if you haven't met it before. You needn't mind, by the way, what you say. She understands nothing."

"How did it happen?"

"I don't quite know. Came on gradually. I took the best advice, naturally, but there was nothing to be done. So we came here. I didn't care about facing things at home where everybody knew us. And I didn't like the idea of a sanatorium. Alice is my wife, you know—sickness or health, for better, for worse, and all that. Come along; dinner's getting cold."

He advanced to the table, leading his wife, whose dim eyes seemed to brighten a little at the sight of food.

"Sit down, my dear, and eat your nice dinner. (She understands that, you see.) You'll excuse her table-manners, won't you? They're not pretty, but you'll get used to them."

He tied a napkin round the neck of the creature and placed food before her in a deep bowl. She snatched at it hungrily, slavering and gobbling as she scooped it up in her fingers and smeared face and hands with the gravy.

Wetherall drew out a chair for his guest opposite to where his wife sat. The sight of her held Langley with a kind of disgusted fascination.

The food—a sort of salmis—was deliciously cooked, but Langley had no appetite. The whole thing was an outrage, to the pitiful woman and to himself. Her seat was directly beneath the Sargent portrait, and his eyes went helplessly from the one to the other.

"Yes," said Wetherall, following his glance. "There is a difference, isn't there?" He himself was eating heartily and apparently enjoying his dinner. "Nature plays sad tricks upon us."

"Is it always like this?"

"No; this is one of her bad days. At times she will be almost human. Of course these people here don't know what to think of it all. They have their own explanation of a very simple medical phenomenon."

"Is there any hope of recovery?"

"I'm afraid not—not of a permanent cure. You are not eating anything."

"I—well, Wetherall, this has been a shock to me."

"Of course. Try a glass of burgundy. I ought not to have asked you to come, but the idea of talking to an educated fellow-creature once again tempted me, I must confess."

"It must be terrible for you."

"I have become resigned. Ah, naughty, naughty!" The idiot had flung half the contents of her bowl upon the table. Wetherall patiently remedied the disaster, and went on:

"I can bear it better here, in this wild place where everything seems possible and nothing unnatural. My people are all dead, so there was nothing to prevent me from doing as I liked about it."

"No. What about your property in the States?"

"Oh, I run over from time to time to keep an eye on things. In fact, I am due to sail next month. I'm glad you caught me. Nobody over there knows how we're fixed, of course. They just know we're living in Europe."

"Did you consult no American doctor?"

"No. We were in Paris when the first symptoms declared themselves. That was shortly after that visit you paid to us." A flash of some emotion to which Langley could not put a name made the doctor's eyes for a moment sinister. "The best men on this side confirmed my own diagnosis. So we came here."

He rang for Martha, who removed the salmis and put on a kind of sweet pudding.

"Martha is my right hand," observed Wetherall. "I don't know what we shall do without her. When I am away, she looks after Alice like a mother. Not that there's much one can do for her, except to keep her fed and warm and clean—and the last is something of a task."

There was a note in his voice which jarred on Langley. Wetherall noticed his recoil and said:

"I won't disguise from you that it gets on my nerves some-times. But it can't be helped. Tell me about yourself. What have you been doing lately?"

Langley replied with as much vivacity as he could assume, and they talked of indifferent subjects till the deplorable being which had once been Alice Wetherall began to mumble and whine fretfully and scramble down from her chair.

"She's cold," said Wetherall. "Go back to the fire, my dear."

He propelled her briskly towards the hearth, and she sank back into the armchair, crouching and complaining and thrusting out her hands towards the blaze. Wetherall brought out brandy and a box of cigars.

"I contrive just to keep in touch with the world, you see," he said. "They send me these from London. And I get the lat-est medical journals and reports. I'm writing a book, you know, on my own subject; so I don't vegetate. I can experi-ment, too—plenty of room for a laboratory, and no Vivisection Acts to bother me. It's a good country to work in. Are you staying here long?"

"I think not very."

"Oh! If you had thought of stopping on, I would have of-fered you the use of this house while I was away. You would find it more comfortable than the *posada*, and I should have no qualms, you know, about leaving you alone in the place with my wife—under the peculiar circumstances."

He stressed the last words and laughed. Langley hardly knew what to say.

"Really, Wetherall—"

"Though, in the old days, *you* might have liked the prospect more and *I* might have liked it less. There was a time, I think, Langley, when you would have jumped at the idea of living alone with—*my wife*."

Langley jumped up.

"What the devil are you insinuating, Wetherall?"

"Nothing, nothing. I was just thinking of the afternoon when you and she wandered away at a picnic and got lost. You remember? Yes, I though you would."

"This is monstrous," retorted Langley. "How dare you say such things—with that poor soul sitting there—?"

"Yes, poor soul. You're a poor thing to look at now, aren't you, my kitten?"

He turned suddenly to the woman. Something in his abrupt gesture seemed to frighten her, and she shrank away from him.

"You devil!" cried Langley. "She's afraid of you. What have you been doing to her? How did she get into this state? I *will* know!"

"Gently," said Wetherall. "I can allow for your natural agitation at finding her like this, but I can't have you coming between me and *my wife*. What a faithful fellow you are, Langley. I believe you still want her—just as you did before when you thought I was dumb and blind. Come now, have you got designs on *my wife*, Langley? Would you like to kiss her, caress her, take her to bed with you—my beautiful wife?"

A scarlet fury blinded Langley. He dashed an inexpert fist at the mocking face. Wetherall gripped his arm, but he broke away. Panic seized him. He fled stumbling against the furniture and rushed out. As he went he heard Wetherall very softly laughing.

The train to Paris was crowded. Langley, scrambling in at the last moment, found himself condemned to the corridor. He sat down on a suitcase and tried to think. He had not been able to collect his thoughts on his wild flight. Even now, he was not quite sure what he had fled from. He buried his head in his hands.

"Excuse me," said a polite voice.

Langley looked up. A fair man in a grey suit was looking down at him through a monocle.

"Fearfully sorry to disturb you," went on the fair man. "I'm just tryin' to barge back to my jolly old kennel. Ghastly crowd, isn't it? Don't know when I've disliked my fellow-creatures more. I say, you don't look frightfully fit. Wouldn't you be better on something more comfortable?"

Langley explained that he had not been able to get a seat. The fair man eyed his haggard and unshaven countenance for a moment and then said:

"Well, look here, why not come and lay yourself down in my bin for a bit? Have you had any grub? No? That's a mistake. Toddle along with me and we'll get hold of a spot of soup and so on. You'll excuse my mentioning it, but you look as if you'd been backing a system that's come unstuck, or something. Not my business, of course, but do have something to eat."

Langley was too faint and sick to protest. He stumbled obediently along the corridor till he was pushed into a first-class sleeper, where a rigidly correct manservant was laying out a pair of mauve silk pyjamas and a set of silver-mounted brushes.

"This gentleman's feeling rotten, Bunter," said the man with the monocle, "so I've brought him in to rest his aching head upon thy breast. Get hold of the commissariat and tell 'em to buzz a plate of soup along and a bottle of something drinkable."

"Very good, my lord."

Langley dropped, exhausted, on the bed, but when the food appeared he ate and drank greedily. He could not remember when he had last made a meal.

"I say," he said, "I wanted that. It's awfully decent of you. I'm sorry to appear so stupid. I've had a bit of a shock."

"Tell me all," said the stranger pleasantly.

The man did not look particularly intelligent, but he seemed friendly and, above all, normal. Langley wondered how the story would sound.

"I'm an absolute stranger to you," he began.

"And I to you," said the fair man. "The chief use of strangers is to tell things to. Don't you agree?"

"I'd like—" said Langley. "The fact is, I've run away from something. It's queer—it's—but what's the use of bothering you with it?"

The fair man sat down beside him and laid a slim hand on his arm.

"Just a moment," he said. "Don't tell me anything if you'd rather not. But my name is Wimsey—Lord Peter Wimsey— and I am interested in queer things."

It was the middle of November when the strange man came to the village. Thin, pale, and silent, with his great black hood flapping about his face, he was surrounded with an atmosphere of mystery from the start. He settled down, not at the inn, but in a dilapidated cottage high up in the mountains, and he brought with him five mule-loads of mysterious baggage and a servant. The servant was almost as uncanny as the master; he was a Spaniard and spoke Basque well enough to act as an interpreter for his employer when necessary; but his words were few, his aspect gloomy and stern, and such brief information as he vouchsafed, disquieting in the extreme. His master, he said, was a wise man; he spent all his time reading books; he ate no flesh; he was of no known country; he spoke the language of the Apostles and had talked with blessed Lazarus after his return from the grave; and when he sat alone in his chamber by night, the angels of God came and conversed with him in celestial harmonies.

This was terrifying news. The few dozen villagers avoided the little cottage, especially at night-time; and when the pale stranger was seen coming down the mountain path, folded in his black robe and bearing one of his magic tomes beneath his arm, the women pushed their children within doors, and made the sign of the cross.

Nevertheless, it was a child that first made the personal acquaintance of the magician. The small son of the Widow Etcheverry, a child of bold and inquisitive disposition, went one evening adventuring into the unhallowed neighbourhood. He was missing for two hours, during which his mother, in a frenzy of anxiety, had called the neighbours about her and summoned the priest, who had unhappily been called away on business to the town. Suddenly, however, the child reappeared, well and cheerful, with a strange story to tell.

He had crept up close to the magician's house (the bold, wicked child, did ever you hear the like?) and climbed into a tree to spy upon the stranger (Jesu-Maria!). And he saw a light in the window, and strange shapes moving about and shadows going to and fro within the room. And then there came a strain of music so ravishing it drew the very heart out of his body, as though all the stars were singing together. (Oh, my precious treasure! The wizard has stolen the heart out of him, alas! alas!) Then the cottage door opened and the wizard came out and with him a great company of familiar spirits. One of them had wings like a seraph and talked in an unknown tongue, and another was like a wee man, no higher than your knee, with a black face and a white beard, and he sat on the wizard's shoulder and whispered in his ear. And the heavenly music played louder and louder. And the wizard had a pale flame all about his head, like the pictures of the saints. (Blessed St. James of Compostella, be merciful to us all! And what then?) Why then he, the boy, had been very much frightened and wished he had not come, but the little dwarf spirit had seen him and jumped into the tree after him, climbing—oh! so fast! And he had tried to climb higher and had slipped and fallen to the ground. (Oh, the poor, wicked, brave, bad boy!)

Then the wizard had come and picked him up and spoken

strange words to him and all the pain had gone away from the places where he had bumped himself (Marvellous! marvellous!) and he had carried him into the house. And inside, it was like the streets of Heaven, all gold and glittering. And the familiar spirits had sat beside the fire, nine in number, and the music had stopped playing. But the wizard's servant had brought him marvellous fruits in a silver dish, like fruits of Paradise, very sweet and delicious, and he had eaten them, and drunk a strange, rich drink from a goblet covered with red and blue jewels. Oh, yes—and there had been a tall crucifix on the wall, big, big, with a lamp burning before it and a strange sweet perfume like the smell in church on Easter Day.

(A crucifix? That was strange. Perhaps the magician was not so wicked, after all. And what next?)

Next, the wizard's servant had told him not to be afraid, and had asked his name and his age and whether he could repeat his Paternoster. So he had said that prayer and the Ave Maria and part of the Credo, but the Credo was long and he had forgotten what came after *"ascendit in coelum."* So the wizard had prompted him and they had finished saying it together. And the wizard had pronounced the sacred names and words without flinching and in the right order, so far as he could tell. And then the servant had asked further about himself and his family, and he had told about the death of the black goat and about his sister's lover, who had left her because she had not so much money as the merchant's daughter. Then the wizard and his servant had spoken together and laughed, and the servant had said: "My master gives this message to your sister: that where there is no love there is no wealth, but he that is bold shall have gold for the asking." And with that, the wizard had put forth his hand into the air and taken from it—out of the empty air, yes, truly—one, two, three, four, five pieces of money and given them to him. And he was afraid to take them till he had made the sign of the cross upon them, and then, as they did not vanish or turn into fiery serpents, he had taken them, and here they were!

So the gold pieces were examined and admired in fear and trembling, and then, by grandfather's advice, placed under the feet of the image of Our Lady, after a sprinkling with Holy Water for their better purification. And on the next morning, as they were still there, they were shown to the priest, who arrived, tardy and flustered upon his last night's summons, and by him pronounced to be good Spanish coin, whereof one piece being devoted to the Church to put all right with Heaven, the rest might be put to secular uses without peril to the soul. After which, the good padre made his hasty way to the cottage, and returned, after an hour, filled with good reports of the wizard.

"For, my children," said he, "this is no evil sorcerer, but a Christian man, speaking the language of the Faith. He and I have conversed together with edification. Moreover, he keeps very good wine and is altogether a very worthy person. Nor did I perceive any familiar spirits or flaming apparitions; but it is true that there is a crucifix and also a very handsome Testament with pictures in gold and colour. *Benedicite*, my children. This is a good and learned man."

And away he went back to his presbytery; and that winter the chapel of Our Lady had a new altar-cloth.

After that, each night saw a little group of people clustered at a safe distance to hear the music which poured out from the wizard's windows, and from time to time a few bold spirits would creep up close enough to peer through the chinks of the shutters and glimpse the marvels within.

The wizard had been in residence about a month, and sat one night after his evening meal in conversation with his servant. The black hood was pushed back from his head, disclosing a sleek poll of fair hair, and a pair of rather humorous grey eyes, with a cynical droop of the lids. A glass of Cockburn 1908 stood on the table at his elbow and from the arm of his chair a red-and-green parrot gazed unwinkingly at the fire.

"Time is getting on, Juan," said the magician. "This business is very good fun and all that — but is there anything doing with the old lady?"

"I think so, my lord. I have dropped a word or two here and there of marvellous cures and miracles. I think she will come. Perhaps even tonight."

"Thank goodness! I want to get the thing over before Wetherall comes back, or we may find ourselves in Queer Street. It will take some weeks, you know, before we are ready to move, even if the scheme works at all. Damn it, what's that?"

Juan rose and went into the inner room, to return in a minute carrying the lemur.

"Micky had been playing with your hair-brushes," he said indulgently, "Naughty one, be quiet! Are you ready for a little practice, my lord?"

"Oh, rather, yes! I'm getting quite a dab at this job. If all else fails, I shall try for an engagement with Maskelyn."

Juan laughed, showing his white teeth. He brought out a set of billiard-balls, coins, and other conjuring apparatus, palming and multiplying them negligently as he went. The other took them from him, and the lesson proceeded.

"Hush!" said the wizard, retrieving a ball which had tiresomely slipped from his fingers in the very act of vanishing. "There's somebody coming up the path."

He pulled his robe about his face and slipped silently into the inner room. Juan grinned, removed the decanter and glasses and extinguished the lamp. In the firelight the great eyes of the lemur gleamed strongly as it hung on the back of the high chair. Juan pulled a large folio from the shelf, lit a scented pastille in a curiously shaped copper vase, and pulled forward a heavy iron cauldron which stood on the hearth. As he piled the logs about it, there came a knock. He opened the door, the lemur running at his heels.

"Whom do you seek, mother?" he asked, in Basque.

"Is the Wise One at home?"

"His body is at home, mother; his spirit holds converse with the unseen. Enter. What would you with us?"

"I have come, as I said—ah, Mary! Is that a spirit?"

"God made spirits and bodies also. Enter and fear not."

The old woman came tremblingly forward.

"Hast thou spoken with him of what I told thee?"

"I have. I have shown him the sickness of thy mistress—her husband's sufferings—all."

"What said he?"

"Nothing; he read in his book."

"Think you he can heal her?"

"I do not know; the enchantment is a strong one; but my master is mighty for good."

"Will he see me?"

"I will ask him. Remain here, and beware thou show no fear, whatever befall."

"I will be courageous," said the old woman, fingering her beads.

Juan withdrew. There was a nerve-shattering interval. The lemur had climbed up to the back of the chair again and swung, teeth-chattering, among the leaping shadows. The parrot cocked his head and spoke a few gruff words from his corner. An aromatic steam began to rise from the cauldron. Then, slowly into the red light, three, four, seven white shapes came stealthily and sat down in a circle about the hearth. Then, a faint music, that seemed to roll in from leagues away. The flame flickered and dropped. There was a tall cabinet against the wall, with gold figures on it that seemed to move with the moving firelight.

Then, out of the darkness, a strange voice chanted in an unearthly tongue that sobbed and thundered.

Martha's knees gave under her. She sank down. The seven white cats rose and stretched themselves, and came sidling slowly about her. She looked up and saw the wizard standing before her, a book in one hand and a silver wand in the other. The upper part of his face was hidden, but she saw his pale lips move and presently he spoke, in a deep, husky tone that vibrated solemnly in the dim room:

" ὦ πέπν, έι μὲν γὰ , πόλεμον πε ὶ τόνδε φυγόντε,
    αἰεὶ δὴ μέλλοιμεν ἀγὴ ω τ' ἀθανάτω τε

ἔσσεθ᾽, οὔτε ᵒεν αὐτὸς ἐνὶ π ὤτοισι μαχοίμην,
οὔτε ᵒέ σε στέλλοιμι μάχην ἐς ᵒνδιάνει αν..."

The great syllables went rolling on. Then the wizard
paused and added, in a kinder tone:

"Great stuff, this Homer. 'It goes so thunderingly as
though it conjured devils.' What do I do next?"

The servant had come back, and now whispered in
Martha's ear.

"Speak now," said he. "The master is willing to help you."

Thus encouraged, Martha stammered out her request.
She had come to ask the Wise Man to help her mistress, who
lay under an enchantment. She had brought an offering—the
best she could find, for she had not liked to take anything of
her master's during his absence. But here were a silver penny,
an oat-cake, and a bottle of wine, very much at the wizard's
service, if such small matters could please him.

The wizard, setting aside his book, gravely accepted the
silver penny, turned it magically into six gold pieces and laid
the offering on the table. Over the oat-cake and the wine he
showed a little hesitation, but at length, murmuring:

"Ergo omnis longo solvit se Teucria luctu"

(a line notorious for its grave spondaic cadence), he metamor-
phosed the one into a pair of pigeons and the other into a curious little crystal tree in a metal pot, and set them beside the
coins. Martha's eyes nearly started from her head, but Juan
whispered encouragingly:

"The good intention gives value to the gift. The master is
pleased. Hush!"

The music ceased on a loud chord. The wizard, speaking
now with greater assurance, delivered himself with fair accuracy of a page or so from Homer's Catalogue of the Ships, and,
drawing from the folds of his robe his long white hand laden
with antique rings, produced from mid-air a small casket of
shining metal, which he proffered to the suppliant.

"The master says," prompted the servant, "that you shall take this casket, and give to your lady of the wafers which it contains, one at every meal. When all have been consumed, seek this place again. And remember to say three Aves and two Paters morning and evening for the intention of the lady's health. Thus, by faith and diligence, the cure may be accomplished."

Martha received the casket with trembling hands.

"*Tendebantque manus ripae ulterioris amore,*" said the wizard, with emphasis. "*Poluphloisboio thalasses. Ne plus ultra. Valete. Plaudite.*"

He stalked away into the darkness, and the audience was over.

"It is working, then?" said the wizard to Juan.

The time was five weeks later, and five more consignments of enchanted wafers had been ceremoniously dispatched to the grim house on the mountain.

"It is working," agreed Juan. "The intelligence is returning, the body is becoming livelier, and the hair is growing again."

"Thank the Lord! It was a shot in the dark, Juan, and even now I can hardly believe that anyone in the world could think of such a devilish trick. When does Wetherall return?"

"In three weeks' time."

"Then we had better fix our grand finale for today fortnight. See that the mules are ready, and go down to the town and get a message off to the yacht."

"Yes, my lord."

"That will give you a week to get clear with the menagerie and the baggage. And—I say, how about Martha? Is it dangerous to leave her behind, do you think?"

"I will try to persuade her to come back with us."

"Do. I should hate anything unpleasant to happen to her. The man's a criminal lunatic. Oh, lord! I'll be glad when this is over. I want to get into a proper suit of clothes again. What Bunter would say if he saw this—"

The wizard laughed, lit a cigar, and turned on the gramophone.

The last act was duly staged a fortnight later.

It had taken some trouble to persuade Martha of the necessity of bringing her mistress to the wizard's house. Indeed, that supernatural personage had been obliged to make an alarming display of wrath and declaim two whole choruses from Euripides before gaining his point. The final touch was put to the terrors of the evening by a demonstration of the ghastly effects of a sodium flame—which lends a very corpse-like aspect to the human countenance, particularly in a lonely cottage on a dark night, and accompanied by incantations and the *Danse Macabre* of Saint-Saens.

Eventually the wizard was placated by a promise, and Martha departed, bearing with her a charm, engrossed upon parchment, which her mistress was to read and thereafter hang about her neck in a white silk bag.

Considered as a magical formula, the document was perhaps a little unimpressive in its language, but its meaning was such as a child could understand. It was in English, and ran:

> You have been ill and in trouble, but your friends are ready to cure you and help you. Don't be afraid, but do whatever Martha tells you, and you will soon be quite well and happy again.

"And even if she can't understand it," said the wizard to his man, "it can't possibly do any harm."

The events of that terrible night have become legend in the village. They tell by the fireside with bated breath how Martha brought the strange, foreign lady to the wizard's house, that she might be finally and for ever freed from the power of the Evil One. It was a dark night and a stormy one, with the wind howling terribly through the mountains.

The lady had become much better and brighter through the wizard's magic—though this, perhaps, was only a fresh glamour and delusion—and she had followed Martha like a little child on that strange and secret journey. They had crept out very quietly to elude the vigilance of old Tomaso, who had strict orders from the doctor never to let the lady stir one step from the house. As for that, Tomaso swore that he had been cast into an enchanted sleep—but who knows? There may have been no more to it than over-much wine. Martha was a cunning woman, and, some said, little better than a witch herself.

Be that as it might, Martha and the lady had come to the cottage, and there the wizard had spoken many things in a strange tongue, and the lady had spoken likewise. Yes—she who for so long had only grunted like a beast, had talked with the wizard and answered him. Then the wizard had drawn strange signs upon the floor round about the lady and himself. And when the lamp was extinguished, the signs glowed awfully, with a pale light of their own. The wizard also drew a circle about Martha herself, and warned her to keep inside it. Presently they heard a rushing noise, like great wings beating, and all the familiars leaped about, and the little white man with the black face ran up the curtain and swung from the pole. Then a voice cried out: "He comes! He comes!" and the wizard opened the door of the tall cabinet with gold images upon it, that stood in the centre of the circle, and he and the lady stepped inside it and shut the doors after them.

The rushing sound grew louder and the familiar spirits screamed and chattered—and then, all of a sudden, there was a thunder-clap and a great flash of light and the cabinet was shivered into pieces and fell down. And lo and behold! the wizard and the lady had vanished clean away and were never more seen or heard of.

This was Martha's story, told the next day to her neighbours. How she had escaped from the terrible house she could not remember. But when, some time after, a group of villagers summoned up courage to visit the place again, they found it bare and empty. Lady, wizard, servant, familiars, furniture, bags, and baggage—all were gone, leaving not a trace behind them, except a few mysterious lines and figures traced on the floor of the cottage.

This was a wonder indeed. More awful still was the disappearance of Martha herself, which took place three nights afterwards.

Next day, the American doctor returned, to find an empty hearth and a legend.

"Yacht ahoy!"

Langley peered anxiously over the rail of the *Abracadabra* as the boat loomed out of the blackness. When the first passenger came aboard, he ran hastily to greet him.

"Is it all right, Wimsey?"

"Absolutely all right. She's a bit bewildered, of course— but you needn't be afraid. She's like a child, but she's getting better every day. Bear up, old man—there's nothing to shock you about her."

Langley moved hesitatingly forward as a muffled female figure was hoisted gently on board.

"Speak to her," said Wimsey. "She may or may not recognize you. I can't say."

Langley summoned up his courage. "Good evening, Mrs. Wetherall," he said, and held out his hand.

The woman pushed the cloak from her face. Her blue eyes gazed shyly at him in the lamplight—then a smile broke out upon her lips.

"Why, I know you—of course I know you. You're Mr. Langley. I'm so glad to see you."

She clasped his hand in hers.

"Well, Langley," said Lord Peter, as he manipulated the syphon, "a more abominable crime it has never been my fortune to discover. My religious beliefs are a little ill-defined, but I hope something really beastly happens to Wetherall in the next world. Say when!"

"You know, there were one or two very queer points about that story you told me. They gave me a line on the thing from the start.

"To begin with, there was this extraordinary kind of decay or imbecility settlin' in on a girl in her twenties—so conveniently, too, just after you'd been hangin' round the Wetherall home and showin' perhaps a trifle too much sensibility, don't you see? And then there was this tale of the conditions clearin' up regularly once a year or so—not like any ordinary brain-trouble. Looked as if it was being controlled by somebody.

"Then there was the fact that Mrs. Wethèrall had been under her husband's medical eye from the beginning, with no family or friends who knew anything about her to keep a check on the fellow. Then there was the determined isolation of her in a place where no doctor could see her and where, even if she had a lucid interval, there wasn't a soul who could understand or be understood by her. Queer, too, that it should be a part of the world where you, with your interests, might reasonably be expected to turn up some day and be treated to a sight of what she had turned into. Then there were Wetherall's well-known researches, and the fact that he kept in touch with a chemist in London.

"All that gave me a theory, but I had to test it before I could be sure I was right. Wetherall was going to America, and that gave me a chance; but of course he left strict orders that nobody should get into or out of his house during his absence. I had, somehow, to establish an authority greater than his over old Martha, who is a faithful soul, God bless her! Hence, exit Lord Peter Wimsey and enter the magician. The treatment was tried and proved successful—hence the elopement and the rescue.

"Well, now, listen—and don't go off the deep end. It's all over now. Alice Wetherall is one of those unfortunate people who suffer from congenital thyroid deficiency. You know the thyroid gland in your throat—the one that stokes the engine and keeps the old brain going. In some people the thing doesn't work properly, and they turn out cretinous imbeciles.

Their bodies don't grow and their minds don't work. But feed 'em the stuff, and they come absolutely all right—cheery and handsome and intelligent and lively as crickets. Only, don't you see, you have to *keep* feeding it to 'em, otherwise they just go back to an imbecile condition.

"Wetherall found this girl when he was a bright young student just learning about the thyroid. Twenty years ago, very few experiments had been made in this kind of treatment, but he was a bit of a pioneer. He gets hold of the kid, works a miraculous cure, and, bein' naturally bucked with himself, adopts her, gets her educated, likes the look of her, and finally marries her. You understand, don't you, that there's nothing fundamentally unsound about those thyroid deficients. Keep 'em going on the little daily dose, and they're normal in every way, fit to live an ordinary life and have ordinary healthy children.

"Nobody, naturally, knew anything about this thyroid business except the girl herself and her husband. All goes well till *you* come along. Then Wetherall gets jealous—"

"He had no cause."

Wimsey shrugged his shoulders.

"Possibly, my lad, the lady displayed a preference—we needn't go into that. Anyhow, Wetherall did get jealous and saw a perfectly marvellous revenge in his power. He carried his wife off to the Pyrenees, isolated her from all help, and then simply sat back and starved her of her thyroid extract. No doubt he told her what he was going to do, and why. It would please him to hear her desperate appeals—to let her feel herself slipping back day by day, hour by hour, into something less than a beast—"

"Oh, God!"

"As you say. Of course, after a time, a few months, she would cease to know what was happening to her. He would still have the satisfaction of watching her—seeing her skin thicken, her body coarsen, her hair fall out, her eyes grow vacant, her speech die away into mere animal noises, her brain go to mush, her habits—"

"Stop it, Wimsey."

"Well, you saw it all yourself. But that wouldn't be enough for him. So, every so often, he would feed her the thyroid again and bring her back sufficiently to realize her own degradation —"

"If only I had the brute here!"

"Just as well you haven't. Well then, one day — by a stroke of luck — Mr. Langley, the amorous Mr. Langley, actually turns up. What a triumph to let him see —"

Langley stopped him again.

"Right-ho! but it was ingenious, wasn't it? So simple. The more I think of it, the more it fascinates me. But it was just that extra refinement of cruelty that defeated him. Because, when you told me the story, I couldn't help recognizing the symptoms of thyroid deficiency, and I thought, 'Just supposing' — so I hunted up the chemist whose name you saw on the parcel, and, after unwinding a lot of red tape, got him to admit that he had several times sent Wetherall consignments of thyroid extract. So then I was almost sure, don't you see.

"I got a doctor's advice and a supply of gland extract, hired a tame Spanish conjurer and some performing cats and things, and barged off complete with disguise and a trick cabinet devised by the ingenious Mr. Devant. I'm a bit of a conjurer myself, and between us we didn't do so badly. The local superstitions helped, of course, and so did the gramophone records. Schubert's 'Unfinished' is first class for producing an atmosphere of gloom and mystery, so are luminous paint and the remnants of a classical education."

"Look here, Wimsey, will she get all right again?"

"Right as ninepence, and I imagine that any American court would give her a divorce on the grounds of persistent cruelty. After that — it's up to you!"

Lord Peter's friends greeted his reappearance in London with mild surprise.

"And what have *you* been doing with yourself?" demanded the Hon. Freddy Arbuthnot.

"Eloping with another man's wife," replied his lordship. "But only," he hastened to add, "in a purely Pickwickian sense. Nothing in it for yours truly. Oh, well! Let's toddle round to the Holborn Empire, and see what George Robey can do for us."

THE QUEEN'S SQUARE

You Jack o' Di'monds, you Jack o' Di'monds," said Mark Sambourne, shaking a reproachful head, "I know you of old." He rummaged beneath the white satin of his costume, panelled with gigantic oblongs and spotted to represent a set of dominoes. "Hang this fancy rig! Where the blazes has the fellow put my pockets? You rob my pocket, yes, you rob-a my pocket, you rob my pocket of silver and go-ho-hold. How much do you make it?" He extracted a fountain-pen and a cheque-book.

"Five-seventeen-six," said Lord Peter Wimsey. "That's right, isn't it, partner?" His huge blue-and-scarlet sleeves rustled as he turned to Lady Hermione Creethorpe, who, in her Queen of Clubs costume, looked a very redoubtable virgin, as, indeed, she was.

"Quite right," said the old lady, "and I consider that very cheap."

"We haven't been playing long," said Wimsey apologetically.

"It would have been more, Auntie," observed Mrs. Wrayburn, "if you hadn't been greedy. You shouldn't have doubled
those four spades of mine."

Lady Hermione snorted, and Wimsey hastily cut in:

"It's a pity we've got to stop, but Deverill will never forgive us if we're not there to dance Sir Roger. He feels strongly
about it. What's the time? Twenty past one. Sir Roger is timed
to start sharp at half past. I supposed we'd better tootle back
to the ballroom."

"I suppose we had," agreed Mrs. Wrayburn. She stood up,
displaying her dress, boldly patterned with the red and black
points of a backgammon board. "It's very good of you," she
added, as Lady Hermione's voluminous skirts swept through
the hall ahead of them, "to chuck your dancing to give Auntie
her bridge. She does so hate to miss it."

"Not at all," replied Wimsey. "It's a pleasure. And in any
case I was jolly glad of a rest. These costumes are dashed hot
for dancing in."

"You make a splendid Jack of Diamonds, though. Such a
good idea of Lady Deverill's, to make everybody come as a
game. It cuts out all those wearisome pierrots and
columbines." They skirted the south-west angle of the ballroom and emerged into the south corridor, lit by a great hanging lantern in four lurid colours. Under the arcading they
paused and stood watching the floor, where Sir Charles Deverill's guests were fox-trotting to a lively tune discoursed by
the band in the musicians' gallery at the far end. "Hullo,
Giles!" added Mrs. Wrayburn, "you look hot."

"I am hot," said Giles Pomfret. "I wish to goodness I
hadn't been so clever about this infernal costume. It's a beautiful billiard-table, but I can't sit down in it." He mopped his
heated brow, crowned with an elegant green lamp-shade. "The
only rest I can get is to hitch my behind on a radiator, and as
they're all in full blast, it's not very cooling. Thank goodness,
I can always make these damned sandwich boards an excuse
to get out of dancing." He propped himself against the nearest
column looking martyred.

PLAN OF THE BALL-ROOM

A. Stair to Dressing-room and Gallery; B, Stair to Gallery; C, Stair to Musicians' Gallery only; D, Settee where Joan Carstairs sat; E, Settee where Jim Playfair sat; F, Where Waits stood; G, Where Ephraim Dodd sat; H, Guests' "Sir Roger"; J, Servants' "Sir Roger"; XX, Hanging Lanterns; O O O O, Arcading.

"Nina Hartford comes off best," said Mrs. Wrayburn. "Water-polo — so sensible — just a bathing-dress and a ball; though I must say it would look better on a less *Restoration* figure. You playing-cards are much the prettiest, and I think the chess-pieces run you close. There goes Gerda Bellingham, dancing with her husband — isn't she *too* marvellous in that red wig? And the bustle and everything — my dear, so attractive. I'm glad they didn't make themselves too Lewis Carroll; Charmian Grayle is the sweetest White Queen — where is she, by the way?"

"I don't like that young woman," said Lady Hermione; "she's fast."

"Dear lady!"

"I've no doubt you think me old-fashioned. Well, I'm glad I am. I say she's fast, and, what's more, heartless. I was watching her before supper, and I'm sorry for Tony Lee. She's been flirting as hard as she can go with Harry Vibart—not to give it a worse name—and she's got Jim Playfair on a string, too. She can't even leave Frank Bellingham alone, though she's staying in his house."

"Oh, I say, Lady H!" protested Sambourne, "you're a bit hard on Miss Grayle. I mean, she's an awfully sporting kid and all that."

"I detest that word 'sporting,'" snapped Lady Hermione. "Nowadays it merely means drunk and disorderly. And she's not such a kid either, young man. In three years' time she'll be a hag, if she goes on at this rate."

"Dear Lady Hermione," said Wimsey, "we can't all be untouched by time, like you."

"You could," retorted the old lady, "if you looked after your stomachs and your morals. Here comes Frank Bellingham—looking for a drink, no doubt. Young people today seem to be positively pickled in gin."

The fox-trot had come to an end, and the Red King was threading his way towards them through a group of applauding couples.

"Hullo, Bellingham!" said Wimsey. "Your crown's crooked. Allow me." He set wig and head-dress to rights with skilful fingers. "Not that I blame you. What crown is safe in these Bolshevik days?"

"Thanks," said Bellingham. "I say, I want a drink."

"What did I tell you?" said Lady Hermione.

"Buzz along, then, old man," said Wimsey. "You've got four minutes. Mind you turn up in time for Sir Roger."

"Right you are. Oh, I'm dancing it with Gerda, by the way. If you see her, you might tell her where I've gone to."

"We will. Lady Hermione, you're honouring me, of course?"

"Nonsense! You're not expecting me to dance at my age? The Old Maid ought to be a wallflower."

"Nothing of the sort. If only I'd had the luck to be born

earlier, you and I should have appeared side by side, as Mat-
rimony. Of course you're going to dance it with me—unless
you mean to throw me over for one of these youngsters."

"I've no use for youngsters," said Lady Hermione. "No
guts. Spindle-shanks." She darted a swift glance at Wimsey's
scarlet hose. "You at least have some suggestion of calves. I
can stand up with you without blushing for you."

Wimsey bowed his scarlet cap and curled wig in deep rev-
erence over the gnarled knuckles extended to him.

"You make me the happiest of men. We'll show them all
how to do it. Right hand, left hand, both hands across, back to
back, round you go and up the middle. There's Deverill going
down to tell the band to begin. Punctual old bird, isn't he?
Just two minutes to go . . . What's the matter, Miss Carstairs?
Lost your partner?"

"Yes—have you seen Tony Lee anywhere?"

"The White King? Not a sign. Nor the White Queen either. I expect they're together somewhere."

"Probably. Poor old Jimmie Playfair is sitting patiently in
the north corridor, looking like Casabianca."

"You'd better go along and console him," said Wimsey,
laughing.

Joan Carstairs made a face and disappeared in the direction of the buffet, just as Sir Charles Deverill, giver of the
party, bustled up to Wimsey and his companions, resplendent
in a Chinese costume patterned with red and green dragons,
bamboos, circles, and characters, and carrying on his shoulder
a stuffed bird with an enormous tail.

"Now, now," he exclaimed, "come along, come along,
come along! All ready for Sir Roger. Got your partner, Wimsey? Ah, yes, Lady Hermione—splendid. You must come and
stand next to your dear mother and me, Wimsey. Don't be
late, don't be late. We want to dance it right through. The
waits will begin at two o'clock—I hope they will arrive in
good time. Dear me, dear me! Why aren't the servants in yet?
I told Watson—I must go and speak to him."

He darted away, and Wimsey, laughing, led his partner up

to the top of the room, where his mother, the Dowager
Duchess of Denver, stood waiting, magnificent as the Queen of
Spades.

"Ah! here you are," said the Duchess placidly. "Dear Sir
Charles—he was getting quite flustered. Such a man for punc-
tuality—he ought to have been a Royalty. A delightful party,
Hermione, isn't it? Sir Roger and the waits—quite medieval—
and a Yule-log in the hall, with the steam-radiators and everything—so oppressive!"

"Tumty, tumty, tiddledy, tumty, tumty, tiddledy," sang
Lord Peter, as the band broke into the old tune. "I do adore
this music. Foot it featly here and there—oh! there's Gerda
Bellingham. Just a moment! Mrs. Bellingham—hi! your royal
spouse awaits your Red Majesty's pleasure in the buffet. Do
hurry him up. He's only got half a minute."

The Red Queen smiled at him, her pale face and black
eyes startlingly brilliant beneath her scarlet wig and crown.

"I'll bring him up to scratch all right," she said, and passed
on, laughing.

"So she will," said the Dowager. "You'll see that young
man in the Cabinet before very long. Such a handsome couple
on a public platform, and very sound, I'm told, about pigs, and
that's so important, the British breakfast-table being what it is."

Sir Charles Deverill, looking a trifle heated, came hurrying back and took his place at the head of the double line of
guests, which now extended three-quarters of the way down
the ballroom. At the lower end, just in front of the Musicians'
Gallery, the staff had filed in, to form a second Sir Roger, at
right angles to the main set. The clock chimed the half-hour.
Sir Charles, craning an anxious neck, counted the dancers.

"Eighteen couples. We're two couples short. How vexa-
tious! Who are missing?"

"The Bellinghams?" said Wimsey. "No, they're here. It's
the White King and Queen, Badminton and Diabolo."

"There's Badminton!" cried Mrs. Wrayburn, signalling
frantically across the room. "Jim! Jim! Bother! He's gone
back again. He's waiting for Charmian Grayle."

"Well, we can't wait any longer," said Sir Charles peevishly. "Duchess, will you lead off?"

The Dowager obediently threw her black velvet train over her arm and skipped away down the centre, displaying an uncommonly neat pair of scarlet ankles. The two lines of dancers, breaking into the hop-and-skip step of the country dance, jigged sympathetically. Below them, the cross lines of black and white and livery coats followed their example with respect. Sir Charles Deverill, dancing solemnly down after the Duchess, joined hands with Nina Hartford from the far end of the line. Tumty, tumty, tiddledy, tumty, tumty, tiddledy ... the first couple turned outward and led the dancers down. Wimsey, catching the hand of Lady Hermione, stooped with her beneath the arch and came triumphantly up to the top of the room, in a magnificent rustle of silk and satin. "My love," sighed Wimsey, "was clad in the black velvet, and I myself in cramoisie." The old lady, well pleased, rapped him over the knuckles with her gilt sceptre. Hands clapped merrily.

"Down we go again," said Wimsey, and the Queen of Clubs and Emperor of the great Mahjongg dynasty twirled and capered in the centre. The Queen of Spades danced up to meet her Jack of Diamonds. "Bézique," said Wimsey; "double Bézique," as he gave both his hands to the Dowager. Tumty, tumty, tiddledy. He again gave his hand to the Queen of Clubs and led her down. Under their lifted arms the other seventeen couples passed. Then Lady Deverill and her partner followed them down—then five more couples.

"We're working nicely to time," said Sir Charles, with his eye on the clock. "I worked it out at two minutes per couple. Ah! here's one of the missing pairs." He waved an agitated arm. "Come into the centre—come along—in here."

A man whose head was decorated with a huge shuttlecock, and Joan Carstairs, dressed as a Diabolo, had emerged from the north corridor. Sir Charles, like a fussy rooster with two frightened hens, guided and pushed them into place between two couples who had not yet done their "hands across," and heaved a sigh of relief. It would have worried him to see them miss their turn. The clock chimed a quarter to two.

"I say, Playfair, have you seen Charmian Grayle or Tony Lee anywhere about?" asked Giles Pomfret of the Badminton costume. "Sir Charles is quite upset because we aren't complete."

"Not a sign of 'em. I was supposed to be dancing this with Charmian, but she vanished upstairs and hasn't come down again. Then Joan came barging along looking for Tony, and we thought we'd better see it through together."

"Here are the waits coming in," broke in Joan Carstairs. "Aren't they sweet? Too-too-truly-rural!"

Between the columns on the north side of the ballroom the waits could be seen filing into place in the corridor, under the command of the Vicar. Sir Roger jigged on his exhausting way. Hands across. Down the centre and up again. Giles Pomfret, groaning, scrambled in his sandwich boards beneath the lengthening arch of hands for the fifteenth time. Tumty, tiddledy. The nineteenth couple wove their way through the dance. Once again, Sir Charles and the Dowager Duchess, both as fresh as paint, stood at the top of the room. The clapping was loudly renewed; the orchestra fell silent; the guests broke up into groups; the servants arranged themselves in a neat line at the lower end of the room; the clock struck two; and the Vicar, receiving a signal from Sir Charles, held his tuning-fork to his ear and gave forth a sonorous A. The waits burst shrilly into the opening bars of "Good King Wenceslas."

It was just as the night was growing darker and the wind blowing stronger that a figure came thrusting its way through the ranks of the singers, and hurried across to where Sir Charles stood; Tony Lee, with his face as white as his costume.

"Charmian . . . in the tapestry room . . . dead . . . strangled."

Superintendent Johnson sat in the library, taking down the evidence of the haggard revellers, who were ushered in upon him one by one. First, Tony Lee, his haunted eyes like dark hollows in a mask of grey paper.

"Miss Grayle had promised to dance with me the last dance before Sir Roger; it was a fox-trot. I waited for her in the passage under the Musicians' Gallery. She never came. I did not search for her. I did not see her dancing with anyone else. When the dance was nearly over, I went out into the garden, by way of the service door under the musicians' stair. I stayed in the garden till Sir Roger de Coverley was over—"

"Was anybody with you, sir?"

"No, nobody."

"You stayed alone in the garden from—yes, from 1:20 past 2 o'clock. Rather disagreeable, was it not, sir, with the snow on the ground?" The Superintendent glanced keenly from Tony's stained and sodden white shoes to his strained face.

"I didn't notice. The room was hot—I wanted air. I saw the waits arrive at about 1:40—I daresay they saw me. I came in a little after 2 o'clock—"

"By the service door again, sir?"

"No; by the garden door on the other side of the house, at the end of the passage which runs along beside the tapestry room. I heard singing going on in the ballroom and saw two men sitting in the little recess at the foot of the staircase on the left-hand side of the passage. I think one of them was the gardener. I went into the tapestry room—"

"With any particular purpose in mind, sir?"

"No—except that I wasn't keen on rejoining the party. I wanted to be quiet." He paused; the Superintendent said nothing. "Then I went into the tapestry room. The light was out. I switched it on and saw—Miss Grayle. She was lying close against the radiator. I thought she had fainted. I went over to her and found she was—dead. I only waited long enough to be sure, and then I went into the ballroom and gave the alarm."

"Thank you, sir. Now, may I ask, what were your relations with Miss Grayle?"

"I-I admired her very much."

"Engaged to her, sir?"

"No, not exactly."

"No quarrel—misunderstanding—anything of that sort?"

"Oh, no!"

Superintendent Johnson looked at him again, and again said nothing, but his experienced mind informed him:

"He's lying."

Aloud he only thanked and dismissed Tony. The White King stumbled drearily out, and the Red King took his place.

"Miss Grayle," said Frank Bellingham, "is a friend of my wife and myself; she was staying at our house. Mr. Lee is also our guest. We all came in one party. I believe there was some kind of understanding between Miss Grayle and Mr. Lee — no actual engagement. She was a very bright, lively, popular girl. I have known her for about six years, and my wife has known her since our marriage. I know of no one who could have borne a grudge against Miss Grayle. I danced with her the last dance but two — it was a waltz. After that came a fox-trot and then Sir Roger. She left me at the end of the waltz; I think she said she was going upstairs to tidy. I think she went out by the door at the upper end of the ballroom. I never saw her again. The ladies' dressing-room is on the second floor, next door to the picture-gallery. You reach it by the staircase that goes up from the garden-passage. You have to pass the door of the tapestry room to get there. The only other way to the dressing-room is by the stair at the east end of the ballroom, which goes up to the picture-gallery. You would then have to pass through the picture-gallery to get to the dressing-room. I know the house well; my wife and I have often stayed here."

Next came Lady Hermione, whose evidence, delivered at great length, amounted to this:

"Charmian Grayle was a minx and no loss to anybody. I am not surprised that someone has strangled her. Women like that ought to be strangled. I would cheerfully have strangled her myself. She has been making Tony Lee's life a burden to him for the last six weeks. I saw her flirting with Mr. Vibart tonight on purpose to make Mr. Lee jealous. She made eyes at Mr. Bellingham and Mr. Playfair. She made eyes at everybody. I should think at least half a dozen people had very good reason to wish her dead."

Mr. Vibart, who arrived dressed in a gaudy Polo costume, and still ludicrously clutching a hobby-horse, said that he had danced several times that evening with Miss Grayle. She was a damn sportin' girl, rattlin' good fun. Well, a bit hot, perhaps, but, dash it all, the poor kid was dead. He might have kissed her once or twice, perhaps, but no harm in that. Well, perhaps poor old Lee did take it a bit hard. Miss Grayle liked pulling Tony's leg. He himself had liked Miss Grayle and was dashed cut-up about the whole beastly business.

Mrs. Bellingham confirmed her husband's evidence. Miss Grayle had been their guest, and they were all on the very best of terms. She felt sure that Mr. Lee and Miss Grayle had been very fond of one another. She had not seen Miss Grayle during the last three dances, but had attached no importance to that. If she had thought about it at all, she would have supposed Miss Grayle was sitting out with somebody. She herself had not been up to the dressing-room since about midnight, and had not seen Miss Grayle go upstairs. She had first missed Miss Grayle when they all stood up for Sir Roger.

Mrs. Wrayburn mentioned that she had seen Miss Carstairs in the ballroom looking for Mr. Lee, just as Sir Charles Deverill went down to speak to the band. Miss Carstairs had then mentioned that Mr. Playfair was in the north corridor, waiting for Miss Grayle. She could say for certain that the time was then 1:28. She had seen Mr. Playfair himself at 1:30. He had looked in from the corridor and gone out again. The whole party had then been standing up together, except Miss Grayle, Miss Carstairs, Mr. Lee, and Mr. Playfair. She knew that, because Sir Charles had counted the couples.

Then came Jim Playfair, with a most valuable piece of evidence.

"Miss Grayle was engaged to me for Sir Roger de Coverley. I went to wait for her in the north corridor as soon as the previous dance was over. That was at 1:25. I sat on the settee in the eastern half of the corridor. I saw Sir Charles go down to speak to the band. Almost immediately afterwards, I saw

Miss Grayle come out of the passage, under the Musicians' Gallery and go up the stairs at the end of the corridor. I called out: 'Hurry up! they're just going to begin.' I do not think she heard me; she did not reply. I am quite sure I saw her. The staircase has open banisters. There is no light in that corner except from the swinging lantern in the corridor, but that is very powerful. I could not be mistaken in the costume. I waited for Miss Grayle till the dance was half over; then I gave it up and joined forces with Miss Carstairs, who had also mislaid her partner."

The maid in attendance on the dressing-room was next examined. She and the gardener were the only two servants who had not danced Sir Roger. She had not quitted the dressing-room at any time since supper, except that she might have gone as far as the door. Miss Grayle had certainly not entered the dressing-room during the last hour of the dance.

The Vicar, much worried and distressed, said that his party had arrived by the garden door at 1:40. He had noticed a man in a white costume smoking a cigarette in the garden. The waits had removed their outer clothing in the garden passage and then gone out to take up their position in the north corridor. Nobody had passed them till Mr. Lee had come in with his sad news.

Mr. Ephraim Dodd, the sexton, made an important addition to this evidence. This aged gentleman was, as he confessed, no singer, but was accustomed to go round with the waits to carry the lantern and collecting box. He had taken a seat in the garden passage "to rest me pore feet." He had seen the gentleman come in from the garden "all in white with a crown on 'is 'ead." The choir were then singing "Bring me flesh and bring me wine." The gentleman had looked about a bit, "made a face, like," and gone into the room at the foot of the stairs. He hadn't been absent "more nor a minute," when he "come out faster than he gone in," and had rushed immediately into the ballroom.

In addition to all this, there was, of course, the evidence of Dr. Pattison. He was a guest at the dance, and had has-

tened to view the body of Miss Grayle as soon as the alarm
was given. He was of opinion that she had been brutally
strangled by someone standing in front of her. She was a tall,
strong girl, and he thought it would have needed a man's
strength to overpower her. When he saw her at five minutes
past two he concluded that she must have been killed within
the last hour, but not within the last five minutes or so. The
body was still quite warm, but, since it had fallen close to the
hot radiator, they could not rely very much upon that indication.

Superintendent Johnson rubbed a thoughtful ear and
turned to Lord Peter Wimsey, who had been able to confirm
much of the previous evidence and, in particular, the exact
times at which various incidents had occurred. The Superintendent knew Wimsey well, and made no bones about taking
him into his confidence.

"You see how it stands, my lord. If the poor young lady
was killed when Dr. Pattison says, it narrows it down a good
bit. She was last seen dancing with Mr. Bellingham at—call it
1:20. At 2 o'clock she was dead. That gives us forty minutes.
But if we're to believe Mr. Playfair, it narrows it down still
further. He says he saw her alive just after Sir Charles went
down to speak to the band, which you put at 1:28. That
means that there's only five people who could possibly have
done it, because all the rest were in the ballroom after that,
dancing Sir Roger. There's the maid in the dressing-room; between you and me, sir, I think we can leave her out. She's a
little slip of a thing, and it's not clear what motive she could
have had. Besides, I've known her from a child, and she isn't
the sort to do it. Then there's the gardener; I haven't seen him
yet, but there again, he's a man I know well, and I'd as soon
suspect myself. Well now, there's this Mr. Tony Lee, Miss
Carstairs, and Mr. Playfair himself. The girl's the least prob-
able, for physical reasons, and besides, strangling isn't a
woman's crime—not as a rule. But Mr. Lee—that's a queer
story, if you like. What was he doing all that time out in the
garden by himself?"

"It sounds to me," said Wimsey, "as if Miss Grayle had given him the push and he had gone into the garden to eat worms."

"Exactly, my lord; and that's where his motive might come in."

'So it might," said Wimsey, "but look here. There's a couple of inches of snow on the ground. If you can confirm the time at which he went out, you ought to be able to see, from his tracks, whether he came in again before Ephraim Dodd saw him. Also, where he went in the interval and whether he was alone."

"That's a good idea, my lord. I'll send my sergeant to make inquiries."

"Then there's Mr. Bellingham. Suppose he killed her after the end of his waltz with her. Did anyone see him in the interval between that and the fox-trot?"

"Quite, my lord. I've thought of that. But you see where *that* leads. It means that Mr. Playfair must have been in a conspiracy with him to do it. And from all we hear, that doesn't seem likely."

"No more it does. In fact, I happen to know that Mr. Bellingham and Mr. Playfair were not on the best of terms. You can wash that out."

"I think so, my lord. And that brings us to Mr. Playfair. It's him we're relying on for the time. We haven't found anyone who saw Miss Grayle during the dance before his—that was the fox-trot. What was to prevent him doing it then? Wait a bit. What does he say himself? Says he danced the fox-trot with the Duchess of Denver." The Superintendent's face fell, and he hunted through his notes again. "She confirms that. Says she was with him during the interval and danced the whole dance with him. Well, my lord, I suppose we can take Her Grace's word for it."

"I think you can," said Wimsey, smiling. "I've known my mother practically since my birth, and have always found her very reliable."

"Yes, my lord. Well, that brings us to the end of the fox-trot. After that, Miss Carstairs saw Mr. Playfair waiting in the north corridor. She says she noticed him several times during the interval and spoke to him. And Mrs. Wrayburn saw him there at 1:30 or thereabouts. Then at 1:45 he and Miss Carstairs came and joined the company. Now, is there anyone who can check all these points? That's the next thing we've got to see to."

Within a very few minutes, abundant confirmation was forthcoming. Mervyn Bunter, Lord Peter's personal man, said that he had been helping to take refreshments along to the buffet. Throughout the interval between the waltz and the fox-trot, Mr. Lee had been standing by the service door beneath the musicians' stair, and half-way through the fox-trot he had been seen to go out into the garden by way of the servants' hall. The police-sergeant had examined the tracks in the snow and found that Mr. Lee had not been joined by any other person, and that there was only the one set of his footprints, leaving the house by the servants' hall and returning by the garden door near the tapestry room. Several persons were also found who had seen Mr. Bellingham in the interval between the waltz and the fox-trot, and who were able to say that he had danced the fox-trot through with Mrs. Bellingham. Joan Carstairs had also been seen continuously throughout the waltz and the fox-trot, and during the following interval and the beginning of Sir Roger. Moreover, the servants who had danced at the lower end of the room were positive that from 1:29 to 1:45 Mr. Playfair had sat continuously on the settee in the north corridor, except for the few seconds during which he had glanced into the ballroom. They were also certain that during that time no one had gone up the staircase at the lower end of the corridor, while Mr. Dodd was equally positive that, after 1:40, nobody except Mr. Lee had entered the garden passage or the tapestry room.

Finally, the circle was closed by William Hoggarty, the gardener. He asserted with the most obvious sincerity that from 1:30 to 1:40 he had been stationed in the garden passage to receive the waits and marshal them to their places. During that time, no one had come down the stair from the picture-gallery or entered the tapestry room. From 1:40 onwards, he had sat beside Mr. Dodd in the passage and nobody had passed him except Mr. Lee.

These points being settled, there was no further reason to doubt Jim Playfair's evidence, since his partners were able to prove his whereabouts during the waltz, the fox-trot, and the intervening interval. At 1:28 or just after, he had seen Charmian Grayle alive. At 2:2 she had been found dead in the tapestry room. During that interval, no one had been seen to enter the room, and every person had been accounted for.

At 6 o'clock, the exhausted guests had been allowed to go to their rooms, accommodation being provided in the house for those who, like the Bellinghams, had come from a distance, since the Superintendent had announced his intention of interrogating them all afresh later in the day.

This new inquiry produced no result. Lord Peter Wimsey did not take part in it. He and Bunter (who was an expert photographer) occupied themselves in photographing the ballroom and adjacent rooms and corridors from every imaginable point of view, for, as Lord Peter said, "You never know what may turn out to be relevant." Late in the afternoon they retired together to the cellar, where with dishes, chemicals, and safe-light hastily procured from the local chemist, they proceeded to develop the plates.

"That's the lot, my lord," observed Bunter at length, sloshing the final plate in the water and tipping it into the hypo. "You can switch the light on now, my lord."

Wimsey did so, blinking in the sudden white glare.

"A very hefty bit of work," said he. "Hullo! What's that plateful of blood you've got there?"

"That's the red backing they put on these plates, my lord, to obviate halation. You may have observed me washing it off before inserting the plate in the developing-dish. Halation, my lord, is a phenomenon—"

Wimsey was not attending.

"But why didn't I notice it before?" he demanded. "That stuff looked to me exactly like clear water."

"So it would, my lord, in the red safe-light. The appearance of whiteness is produced," added Bunter sententiously, "by the reflection of *all* the available light. When all the available light is red, red and white are, naturally, indistinguishable. Similarly, in a green light—"

"Good God!" said Wimsey. "Wait a moment, Bunter, I must think this out . . . Here! damn those plates—let them be. I want you upstairs."

He led the way at a canter to the ballroom, dark now, with the windows in the south corridor already curtained and only the dimness of the December evening filtering through the high windows of the clerestory above the arcading. He first turned on the three great chandeliers in the ballroom itself. Owing to the heavy oak panelling that rose to the roof at both ends and all four angles of the room, these threw no light at all upon the staircase at the lower end of the north corridor. Next, he turned on the light in the four-sided hanging lantern, which hung in the north corridor above and between the two settees. A vivid shaft of green light immediately flooded the lower half of the corridor and the staircase; the upper half was bathed in strong amber, while the remaining sides of the lantern showed red towards the ballroom and blue towards the corridor wall.

Wimsey shook his head.

"Not much room for error there. Unless—I know! Run, Bunter, and ask Miss Carstairs and Mr. Playfair to come here a moment."

While Bunter was gone, Wimsey borrowed a step-ladder from the kitchen and carefully examined the fixing of the lantern. It was a temporary affair, the lantern being supported by a hook screwed into a beam and lit by means of a flex run from the socket of a permanent fixture at a little distance.

"Now, you two," said Wimsey, when the two guests arrived, "I want to make a little experiment. Will you sit down on this settee, Playfair, as you did last night. And you, Miss Carstairs—I picked you out to help because you're wearing a white dress. Will you go up the stairs at the end of the corridor as Miss Grayle did last night. I want to know whether it looks the same to Playfair as it did then—bar all the other people, of course."

He watched them as they carried out this manoeuvre. Jim Playfair looked puzzled.

"It doesn't seem quite the same, somehow. I don't know what the difference is, but there is a difference."

Joan, returning, agreed with him.

"I was sitting on that other settee part of the time," she said, "and it looks different to me. I think it's darker."

"Lighter," said Jim.

"Good!" said Wimsey. "That's what I wanted you to say. Now, Bunter, swing that lantern through a quarter-turn to the left."

The moment this was done, Joan gave a little cry.

"That's it! That's it! The blue light! I remember thinking how frosty-faced those poor waits looked as they came in."

"And you, Playfair?"

"That's right," said Jim, satisfied. "The light was red last night. *I* remember thinking how warm and cosy it looked."

Wimsey laughed.

"We're on to it, Bunter. What's the chessboard rule? *The Queen stands on a square of her own colour.* Find the maid who looked after the dressing-room, and ask her whether Mrs. Bellingham was there last night between the fox-trot and Sir Roger."

In five minutes Bunter was back with his report.

"The maid says, my lord, that Mrs. Bellingham did not come into the dressing-room at that time. But she saw her come out of the picture-gallery and run downstairs towards the tapestry room just as the band struck up Sir Roger."

"And that," said Wimsey, "was at 1:29."

"Mrs. Bellingham?" said Jim. "But you said you saw her yourself in the ballroom before 1:30. She couldn't have had time to commit the murder."

"No, she couldn't," said Wimsey. "But Charmian Grayle was dead long before that. It was the Red Queen, not the White, you saw upon the staircase. Find out why Mrs. Bellingham lied about her movements, and then we shall know the truth."

"A very sad affair, my lord," said Superintendent Johnson, some hours later. "Mr. Bellingham came across with it like a gentleman as soon as we told him we had evidence against his wife. It appears that Miss Grayle knew certain facts about him which would have been very damaging to his political career. She'd been getting money out of him for years. Earlier in the evening she surprised him by making fresh demands. During the last waltz they had together, they went into the tapestry room and a quarrel took place. He lost his temper and laid hands on her. He says he never meant to hurt her seriously, but she started to scream and he took hold of her throat to silence her and—sort of accidentally—throttled her. When he found what he'd done, he left her there and came away, feeling, as he says, all of a daze. He had the next dance with his wife. He told her what had happened, and then discovered that he'd left the little sceptre affair he was carrying in the room with the body. Mrs. Bellingham—she's a brave woman—undertook to fetch it back. She slipped through the dark passage under the Musicians' Gallery—which was empty—and up the stair to the picture-gallery. She did not hear Mr. Playfair speak to her. She ran through the gallery and down the other stair, secured the sceptre, and hid it under her own dress. Later, she heard from Mr. Playfair about what he saw, and realized that in the red light he had mistaken her for the White Queen. In the early hours of this morning, she slipped downstairs and managed to get the lantern shifted round. Of course, she's an accessory after the fact, but she's the kind of wife a man would like to have. I hope they let her off light."

"Amen!" said Lord Peter Wimsey.

THE NECKLACE OF PEARLS

Sir Septimus Shale was accustomed to assert his authority once in the year and once only. He allowed his young and fashionable wife to fill his house with diagrammatic furniture made of steel; to collect advanced artists and anti-grammatical poets; to believe in cocktails and relativity and to dress as extravagantly as she pleased; but he did insist on an old-fashioned Christmas. He was a simple-hearted man, who really liked plum-pudding and cracker mottoes, and he could not get it out of his head that other people, "at bottom," enjoyed these things also. At Christmas, therefore, he firmly retired to his country house in Essex, called in the servants to hang holly and mistletoe upon the cubist electric fittings; loaded the steel sideboard with delicacies from Fortnum & Mason; hung up stockings at the heads of the polished walnut bedsteads; and even, on this occasion only, had the electric radiators removed from the modernist grates and installed wood fires and a Yule log. He then gathered his family and friends about him, filled them with as much Dickensian good fare as he could persuade them to swallow, and, after their Christmas dinner, set them down to play "Charades" and "Clumps" and "Animal, Vegetable, and Mineral" in the drawing-room, concluding these diversions by "Hide-and-Seek" in the dark all over the house. Because Sir Septimus was a very rich man, his guests fell in with this invariable programme, and if they were bored, they did not tell him so.

Another charming and traditional custom which he followed was that of presenting to his daughter Margharita a pearl on each successive birthday—this anniversary happening to coincide with Christmas Eve. The pearls now numbered twenty, and the collection was beginning to enjoy a certain celebrity, and had been photographed in the Society papers. Though not sensationally large—each one being about the size of a marrow-fat pea—the pearls were of very great value. They were of exquisite colour and perfect shape and matched to a hair's-weight. On this particular Christmas Eve, the presentation of the twenty-first pearl had been the occasion of a very special ceremony. There was a dance and there were speeches. On the Christmas night following, the more restricted family party took place, with the turkey and the Victorian games. There were eleven guests, in addition to Sir Septimus and Lady Shale and their daughter, nearly all related or connected to them in some way: John Shale, a brother with his wife and their son and daughter Henry and Betty; Betty's fiancé, Oswald Truegood, a young man with parliamentary ambitions; George Comphrey, a cousin of Lady Shale's, aged about thirty and known as a man about town; Lavinia Prescott, asked on George's account; Joyce Trivett, asked on Henry Shale's account; Richard and Beryl Dennison, distant relations of Lady Shale, who lived a gay and expensive life in town on nobody precisely knew what resources; and Lord Peter Wimsey, asked, in a touching spirit of unreasonable hope, on Margharita's account. There were also, of course, William Norgate, secretary to Sir Septimus, and Miss Tomkins, secretary to Lady Shale, who had to be there be-

cause, without their calm efficiency, the Christmas arrangements could not have been carried through.

Dinner was over—a seemingly endless succession of soup,
fish, turkey, roast beef, plum-pudding, mince-pies, crystallized
fruit, nuts, and five kinds of wine, presided over by Sir Septimus, all smiles, by Lady Shale, all mocking deprecation, and
by Margharita, pretty and bored, with the necklace of twenty-
one pearls gleaming softly on her slender throat. Gorged and
dyspeptic and longing only for the horizontal position, the
company had been shepherded into the drawing-room and set
to play "Musical Chairs" (Miss Tomkins at the piano), "Hunt
the Slipper" (slipper provided by Miss Tomkins), and "Dumb
Crambo" (costumes by Miss Tomkins and Mr. William Norgate). The back drawing-room (for Sir Septimus clung to
these old-fashioned names) provided an admirable dressing-
room, being screened by folding doors from the large drawing-
room in which the audience sat on aluminum chairs,
scrabbling uneasy toes on a floor of black glass under the
tremendous illumination of electricity reflected from a brass
ceiling.

It was William Norgate who, after taking the temperature
of the meeting, suggested to Lady Shale that they should play
at something less athletic. Lady Shale agreed and, as usual,
suggested bridge. Sir Septimus, as usual, blew the suggestion
aside.

"Bridge? Nonsense! Nonsense! Play bridge every day of
your lives. This is Christmas time. Something we can all play
together. How about 'Animal, Vegetable, and Mineral?' "

This intellectual pastime was a favourite with Sir Septimus; he was rather good at putting pregnant questions. After
a brief discussion, it became evident that this game was an inevitable part of the programme. The party settled down to it,
Sir Septimus undertaking to "go out" first and set the thing
going.

Presently they had guessed among other things Miss
Tomkins's mother's photograph, a gramophone record of "I
want to be happy" (much scientific research into the exact

composition of records, settled by William Norgate out of the *Encyclopaedia Britannica)*, the smallest stickleback in the stream at the bottom of the garden, the new planet Pluto, the scarf worn by Mrs. Dennison (very confusing, because it was not silk, which would be animal, or artificial silk, which would be vegetable, but made of spun glass—mineral, a very clever choice of subject), and had failed to guess the Prime Minister's wireless speech—which was voted not fair, since nobody could decide whether it was animal by nature or a kind of gas. It was decided that they should do one more word and then go on to "Hide-and-Seek." Oswald Truegood had retired into the back room and shut the door behind him while the party discussed the next subject of examination, when suddenly Sir Septimus broke in on the argument by calling to his daughter:

"Hullo, Margy! What have you done with your necklace?"

"I took it off, Dad, because I thought it might get broken in 'Dumb Crambo.' It's over here on this table. No, it isn't. Did you take it, mother?"

"No, I didn't. If I'd seen it, I should have. You are a careless child."

"I believe you've got it yourself, Dad. You're teasing."

Sir Septimus denied the accusation with some energy. Everybody got up and began to hunt about. There were not many places in that bare and polished room where a necklace could be hidden. After ten minutes' fruitless investigation, Richard Dennison, who had been seated next to the table where the pearls had been placed, began to look rather uncomfortable.

"Awkward, you know," he remarked to Wimsey.

At this moment, Oswald Truegood put his head through the folding-doors and asked whether they hadn't settled on something by now, because he was getting the fidgets.

This directed the attention of the searchers to the inner room. Margharita must have been mistaken. She had taken it in there, and it had got mixed up with the dressing-up clothes somehow. The room was ransacked. Everything was lifted up and shaken. The thing began to look serious. After half an hour of desperate energy it became apparent that the pearls were nowhere to be found.

"They must be somewhere in these two rooms, you know," said Wimsey. "The back drawing-room has no door and nobody could have gone out of the front drawing-room without being seen. Unless the windows—"

No. The windows were all guarded on the outside by heavy shutters which it needed two footmen to take down and replace. The pearls had not gone out that way. In fact, the mere suggestion that they had left the drawing-room at all was disagreeable. Because—because—

It was William Norgate, efficient as ever, who coldly and boldly, faced the issue.

"I think, Sir Septimus, it would be a relief to the minds of everybody present if we could all be searched."

Sir Septimus was horrified, but the guests, having found a leader, backed up Norgate. The door was locked, and the search was conducted—the ladies in the inner room and the men in the outer.

Nothing resulted from it except some very interesting information about the belongings habitually carried about by the average man and woman. It was natural that Lord Peter Wimsey should possess a pair of forceps, a pocket lens, and a small folding foot-rule—was he not a Sherlock Holmes in high life? But that Oswald Truegood should have two liver-pills in a screw of paper and Henry Shale a pocket edition of *The Odes of Horace* was unexpected. Why did John Shale distend the pockets of his dress-suit with a stump of red sealing-wax, an ugly little mascot, and a five-shilling piece? George Comphrey had a pair of folding scissors, and three wrapped lumps of sugar, of the sort served in restaurants and dining-cars—evidence of a not uncommon form of kleptomania; but that the tidy and exact Norgate should burden himself with a reel of white cotton, three separate lengths of string, and twelve safety-pins on a card seemed really remarkable till one remembered that he had superintended all the Christmas decorations. Richard

Dennison, amid some confusion and laughter, was found to cherish a lady's garter, a powder-compact, and half a potato; the last-named, he said, was a prophylactic against rheumatism (to which he was subject), while the other objects belonged to his wife. On the ladies' side, the more striking exhibits were a little book on palmistry, three invisible hair-pins, and a baby's photograph (Miss Tomkins); a Chinese trick cigarette-case with a secret compartment (Beryl Dennison); a *very* private letter and an outfit for mending stocking-ladders (Lavinia Prescott); and a pair of eyebrow tweezers and a small packet of white powder, said to be for headaches (Betty Shale). An agitating moment followed the production from Joyce Trivett's handbag of a small string of pearls—but it was promptly remembered that these had come out of one of the crackers at dinnertime, and they were, in fact, synthetic. In short, the search was unproductive of anything beyond a general shamefacedness and the discomfort always produced by undressing and re-dressing in a hurry at the wrong time of the day.

It was then that somebody, very grudgingly and haltingly, mentioned the horrid word "Police." Sir Septimus, naturally, was appalled by the idea. It was disgusting. He would not allow it. The pearls must be somewhere. They must search the rooms again. Could not Lord Peter Wimsey, with his experience of—er—mysterious happenings, do something to assist them?

"Eh?" said his lordship. "Oh, by Jove, yes—by all means, certainly. That is to say, provided nobody supposes—eh, what? I mean to say, you don't know that I'm not a suspicious character, do you, what?"

Lady Shale interposed with authority.

"We don't think *anybody* ought to be suspected," she said, "but, if we did, we'd know it couldn't be you. You know *far* too much about crimes to want to commit one."

"All right," said Wimsey. "But after the way the place has been gone over—" He shrugged his shoulders.

"Yes, I'm afraid you won't be able to find any footprints," said Margharita. "But we may have overlooked something."

Wimsey nodded.

"I'll try. Do you all mind sitting down on your chairs in the outer room and staying there. All except one of you — I'd better have a witness to anything I do or find. Sir Septimus — you'd be the best person, I think."

He shepherded them to their places and began a slow circuit of the two rooms, exploring every surface, gazing up to the polished brazen ceiling, and crawling on hands and knees in the approved fashion across the black and shining desert of the floors. Sir Septimus followed, staring when Wimsey stared, bending with his hands upon his knees when Wimsey crawled, and puffing at intervals with astonishment and chagrin. Their progress rather resembled that of a man taking out a very inquisitive puppy for a very leisurely constitutional. Fortunately, Lady Shale's taste in furnishing made investigation easier; there were scarcely any nooks or corners where anything could be concealed.

They reached the inner drawing-room, and here the dressing-up clothes were again minutely examined, but without result. Finally, Wimsey lay down flat on his stomach to squint under a steel cabinet which was one of the very few pieces of furniture which possessed short legs. Something about it seemed to catch his attention. He rolled up his sleeve and plunged his arm into the cavity, kicked convulsively in the effort to reach farther than was humanly possible, pulled out from his pocket and extended his folding foot-rule, fished with it under the cabinet, and eventually succeeded in extracting what he sought.

It was a very minute object — in fact, a pin. Not an ordinary pin, but one resembling those used by entomologists to impale extremely small moths on the setting-board. It was about three-quarters of an inch in length, as fine as a very fine needle, with a sharp point and a particularly small head.

"Bless my soul!" said Sir Septimus. "What's that?"

"Does anybody here happen to collect moths or beetles or anything?" asked Wimsey, squatting on his haunches and examining the pin.

"I'm pretty sure they don't," replied Sir Septimus. "I'll ask them."

"Don't do that." Wimsey bent his head and stared at the floor, from which his own face stared meditatively back at him.

"I see," said Wimsey presently. "That's how it was done. All right, Sir Septimus. I know where the pearls are, but I don't know who took them. Perhaps it would be as well—for everybody's satisfaction—just to find out. In the meantime they are perfectly safe. Don't tell anyone that we've found this pin or that we've discovered anything. Send all these people to bed. Lock the drawing-room door and keep the key, and we'll get our man—or woman—by breakfast-time."

"God bless my soul," said Sir Septimus, very much puzzled.

Lord Peter Wimsey kept careful watch that night upon the drawing-room door. Nobody, however, came near it. Either the thief suspected a trap or he felt confident that any time would do to recover the pearls. Wimsey, however, did not feel that he was wasting his time. He was making a list of people who had been left alone in the back drawing-room during the playing of "Animal, Vegetable, and Mineral." The list ran as follows:

> Sir Septimus Shale
> Lavinia Prescott
> William Norgate
> Joyce Trivett and Henry Shale (together, because they had claimed to be incapable of guessing anything un-aided)
> Mrs. Dennison
> Betty Shale
> George Comphrey
> Richard Dennison
> Miss Tomkins
> Oswald Truegood

He also made out a list of the persons to whom pearls might be useful or desirable. Unfortunately, this list agreed in almost all respects with the first (always excepting Sir Septimus) and so was not very helpful. The two secretaries had both come well recommended, but that was exactly what they would have done had they come with ulterior designs; the Dennisons were notorious livers from hand to mouth; Betty Shale carried mysterious white powders in her handbag, and was known to be in with a rather rapid set in town; Henry was a harmless dilettante, but Joyce Trivett could twist him round her little finger and was what Jane Austen liked to call "expensive and dissipated;" Comphrey speculated; Oswald Truegood was rather frequently present at Epsom and Newmarket—the search for motives was only too fatally easy.

When the second housemaid and the under-footman appeared in the passage with household implements, Wimsey abandoned his vigil, but he was down early to breakfast. Sir Septimus with his wife and daughter were down before him, and a certain air of tension made itself felt. Wimsey, standing on the hearth before the fire, made conversation about the weather and politics.

The party assembled gradually, but, as though by common consent, nothing was said about pearls until after breakfast, when Oswald Truegood took the bull by the horns.

"Well now!" said he. "How's the detective getting along? Got your man, Wimsey?"

"Not yet," said Wimsey easily.

Sir Septimus, looking at Wimsey as though for his cue, cleared his throat and dashed into speech.

"All very tiresome," he said, "all very unpleasant. Hr'rm. Nothing for it but the police, I'm afraid. Just at Christmas, too. Hr'rm. Spoilt the party. Can't stand seeing all this stuff about the place." He waved his hand towards the festoons of evergreens and coloured paper that adorned the walls. "Take it all down, eh, what? No heart in it. Hr'rm. Burn the lot."

"What a pity, when we worked so hard over it," said Joyce.

"Oh, leave it, Uncle," said Henry Shale. "You're bothering too much about the pearls. They're sure to turn up."

"Shall I ring for James?" suggested William Norgate.

"No," interrupted Comphrey, "let's do it ourselves. It'll give us something to do and take our minds off our troubles."

"That's right," said Sir Septimus. "Start right away. Hate the sight of it."

He savagely hauled a great branch of holly down from the mantelpiece and flung it, crackling, into the fire.

"That's the stuff," said Richard Dennison. "Make a good old blaze!" He leapt up from the table and snatched the mistletoe from the chandelier. "Here goes! One more kiss for somebody before it's too late."

"Isn't it unlucky to take it down before the New Year?" suggested Miss Tomkins.

"Unlucky be hanged. We'll have it all down. Off the stairs and out of the drawing-room too. Somebody go and collect it."

"Isn't the drawing-room locked?" asked Oswald.

"No. Lord Peter says the pearls aren't there, wherever else they are, so it's unlocked. That's right, isn't it, Wimsey?"

"Quite right. The pearls were taken out of these rooms. I can't tell yet how, but I'm positive of it. In fact, I'll pledge my reputation that wherever they are, they're not up there."

"Oh, well," said Comphrey, "in that case, have at it! Come along, Lavinia—you and Dennison do the drawing-room and I'll do the back room. We'll have a race."

"But if the police are coming in," said Dennison, "oughtn't everything to be left just as it is?"

"Damn the police!" shouted Sir Septimus. "They don't want evergreens."

Oswald and Margharita were already pulling the holly and ivy from the staircase, amid peals of laughter. The party dispersed. Wimsey went quietly upstairs and into the drawing-room, where the work of demolition was taking place at a great rate, George having bet the other two ten shillings to a tanner that they would not finish their part of the job before he finished his.

"You mustn't help," said Lavinia, laughing to Wimsey. "It wouldn't be fair."

Wimsey said nothing, but waited till the room was clear. Then he followed them down again to the hall, where the fire was sending up a great roaring and spluttering, suggestive of Guy Fawkes' night. He whispered to Sir Septimus, who went forward and touched George Comphrey on the shoulder.

"Lord Peter wants to say something to you, my boy," he said.

Comphrey started and went with him a little reluctantly, as it seemed. He was not looking very well.

"Mr. Comphrey," said Wimsey, "I fancy these are some of your property." He held out the palm of his hand, in which rested twenty-two fine, small-headed pins.

"Ingenious," said Wimsey, "but something less ingenious would have served his turn better. It was very unlucky, Sir Septimus, that you should have mentioned the pearls when you did. Of course, he hoped that the loss wouldn't be discovered till we'd chucked guessing games and taken to "Hide-and-Seek." Then the pearls might have been anywhere in the house, we shouldn't have locked the drawing-room door, and he could have recovered them at his leisure. He had had this possibility in his mind when he came here, obviously, and that was why he brought the pins, and Miss Shale's taking off the necklace to play 'Dumb Crambo' gave him his opportunity.

"He had spent Christmas here before, and knew perfectly well that 'Animal, Vegetable, and Mineral' would form part of the entertainment. He had only to gather up the necklace from the table when it came to his turn to retire, and he knew he could count on at least five minutes by himself while we were all arguing about the choice of a word. He had only to snip the pearls from the string with his pocket-scissors, burn the string in the grate, and fasten the pearls to the mistletoe with the fine pins. The mistletoe was hung on the chandelier, pretty high — it's a lofty room — but he could easily reach it by standing on the glass table, which wouldn't show footmarks, and it was al-most certain that nobody would think of examining the mistle-toe for extra berries. I shouldn't have thought of it myself if I hadn't found that pin which he had dropped. That gave me the idea that the pearls had been separated and the rest was easy. I took the pearls off the mistletoe last night—the clasp was there, too, pinned among the holly-leaves. Here they are. Comphrey must have got a nasty shock this morning. I knew he was our man when he suggested that the guests should tackle the decorations themselves and that he should do the back drawing-room—but I wish I had seen his face when he came to the mistletoe and found the pearls gone."

"And you worked it all out when you found the pin?" said Sir Septimus.

"Yes; I knew then where the pearls had gone to."

"But you never even looked at the mistletoe."

"I saw it reflected in the black glass floor, and it struck me then how much the mistletoe berries looked like pearls."

IN THE TEETH OF
THE EVIDENCE

Well, old son," said Mr. Lamplough, "and what can we do for you to-day?"

"Oh, some of your whizz-bang business, I suppose," said Lord Peter Wimsey, seating himself resentfully in the green velvet torture-chair and making a face in the direction of the drill. "Jolly old left-hand upper grinder come to bits on me. I was only eating an omelette, too. Can't understand why they always pick these moments. If I'd been cracking nuts or chewing peppermint jumbles I could understand it."

"Yes?" said Mr. Lamplough, soothingly. He drew an electric bulb, complete with mirror, as though by magic out of a kind of Maskelyne-and-Devant contraption on Lord Peter's left; a trail of flex followed it, issuing apparently from the bowels of the earth. "Any pain?"

"No *pain*," said Wimsey, irritably, "unless you count a sharp edge fit to saw your tongue off. Point is, why should it go pop like that? I wasn't doing anything to it."

"No?" said Mr. Lamplough, his manner hovering between

the professional and the friendly, for he was an old Winchester man and a member of one of Wimsey's clubs, and had frequently met him on the cricket-field in the days of their youth. "Well, if you'll stop talking half a moment, we'll have a look at it. Ah!"

"Don't say, 'Ah!' like that, as if you'd found pyorrhoea and necrosis of the jaw and were gloating over it, you damned old ghoul. Just carve it out and stop it up and be hanged to you. And, by the way, what have you been up to? Why should I meet an inspector of police on your doorstep? You needn't pretend he came to have his bridgework attended to, because I saw his sergeant waiting for him outside."

"Well, it was rather curious," said Mr. Lamplough, dexterously gagging his friend with one hand and dabbing cotton-wool into the offending cavity with the other. "I suppose I oughtn't to tell you, but if I don't, you'll get it all out of your friends at Scotland Yard. They wanted to see my predecessor's books. Possibly you noticed that bit in the papers about a dental man being found dead in a blazing garage on Wimbledon Common?"

"Yonk—ugh?" said Lord Peter Wimsey.

"Last night," said Mr. Lamplough. "Pooped off about nine pipemma, and it took them three hours to put it out. One of those wooden garages—and the big job was to keep the blaze away from the house. Fortunately it's at the end of the row, with nobody at home. Apparently this man Prendergast was all alone there—just going off for a holiday or something—and he contrived to set himself and his car and his garage alight last night and was burnt to death. In fact, when they found him, he was so badly charred that they couldn't be sure it was he. So, being sticklers for routine, they had a look at his teeth."

"Oh, yes?" said Wimsey, watching Mr. Lamplough fitting a new drill into its socket. "Didn't anybody have a go at putting the fire out?"

"Oh, yes—but as it was a wooden shed, full of petrol, it simply went up like a bonfire. Just a little bit over this way, please. That's splendid." Gr-r-r, whizz, gr-r-r. "As a matter of fact, they seem to think it might just possibly be suicide. The man's married, with three children, and immured and all that sort of thing." Whizz, gr-r-r, buzz, gr-r-r, whizz. "His family's down at Worthing, staying with his mother-in-law or something. Tell me if I hurt you." Gr-r-r. "And I don't suppose he was doing any too well. Still, of course, he may easily have had an accident when filling up. I gather he was starting off that night to join them."

"A—ow—oo—oo—uh—ihi—ih?" inquired Wimsey naturally enough.

"How do I come into it?" said Mr. Lamplough, who, from long experience was expert in the interpretation of mumblings. "Well, only because the chap whose practice I took over here did this fellow Prendergast's dental work for him." Whizz. "He died, but left his books behind him for my guidance, in case any of his old patients should feel inclined to trust me." Gr-r-r, whizz. "I'm sorry. Did you feel that? As a matter of fact, some of them actually do. I suppose it's an instinct to trundle round to the same old place when you're in pain, like the dying elephants. Will you rinse, please?"

"I see," said Wimsey, when he had finished washing out chips of himself and exploring his ravaged molar with his tongue. "How odd it is that these cavities always seem so large. I feel as if I could put my head into this one. Still, I suppose you know what you're about. And are Prendergast's teeth all right?"

"Haven't had time to hunt through the ledger, yet, but I've said I'll go down to have a look at them as soon as I've finished with you. It's my lunch-time anyway, and my two o'clock patient isn't coming, thank goodness. She usually brings five spoilt children, and they all want to sit round and watch, and play with the apparatus. One of them got loose last time and tried to electrocute itself on the X-ray plant next door. And she thinks that children should be done at half-price. A little wider if you can manage it." Gr-r-r. "Yes, that's very nice. Now we can dress that and put in a temporary. Rinse please."

"Yes," said Wimsey, "and for goodness' sake make it firm and not too much of your foul oil of cloves. I don't want bits to come out in the middle of dinner. You can't imagine the nastiness of caviar flavoured with cloves."

"No?" said Mr. Lamplough. "You may find this a little cold." Squirt, swish. "Rinse, please. You may notice it when the dressing goes in. Oh, you did notice it? Good. That shows that the nerve's all right. Only a little longer now. There! Yes, you may get down now. Another rinse? Certainly. When would you like to come in again?"

"Don't be silly, old horse," said Wimsey. "I am coming out to Wimbledon with you straight away. You'll get there twice as fast if I drive you. I've never had a corpse-in-blazing-garage before, and I want to learn."

There is nothing really attractive about corpses in blazing garages. Even Wimsey's war experience did not quite reconcile him to the object that lay on the mortuary slab in the police station. Charred out of all resemblance to humanity, it turned even the police surgeon pale, while Mr. Lamplough was so overcome that he had to lay down the books he had brought with him and retire into the open to recover himself. Meanwhile Wimsey, having put himself on terms of mutual confidence and esteem with the police officials, thoughtfully turned over the little pile of blackened odds and ends that represented the contents of Mr. Prendergast's pockets. There was nothing remarkable about them. The leather note-case still held the remains of a thickish wad of notes—doubtless cash in hand for the holiday at Worthing. The handsome gold watch (obviously a presentation) had stopped at seven minutes past nine. Wimsey remarked on its good state of preservation. Sheltered between the left arm and the body—that seemed to be the explanation.

"Looks as though the first sudden blaze had regularly overcome him," said the police inspector. "He evidently made no attempt to get out. He'd simply fallen forward over the wheel, with his head on the dashboard. That's why the face is so disfigured. I'll show you the remains of the car presently if you're interested, my lord. If the other gentleman's feeling better we may as well take the body first."

Taking the body was a long and unpleasant job. Mr. Lamplough, nerving himself with an effort and producing a pair of forceps and a probe, went gingerly over the jaws—reduced almost to their bony structure by the furnace heat to which they had been exposed—while the police surgeon checked entries in the ledger. Mr. Prendergast had a dental history extending back over ten years in the ledger, and had already had two or three fillings done before that time. These had been noted at the time when he first came to Mr. Lamplough's predecessor.

At the end of a long examination, the surgeon looked up from the notes he had been making.

"Well, now," he said, "let's check that again. Allowing for renewal of old work, I think we've got a pretty accurate picture of the present state of his mouth. There ought to be nine fillings in all. Small amalgam filling in right lower back wisdom tooth; big amalgam ditto in right lower back molar; amalgam fillings in right upper first and second bicuspids at point of contact; right upper incisor crowned—that all right?"

"I expect so," said Mr. Lamplough, "except that the right upper incisor seems to be missing altogether, but possibly the crown came loose and fell out." He probed delicately. "The jaw is very brittle—I can't make anything of the canal—but there's nothing against it."

"We may find the crown in the garage," suggested the Inspector.

"Fused porcelain filling in left upper canine," went on the surgeon; "amalgam fillings in left upper first bicuspid and lower second bicuspid and left lower thirteen-year-old molar. That seems to be all. No teeth missing and no artificials. How old was this man, Inspector?"

"About forty-five, Doc."

"My age. I only wish I had as good a set of teeth," said the surgeon. Mr. Lamplough agreed with him.

"Then I take it, this is Mr. Prendergast all right," said the Inspector.

"Not a doubt of it, I should say," replied Mr. Lamplough; "though I should like to find that missing crown."

"We'd better go round to the house, then," said the Inspector. "Well, yes, thank you, my lord, I shouldn't mind a lift in that. Some car. Well, the only point now is, whether it was accident or suicide. Round to the right my lord, and then second on the left — I'll tell you as we go."

"A bit out of the way for a dental man," observed Mr. Lamplough, as they emerged upon some scattered houses near the Common.

The Inspector made a grimace.

"I thought the same, sir, but it appears Mrs. Prendergast persuaded him to come here. So good for the children. Not so good for the practice, though. If you ask me, I should say Mrs. P. was the biggest argument we have for suicide. Here we are."

The last sentence was scarcely necessary. There was a little crowd about the gate of a small detached villa at the end of a row of similar houses. From a pile of dismal debris in the garden a smell of burning still rose, disgustingly. The Inspector pushed through the gate with his companions, pursued by the comments of the bystanders.

"That's the Inspector . . . that's Dr. Maggs . . . that'll be another doctor, him with the little bag . . . who's the bloke in the eye-glass? . . . Looks a proper nobleman, don't he, Florrie? . . . Why he'll be the insurance bloke . . . Coo! Look at his grand car . . . that's where the money goes. . . . That's a Rolls, that is . . . no, silly, it's a Daimler. . . . Ow, well, it's all advertisement these days."

Wimsey giggled indecorously all the way up the garden path. The sight of the skeleton car amid the sodden and fire-blackened remains of the garage sobered him. Two police constables, crouched over the ruin with a sieve, stood up and saluted.

"How are you getting on, Jenkins?"

"Haven't got anything very much yet, sir, bar an ivory cigarette-holder. This gentleman"—indicating a stout, bald man in spectacles, who was squatting among the damaged coach-work, "is Mr. Tolley, from the motorworks, come with a note from the Superintendent, sir."

"Ah, yes. Can you give any opinion about this, Mr. Tolley? Dr. Maggs you know. Mr. Lamplough, Lord Peter Wimsey. By the way, Jenkins, Mr. Lamplough has been going into the corpse's dentistry, and he's looking for a lost tooth. You might see if you can find it. Now, Mr. Tolley?"

"Can't see much doubt about how it happened," said Mr. Tolley, picking his teeth thoughtfully. "Regular death-traps, these little saloons, when anything goes wrong unexpectedly. There's a front tank, you see, and it looks as though there might have been a bit of a leak behind the dash, somewhere. Possibly the seam of the tank had got strained a bit, or the union had come loose. It's loose now, as a matter of fact, but that's not unusual after a fire, Rouse case or no Rouse case. You can get quite a lot of slow dripping from a damaged tank or pipe, and there seems to have been a coconut mat round the controls, which would prevent you from noticing. There'd be a smell, of course, but these little garages do often get to smell of petrol, and he kept several cans of the stuff here. More than the legal amount—but *that's* not unusual either. Looks to me as though he'd filled up his tank—there are two empty tins near the bonnet, with the caps loose—got in, shut the door, started up the car, perhaps, and then lit a cigarette. Then, if there were any petrol fumes about from a leak, the whole show would go up in his face—whoosh!"

"How was the ignition?"

"Off. He may never have switched it on, but it's quite likely he switched it off again when the flames went up. Silly thing to do, but lots of people *do* do it. The proper thing, of course, is to switch off the petrol and leave the engine running so as to empty the carburettor, but you don't always think straight when you're being burnt alive. Or he may have meant to turn off the petrol and been overcome before he could manage it. The tank's over here to the left, you see."

"On the other hand," said Wimsey, "he may have committed suicide and faked the accident."

"Nasty way of committing suicide."

"Suppose he'd taken poison first."

"He'd have had to stay alive long enough to fire the car."

"That's true. Suppose he'd shot himself—would the flash from the—no, that's silly—you'd have found the weapon in the case. Or a hypodermic? Same objection. Prussic acid might have done it—I mean, he might just have had time to take a tablet and then fire the car. Prussic acid's pretty quick, but it isn't absolutely instantaneous."

"I'll have a look for it, anyway," said Dr. Maggs.

They were interrupted by the constable.

"Excuse me, sir, but I think we've found the tooth. Mr. Lamplough says this is it."

Between his pudgy finger and thumb he held up a small, bony object, from which a small stalk of metal still protruded.

"That's a right upper incisor crown all right by the look of it," said Mr. Lamplough. "I suppose the cement gave way with the heat. Some cements are sensitive to heat, some, on the other hand, to damp. Well, that settles it, doesn't it?"

"Yes—well, we shall have to break it to the widow. Not that she can be in very much doubt, I imagine."

Mrs. Prendergast—a very much made-up lady with a face set in lines of habitual peevishness—received the news with a burst of loud sobs. She informed them, when she was sufficiently recovered, that Arthur had always been careless about petrol, that he smoked too much, that she had often warned him about the danger of small saloons, that she had told him he ought to get a bigger car, that the one he had was not really large enough for her and the whole family, that he *would* drive at night, though she had always said it was dangerous, and that if he'd listened to her, it would never have happened.

"Poor Arthur was not a good driver. Only last week, when he was taking us down to Worthing, he drove the car right up on a bank in trying to pass a lorry, and frightened us all dread-fully."

"Ah!" said the Inspector. "No doubt that's how the tank got strained." Very cautiously he inquired whether Mr. Pren-dergast could have had any reason for taking his own life. The widow was indignant. It was true that the practice had been declining of late, but Arthur would never had been so wicked as to do such a thing. Why, only three months ago, he had taken out a life-insurance for £500 and he'd never have inval-idated it by committing suicide within the term stipulated by the policy. Inconsiderate of her as Arthur was, and whatever injuries he had done her as a wife, he wouldn't rob his inno-cent children.

The Inspector pricked up his ears at the word "injuries." What injuries?

Oh, well, of course, she'd known all the time that Arthur was carrying on with that Mrs. Fielding. You couldn't deceive her with all this stuff about teeth needing continual attention. And it was all very well to say that Mrs. Fielding's house was better run than her own. *That* wasn't surprising—a rich widow with no children and no responsibilities, of course she could afford to have everything nice. You couldn't espect a busy wife to do miracles on such a small housekeeping al-lowance. If Arthur had wanted things different, he should have been more generous, and it was easy enough for Mrs. Fielding to attract men, dressed up like a fashion-plate and no better than she should be. She'd told Arthur that if it didn't stop she'd divorce him. And since then he'd taken to spending all his evenings in Town, and what was he doing there—

The Inspector stemmed the torrent by asking for Mrs. Fielding's address.

"I'm sure I don't know," said Mrs. Prendergast. "She did live at Number 57, but she went aboard after I made it clear I wasn't going to stand any more of it. It's very nice to be some people, with plenty of money to spend. I've never been abroad since our honeymoon, and that was only to Boulogne."

At the end of this conversation, the Inspector sought Dr.

Maggs and begged him to be thorough in his search for prussic acid.

The remaining testimony was that of Gladys, the general servant. She had left Mr. Prendergast's house the day before at 6 o'clock. She was to have taken a week's holiday while the Prendergasts were at Worthing. She had thought that Mr. Prendergast had seemed worried and nervous the last few days, but that had not surprised her, because she knew he disliked staying with his wife's people. She (Gladys) had finished her work and put out a cold supper and then gone home with her employer's permission. He had a patient—a gentleman from Australia, or some such a place, who wanted his teeth attended to in a hurry before going off on his travels again. Mr. Prendergast had explained that he would be working late, and would shut up the house himself, and she need not wait. Further inquiry showed that Mr. Prendergast had "scarcely touched" his supper, being, presumably, in a hurry to get off. Apparently, then, the patient had been the last person to see Mr. Prendergast alive.

The dentist's appointment-book was next examined. The patient figured there as "Mr. Williams 5.30," and the address-book placed Mr. Williams at a small hotel in Bloomsbury. The manager of the hotel said that Mr. Williams had stayed there for a week. He had given no address except "Adelaide," and had mentioned that he was revisiting the old country for the first time after twenty years and had no friends in London. Unfortunately, he could not be interviewed. At about half-past ten the previous night, a messenger had called, bringing his car, to pay his bill and remove his luggage. No address had been left for forwarding letters. It was not a district messenger, but a man in a slouch hat and heavy dark overcoat. The night-porter had not seen his face very clearly, as only one light was on in the hall. He had told them to hurry up, as Mr. Williams wanted to catch the boat-train from Waterloo. Inquiry at the booking-office showed that a Mr. Williams had actually travelled on that train, being booked to Paris. The ticket had been taken that same night. So Mr. Williams had disappeared into the blue, and even if they could trace him, it seemed unlikely that he could throw much light on Mr. Prendergast's state of mind immediately previous to the disaster. It seemed a little odd, at first, that Mr. Williams, from Adelaide, staying in Bloomsbury, should have travelled to Wimbledon to get his teeth attended to, but the simple explanation was the likeliest: namely, that the friendless Williams had struck up an acquaintance with Prendergast in a café or some such place, and that a casual mention of his dental necessities had led to a project of mutual profit and assistance.

After which, nothing seemed to be left but for the coroner to bring in a verdict of Death by Misadventure and for the widow to send in her claim to the Insurance Company, when Dr. Maggs upset the whole scheme of things by announcing that he had discovered traces of a large injection of hyoscine in the body, and what about it? The Inspector, on hearing this, observed callously that he was not surprised. If ever a man had an excuse for suicide, he thought it was Mrs. Prendergast's husband. He thought that it would be desirable to make a careful search among the scorched laurels surrounding what had been Mr. Prendergast's garage. Lord Peter Wimsey agreed, but committed himself to the prophecy that the syringe would not be found.

Lord Peter Wimsey was entirely wrong. The syringe was found next day, in a position suggesting that it had been thrown out of the window of the garage after use. Traces of the poison were discovered to be present in it. "It's a slow-working drug," observed Dr. Maggs. "No doubt he jabbed himself, threw the syringe away, hoping it would never be looked for, and then, before he lost consciousness, climbed into the car and set light to it. A clumsy way of doing it."

"A damned ingenious way of doing it," said Wimsey. "I don't believe in that syringe, somehow." He rang up his dentist. "Lamplough, old horse," he said, "I wish you'd do something for me. I wish you'd go over those teeth again. No—not my teeth; Prendergast's."

"Oh, blow it!" said Mr. Lamplough, uneasily.

"No, but I wish you would," said his lordship.

The body was sill unburied. Mr. Lamplough, grumbling very much, went down to Wimbledon with Wimsey, and again went through his distasteful task. This time he started on the left side.

"Lower thirteen-year-old molar and second bicuspid filled amalgam. The fire's got at those a bit, but they're all right. First upper bicuspid—bicuspids are stupid sort of teeth—always the first to go. That filling looks to have been rather carelessly put in—not what I should call good work; it seems to extend over the next tooth—possibly the fire did that. Left upper canine, cast porcelain filling on anterior face—"

"Half a jiff," said Wimsey, "Maggs' note says 'fused porcelain.' Is it the same thing?"

"No. Different process. Well, I suppose its fused porcelain—difficult to see. I should have said it was cast, myself, but that's as may be."

"Let's verify it in the ledger. I wish Maggs had put the dates in—goodness knows how far I shall have to hunt back, and I don't understand this chap's writing or his dashed abbreviations."

"You won't have to go back very far if it's cast. The stuff only came in about 1928, from America. There was quite a rage for it then, but for some reason it didn't take on extraordinarily well over here. But some men use it."

"Oh, then it isn't cast," said Wimsey. "There's nothing here about canines, back to '28. Let's make sure; '27, '26, '25, '24, '23. Here you are. Canine, something or other."

"That's it," said Lamplough, coming to look over his shoulder. "Fused porcelain. I must be wrong, then. Easily see by taking it out. The grain's different, and so is the way it's put in."

"How, different?"

"Well," said Mr. Lamplough, "one's a cast, you see."

"And the other's fused. I did grasp that much. Well, go ahead and take it out."

"Can't very well; not here."

"Then take it home and do it there. Don't you see, Lamplough, how important it is? If it is cast porcelain, or whatever you call it, it *can't* have been done in '23. And if it was removed later, then another dentist must have done it. And he may have done other things—and in that case, those things ought to be there, and they're not. Don't you *see?*"

"I see you're getting rather agitato," said Mr. Lamplough; "all I can say is, I refuse to have this thing taken along to my surgery. Corpses aren't popular in Harley Street."

In the end, the body was removed, by permission, to the dental department of the local hospital. Here Mr. Lamplough, assisted by the staff dental expert, Dr. Maggs, and the police, delicately extracted the filling from the canine.

"If that," said he triumphantly, "is not cast porcelain I will extract all my own teeth without an anæsthetic and swallow them. What do you say, Benton?"

The hospital dentist agreed with him. Mr. Lamplough, who had suddenly developed an eager interest in the problem, nodded, and inserted a careful probe between the upper right bicuspids, with their adjacent fillings.

"Come and look at this, Benton. Allowing for the action of the fire and all this muck, wouldn't you have said this was a very recent filling? There, at the point of contact. Might have been done yesterday. And—here—wait a minute. Where's the lower jaw gone to? Get that fitted up. Give me a bit of carbon. Look at the tremendous bite there ought to be here, with that big molar coming down on to it. That filling's miles too high for the job. Wimsey—when was this bottom right-hand back molar filled?"

"Two years ago," said Wimsey.

"That's impossible," said the two dentists together, and Mr. Benton added:

"If you clean away the mess, you'll see it's a new filling. Never been bitten on, I should say. Look here, Mr. Lamplough, there's something odd here."

"Odd? I should say there was. I never thought about it when I was checking it up yesterday, but look at this old cavity in the lateral here. Why didn't he have that filled when all this other work was done? Now it's cleaned out you can see it plainly. Have you got a long probe? It's quite deep and must have given him jip. I say, Inspector, I want to have some of these fillings out. Do you mind?"

"Go ahead," said the Inspector, "we've got plenty of witnesses."

With Mr. Benton supporting the grisly patient and Mr. Lamplough manipulating the drill, the filling of one of the molars was speedily drilled out, and Mr. Lamplough said: "Oh, gosh!"—which, as Lord Peter remarked, just showed you what a dentist meant when he said "Ah!"

"Try the bicuspids," suggested Mr. Benton.

"Or this thirteen-year-old," chimed in his colleague.

"Hold hard, gentlemen," protested the Inspector, "don't spoil the specimen altogether."

Mr. Lamplough drilled away without heeding him. Another filling came out, and Mr. Lamplough said "Gosh!" again.

"It's all right," said Wimsey, grinning, "you can get out your warrant, Inspector."

"What's that, my lord?"

"Murder," said Wimsey.

"Why?" said the Inspector. "Do these gentlemen mean that Mr. Prendergast got a new dentist who poisoned his teeth for him?"

"No," said Mr. Lamplough; "at least, not what you mean by poisoning. But I've never seen such work in my life. Why, in two places the man hasn't even troubled to clear out the decay at all. He's just enlarged the cavity and stopped it up again anyhow. Why this chap didn't get thundering abscesses I don't know."

"Perhaps," said Wimsey, "the stoppings were put in too recently. Hullo! what now?"

"This one's all right. No decay here. Doesn't look as if there ever had been, either. But one can't tell about that."

"I dare say there never was. Get your warrant out, Inspector."

"For the murder of Mr. Prendergast? And against whom?"

"No. Against Arthur Prendergast for the murder of one, Mr. Williams, and, incidentally, for arson and attempted fraud. And against Mrs. Fielding too, if you like, for conspiracy. Though you mayn't be able to prove that part of it."

It turned out, when they found Mr. Prendergast in Rouen, that he had thought out the scheme well in advance. The one thing he had had to wait for had been to find a patient of his own height and build, with a good set of teeth and few home ties. When the unhappy Williams had fallen into his clutches, he had few preparations to make. Mrs. Prendergast had to be packed off to Worthing — a journey she was ready enough to take at any time — and the maid given a holiday. Then the necessary dental accessories had to be prepared and the victim invited out to tea at Wimbledon. Then the murder — a stunning blow from behind, followed by an injection. Then, the slow and horrid process of faking the teeth to correspond with Mr. Prendergast's own. Next, the exchange of clothes and the body carried down and placed in the car. The hypodermic put where it might be overlooked on a casual inspection and yet might plausibly be found if the presence of the drug should be discovered; ready, in the one case, to support a verdict of Accident and, in the second, of Suicide. Then the car soaked in petrol, the union loosened, the cans left about. The garage door and window left open, to lend colour to the story and provide a draught, and, finally, light set to the car by means of a train of petrol laid through the garage door. Then, flight to the station through the winter darkness and so by underground to London. The risk of being recognised on the underground was small, in Williams's hat and clothes and with a scarf wound about the lower part of the face. The next step was to pick up Williams's luggage and take the boat-train to join the wealthy and enamoured Mrs. Fielding in France. After which, Williams and Mrs. Williams could have returned to England, or not, as they pleased.

"Quite a student of criminology," remarked Wimsey, at the conclusion of this little adventure. "He'd studied Rouse and Furnace all right, and profited by their mistakes. Pity he overlooked that matter of the cast porcelain. Makes a quicker job, does it, Lamplough? Well, more haste, less speed. I do wonder, though, at what point of the proceedings Williams actually died."

"Shut up," said Mr. Lamplough, "and, by the way, I've still got to finish that filling for you."

ABSOLUTELY ELSEWHERE

Lord Peter Wimsey sat with Chief-Inspector Parker, of the C.I.D., and Inspector Henley, of the Baldock police, in the library at "The Lilacs."

"So you see," said Parker, "that all the obvious suspects were elsewhere at the time."

"What do you mean by 'elsewhere'?" demanded Wimsey, peevishly. Parker had hauled him down to Wapley, on the Great North Road, without his breakfast, and his temper had suffered. "Do you mean that they couldn't have reached the scene of the murder without travelling at over 186,000 miles a second? Because, if you don't mean that, they weren't absolutely elsewhere. They were only relatively and apparently elsewhere."

"For heaven's sake, don't go all Eddington. Humanly speaking, they were elsewhere, and if we're going to nail one of them we shall have to do it without going into their Fitzgerald contractions and coefficients of spherical curvature. I think, Inspector, we had better have them in one by one, so that I can hear all their stories again. You can check them up if they depart from their original statements at any point. Let's take the butler first."

The Inspector put his head out into the hall and said: "Hamworthy."

The butler was a man of middle age, whose spherical curvature was certainly worthy of consideration. His large face was pale and puffy, and he looked unwell. However, he embarked on his story without hesitation.

"I have been in the late Mr. Grimbold's service for twenty years, gentlemen, and have always found him a good master. He was a strict gentleman, but very just. I know he was considered very hard in business matters, but I suppose he had to be that. He was a bachelor, but he brought up his two nephews, Mr. Harcourt and Mr. Neville, and was very good to them. In his private life I should call him a kind and considerate man. His profession? Yes, I suppose you would call him a money-lender.

"About the events of last night, sir, yes. I shut up the house at 7:30 as usual. Everything was done exactly to time, sir, — Mr. Grimbold was very regular in his habits. I locked all the windows on the ground floor, as was customary during the winter months. I am quite sure I didn't miss anything out. They all have burglar-proof bolts and I should have noticed if they had been out of order. I also locked and bolted the front door and put up the chain."

"How about the conservatory door?"

"That, sir, is a Yale lock. I tried it, and saw that it was shut. No, I didn't fasten the catch. It was always left that way, sir, in case Mr. Grimbold had business which kept him in Town late, so that he could get in without disturbing the household."

"But he had no business in Town last night?"

"No, sir, but it was always left that way. Nobody could get in without the key, and Mr. Grimbold had that on his ring."

"Is there no other key in existence?"

"I believe"—the butler coughed—"I believe, sir, though I

do not know, that there is *one*, sir, — in the possession of — of a lady, sir, who is at present in Paris."

"I see. Mr. Grimbold was about sixty years old, I believe. Just so. What is the name of this lady?"

"Mrs. Winter, sir. She lives at Wapley, but since her husband died last month, sir, I understand she has been residing abroad."

"I see. Better make a note of that, Inspector. Now, how about the upper rooms and the back door?"

"The upper-room windows were all fastened in the same way, sir, except Mr. Grimbold's bedroom and the cook's room and mine, sir; but they couldn't be reached without a ladder, and the ladder is locked up in the tool-shed."

"That's all right," put in Inspector Henley. "We went into that last night. The shed was locked and, what's more, there were unbroken cobwebs between the ladder and the wall."

"I went through all the rooms at half-past seven, sir, and there was nothing out of order."

"You may take it from me," said the Inspector, again, "that there was no interference with any of the locks. Carry on, Hamworthy."

"Yes, sir. While I was seeing to the house, Mr. Grimbold came down into the library for his glass of sherry. At 7:45 the soup was served and I called Mr. Grimbold to dinner. He sat at the end of the table as usual, facing the serving-hatch."

"With his back to the library door," said Parker, making a mark on a rough plan of the room, which lay before him. "Was that door shut?"

"Oh, yes, sir. All the doors and windows were shut."

"It looks a dashed draughty room," said Wimsey. "Two doors and a serving-hatch and two french windows."

"Yes, my lord; but they are all very well-fitting, and the curtains were drawn."

His lordship moved across to the connecting door and opened it.

"Yes," he said; "good and heavy and moves in sinister si-

lence. I like these thick carpets, but the pattern's a bit fierce."
He shut the door noiselessly and returned to his seat.

"Mr. Grimbold would take about five minutes over his
soup, sir. When he had done, I removed it and put on the fish.
I did not have to leave the room; everything comes through
the serving-hatch. The wine—that is, the Chablis—was already on the table. That course was only a small portion of
turbot, and would take Mr. Grimbold about five minutes
again. I removed that, and put on the roast pheasant. I was
just about to serve Mr. Grimbold with the vegetables, when
the telephone-bell rang. Mr. Grimbold said: 'You'd better see
who it is. I'll help myself.' It was not the cook's business, of
course, to answer the telephone."

"Are there no other servants?"

"Only the woman who comes in to clean during the day,
sir. I went out to the instrument, shutting the door behind me."

"Was that this telephone or the one in the hall?"

"The one in the hall, sir. I always used that one, unless I
happened to be actually in the library at the time. The call was
from Mr. Neville Grimbold in Town, sir. He and Mr. Harcourt
have a flat in Jermyn Street. Mr. Neville spoke, and I recognised his voice. He said: 'Is that you, Hamworthy? Wait a moment. Mr. Harcourt wants you.' He put the receiver down and
then Mr. Harcourt came on. He said: 'Hamworthy, I want to
run down to-night to see my uncle, if he's at home.' I said:
'Yes, sir, I'll tell him.' The young gentlemen often come down
for a night or two, sir. We keep their bedrooms ready for them.
Mr. Harcourt said he would be starting at once and expected
to get down by about half-past nine. While he was speaking I
heard the big grandfather-clock up in their flat chime the
quarters and strike eight, and immediately after, our own hall-
clock struck, and then I heard the Exchange say 'Three minutes.' So the call must have come through at three minutes to
eight, sir."

"Then there's no doubt about the time. That's a comfort.
What next, Hamworthy?"

"Mr. Harcourt asked for another call and said: 'Mr.

Neville has got something to say,' and then Mr. Neville came back to the 'phone. He said he was going up to Scotland shortly, and wanted me to send up a country suit and some stockings and shirts that he had left down here. He wanted the suit sent to the cleaner's first, and there were various other instructions, so that he asked for another three minutes. That would be at 8.3, sir, yes. And about a minute after that, while he was still speaking, the front-door bell rang. I couldn't very well leave the 'phone, so the caller had to wait, and at five past eight he rang the bell again. I was just going to ask Mr. Neville to excuse me, when I saw Cook come out of the kitchen and go through the hall to the front door. Mr. Neville asked me to repeat his instructions, and then the Exchange interrupted us again, so he rang off, and when I turned round I saw Cook just closing the library door. I went to meet her, and she said: 'Here's that Mr. Payne again, wanting Mr. Grimbold. I've put him in the library, but I don't like the looks of him.' So I said: 'All right; I'll fix him,' and Cook went back to the kitchen."

"One moment," said Parker. "Who's Mr. Payne?"

"He's one of Mr. Grimbold's clients, sir. He lives about five minutes away, across the fields, and he's been here before, making trouble. I think he owes Mr. Grimbold money, sir, and wanted more time to pay."

"He's here, waiting in the hall," added Henley.

"Oh?" said Wimsey. "The unshaven party with the scowl and the ash-plant, and the blood-stained coat?"

"That's him, my lord," said the butler. "Well, sir,"—he turned to Parker again, "I started to go along to the library, when it come over me sudden-like that I'd never taken in the claret—Mr. Grimbold would be getting very annoyed. So I went back to my pantry—you see where that is, sir,—and fetched it from where it was warming before the fire. I had a little hunt then for the salver, sir, till I found I had put down my evening paper on top of it, but I wasn't more than a minute, sir, before I got back into the dining-room. And then, sir"—the butler's voice faltered—"then I saw Mr. Grimbold fallen forward on the table, sir, all across his plate, like. I thought he must have been took ill, and I hurried up to him and found—I found he was dead, sir, with a dreadful wound in his back."

"No weapon anywhere?"

"Not that I could see, sir. There was a terrible lot of blood. It made me feel shockingly faint, sir, and for a minute I didn't hardly know what to do. As soon as I could think of anything, I rushed over to the serving-hatch and called Cook. She came hurrying in and let out an awful scream when she saw the master. Then I remembered Mr. Payne and opened the library door. He was standing there, and he began at once, asking how long he'd have to wait. So I said: 'Here's an awful thing! Mr. Grimbold has been murdered!' and he pushed past me into the dining-room, and the first thing he said was: 'How about those windows?' He pulled back the curtain of the one nearest the library, and there was the window standing open. 'This is the way he went,' he said, and started to rush out. I said, 'no, you don't'—thinking he meant to get away, and I hung on to him. He called me a lot of names, and then he said: 'Look here, my man, be reasonable. The fellow's getting away all this time. We must have a look for him.' So I said, 'Not without I go with you.' And he said, 'All right.' So I told Cook not to touch anything but to ring up the police, and Mr. Payne and I went out after I'd fetched my torch from the pantry."

"Did Payne go with you to fetch it?"

"Yes, sir. Well, him and me went out and we searched about in the garden, but we couldn't see any footprints or anything, because it's an asphalt path all round the house and down to the gate. And we couldn't see any weapon, either. So then he said: 'We'd better go back and get the car and search the roads,' but I said: 'No, he'll be away by then,' because it's only a quarter of a mile from our gate to the Great North Road, and it would take us five or ten minutes before we could start. So Mr. Payne said: 'Perhaps you're right,' and came back to the house with me. Well, then, sir, the constable came from Wapley, and after a bit, the Inspector here and Dr. Crofts from Baldock, and they made a search and asked a lot of questions, which I answered to the best of my ability, and I can't tell you no more, sir."

"Did you notice," asked Parker, "whether Mr. Payne had any stains of blood about him?"

"No, sir, — I can't say that he had. When I first saw him, he was standing in here, right under the light, and I think I should have seen it if there was anything, sir. I can't say fairer than that."

"Of course you've searched this room, Inspector, for bloodstains or a weapon or for anything such as gloves or a cloth, or anything that might have been used to protect the murderer from bloodstains?"

"Yes, Mr. Parker. We searched very carefully."

"Could anybody have come downstairs while you were in the dining-room with Mr. Grimbold?"

"Well, sir, I suppose they might. But they'd have to have got into the house before half-past seven, sir, and hidden themselves somewhere. Still, there's no doubt it might have happened that way. They couldn't come down by the back stairs, of course, because they'd have had to pass the kitchen, and Cook would have heard them, the passage being flagged, sir, but the front stairs — well, I don't know hardly what to say about that."

"That's how the man got in, depend upon it," said Parker. "Don't look so distressed, Hamworthy. You can't be expected to search all the cupboards in the house every evening for concealed criminals. Now I think I had better see the two nephews. I suppose they and their uncle got on together all right?"

"Oh, yes, sir. Never had a word of any sort. It's been a great blow to them, sir. They were terribly upset when Mr. Grimbold was ill in the summer —"

"He was ill, was he?"

"Yes, sir, with his heart, last July. He took a very bad turn, sir, and we had to send for Mr. Neville. But he pulled round wonderfully, sir, — only he never seemed to be quite such a cheerful gentleman afterwards. I think it made him feel he wasn't getting younger, sir. But I'm sure nobody ever thought he'd be cut off like this."

"How is his money left?" asked Parker.

"Well, sir, that I don't know. I believe it would be divided between the two gentlemen, sir—not but what they have plenty of their own. But Mr. Harcourt would be able to tell you, sir. He's the executor."

"Very well, we'll ask him. Are the brothers on good terms?"

"Oh, yes, indeed, sir. Most devoted. Mr. Neville would do anything for Mr. Harcourt—and Mr. Harcourt for him, I'm sure. A very pleasant pair of gentlemen, sir. You couldn't have nicer."

"Thanks, Hamworthy. That will do for the moment, unless anybody else has anything to ask?"

"How much of the pheasant was eaten, Hamworthy?"

"Well, my lord, not a great deal of it—I mean, nothing like all of what Mr. Grimbold had on his plate. But he'd ate some of it. It might have taken three or four minutes or so to eat what he had done, my lord, judging by what I helped him to."

"There was nothing to suggest that he had been interrupted, for example, by somebody coming to the windows, or of his having got up to let the person in?"

"Nothing at all, my lord, that I could see."

"The chair was pushed in close to the table when I saw him," put in the Inspector, "and his napkin was on his knees and the knife and fork lying just under his hands, as though he had dropped them when the blow came. I understand that the body was not disturbed."

"No, sir. I never moved it—except, of course, to make sure that he was dead. But I never felt any doubt of that, sir, when I saw that dreadful wound in his back. I just lifted his head and let it fall forward again, same as before."

"All right, then, Hamworthy. Ask Mr. Harcourt to come in."

Mr. Harcourt Grimbold was a brisk-looking man of about thirty-five. He explained that he was a stockbroker and his brother Neville an official in the Ministry of Public Health, and that they had been brought up by their uncle from the ages of eleven and ten respectively. He was aware that his uncle had had many business enemies, but for his own part he had received nothing from him but kindness.

"I'm afraid I can't tell you much about this terrible business, as I didn't get here till 9:45 last night, when, of course, it was all over."

"That was a little later than you hoped to be here?"

"Just a little. My tail-lamp went out between Welwyn Garden City and Welwyn, and I was stopped by a bobby. I went to a garage in Welwyn, where they found that the lead had come loose. They put it right, and that delayed me for a few minutes more."

"It's about forty miles from here to London?"

"Just over. In the ordinary way, at that time of night, I should reckon an hour and a quarter from door to door. I'm not a speed merchant."

"Did you drive yourself?"

"Yes. I have a chauffeur, but I don't always bring him down here with me."

"When did you leave London?"

"About 8:20, I should think. Neville went round to the garage and fetched the car as soon as he'd finished telephoning, while I put my toothbrush and so on in my bag."

"You didn't hear about the death of your uncle before you left?"

"No. They didn't think of ringing me up, I gather, till after I had started. The police tried to get Neville later on, but he'd gone round to the club, or something. I 'phoned him myself after I got here, and he came down this morning."

"Well, now, Mr. Grimbold, can you tell us anything about your late uncle's affairs?"

"You mean his will? Who profits, and that kind of thing? Well, I do, for one, and Neville, for another. And Mrs.—have you heard of a Mrs. Winter?"

"Something, yes."

"Well, she does, for a third. And then, of course, old Hamworthy gets a nice little nest-egg, and the cook gets something, and there is a legacy of £500 to the clerk at my uncle's London office. But the bulk of it goes to us and to Mrs. Winter. I know what you're going to ask—how much is it? I haven't the faintest idea, but I know it must be something pretty considerable. The old man never let on to a soul how much he really was worth, and we never bothered about it. I'm turning over a good bit, and Neville's salary is a heavy burden on a long-suffering public, so we only had a mild, academic kind of interest in the question."

"Do you suppose Hamworthy knew he was down for a legacy?"

"Oh, yes—there was no secret about that. He was to get £100 and a life-interest in £200 a year, provided, of course, he was still in my uncle's service when he—my uncle, I mean—died."

"And he wasn't under notice, or anything?"

"N-no. No. Not more than usual. My uncle gave everybody notice about once a month, to keep them up to the mark. But it never came to anything. He was like the Queen of Hearts in *Alice*—he never executed nobody, you know."

"I see. We'd better ask Hamworthy about that, though. Now, this Mrs. Winter. Do you know anything about her?"

"Oh, yes. She's a nice woman. Of course, she was Uncle William's mistress for donkey's years, but her husband was practically potty with drink, and you could scarcely blame her. I wired her this morning and here's her reply, just come."

He handed Parker a telegram, despatched from Paris, which read: "Terribly shocked and grieved. Returning immediately. Love and sympathy. Lucy."

"You are on friendly terms with her, then?"

"Good Lord, yes. Why not? We were always damned sorry for her. Uncle William would have taken her away with him somewhere, only she wouldn't leave Winter. In fact, I think they had practically settled that they were to get married now that Winter has had the grace to peg out. She's only about thirty-eight, and it's time she had some sort of show in life, poor thing."

"So, in spite of the money, she hadn't really very much to gain by your uncle's death?"

"Not a thing. Unless, of course, she wanted to marry somebody younger, and was afraid of losing the cash. But I believe she was honestly fond of the old boy. Anyhow, she couldn't have done the murder, because she's in Paris."

"H'm!" said Parker. "I suppose she is. We'd better make sure, though. I'll ring through to the Yard and have her looked out for at the ports. Is this 'phone through to the Exchange?"

"Yes," said the Inspector. "It doesn't have to go through the hall 'phone; they're connected in parallel."

"All right. Well, I don't think we need trouble you further, at the moment, Mr. Grimbold. I'll put my call through, and after that we'll send for the next witness. . . . Give me White-hall 1212, please. . . . I suppose the time of Mr. Harcourt's call from town has been checked, Inspector?"

"Yes, Mr. Parker. It was put in at 7:57 and renewed at 8 o'clock and 8:03. Quite an expensive little item. And we've also checked up on the constable who spoke to him about his lights and the garage that put them right for him. He got into Welwyn at 9:05 and left again about 9:15. The number of the car is right, too."

"Well, he's out of it in any case, but it's just as well to check all we can. . . . Hullo, is that Scotland Yard? Put me through to Chief-Inspector Hardy. Chief-Inspector Parker speaking."

As soon as he had finished with his call, Parker sent for Neville Grimbold. He was rather like his brother, only a little slimmer and a little more suave in speech, as befitted a Civil Servant. He had nothing to add, except to confirm his brother's story and to explain that he had gone to a cinema from 8:20 to about 10 o'clock, and then on to his club, so that he had heard nothing about the tragedy till later in the evening.

The cook was the next witness. She had a great deal to say, but nothing very convincing to tell. She had not happened to see Hamworthy go to the pantry for the claret, otherwise she confirmed his story. She scouted the idea that somebody had been concealed in one of the upper rooms, because the daily woman, Mrs. Crabbe, had been in the house till nearly dinner-time, putting camphor-bags in all the wardrobes; and, anyhow, she had no doubt but what "that Payne" had stabbed Mr. Grimbold—"a nasty, murdering beast." After which, it only remained to interview the murderous Mr. Payne.

Mr. Payne was almost aggressively frank. He had been treated very harshly by Mr. Grimbold. What with exorbitant usury and accumulated interest added to the principal, he had already paid back about five times the original loan, and now Mr. Grimbold had refused him any more time to pay, and had announced his intention of foreclosing on the security, namely, Mr. Payne's house and land. It was all the more brutal because Mr. Payne had every prospect of being able to pay off the entire debt in six months' time, owing to some sort of interest or share in something or other which was confidently expected to turn up trumps. In his opinion, old Grimbold had refused to renew on purpose, so as to prevent him from paying—what *he* wanted was the property. Grimbold's death was the saving of the situation, because it would postpone settlement till after the confidently-expected trumps had turned up. Mr. Payne would have murdered old Grimbold with pleasure, but he hadn't done so, and in any case he wasn't the sort of man to stab anybody in the back, though, if the money-lender had been a younger man, he, Payne, would have been happy to break all his bones for him. There it was, and they could take it or leave it. If that old fool, Hamworthy, hadn't got in his way, he'd have laid hands on the murderer all right—if Hamworthy was a fool which he doubted. Blood? Yes, there was blood on his coat. He had got that in struggling with Hamworthy at the window. Hamworthy's hands had been all over blood when he made his appearance in the library. No doubt he had got it from the corpse. He, Payne, had taken care not to change his clothes, because, if he had done so, somebody would have tried to make out that he was hiding something. Actually, he had not been home, or asked to go home, since the murder. Mr. Payne added that he objected strongly to the attitude taken up by the local police, who had treated him with undisguised hostility. To which Inspector Henley replied that Mr. Payne was quite mistaken.

"Mr. Payne," said Lord Peter, "will you tell me one thing? When you heard the commotion in the dining-room, and the cook screaming, and so on, why didn't you go in at once to find out what was the matter?"

"Why?" retorted Mr. Payne. "Because I never heard anything of the sort, that's why. The first thing I knew about it was seeing the butler-fellow standing there in the doorway, waving his bloody hands about and gibbering."

"Ah!" said Wimsey. "I thought it was a good, solid door. Shall we ask the lady to go in and scream for us now, with the dining-room window open?"

The Inspector departed on this errand, while the rest of the company waited anxiously to count the screams. Nothing happened, however, till Henley put his head in and asked, what about it?

"Nothing," said Parker.

"It's a well-built house," said Wimsey. "I suppose any sound coming through the window would be muffled by the conservatory. Well, Mr. Payne, if you didn't hear the screams it's not surprising that you didn't hear the murderer. Are those all your witnesses, Charles? Because I've got to get back to London to see a man about a dog. But I'll leave you two suggestions with my blessing. One is, that you should look for a car, which was parked within a quarter of a mile of this house last night, between 7:30 and 8:15; the second is, that you should all come and sit in the dining-room to-night, with the doors and windows shut, and watch the french windows. I'll give Mr. Parker a ring about eight. Oh, and you might lend me the key of the conservatory door. I've got a theory about it."

The Chief Inspector handed over the key, and his lordship departed.

The party assembled in the dining-room was in no very companionable mood. In fact, all the conversation was supplied by the police, who kept up a chatty exchange of fishing reminiscences, while Mr. Payne glowered, the two Grimbolds smoked cigarette after cigarette, and the cook and the butler balanced themselves nervously on the extreme edges of their chairs. It was a relief when the telephone-bell rang.

Parker glanced at his watch as he got up to answer it. "Seven-fifty-seven," he observed, and saw the butler pass his handkerchief over his twitching lips. "Keep your eye on the windows." He went out into the hall.

"Hullo!" he said.

"Is that Chief-Inspector Parker?" asked a voice he knew well. "This is Lord Peter Wimsey's man speaking from his lordship's rooms in London. Would you hold the line a moment? His lordship wishes to speak to you."

Parker heard the receiver set down and lifted again. Then Wimsey's voice came through: "Hullo, old man? Have you found that car yet?"

"We've heard of *a* car," replied the Chief Inspector cautiously, "at a Road-House on the Great North Road, about five minutes' walk from the house."

"Was the number A B J 28?"

"Yes. How did you know?"

"I thought it might be. It was hired from a London garage at five o'clock yesterday afternoon and brought back just before ten. Have you traced Mrs. Winter?"

"Yes, I think so. She landed from the Calais boat this evening. So apparently she's O.K."

"I thought she might be. Now, listen. Do you know that Harcourt Grimbold's affairs are in a bit of a mess? He nearly had a crisis last July, but somebody came to his rescue — possibly Uncle, don't you think? All rather fishy, my informant saith. And I'm told, very confidentially, that he's got badly caught over the Biggars-Whitlow crash. But of course he'll have no difficulty in raising money now, on the strength of Uncle's will. But I imagine the July business gave Uncle William a jolt. I expect —"

He was interrupted by a little burst of tinkling music, followed by the eight silvery strokes of a bell.

"Hear that? Recognise it? That's the big French clock in my sitting-room. . . . What? All right, Exchange, give me another three minutes. Bunter wants to speak to you again."

The receiver rattled, and the servant's suave voice took up the tale.

"His lordship asks me to ask you, sir, to ring off at once and go straight into the dining-room."

Parker obeyed. As he entered the room, he got an instantaneous impression of six people, sitting as he had left them, in an expectant semi-circle, their eyes strained towards the french windows. Then the library door opened noiselessly and Lord Peter Wimsey walked in.

"Good God!" exclaimed Parker, involuntarily. "How did you get here?" The six heads jerked round suddenly.

"On the back of the light waves," said Wimsey, smoothing back his hair. "I have travelled eighty miles to be with you, at 186,000 miles a second."

"It was rather obvious, really," said Wimsey, when they had secured Harcourt Grimbold (who fought desperately) and his brother Neville (who collapsed and had to be revived with brandy). "It had to be those two; they were so very much elsewhere—almost absolutely elsewhere. The murder could only have been committed between 7:57 and 8:06, and there had to be a reason for that prolonged 'phone-call about something that Harcourt could very well have explained when he came. And the murderer had to be in the library before 7:57, or he would have been seen in the hall—unless Grimbold had let him in by the french window, which didn't appear likely.

"Here's how it was worked. Harcourt set off from Town in a hired car about six o'clock, driving himself. He parked the car at the Road-House, giving some explanation. I suppose he wasn't known there?"

"No; it's quite a new place; only opened last month."

"Ah! Then he walked the last quarter-mile on foot, arriving here at 7:45. It was dark, and he probably wore goloshes, so as not to make a noise coming up the path. He let himself into the conservatory with a duplicate key."

"How did he get that?"

"Pinched Uncle William's key off his ring last July, when the old boy was ill. It was probably the shock of hearing that his dear nephew was in trouble that caused the illness. Harcourt was here at the time—you remember it was only Neville that had to be 'sent for'—and I suppose Uncle paid up then, on conditions. But I doubt if he'd have done as much again—especially as he was thinking of getting married. And I expect, too, Harcourt thought that Uncle might easily alter his will after marriage. He might even have founded a family, and what would poor Harcourt do then, poor thing? From every point of view, it was better that Uncle should depart this life. So the duplicate key was cut and the plot thought out, and Brother Neville, who would 'do anything for Mr. Harcourt,' was roped in to help. I'm inclined to think that Harcourt must have done something rather worse than merely lose money, and Neville may have troubles of his own. But where was I?"

"Coming in at the conservatory door."

"Oh, yes—that's the way I came to-night. He'd take cover in the garden and would know when Uncle William went into the dining-room, because he'd see the library light go out. Remember, he knew the household. He came in, in the dark, locking the outer door after him, and waited by the telephone till Neville's call came through from London. When the bell stopped ringing, he lifted the receiver in the library. As soon as Neville had spoken his little piece, Harcourt chipped in. Nobody could hear him through these sound-proof doors, and Hamworthy couldn't possibly tell that his voice wasn't coming from London. In fact, it *was* coming from London, because, as the 'phones are connected in parallel, it could only come by way of the Exchange. At eight o'clock, the grandfather clock in Jermyn Street struck—further proof that the London line was open. The minute Harcourt heard that, he called on Neville to speak again, and hung up under cover of the rattle

of Neville's receiver. Then Neville detained Hamworthy with
a lot of rot about a suit, while Harcourt walked into the dining-
room, stabbed his uncle and departed by the window. He had
five good minutes in which to hurry back to his car and drive
off—and Hamworthy and Payne actually gave him a few minutes more by suspecting and hampering one another."

"Why didn't he go back through the library and conservatory?"

"He hoped everybody would think that the murderer had
come in by the window. In the meantime, Neville left London
at 8:20 in Harcourt's car, carefully drawing the attention of a
policeman and a garage man to the licence number as he
passed through Welwyn. At an appointed place outside Welwyn he met Harcourt, primed him with his little story about
tail-lights, and changed cars with him. Neville returned to
town with the hired 'bus; Harcourt came back here with his
own car. But I'm afraid you'll have a little difficulty in finding
the weapon and the duplicate key and Harcourt's blood-stained
gloves and coat. Neville probably took them back, and they
may be anywhere. There's a good, big river in London."

STRIDING FOLLY

Shall I expect you next Wednesday for our game as usual?" asked Mr. Mellilow.

"Of course, of course," replied Mr. Creech. "Very glad there's no ill feeling, Mellilow. Next Wednesday as usual. Unless . . ." his heavy face darkened for a moment, as though at some disagreeable recollection. "There may be a man coming to see me. If I'm not here by nine, don't expect me. In that case, I'll come on Thursday."

Mr. Mellilow let his visitor out through the french window and watched him across the lawn to the wicket-gate leading to the Hall grounds. It was a clear October night, with a gibbous moon going down the sky. Mr. Mellilow slipped on his goloshes (for he was careful of his health and the grass was wet) and himself went down past the sundial and the fishpond and through the sunk garden till he came to the fence that bounded his tiny freehold on the southern side. He leaned his arms on the rail and gazed across the little valley at the tumbling river and the wide slope beyond, which was crowned, at a mile's distance, by the ridiculous stone tower known as the Folly. The valley, the slope, and the tower all belonged to Striding Hall. They lay there, peaceful and lovely in the moonlight, as though nothing could ever disturb their fantastic solitude. But Mr. Mellilow knew better.

He had bought the cottage to end his days in, thinking that here was a corner of England the same yesterday, today, and for ever. It was strange that he, a chess player, should not have been able to see three moves ahead. The first move had been the death of the old squire. The second had been the purchase by Creech of the whole Striding property. Even then, he had not been able to see why a rich business man—unmarried and with no rural interests—should have come to live in a post so remote. True, there were three considerable towns at a few miles' distance, but the village itself was on the road to nowhere. Fool! He had forgotten the Grid! It had come, like a great, ugly chessrook swooping from an unconsidered corner, marching over the country, straddling four, six, eight parishes at a time, planting hideous pylons to mark its progress, and squatting now at Mr. Mellilow's very door.

For Creech had just calmly announced that he was selling the valley to the Electrical Company; and there would be a huge power-plant on the river and workmen's bungalows on the slope, and then Development—which, to Mr. Mellilow, was another name for the devil. It was ironical that Mr. Mellilow, alone in the village, had received Creech with kindness, excusing his vulgar humour and insensitive manners, because he thought Creech was lonely and believed him to be well-meaning, and because he was glad to have a neighbour who could give him a weekly game of chess.

Mr. Mellilow came in sorrowful, and restored his goloshes to their usual resting-place on the verandah by the french window. He put the chessmen away and the cat out and locked up the cottage—for he lived quite alone, with a woman coming in by the day. Then he went up to bed with his mind full of the Folly, and presently he fell asleep and dreamed.

He was standing in a landscape whose style seemed very

familiar to him. There was a wide plain, intersected with hedgerows, and crossed in the middle distance by a river, over which was a small stone bridge. Enormous blue-black thunder-clouds hung heavy overhead, and the air had the electric stillness of something stretched to snapping-point. Far off, be-yond the river, a livid streak of sunlight pierced the clouds and lit up with theatrical brilliance a tall, solitary tower. The scene had a curious unreality, as though of painted canvas. It was a picture, and he had an odd conviction that he recognized the handling and could put a name to the artist. " 'Smooth and tight,' " were the words that occurred to him. And then, " 'It's bound to break before long.' " And then, " 'I ought not to have come out without my galoshes.' "

It was important, it was imperative that he should get to the bridge. But the faster he walked, the greater the distance grew, and without his goloshes the going was very difficult. Sometimes he was bogged to the knee, sometimes he floun-dered on steep banks of shifting shale; and the air was not merely oppressive—it was *hot* like the inside of an oven. He was running now, with the breath labouring in his throat, and when he looked up he was astonished to see how close he was to the tower. The bridge was fantastically small, dwindled to a pinpoint on the horizon, but the tower fronted him just across the river, and close on his right was a dark wood, which had not been there before.

Something flickered on the wood's edge, out and in again, shy and swift as a rabbit; and now the wood was between him and the bridge and the tower behind it, still glowing in that unnatural streak of sunlight. He was at the river's brink, but the bridge was nowhere to be seen—and the tower, the tower was moving. It had crossed the river. It had taken the wood in one gigantic leap. It was no more than fifty yards off, im-mensely high, shining, and painted. Even as he ran, dodging and twisting, it took another field in its stride, and when he turned to flee it was there before him. It was a double tower—twin towers—a tower and its mirror image, advancing with a swift and awful stealth from either side to crush him. He was pinned now between them, panting. He saw their smooth, yellow sides tapering up to heaven, and about their feet went a montrous stir, like the quiver of a crouching cat.

Then the low sky burst like a sluice and through the drench of the rain he leapt at a doorway in the foot of the tower before him and found himself climbing the familiar stair of Striding Folly. "My goloshes will be here," he said, with a passionate sense of relief. The lightning stabbed suddenly through a loop-hole and he saw a black crow lying dead upon the stairs. Then thunder . . . like the rolling of drums.

The daily woman was hammering upon the door. "You *have* slept in," she said, "and no mistake."

Mr. Mellilow, finishing his supper on the following Wednesday, rather hoped that Mr. Creech would not come. He had thought a good deal during the week about the electric power scheme, and the more he thought about it, the less he liked it. He had discovered another thing which had increased his dislike. Sir Henry Hunter, who owned a good deal of land on the other side of the market town, had, it appeared, offered the company a site more suitable than Striding in every way on extremely favourable terms. The choice of Striding seemed inexplicable, unless on the supposition that Creech had bribed the surveyor. Sir Henry voiced his suspicions without any mincing of words. He admitted, however, that he could prove nothing.

"But he's crooked," he said. "I have heard things about him in Town. Other things. Ugly rumours."

Mr. Mellilow suggested that the deal might not, after all, go through.

"You're an optimist," said Sir Henry. "Nothing stops a fellow like Creech. Except death. He's a man with enemies. . . ." He broke off, adding darkly: "Let's hope he breaks his damned neck one of these days—and the sooner the better."

Mr. Mellilow was uncomfortable. He did not like to hear about crooked transactions. Business men, he supposed, were like that; but if they were, he would rather not play games with them. It spoilt things, somehow. Better, perhaps, not to think too much about it. He took up the newspaper, determined to occupy his mind, while waiting for Creech, with that day's chess problem. White to play and mate in three.

He had just become pleasantly absorbed when a knock came at the front door. Creech? As early as eight o'clock? Surely not. And in any case, he would have come by the lawn and the french window. But who else would visit the cottage of an evening? Rather disconcerted, he rose to let the visitor in. But the man who stood on the threshold was a stranger.

"Mr. Mellilow?"

"Yes, my name is Mellilow. What can I do for you?"

(A motorist, he supposed, enquiring his way or wanting to borrow something.)

"Ah! that is good. I have come to play chess with you."

"To play chess?" repeated Mr. Mellilow, astonished.

"Yes; I am a commercial traveller. My car has broken down in the village. I have to stay at the inn, and I ask the good Potts if there is anyone who can give me a game of chess to pass the evening. He tells me Mr. Mellilow lives here and plays well. Indeed, I recognize the name. Have I not read *Mellilow on Pawn-Play?* It is yours, no?"

Rather flattered, Mr. Mellilow admitted the authorship of this little work.

"So. I congratulate you. And you will do me the favour to play with me, hey? Unless I intrude, or you have company."

"No," said Mr. Mellilow. "I am more or less expecting a friend, but he won't turn up till nine and perhaps he won't come at all."

"If he come, I go," said the stranger. "It is very good of you." He had somehow oozed his way into the house without any direct invitation and was removing his hat and overcoat. He was a big man with a short, thick, curly beard and tinted spectacles, and he spoke in a deep voice with a slight foreign accent. "My name," he added, "is Moses. I represent Messrs. Cohen and Gold of Farringdon Street, the manufacturers of electrical fittings."

He grinned widely, and Mr. Mellilow's heart contracted.

Such haste seemed almost indecent. Before the site was even taken! He felt an unreasonable resentment against this harmless Jew. Then he rebuked himself. It was not the man's fault. "Come in," he said, with more cordiality in his voice than he really felt, "I shall be very glad to give you a game."

"I am very grateful," said Mr. Moses, squeezing his great bulk through into the sitting-room. "Ha! You are working out the *Record's* three-mover. It is elegant but not profound. You will not take long to break his back. You permit that I disturb?"

Mr. Mellilow nodded, and the stranger began to arrange the board for play.

"You have hurt your hand?" inquired Mr. Mellilow.

"It is nothing," replied Mr. Moses, turning back the glove he wore and displaying a quantity of sticking-plaster. "I break my knuckles trying to start the dam' car. She kick me. Bah! A trifle. I wear a glove to protect him. So, we begin?"

"Won't you have something to drink fist?"

"No, no, thank you very much. I have refreshed myself already at the inn. Too many drinks are not good. But do not let that prevent you."

Mr. Mellilow helped himself to a modest whisky and soda and sat down to the board. He won the draw and took the white pieces, playing his king's pawn to king's fourth.

"So!" said Mr. Moses, as the next few moves and countermoves followed their prescribed course, "the *giuoco piano*, hey? Nothing spectacular. We try the strength. When we know what we have each to meet, then the surprises will begin."

The first game proceeded cautiously. Whoever Mr. Moses might be, he was a sound and intelligent player, not easily stampeded into indiscretions. Twice Mr. Mellilow baited a delicate trap; twice, with a broad smile, Mr. Moses stepped daintily out between the closing jaws. The third trap was set more carefully. Gradually, and fighting every step of the way, black was forced behind his last defences. Yet another five minutes, and Mr. Mellilow said gently: "Check;" adding, "and mate in four." Mr. Moses nodded. "That was good." He glanced at the clock. "One hour. You give me my revenge, hey? Now we know one another. Now we shall see."

Mr. Mellilow agreed. Ten minutes past nine. Creech would not come now. The pieces were set up again. This time, Mr. Moses took white, opening with the difficult and dangerous Steinitz gambit. Within a few minutes Mr. Mellilow realized that, up till now, his opponent had been playing with him in a double sense. He experienced that eager and palpitating excitement which attends the process of biting off more than one can chew. By half-past nine, he was definitely on the defensive; at a quarter to ten, he thought he spied a way out; five minutes later, Mr. Moses said, suddenly, "It grows late: we must begin to push a little," and thrust forward a knight, leaving his queen *en prise.*

Mr. Mellilow took prompt advantage of the oversight — and became aware, too late, that he was menaced by the advance of a white rook.

Stupid! How had he come to overlook that? There was an answer, of course . . . but he wished the little room were not so hot and that the stranger's eyes were not so inscrutable behind the tinted glasses. If he could manœuvre his king out of harm's way for the moment and force his pawn through, he had still a chance. The rook moved in upon him as he twisted and dodged; it came swooping and striding over the board, four, six, eight squares at a time; and now the second white rook had darted out from its corner; they were closing in upon him — a double castle, twin castles, a castle and its mirror image: O God! It was his dream of striding towers, smooth and yellow and painted. Mr. Mellilow wiped his forehead.

"Check!" said Mr. Moses. And again, "Check!" And then, "Checkmate!"

Mr. Mellilow pulled himself together. This would never do. His heart was thumping as though he had been running a race. It was ridiculous to be so much overwrought by a game of chess; and if there was one kind of man in the world that he despised, it was a bad loser. The stranger was uttering some

polite commonplace—he could not tell what—and replacing
the pieces in their box.

"I must go now," said Mr. Moses. "I thank you very much
for the pleasure you have so kindly given me. . . . Pardon me,
you are a little unwell?"

"No, no," said Mr. Mellilow. "It is the heat of the fire and
the lamp. I have enjoyed our games very much. Won't you
take anything before you go?"

"No, I thank you. I must be back before the good Potts
locks me out. Again, my hearty thanks."

He grasped Mr. Mellilow's hand in his gloved grip and
passed out quickly into the hall. In another moment he had
seized hat and coat and was gone. His footsteps died away
along the cobbled path.

Mr. Mellilow returned to the sitting-room. A curious
episode; he could scarcely believe that it had really happened.
There lay the empty board, the pieces in their box, the *Record*
on the old oak chest with a solitary tumbler beside it; he might
have dozed off and dreamed the whole thing, for all the trace
the stranger's visit had left. Certainly the room was very hot.
He threw the french window open. A lop-sided moon had
risen, chequering the valley and the slope beyond with patches
of black and white. High up, and distant, the Folly made a
pale streak upon the sky. Mr. Mellilow thought he would walk
down to the bridge to clear his head. He groped in the accustomed corner for his goloshes. They were not there. "Where
on earth has that woman put them?" muttered Mr. Mellilow.
And he answered himself, irrationally but with complete conviction, "My goloshes are up at the Folly."

His feet seemed to move of their own accord. He was
through the garden now, walking quickly down the field to the
little wooden foot-bridge. His goloshes were at the Folly. It was
imperative that he should fetch them back; the smallest delay
would be fatal. "This is ridiculous," thought Mr. Mellilow to
himself. "It is that foolish dream running in my head. Mrs.
Gibbs must have taken them away to clean them. but while I
am here, I may as well go on; the walk will do me good."

The power of the dream was so strong upon him that he was almost surprised to find the bridge in its accustomed place. He put his hand on the rail and was comforted by the roughness of the untrimmed bark. Half a mile uphill now to the Folly. Its smooth sides shone in the moonlight, and he turned suddenly, expecting to see the double image striding the fields behind him. Nothing so sensational was to be seen, however. He breasted the slope with renewed courage. Now he stood close beneath the tower—and with a little shock he saw that the door at its base stood open.

He stepped inside, and immediately the darkness was all about him like a blanket. He felt with his foot for the stair and groped his way up between the newel and the wall. Now in gloom, not in the gleam of a loophole, the spiral seemed to turn endlessly. Then, as his head rose into the pale glimmer of the fourth window, he saw a shapeless blackness sprawled upon the stair. With a sudden dreadful certainty that *this* was what he had come to see, he mounted further and stooped over it. Creech was lying there, dead. Close beside the body lay a pair of goloshes. As Mr. Mellilow moved to pick them up, something rolled beneath his foot. It was a white chessrook.

The police-surgeon said that Creech had been dead since about nine o'clock. It was proved that at eight-fifty he had set out towards the wicket-gate to play chess with Mr. Mellilow. And in the morning light the prints of Mr. Mellilow's goloshes were clear, leading down the gravelled path on the far side of the lawn, past the sundial and the fish-pond, and through the sunk garden and so over the muddy field and the footbridge, and up the slope to the Folly. Deep footprints they were, and close together, such as a man might make who carried a monstrous burden. A good mile to the Folly and half of it uphill. The doctor looked inquiringly at Mr. Mellilow's spare form.

"Oh, yes," said Mr. Mellilow. "I could have carried him. It's a matter of knack, not strength. You see—" he blushed faintly, "I'm not really a gentleman. My father was a miller and I spent my whole boyhood carrying sacks. Only I was always fond of my books, and so I managed to educate myself and earn a little money. It would be silly to pretend I couldn't have carried Creech. But I didn't do it, of course."

"It's unfortunate," said the superintendent, "that we can't find no trace of this man Moses." His voice was the most unpleasant Mr. Mellilow had ever heard—a sceptical voice with an edge like a saw. "He never come down to the Feathers, that's a certainty. Potts never set eyes on him, let alone sent him up here with a tale about chess. Nor nobody saw no car neither. An odd gentleman this Mr. Moses seem to have been. No footmarks to the front door? Well, it's cobbles, so you wouldn't expect none. That his glass of whisky by any chance, sir? . . . Oh? he wouldn't have a drink, wouldn't he? Ah! And you played two games of chess in this very room? Ah! very absorbing pursoot, so I'm told. You didn't hear poor Mr. Creech come up the garden?"

"The window was shut," said Mr. Mellilow, "and the curtains drawn. And Mr. Creech always walked straight over the grass from the wicket-gate."

"H'm!" said the superintendent. "So he comes, or somebody comes, right up on to the verandah and sneaks a pair of goloshes; and you and this Mr. Moses are so occupied you don't hear nothing."

"Come, superintendent," said the Chief Constable, who was sitting on Mr. Mellilow's oak chest and looked rather uncomfortable. "I don't think that's impossible. The man might have worn tennis-shoes or something. How about fingerprints on the chessmen?"

"He wore a glove on his right hand," said Mr. Mellilow unhappily. "I remember that he didn't use his left hand at all— not even when taking a piece."

"A very remarkable gentleman," said the superintendent again. "No finger-prints, no foot-prints, no drinks, no eyes visible, no features to speak of, pops in and out without leaving no trace—a kind of vanishing gentleman." Mr. Mellilow made a helpless gesture. "These the chessmen you was using?" Mr. Mellilow nodded, and the superintendent turned the box upside-down upon the board, carefully extending a vast enclosing paw to keep the pieces from rolling away. "Let's see. Two big 'uns with spikes. Four chaps with split-open 'eads. Four 'orses. Two black 'uns—what d'you call these? Rooks, eh? Look more like churches to me. One white church—rook if you like. What's gone with the other one? Or don't these rook-affairs go in pairs like the rest?"

"They must be both there," said Mr. Mellilow. "He was using two white rooks in the end-game. He mated me with them—I remember. . . ."

he remembered only too well. The dream and the double castle moving to crush him. He watched the superintendent feeling in his pocket and suddenly knew the name of the terror that had flickered in and out of the black wood.

The superintendent set down the white rook that had lain by the corpse at the Folly. Colour, height, and weight matched with the rook on the board.

"Staunton men," said the Chief Constable, "all of a pattern."

But the superintendent, with his back to the french window, was watching Mr. Mellilow's grey face.

"He must have put it in his pocket," said Mr. Mellilow. "He cleared the pieces away at the end of the game."

"But he couldn't have taken it up to Striding Folly," said the superintendent, "nor he couldn't have done the murder, by your own account."

"Is it possible that you carried it up to the Folly yourself," asked the Chief Constable, "and dropped it there when you found the body?"

"The gentleman has said that he saw this man Moses put it away," said the superintendent.

They were watching him now, all of them. Mr. Mellilow clasped his head in his hands. His forehead was drenched. "Something must break soon," he thought.

Like a thunderclap there came a blow on the window; the superintendent leapt nearly out of his skin.

"Lord, my lord!" he complained, opening the window and letting a gust of fresh air into the room, "how you startled me!"

Mr. Mellilow gasped. Who was this? His brain wasn't

working properly. That friend of the Chief Constable's, of course, who had disappeared somehow during the conversation. Like the bridge in his dream. Disappeared. Gone out of the picture.

"Absorbin' game, detectin'," said the Chief Constable's friend. "Very much like chess. People come creepin' right up on to the verandah and you never even notice them. In broad daylight, too. Tell me, Mr. Mellilow—what made you go up last night to the folly?"

Mr. Mellilow hesitated. This was the point in his story that he had made no attempt to explain. Mr. Moses had sounded unlikely enough; a dream about goloshes would sound more unlikely still.

"Come now," said the Chief Constable's friend, polishing his monocle on his handkerchief and replacing it with an exaggerated lifting of the eyebrows. "What was it? Woman, woman, lovely woman? Meet me by moonlight and all that kind of thing?"

"Certainly not," said Mr. Mellilow indignantly. "I wanted a breath of fresh—" He stopped, uncertainly. There was something in the other man's childish-foolish face that urged him to speak the reckless truth. "I had a dream," he said.

The superintendent shuffled his feet, and the Chief Constable crossed one leg awkwardly over the other.

"Warned of God in a dream," said the man with the monocle, unexpectedly. "What did you dream of?" He followed Mr. Mellilow's glance at the board. "Chess?"

"Of two moving castles," said Mr. Mellilow, "and the dead body of a black crow."

"A pretty piece of used and inverted symbolism," said the other. "The dead body of a black crow becomes a dead man with a white rook."

"But that came afterwards," said the Chief Constable.

"So did the end-game with the two rooks," said Mr. Mellilow.

"Our friend's memory works both ways," said the man with the monocle, "like the White Queen's. She, by the way,

could believe as many as six impossible things before breakfast. So can I. Pharaoh, tell your dream."

"Time's getting on, Wimsey," said the Chief Constable.

"Let time pass," retorted the other, "for, as a great chess-
player observed, it helps more than reasoning."

"What player was that?" demanded Mr. Mellilow.

"A lady," said Lord Peter Wimsey, "who played with living men and mated kings, popes, and emperors."

"Oh," said Mr. Mellilow. "Well—" He told his tale from
the beginning, making no secret of his grudge against Creech
and his nightmare fancy of the striding electric pylons. "I
think," he said, "that was what gave me the dream." And he
went on to his story of the goloshes, the bridge, the moving
towers, and death on the stairs at the Folly.

"A damned lucky dream for you," said Wimsey. "But I see
now why they chose you. Look! It is all clear as daylight. If
you had had no dream—if the murderer had been able to
come back later and replace your goloshes—if someone else
had found the body in the morning with the chess-rook beside
it and your tracks leading back and home again, that might
have been mate in one move. There are two men to look for,
superintendent. One of them belongs to Creech's household,
for he knew that Creech came every Wednesday through the
wicket-gate to play chess with you; and he knew that Creech's
chessmen and yours were twin sets. The other was a
stranger—probably the man whom Creech half-expected to
call upon him. One lay in wait for Creech and strangled him
near the wicket-gate as he arrived; fetched your goloshes from
the vernadah, and carried the body down to the Folly. And the
other came here in disguise to hold you in play and give you
an alibi that no one could believe. The one man is strong in his
hands and strong in the back—a sturdy, stocky man with feet
no bigger than yours. The other is a big man, with noticeable
eyes and probably clean-shaven, and he plays brilliant chess.
Look among Creech's enemies for those two men and ask
them where they were between eight o'clock and ten-thirty
last night."

"Why didn't the strangler bring back the goloshes?" asked the Chief Constable.

"Ah!" said Wimsey; "that was where the plan went wrong. I think he waited up at the Folly to see the light go out in the cottage. He thought it would be too great a risk to come up twice on to the verandah while Mr. Mellilow was there."

"Do you mean," asked Mr. Mellilow, "that he was there, in the Folly, watching me, when I was groping up those black stairs?"

"He may have been," said Wimsey. "But probably, when he saw you coming up the slope, he knew that things had gone wrong and fled away in the opposite direction, to the high road that runs behind the Folly. Mr. Moses, of course, went, as he came, by the road that passes Mr. Mellilow's door, removing his disguise in the nearest convenient place."

"That's all very well, my lord," said the superintendent, "but where's the proof of it?"

"Everywhere," said Wimsey. "Go and look at the tracks again. There's one set going outwards in goloshes, deep and short, made when the body was carried down. One made later, in walking shoes, which is Mr. Mellilow's track going outwards towards the Folly. And the third is Mr. Mellilow again, coming back, the track of a man running very fast. Two out and only one in. Where is the man who went out and never came back?"

"Yes," said the superintendent doggedly. "But suppose Mr. Mellilow made that second lot of tracks himself to put us off the scent, like? I'm not saying he did, mind you, but why couldn't he have?"

"Because," said Wimsey, "he had no time. The in-and-out tracks left by the shoes were made *after* the body was carried down. There is no other bridge for three miles on either side, and the river runs waist-deep. It can't be forded; so it must be crossed by the bridge. But at half-past ten Mr. Mellilow was in the Feathers, on *this* side of the river, ringing up the police. It couldn't be done, Super, unless he had wings. The bridge is there to prove it; for the bridge was crossed three times only."

"The bridge," said Mr. Mellilow, with a great sigh. "I knew in my dream there was something important about that. I knew I was safe if only I could get to the bridge."

THE HAUNTED POLICEMAN

ood God!" said his lordship.
"Did I do that?"

"All the evidence points that way," replied his wife.

"Then I can only say that I never knew so convincing a
body of evidence produce such an inadequate result."

The nurse appeared to take this reflection personally. She
said in a tone of rebuke:

"He's a *beautiful* boy."

"H'm," said Peter. He adjusted his eyeglass more carefully.
"Well, you're the expert witness. Hand him over."

The nurse did so with a dubious air. She was relieved to
see that this disconcerting parent handled the child compe-
tently; as, in a man who was an experienced uncle, was not,
after all, so very surprising. Lord Peter sat down gingerly on
the edge of the bed.

"Do you feel it's up to standard?" he inquired with some
anxiety. "Of course, *your* workmanship's always sound—but
you never know with these collaborate efforts."

"I think it'll do," said Harriet drowsily.

"Good." He turned abruptly to the nurse. "All right; we'll keep it. Take it and put it away, and tell 'em to invoice it to me. It's a very interesting addition to you, Harriet; but it would have been a hell of a rotten substitute." His voice wavered a little, for the last twenty-four hours had been very trying ones, and he had had the fright of his life.

The doctor, who had been doing something in the other room entered in time to catch the last words.

"There was never any likelihood of that, you goop," he said, cheerfully. "Now, you've seen all there is to be seen, and you'd better run away and play." He led his charge firmly to the door. "Go to bed," he advised him in kindly accents; "you look all in."

"I'm all right," said Peter. "I haven't been doing anything. And look here—" he stabbed a belligerent finger in the direction of the adjoining room, "tell those nurses of yours, if I want to pick my son up, I'll pick him up. If his mother wants to kiss him, she can damn well kiss him. I'll have none of your infernal hygiene in *my* house."

"Very well," said the doctor, "just as you like. Anything for a quiet life. I rather believe in a few healthy germs myself. Builds up resistance. No, thanks, I won't have a drink. I've got to go on to another one, and an alcoholic breath impairs confidence."

"Another one?" said Peter, aghast.

"One of my hospital mothers. You're not the only fish in the sea by a long chalk. One born every minute."

"God! What a hell of a world." They passed down the great curved stair. In the hall a sleepy footman clung, yawning, to his post of duty.

"All right, William," said Peter. "Buzz off now; I'll lock up." He let the doctor out. "Good night—and thanks very much, old man. I'm sorry I swore at you."

"They mostly do," replied the doctor philosophically. "Well, bung-ho, Flim. I'll look in again later, just to earn my fee, but I shan't be wanted. You've married into a good tough family, and I congratulate you."

The car, spluttering and protesting a little after its long wait in the cold, drove off, leaving Peter alone on the doorstep. Now that it was all over and he could go to bed, he felt extraordinarily wakeful. He would have liked to go to a party. He leaned back against the wrought-iron railings and lit a cigarette, staring vaguely into the lamp-lit dusk of the Square. It was thus that he saw the policeman.

The blue-uniformed figure came up from the direction of South Audley Street. He, too, was smoking, and he walked, not with the firm tramp of a constable on his beat, but with the hesitating step of a man who has lost his bearings. When he came in sight, he had pushed back his helmet and was rubbing his head in a puzzled manner. Official habit made him look sharply at the bare-headed gentleman in evening dress, abandoned on a doorstep at three in the morning, but since the gentleman appeared to be sober and bore no signs of being about to commit a felony, he averted his gaze and prepared to pass on.

" 'Morning, Officer," said the gentleman, as he came abreast with him.

" 'Morning, sir," said the policeman.

"You're off duty early," pursued Peter, who wanted somebody to talk to. "Come in and have a drink."

This offer reawakened all the official suspicion.

"Not just now, sir, thank you," replied the policeman guardedly.

"Yes, now. That's the point." Peter tossed away his cigarette-end. It described a fiery arc in the air and shot out a little train of sparks as it struck the pavement. "I've got a son."

"Oh, ah!" said the policeman, relieved by this innocent confidence. "Your first, eh?"

"And last, if I know anything about it."

"That's what my brother says, every time," said the policeman. "Never no more, he says. He's got eleven. Well, sir, good luck to it. I see how you're situated, and thank you kindly, but after what the Sergeant said I dunno as I better. Though if I was to die this moment, not a drop 'as passed me lips since me supper beer."

Peter put his head on one side and considered this.

"The Sergeant said you were drunk?"

"He did, sir."

"And you were not?"

"No, sir. I saw everything just the same as I told him, though what's become of it now is more than I can say. But drunk I was not, sir, no more than you are yourself."

"Then," said Peter, "as Mr. Joseph Surface remarked to Lady Teazle, what is troubling you is the consciousness of your own innocence. He insinuated that you have looked on the wine when it was red—you'd better come in and make it so. You'll feel better."

The policeman hesitated.

"Well, sir, I dunno. Fact is, I've had a bit of a shock."

"So've I," said Peter. "Come in for God's sake and keep me company."

"Well, sir—" said the policeman again. He mounted the steps slowly.

The logs in the hall chimney were glowing a deep red through their ashes. Peter raked them apart, so that the young flame shot up between them. "Sit down," he said; "I'll be back in a moment."

The policeman sat down, removed his helmet, and stared about him, trying to remember who occupied the big house at the corner of the Square. The engraved coat of arms upon the great silver bowl on the chimney-piece told him nothing, even though it was repeated in colour upon the backs of two tapestried chairs: three white mice skipping upon a black ground. Peter, returning quietly from the shadows beneath the stair, caught him as he traced the outlines with a thick finger.

"A student of heraldry?" he said. "Seventeenth century work and not very graceful. You're new to this beat, aren't you? My name's Wimsey."

He put down a tray on the table.

"If you'd rather have beer or whisky, say so. These bottles are only a concession to my mood."

The policeman eyed the long necks and bulging silver-wrapped corks with curiosity. "Champagne?" he said. "Never tasted it, sir. But I'd like to try the stuff."

"You'll find it thin," said Peter, "but if you drink enough of it, you'll tell me the story of your life." The cork popped, and the wine frothed out into the wide glasses.

"Well!" said the policeman. "Here's to your good lady, sir, and the new young gentleman. Long life and all the best. A bit in the nature of cider, ain't it, sir?"

"Just a trifle. Give me your opinion after the third glass, if you can put up with it so long. And thanks for your good wishes. You a married man?"

"Not yet, sir. Hoping to be when I get promotion. If only the Sergeant—but that's neither here nor there. You been married long, sir, if I may ask?"

"Just over a year."

"Ah! and do you find it comfortable, sir?"

Peter laughed.

"I've spent the last twenty-four hours wondering why, when I'd had the blazing luck to get on to a perfectly good thing, I should be fool enough to risk the whole show on a damned silly experiment."

The policeman nodded sympathetically.

"I see what you mean, sir. Seems to me, life's like that. If you don't take risks, you get nowhere. If you do, they may go wrong, and then where are you? And 'alf the time, when things happen, they happen first, before you can even think about 'em."

"Quite right," said Peter, and filled the glasses again. He found the policeman soothing. True to his class and training, he turned naturally in moments of emotion to the company of the common man. Indeed, when the recent domestic crisis had threatened to destroy his nerve, he had headed for the butler's pantry with the swift instinct of the homing pigeon. There, they had treated him with great humanity, and allowed him to clean the silver.

With a mind oddly clarified by champagne and lack of sleep, he watched the constable's reaction to Pol Roger 1926.

The first glass had produced a philosophy of life; the second produced a name—Alfred Burt—and further hints of some mysterious grievance against the Station Sergeant; the third glass, as prophesied, produced the story.

"You were right, sir" (said the policeman) "when you spotted I was new to the beat. I only come on it at the beginning of the week, and that accounts for me not being acquainted with you, sir, nor with most of the residents about here. Jessop, now, he knows everybody, and so did Pinker—but he's been took off to another division. You'd remember Pinker—big chap, make two o' me, with a sandy moustache. Yes, I thought you would.

"Well, sir, as I was saying, me knowing the district in a general way, but not, so to speak, like the palm o' me 'and, might account for me making a bit of a fool of myself, but it don't account for me seeing what I did see. See it I did, and not drunk nor nothing like it. And as for making a mistake in the number, well, that might happen to anybody. All the same, sir, thirteen was the number I see, plain as the nose on your face."

"You can't put it stronger than that," said Peter, whose nose was of a kind difficult to overlook.

"You know Merriman's End, sir?"

"I think I do. Isn't it a long cul-de-sac running somewhere at the back of South Audley Street, with a row of houses on one side and a high wall on the other?"

"That's right, sir. Tall, narrow houses they are, all alike, with deep porches and pillars to them."

"Yes. Like an escape from the worst square in Pimlico. Horrible. Fortunately, I believe the street was never finished, or we should have had another row of the monstrosities on the opposite side. This house is pure eighteenth century. How does it strike you?"

P.C. Burt contemplated the wide hall—the Adam fireplace and panelling with their graceful shallow mouldings, the pedimented doorways, the high roundheaded window lighting hall and gallery, the noble proportions of the stair. He sought for a phrase.

"It's a gentleman's house," he pronounced at length. "Room to breathe, if you see what I mean. Seems like you couldn't act vulgar in it." He shook his head. "Mind you, I wouldn't call it cosy. It ain't the place I'd choose to sit down to a kipper in me shirt-sleeves. But it's got class. I never thought about it before, but now you mention it I see what's wrong with them other houses in Merriman's End. They're sort of squeezed-like. I been into more'n one o' them to-night, and that's what they are: they're squeezed. But I was going to tell you about that.

"Just upon midnight it was" (pursued the policeman) "when I turns into Merriman's End in the ordinary course of my dooties. I'd got pretty near down towards the far end, when I see a fellow lurking about in a suspicious way under the wall. There's back gates there, you know, sir, leading into some gardens, and this chap was hanging about inside one of the gateways. A rough-looking fellow, in a baggy old coat—might a-been a tramp off the Embankment. I turned my light on him—that street's not very well lit, and it's a dark night—but I couldn't see much of his face, because he had on a ragged old hat and a big scarf round his neck. I thought he was up to no good, and I was just about to ask him what he was doing there, when I hear a most awful yell come out o' one o' them houses opposite. Ghastly it was, sir. 'Help!' it said. 'Murder! Help!,' fit to freeze your marrow."

"Man's voice or woman's?"

"Man's, sir, I think. More of a roaring kind of yell, if you take my meaning. I says, 'Hullo! What's up there? Which house is it?' The chap says nothing, but he points, and him and me runs across together. Just as we gets to the house there's a noise like as if someone was being strangled just inside, and a thump, as it might be something falling against the door."

"Good God!" said Peter.

"I gives a shout and rings the bell. 'Hoy!' I says. 'What's up here?' and then I knocks on the door. There's no answer, so I rings and knocks again. Then the chap who was with me, he pushed open the letter-flap and squints through it."

"Was there a light in the house?"

"It was all dark, sir, except the fan-light over the door. That was lit up bright, and when I looks up, I see the number of the house — No. 13, painted plain as you like on the transom. Well, this chap peers in, and all of a sudden he gives a kind of gurgle and falls back. 'Here!' I says, 'what's amiss? Let me have a look.' So I puts me eye to the flap and I looks in."

P.C. Burt paused and drew a long breath. Peter cut the wire of the second bottle.

"Now, sir," said the Policeman, "believe me or believe me not, I was as sober at that moment as I am now. I can tell you everything I see in that house, same as if it was wrote up there on that wall. Not as it was a great lot, because the flap wasn't all that wide, but by squinnying a bit, I could make shift to see right across the hall and a piece on both sides and part way up the stairs. And here's what I see, and you take notice of every word, on account of what came after."

He took another gulp of the Pol Roger to loosen his tongue and continued:

"There was the floor of the hall. I could see that very plain. All black and white squares it was, like marble, and it stretched back a good long way. About half-way along, on the left, was the staircase, with a red carpet, and the figure of a white naked woman at the foot, carrying a big pot full of blue and yellow flowers. In the wall next the stairs there was an open door, and a room all lit up. I could just see the end of a table, with a lot of glass and silver on it. Between that door and the front door there was a big black cabinet, shiny, with gold figures painted on it, like them things they had at the Exhibition. Right at the back of the hall there was a place like a conservatory, but I couldn't see what was in it, only it looked very gay. There was a door on the right, and that was open, too. A very pretty drawing-room, by what I could see of it, with pale blue paper and pictures on the walls. There were pictures in the hall, too, and a table on the right with a copper bowl, like as it might be for visitors' cards to be put in. Now,

I see all that, sir, and I put it to you, if it hadn't a-been there, how could I describe it so plain?"

"I have known people describe what wasn't there," said Peter thoughtfully, "but it was seldom anything of that kind. Rats, cats, and snakes I have heard of, and occasionally naked female figures; but delirious lacquer cabinets and hall-tables are new to me."

"As you say, sir," agreed the policeman, "and I see you believe me so far. But here's something else, what you mayn't find quite so easy. There was a man laying in that hall, sir, as sure as I sit here, and he was dead. He was a big man and clean-shaven, and he wore evening dress. Somebody had stuck a knife into his throat. I could see the handle of it—it looked like a carving-knife, and the blood had run out, all shiny, over the marble squares."

The policeman looked at Peter, passed his handkerchief over his forehead, and finished the fourth glass of champagne.

"His head was up against the end of the hall-table," he went on, "and his feet must have been up against the door, but I couldn't see anything quite close to me, because of the letter-box. You understand, sir, I was looking through the wire cage of the box, and there was something inside—letters, I suppose, that cut off my view downwards. But I see all the rest—in front and a bit of both sides; and it must have been regularly burnt in upon me brain, as they say, for I don't suppose I was looking more than a quarter of a minute or so. Then all the lights went out at once, same as if somebody had turned off the main switch. So I looks round, and I don't mind telling you I felt a bit queer. And *when* I looks round, lo and behold! My bloke in the muffler had hopped it."

"The devil he had," said Peter.

"Hopped it," repeated the policeman, "and there I was. And just there, sir, is where I made my big mistake, for I thought he couldn't a-got far, and I started off up the street after him. But I couldn't see him, and I couldn't see nobody. All the houses was dark, and it come over me what a sight of funny things may go on, and nobody take a mite o' notice. The

way I'd shouted and banged on the door, you'd a-thought it'd
a-brought out every soul in the street, not to mention that
awful yelling. But there—you may have noticed it yourself, sir.
A man may leave his ground-floor windows open, or have his
chimney a-fire, and you may make noise enough to wake the
dead, trying to draw his attention, and nobody give no heed.
He's fast asleep, and the neighbours say, 'Blast that row, but,
it's no business of mine,' and stick their 'eads under the bed-
clothes."

"Yes," said Peter. "London's like that."

"That's right, sir. A village is different. You can't pick up a
pin there without somebody coming up to ask where you got
it from—but London keeps itself to itself. . . . Well, something'll have to be done, I thinks to myself, and I blows me
whistle. They heard that all right. Windows started to go up
all along the street. That's London, too."

Peter nodded. "London will sleep through the last trump.
Puddley-in-the-Rut and Doddering-in-the-Dumps will look
down their noses and put on virtuous airs. But God, who is
never surprised, will say to his angel, 'Whistle 'em up,
Michael, whistle 'em up; East and West will rise from the dead
at the sound of the policeman's whistle.' "

"Quite so, sir," said P.C. Burt; and wondered for the first
time whether there might not be something in this champagne
stuff after all. He waited for a moment and then resumed:

"Well, it so happened that just when I sounded my whistle, Withers—that's the man on the other beat—was in Audley
Square, coming to meet me. You know, sir, we has times for
meeting one another, arranged different-like every night; and
twelve o'clock in the Square was our rendy-voos to-night. So
up he comes in, you might say, no time at all, and finds me
there, with everyone a-hollering at me from the windows to
know what was up. Well, naturally I didn't want the whole
bunch of 'em running out into the street and our man getting
away in the crowd, so I just tells 'em there's nothing, only a bit
of an accident farther along. And then I see Withers and glad
enough I was. We stands there at the top o' the street, and I

tells him there's a dead man laying in the hall at Number 13, and it looks to me like murder. 'Number 13?' he says, 'you can't mean Number 13. There ain't no Number 13 in Merriman's end, you fathead; it's all even numbers.' And so it is, sir, for the houses on the other side were never built, so there's no odd numbers at all, barrin' Number 1, as is the big house on the corner.

"Well, that give me a bit of a jolt. I wasn't so much put out at not having remembered about the numbers, for as I tell you, I never was on the beat before this week. No; but I knew I'd seen that there number writ up plain as pie on the fanlight, and I didn't see how I could have been mistaken. But when Withers heard the rest of the story, he thought maybe I'd misread it for Number 12. It couldn't be 18, for there's only sixteen houses in the road; nor it couldn't be 16 neither, for I knew it wasn't the end house. But we thought it might be 12 or 10; so away we goes to look.

"We didn't have no difficulty about getting in at Number 12. There was a very pleasant old gentleman came down in his dressing-gown, asking what the disturbance was, and could he be of use. I apologized for disturbing him, and said I was afraid there'd been an accident in one of the houses, and had he heard anything. Of course, the minute he opened the door I could see it wasn't Number 12 we wanted; there was only a little hall with polished boards, and the walls plain panelled — all very bare and neat — and no black cabinet nor naked woman nor nothing. The old gentleman said, yes, his son had heard somebody shouting and knocking a few minutes earlier. He'd got up and put his head out of the window, but couldn't see nothing, but they both thought from the sound it was Number 14 forgotten his latchkey again. So we thanked him very much and went on to Number 14.

"We had a bit of a job to get Number 14 downstairs. A fiery sort of gentleman he was, something in the military way I thought, but he turned out to be a retired Indian Civil servant. A dark gentleman, with a big voice, and his servant was dark, too — some sort of a nigger. The gentleman wanted to know what the blazes all this row was about, and why a decent citizen wasn't allowed to get his proper sleep. He supposed that young fool at Number 12 was drunk again. Withers had to speak a bit sharp to him; but at last the nigger came down and let us in. Well, we had to apologize once more. The hall was not a bit like—the staircase was on the wrong side, for one thing, and though there was a statue at the foot of it, it was some kind of a heathen idol with a lot of heads and arms, and the walls were covered with all sorts of brass stuff and native goods—you know the kind of thing. There was a black and white linoleum on the floor, and that was about all there was to it. The servant had a soft sort of way with him I didn't half like. He said he slept at the back and had heard nothing till his master rang for him. Then the gentleman came to the top of the stairs and shouted out it was no use disturbing him; the noise came from Number 12 as usual, and if that young man didn't stop his blanky Bohemian goings-on, he'd have the law on his father. I asked if he'd seen anything, and he said, no, he hadn't. Of course, sir, me and that other chap was inside the porch, and you can't see anything what goes on inside those porches from the other houses, because they're filled in at the sides with coloured glass—all the lot of them."

Lord Peter Wimsey looked at the policeman and then looked at the bottle, as though estimating the alcoholic contents of each. With deliberation, he filled both glasses again.

"Well, sir," said P.C. Burt, after refreshing himself, "by this time Withers was looking at me in rather an old-fashioned manner. However, he said nothing, and we went back to Number 10, where there was two maiden ladies and a hall full of stuffed birds and wallpaper like a florists' catalogue. The one who slept in the front was deaf as a post, and the one who slept at the back hadn't heard nothing. But we got hold of their maids, and the cook said she'd heard the voice calling 'Help!' and thought it was in Number 12, and she'd hid her head in the pillow and said her prayers. The housemaid was a sensible girl. She'd looked out when she'd heard me knocking. She couldn't see anything at first, owing to us being in the porch, but she thought something must be going on, so, not wishing to catch cold, she went back to put on her bedroom slippers. When she got back to the window she was just in time to see a man running up the road. He went very quick and very silent, as if he had goloshes on, and she could see the ends of his muffler flying out behind him. She saw him run out of the street and turn to the right, and then she heard me coming along after him. Unfortunately, her eye being on the man, she didn't notice which porch I came out of. Well, that showed I wasn't inventing the whole story at any rate, because there was my bloke in the muffler. The girl didn't recognize him at all, but that wasn't surprising, because she'd only just entered the old ladies' service. Besides, it wasn't likely the man had anything to do with it, because he was outside with me when the yelling started. My belief is he was the sort as doesn't care to have his pockets examined too close, and the minute my back was turned he thought he'd be better and more comfortable elsewhere.

"Now there ain't no need" (continued the policeman) "for me to trouble you, sir, with all them houses what we went into. We made inquiries at the whole lot, from Number 2 to Number 16, and there wasn't one of them had a hall in any ways conformable to what that chap and I saw through the letter-box. Nor there wasn't a soul in 'em could give us any help more than what we'd had already. You see, sir, though it took me a bit o' time telling, it all went very quick. There was the yells; they didn't last beyond a few seconds or so, and before they was finished, we was across the road and inside the porch. Then there was me shouting and knocking; but I hadn't been long at that afore the chap with me looks through the box. Then I had my look inside, for fifteen seconds it might be, and while I'm doing that, my chap's away up the street. Then I runs after him, and then I blows me whistle. The whole thing might take a minute, or a minute and a half maybe. Not more.

"Well, sir; by the time we'd been into every house in Merriman's End, I was feeling a bit queer again, I can tell you, and Withers, he was looking queerer. He says to me, 'Burt,' he says, 'is this your idea of a joke? Because if so, the 'Olborn Empire's where you ought to be, not the police force.' So I tells him over again, most solemn, what I see — 'and,' I says, 'if only we could lay hands on that chap in the muffler, he could tell you he seen it, too. And what's more,' I says, 'do you think I'd risk me job, playing a silly trick like that?' He says, 'Well, it beats me,' he says. 'If I didn't know you was a sober kind of chap, I'd say you was seein' things.' 'Things?' I says to him, 'I see that there corpse a-layin' there with the knife in his neck, and that was enough for me. 'Orrible, he looked, and the blood all over the floor.' 'Well,' he says, 'maybe he wasn't dead after all, and they've cleared him out of the way.' 'And cleared the house away, too, I suppose,' I said to him. So Withers says, in an odd sort o' voice, 'You're sure about the house? You wasn't letting your imagination run away with you over naked females and such?' That was a nice thing to say. I said, 'No, I wasn't. There's been some monkey business going on in this street and I'm going to get to the bottom of it, if we has to comb-out London for that chap in the muffler.' 'Yes,' says Withers, nasty-like, 'it's a pity he cleared off so sudden.' 'Well,' I says, 'you can't say I imagined *him*, anyhow, because that there girl saw him, and a mercy she did,' I said, 'or you'd be saying next I ought to be in Colney Hatch.' 'Well,' he says, 'I dunno what you think you're going to do about it. You better ring up the station and ask for instructions.'

"Which I did. And Sergeant Jones, he came down himself, and he listens attentive-like to what we both has to say, and then he walks along the street, slow-like, from end to end. And then he comes back and says to me, 'Now, Burt,' he says, 'just you describe that hall to me again, careful.' Which I does, same as I described it to you, sir. And he says, 'You're sure there was the room on the left of the stairs with the glass and silver on the table; and the room on the right with the pictures in it?' And I says, 'Yes, Sergeant, I'm quite sure of that.' And Withers says, 'Ah!' in a kind of got-you-now voice, if you take my meaning. And the Sergeant says, 'Now, Burt,' he says, 'pull yourself together and take a look at these here houses.

Don't you see they're all single-fronted? There ain't one on 'em has rooms *both* sides o' the front hall. Look at the windows, you fool,' he says."

Lord Peter poured out the last of the champagne.

"I don't mind telling you, sir" (went on the policeman), "that I was fair knocked silly. To think of me never noticing that! Withers had noticed it all right, and that's what made him think I was drunk or barmy. But I stuck to what I'd seen. I said, there must be two of them houses knocked into one, somewhere; but that didn't work, because we'd been into all of them, and there wasn't no such thing—not without there was one o' them concealed doors like you read about in crook stories. 'Well, anyhow,' I says to the Sergeant, 'the yells was real all right, because other people heard 'em. Just you ask, and they'll tell you.' So the Sergeant says, 'Well, Burt, I'll give you every chance.' So he knocked up Number 12 again—not wishing to annoy Number 14 any more than he was already— and this time the son comes down. An agreeable gentleman he was, too; not a bit put out. He says, Oh, yes, he'd heard the yells and his father'd heard them too. 'Number 14,' he says, 'that's where the trouble is. A very odd bloke, is Number 14, and I shouldn't be surprised if he beats that unfortunate servant of his. The Englishman abroad, you know! The outposts of Empire and all that kind of thing. They're rough and ready—and then the curry in them parts is bad for the liver.' So I was for inquiring at Number 14 again; but the Sergeant, he loses patience and says, 'You know quite well,' he says, 'it ain't Number 14, and in my opinion, Burt, you're either dotty or drunk. You best go home straight away,' he says, 'and sober up, and I'll see you again when you can give a better account of yourself.' So I argues a bit, but it ain't no use, and away he goes, and Withers goes back to his beat. And I walks up and down a bit till Jessop comes to take over, and then I comes away, and that's when I sees you, sir.

"But I ain't drunk, sir—at least, I wasn't then, though there do seem to be a kind of a swimming in me head at this moment. Maybe that stuff's stronger than it tastes. But I wasn't drunk then, and I'm pretty sure I'm not dotty. I'm haunted, sir, that's what it is—haunted. It might be there was someone killed in one of them houses a many years ago, and that's what I see to-night. Perhaps they changed the numbering of the street on account of it—I've heard tell of such things—and when the same night comes round the house goes back to what it was before. But there I am, with a black mark against me, and it ain't a fair trick for no ghost to go getting a plain man into trouble. And I'm sure, sir, you'll agree with me."

The policeman's narrative had lasted some time, and the hands of the grandfather clock stood at a quarter to five. Peter Wimsey gazed benevolently at his companion, for whom he was beginning to feel a positive affection. He was, if anything, slightly more drunk than the policeman, for he had missed tea and had no appetite for his dinner; but the wine had not clouded his wits; it had only increased excitability and postponed sleep. He said:

"When you looked through the letter-box, could you see any part of the ceiling, or the lights?"

"No, sir; on account, you see, of the flap. I could see right and left and straight forward; but not upwards, and none of the near part of the floor."

"When you looked at the house from outside, there was no light except through the fanlight. But when you looked through the flap, all the rooms were lit, right and left and at the back?"

"That's so, sir."

"Are there back doors to the houses?"

"Yes, sir. Coming out of Merriman's End, you turn to the right, and there's an opening a little way along which takes you to the back doors."

"You seem to have a very distinct visual memory. I wonder if your other kinds of memory are as good. Can you tell me, for instance, whether any of the houses you went into had any particular smell? Especially 10, 12, and 14?"

"Smell, sir?" The policeman closed his eyes to stimulate recollection. "Why, yes, sir. Number 10, where the two ladies live, that had a sort of an old-fashioned smell. I can't put me tongue to it. Not lavender—but something as ladies keeps in bowls and such—rose-leaves and what not. Pot-pourri, that's the stuff. Pot-pourri. And Number 12—well, no, there was nothing particular there, except I remember thinking they must keep pretty good servants, though we didn't see anybody except the family. All that floor and panelling was polished beautiful—you could see your face in it. Beeswax and turpentine, I says to meself. And elbow-grease. What you'd call a clean house with a good, clean smell. But Number 14—that was different. I didn't like the smell of that. Stuffy, like as if the nigger had been burning some o' that there incense to his idols, maybe. I never could abide niggers."

"Ah!" said Peter. "What you say is very suggestive." He placed his finger-tips together and shot his last question over them:

"Ever been inside the National Gallery?"

"No, sir," said the policeman, astonished. "I can't say as I ever was."

"That's London again," said Peter. "We're the last people in the world to know anything of our great metropolitan institutions. Now, what is the best way to tackle this bunch of toughs, I wonder? It's a little early for a call. Still, there's nothing like doing one's good deed before breakfast, and the sooner you're set right with the Sergeant, the better. Let me see. Yes—I think that may do it. Costume pieces are not as a rule in my line, but my routine has been so much upset already, one way and another, that an irregularity more or less will hardly matter. Wait there for me while I have a bath and change. I may be a little time; but it would hardly be decent to get there before six."

The bath had been an attractive thought, but was perhaps ill advised, for a curious languor stole over him with the touch of the hot water. The champagne was losing its effervescence. It was with an effort that he dragged himself out and reawakened himself with a cold shower. The matter of dress required a little thought. A pair of grey flannel trousers was easily found, and though they were rather too well creased for the part he meant to play, he thought that with luck they would probably pass unnoticed. The shirt was a difficulty. His collection of shirts was a notable one, but they were mostly of an inconspicuous and gentlemanly sort. He hesitated for some time over a white shirt with an open sports collar, but decided at length upon a blue one, bought as an experiment and held to be not quite successful. A red tie, if he had possessed such a thing, would have been convincing. After some consideration, he remembered that he had seen his wife in a rather wide Liberty tie, whose prevailing colour was orange. That, he felt, would do if he could find it. On her it had looked rather well; on him, it would be completely abominable. He went through into the next room; it was queer to find it empty. A peculiar sensation came over him. Here *he* was, rifling his wife's drawers, and there *she* was, spirited out of reach at the top of the house with a couple of nurses and an entirely new baby, which might turn into goodness knew what.

He sat down before the glass and stared at himself. He felt as though he ought to have changed somehow in the night; but he only looked unshaven and, he thought, a trifle intoxicated. Both were quite good things to look at the moment, though hardly suitable for the father of a family. He pulled out all the drawers in the dressing-table; they emitted vaguely familiar smells of face-powder and handkerchief sachet. He tried the big built-in wardrobe: frocks, costumes and trays full of underwear, which made him feel sentimental. At last he struck a promising vein of gloves and stockings. The next tray held ties, the orange of the desired Liberty creation gleaming in a friendly way among them. He put it on, and observed with pleasure that the effect was Bohemian beyond description. He wandered out again, leaving all the drawers open behind him as though a burglar had passed through the room. An ancient tweed jacket of his own, of a very countrified pattern, suitable only for fishing in Scotland, was next unearthed, together with a pair of brown canvas shoes. He secured his trousers by a belt, searched for and found an old soft-brimmed felt hat of no recognizable colour, and, after removing a few trout-flies from the hat-band and tucking his shirt-sleeves well up inside the coat-sleeve, decided that he would do. As an after-thought, he returned to his wife's room and selected a wide woollen scarf in a shade of greenish blue. Thus equipped, he came downstairs again, to find P.C. Burt fast asleep, with his mouth open and snoring.

Peter was hurt. Here he was, sacrificing himself in the interests of this stupid policeman, and the man hadn't the common decency to appreciate it. However, there was no point in waking him yet. He yawned horribly and sat down.

It was the footman who wakened the sleepers at half-past six. If he was surprised to see his master, very strangely attired, slumbering in the hall in the company with a large policeman, he was too well trained to admit the fact even to himself. He merely removed the tray. The faint clink of glass roused Peter, who slept like a cat at all times.

"Hullo, William," he said. "Have I overslept myself? What's the time?"

"Five and twenty to seven, my lord."

"Just about right." He remembered that the footman slept on the top floor. "All quiet on the Western Front, William?"

"Not altogether quiet, my lord." William permitted himself a slight smile. "The young master was lively about five. But all satisfactory, I gather from Nurse Jenkyn."

"Nurse Jenkyn? Is that the young one? Don't let yourself be run away with, William. I say, just give P.C. Burt a light prod in the ribs, would you? He and I have business together."

In Merriman's End the activities of the morning were beginning. The milkman came jingling out of the cul-de-sac; lights were twinkling in upper rooms; hands were withdrawing curtains; in front of Number 10 the housemaid was already scrubbing the steps. Peter posted his policeman at the top of the street.

"I don't want to make my first appearance with official accompaniment," he said. "Come along when I beckon. What, by the way, is the name of the agreeable gentleman in Number 12? I think he may be of some assistance to us."

"Mr. O'Halloran, sir."

The policeman looked at Peter expectantly. He seemed to have abandoned all initiative and to place implicit confidence in this hospitable and eccentric gentleman. Peter slouched down the street with his hands in his trousers pocket, and his shabby hat pulled rakishly over his eyes. At Number 12 he paused and examined the windows. Those on the ground floor were open; the house was awake. He marched up the steps, took a brief glance through the flap of the letter-box, and rang the bell. A maid in a neat blue dress and white cap and apron opened the door.

"Good morning," said Peter, slightly raising the shabby hat; "is Mr. O'Halloran in?" He gave the *r* a soft continental roll. "Not the old gentleman. I mean young Mr. O'Halloran?"

"He's in," said the maid doubtfully, "but he isn't up yet."

"Oh!" said Peter. "Well, it is a little early for a visit. But I desire to see him urgently. I am—there is a little trouble where I live. Could you entreat him—would you be so kind? I have walked all the way," he added, pathetically, and with perfect truth.

"Have you, sir?" said the maid. She added kindly, "You do look tired, sir, and that's a fact."

"It is nothing," said Peter. "It is only that I forgot to have any dinner. But if I can see Mr. O'Halloran it will be all right."

"You'd better come in, sir," said the maid. "I'll see if I can wake him." She conducted the exhausted stranger in and offered him a chair. "What name shall I say, sir?"

"Petrovinsky," said his lordship, hardily. As he had rather expected, neither the unusual name nor the unusual clothes of this unusually early visitor seemed to cause very much surprise. The maid left him in the tidy little panelled hall and went upstairs without so much as a glance at the umbrella-stand.

Left to himself, Peter sat still noticing that the hall was remarkably bare of furniture, and was lit by a single electric pendant almost immediately inside the front door. The letter-box was the usual wire-cage, the bottom of which had been carefully lined with brown paper. From the back of the house came a smell of frying bacon.

Presently there was the sound of somebody running downstairs. A young man appeared in a dressing-gown. He called out as he came: "Is that you, Stefan? Your name came up as Mr. Whiskey. Has Marfa run away again, or — What the hell? Who the devil are you, sir?"

"Wimsey," said Peter, mildly, "not Whisky; Wimsey, the policeman's friend. I just looked in to congratulate you on a mastery of the art of false perspective which I thought had perished with the ingenious Van Hoogstraaten, or at least with Grace and Lambelet."

"Oh!" said the young man. He had a pleasant countenance, with humorous eyes and ears pointed like a faun's. He laughed a little ruefully. "I suppose my beautiful murder is out. It was too good to last. Those bobbies! I hope to god they gave Number 14 a bad night. May I ask how you came to be involved in the matter?"

"I," said Peter, "am the kind of person in whom distressed constables confide — I cannot imagine why. And when I had the picture of that sturdy blue-clad figure, led so persuasively by a Bohemian stranger and invited to peer through a hole, I was irresistibly transported in mind to the National Gallery. Many a time have I squinted sideways through those holes into the little black box, and admired that Dutch interior of many vistas painted so convincingly on the four flat sides of the box. How right you were to preserve your eloquent silence! Your Irish tongue would have given you away. The servants, I gather, were purposely kept out of sight."

"Tell me," said Mr. O'Halloran, seating himself sideways upon the hall table, "do you know by heart the occupation of every resident in this quarter of London? I do not paint under my own name."

"No," said Peter. "Like the good Dr. Watson, the constable could observe, though he could not reason from his observation; it was the smell of turpentine that betrayed you. I gather that at the time of his first call the apparatus was not very far off."

"It was folded together and lying under the stairs," replied the painter. "It has since been removed to the studio. My father had only just had time to get it out of the way and hitch down the 'Number 13' from the fan-light before the police reinforcements arrived. He had not even time to put back this table I am sitting on; a brief search would have discovered it in the dining-room. My father is a remarkable sportsman; I cannot too highly recommend the presence of mind he displayed while I was hareing round the houses and leaving him to hold the fort. It would have been so simple and so unenterprising to explain; but my father, being an Irishman, enjoys treading on the coat-tails of authority."

"I should like to meet your father. The only thing I do not thoroughly understand is the reason of this elaborate plot. Were you by any chance executing a burglary round the corner, and keeping the police in play while you did it?"

"I never thought of that," said the young man, with regret in his voice. "No. The bobby was not the predestined victim. He happened to be present at a full-dress rehearsal, and the joke was too good to be lost. The fact is, my uncle is Sir Lucius Preston, the R.A."

"Ah!" said Peter, "the light begins to break."

"My own style of draughtsmanship," pursued Mr. O'Halloran, "is modern. My uncle has on several occasions informed me that I draw like that only because I do not know how to draw. The idea was that he should be invited to dinner tomorrow and regaled with a story of the mysterious 'Number 13,' said to appear from time to time in this street and to be haunted by strange noises. Having thus detained him till close upon midnight, I should have set out to see him to the top of the street. As we went along, the cries would have broken out. I should have led him back—"

"Nothing," said Peter, "could be clearer. After the preliminary shock he would have been forced to confess that your draughtsmanship was a triumph of academic accuracy."

"I hope," said Mr. O'Halloran, "the performance may still go forward as originally intended." He looked with some anxiety at Peter, who replied:

"I hope so, indeed. I also hope that your uncle's heart is a strong one. But may I, in the meantime, signal to my unfortunate policeman and relieve his mind? He is in danger of losing his promotion, though a suspicion that he was drunk on duty."

"Good God!" said Mr. O'Halloran. "No—I don't want that to happen. Fetch him in."

The difficulty was to make P.C. Burt recognize in the daylight what he had seen by night through the letter-flap. Of the framework of painted canvas, with its forms and figures oddly foreshortened and distorted, he could make little. Only when the thing was set up and lighted in the curtained studio was he at length reluctantly convinced.

"It's wonderful," he said. "It's like Maskelyn and Devant. I wish the sergeant could a-seen it."

"Lure him down here to-morrow night," said Mr. O'Halloran. "Let him come as my uncle's bodyguard. You—" he turned to Peter—"you seem to have a way with policemen. Can't you inveigle the fellow along? Your impersonation of starving and disconsolate Bloomsbury is fully as convincing as mine. How about it?"

"I don't know," said Peter. "The costume gives me pain. Besides, is it kind to a p.b. policeman? I give you the R.A., but when it comes to the guardians of the law—damn it all! I'm a family man, and I must have *some* sense of responsibility."

TALBOYS

This story, written in 1942 and recently discovered, appears here in print for the first time

Father!"

"Yes, my son."

"You know those peaches of Mr. Puffett's, the whacking great big ones you said I wasn't to take?"

"Well?"

"Well, I've tooken them."

Lord Peter Wimsey rolled over on his back and stared at his offspring in consternation. His wife laid down her sewing.

"Oh, Bredon, how naughty! Poor Mr. Puffett was going to exhibit them at the Flower Show."

"Well, Mummy, I didn't mean to. It was a dare."

Having offered this explanation for what it was worth, Master Bredon Wimsey again turned candid eyes upon his father, who groaned and sat up.

"And *must* you come and tell me about it? I hope, Bredon, you are not developing into a prig."

"Well, Father, Mr. Puffett saw me. An' he's coming up to have a word with you when he's put on a clean collar."

"Oh, I see," said his lordship, relieved. "And you thought you'd better come and get it over before my temper became further inflamed by hearing his version of the matter?"

"Yes, please, sir."

"That is rational, at any rate. Very well, Bredon. Go up into my bedroom and prepare for execution. You will find the cane behind the dressing-table."

"Yes, Father. You won't be long, will you, sir?"

"I shall allow precisely the right time for apprehension and remorse. Off with you!"

The culprit vanished hastily in the direction of the house; the executioner heaved himself to his feet and followed at a leisurely pace, rolling up his sleeves as he went with a certain grimness.

"My dear!" exclaimed Miss Quirk. She gazed in horror through her spectacles at Harriet, who had placidly returned to her patchwork. "Surely, *surely* you don't allow him to cane that mite of a child."

"Allow?" said Harriet, amused. "That's hardly the right word, is it?"

"But Harriet, dear, he oughtn't to do it. You don't realise how dangerous it is. He may ruin the boy's character for life. One must reason with these little people, not break their spirit by brutality. When you inflict pain and humiliation on a child like that, you make him feel helpless and inferior, and all that suppressed resentment will break out later in the most extraordinary and shocking ways."

"Oh, I don't think he resents it," said Harriet. "He's devoted to his father."

"Well, if he is," retorted Miss Quirk, "it must be a sort of masochism, and it ought to be stopped—I mean, it ought to be led gently in some other direction. It's unnatural. How could anyone feel a *healthy* devotion for a person who beats him?"

"I can't think; but it often seems to happen. Peter's mother used to lay into him with a slipper, and they've always been the best of friends."

"If I had a child belonging to me," said Miss Quirk, "I would never permit anybody to lay a hand on him. All my little nephews and nieces have been brought up on enlightened modern lines. They never even hear the word 'don't.' Now, you see what happens. Just *because* your boy was told *not* to pick the peaches, he picked them. If he hadn't been forbidden to do it, he wouldn't have been disobedient."

"No," said Harriet, "I suppose that's quite true. He would have picked the peaches just the same, but it wouldn't have been disobedience."

"Exactly," cried Miss Quirk, triumphantly. "You see—you manufacture a crime and then punish the poor child for it. Besides if it hadn't been for the prohibition, he'd have left the fruit alone."

"You don't know Bredon. He never leaves anything alone."

"Of course not," said Miss Quirk, "and he never will, so long as you surround him with prohibitions. His meddling with what doesn't belong to him is just an act of defiance."

"He's not defiant very often," said Harriet, "but of course it's very difficult to refuse a dare from a big boy like George Waggett. I expect it was George; it usually is."

"No doubt," observed Miss Quirk, "the village children are all brought up in an atmosphere of faultfinding and defiance. That kind of thing is contagious. Democratic principles are all very well, but I should scarcely have thought it wise to expose your little boy to contamination."

"Would you forbid him to play with George Waggett?"

Miss Quirk was not to be caught.

"I should never *forbid* anything. I should endeavor to suggest some more suitable companion. Bredon could be encouraged to look after his little brother; that would give him a useful outlet for his energies and allow him to feel himself important."

"Oh, but he's really good with Roger," said Harriet, equably. She looked up, to see chastiser and chastised emerging from the house, hand in hand. "They seem to be quite good friends. Bredon was rather uplifted when he was promoted to a cane; he thinks it dignified and grown-up. . . . Well, ruffian, how many did you get?"

"Three," said Master Bredon confidentially. "Awful hard ones. One for being naughty, an' one for being young ass enough to be caught, and one for making a 'fernal nuisance of myself on a hot day."

"Oh, dear," said Miss Quirk, appalled by the immorality of all this. "And are you sorry for having taken poor Mr. Puffett's peaches, so that he can't get a prize at the Show?"

Bredon looked at her in astonishment.

"We've done all that," he said, with a touch of indignation. His father thought it well to intervene.

"It's a rule in this household," he announced, "that once we've been whacked, nothing more can be said. The topic is withdrawn from circulation."

"Oh," said Miss Quirk. She still felt that something ought to be done to compensate the victim of brutality and relieve his repressions. "Well, as you're a good boy, would you like to come and sit on my knee?"

"No, thank you," said Bredon. Training, or natural politeness, prompted him to amplify the refusal. "Thank you very much all the same."

"A more tactless suggestion," said Peter, "I never heard." He dropped into a deck-chair, picked up his son and heir by the waist-belt and slung him face downwards across his knees. "You'll have to eat your tea on all fours, like Nebuchadnezzar."

"Who was Nebuchadnezzar?"

"Nebuchadnezzar, the King of the Jews—" began Peter. His version of that monarch's iniquities was interrupted by the appearance, from behind the house, of a stout figure, unsuitably clad for the season in sweater, corduroy trousers and bowler hat. "The curse is come upon me, cried the Lady of Shalott."

"Who was the Lady of Shalott?"

"I'll tell you at bedtime. Here is Mr. Puffett, breathing out threatenings and slaughter. We must now stand up and face the music. 'Afternoon, Puffett."

" 'Arternoon, me lord and me lady," said Mr. Puffett. He removed his bowler and mopped his streaming brow. "And miss," he added, with a vague gesture in Miss Quirk's direction. "I made bold, me lord, to come round—"

"That," said Peter, "was very kind of you. Otherwise, of course, we should have come to see you and say we were sorry. We were overcome by a sudden irresistible impulse, attributable, we think, to the beauty of the fruit and the exciting nature of the enterprise. We hope very much that we have left enough for the Flower Show, and we will be careful not to do it again. We should like to mention that a measure of justice has already been done, in the shape of three of the juiciest, but if there is anything further coming to us, we shall try to receive it in a becoming spirit of penitence."

"Well, there!" said Mr. Puffett. "If I didn't say to Jinny, 'Jinny,' I says, 'I 'ope the young gentleman doesn't tell 'is lordship. He'll be main angry,' I says, 'and I wouldn't wonder if 'e didn't wallop 'im.' 'Oh, Dad,' she says, 'run up quick, never mind your Sunday coat, and tell 'is lordship as 'e didn't take only two peaches and there's plenty left,' she says. So I comes as quick as I can, only I 'ad ter wash, what with doin' out the pigsties, and jest to put on a clean collar; but not bein' as young as I was, and gettin' stout-like, I don't get up the 'ill as quick as I might. There wasn't no call to thrash the young gentleman, me lord, me 'avin' caught 'im afore much 'arm was done. Boys will be boys—and I'll lay what you like it was some of them other young devils put 'im up to it, begging your pardon, me lady."

"Well, Bredon," said his father, "it's very kind of Mr. Puffett to take that view of it. Suppose you go with him up to the house and ask Bunter to draw him a glass of beer. And on the way, you may say whatever your good feeling may suggest."

He waited till the oddly-assorted couple were half-way across the lawn, and then called, "Puffett?"

"Me lord?" said Mr. Puffett, returning alone.

"Was there really much damage done?"

"No, me lord. Only two peaches, like I said. I jest popped

out from be'ind the potting-shed in time, and 'e was off like one o'clock."

"Thank heaven! From what he said, I was afraid he had wolfed the lot. And, look here, Puffett. Don't ask him who put him up to it. I shouldn't imagine he'd tell, but he might fancy he was a bit of a hero for refusing."

"I get you," said Mr. Puffett. " 'E's a proper 'igh-sperrited young gentleman, ain't 'e?" He winked, and went ponderously to rejoin his penitent robber.

The episode was considered closed; and everybody (except Miss Quirk) was surprised when Mr. Puffett arrived next morning at breakfast-time and announced without preliminary:

"Beg pardon, me lord, but all my peaches 'as bin took in the night, and I'd be glad to know 'oo done it."

"All your peaches taken, Puffett?"

"Every blessed one of 'em, me lord, practically speakin'. And the Flower Show termorrer."

"Coo!" said Master Bredon. He looked up from his plate, and found Miss Quirk's eye fixed upon him.

"That's a dirty trick," said his lordship. "Have you any idea who it was? Or would you like me to come and look into the matter for you?"

Mr. Puffett turned his bowler hat slowly over between his large hands.

"Not wishin' yer lordship ter put yerself out," he said slowly. "But it jest crossed me mind aṣ summun at the 'ouse might be able ter throw light, as it were, upon the subjick."

"I shouldn't think so," said Peter, "but it's easy to ask. Harriet, do you by any chance know anything about the disappearance of Puffett's peaches?"

Harriet shook her head.

"Not a thing. Roger, dear, please eat your egg not quite so splashily. You've given yourself a moustache like Mr. Billing's."

"Can you give us any help, Bredon?"

"No."

"No, what?"

"No sir. Please, Mummy, may I get down?"

"Just a minute, darling. You haven't folded up your napkin."

"Oh, sorry."

"Miss Quirk?"

Miss Quirk was so much aghast at hearing this flat denial that she had remained staring at the eldest Master Wimsey, and started on hearing herself addressed.

"Do *I* know anything? Well!" She hesitated. "Now, Bredon, am I to tell Daddy? Wouldn't you rather do it yourself?" Bredon shot a quick look at his father, but made no answer. That was only to be expected. Beat a child, and you make him a liar and a coward. "Come now," said Miss Quirk, coaxingly, "it would be *ever* so much nicer and better and braver to own up, don't you think? It'll make Mummy and Daddy very very sad if you leave it to *me* to tell them."

"To tell us what?" inquired Harriet.

"My dear Harriet," said Miss Quirk, annoyed by this foolish question, "if I tell you *what*, then I've told you, haven't I? And I'm quite *sure* Bredon would much rather tell you himself."

"Bredon," said his father, "have you any idea what Miss Quirk thinks you ought to tell us? Because, if so, you could tell us and we could get on."

"No, sir. I don't know anything about Mr. Puffett's peaches. May I get down *now*, Mummy, please?"

"Oh, Bredon!" cried Miss Quirk, reproachingly. "When I saw you, you know, with my own eyes! Ever so early—at five o'clock this morning. Now, won't you say what you were doing?"

"Oh, that!" said Bredon and blushed. Mr. Puffett scratched his head.

"What were you doing?" asked Harriet gently. "Not anything naughty, darling, were you? Or is it a secret?"

Bredon nodded. "Yes, it's a secret. Something we were doing." He sighed. "I don't think it's naughty, Mum."

"I expect it is though," said Peter in a resigned tone. "Your secrets so often are. Quite unintentionally, no doubt, but they do have a tendency that way. Be warned in time, Bredon, and undo it, or stop doing it, before I discover it. I understand it had nothing to do with Mr. Puffett's peaches?"

"Oh, no, Father. Please, Mummy, may I—?"

"Yes, dear, you may get down. But you must ask Miss Quirk to excuse you."

"Please, Miss Quirk, will you excuse me?"

"Yes, certainly," said Miss Quirk in a mournful tone. Bredon scrambled down hastily, said, "I'm *very* sorry about your peaches, Mr. Puffett," and made his escape.

"I am sorry to have to say it," said Miss Quirk, "but I think, Mr. Puffett, you will find your peaches in the woodshed. I woke up early this morning, and I saw Bredon and another little boy crossing the yard, carrying something between them in a bucket. I waved at them from the window, and they hurried off to the woodshed in what I *can* only call a furtive kind of way."

"Well, Puffett," said his lordship, "I'm sorry about this. Shall I come up and take a look at the place? Or do you wish to search the woodshed? I am quite sure you will not find your peaches there, though I should hesitate to say what else you might not find."

"I'd be grateful," replied Mr. Puffett, "to 'ave yer advice, me lord, if so be as you could spare the time. What beats me, it's a wide bed, and yet there ain't no footprints, in a manner of speaking, except as it might be young master's, there. Which, footprints bein' in a manner your lordship's walk in life, I made bold to come. But, Master Bredon 'avin' said it weren't him, I reckon them marks'll be wot 'e left yesterday, though 'ow a man or boy either could cross that there bed of damp earth and not leave no sign of 'imself, unless 'e wos a bird, is more than I can make out, nor Jinny neither."

Mr. Tom Puffett was proud of his walled garden. He had built the wall himself (for he was a builder by trade), and it was a handsome brick structure, ten feet high, and topped on all four sides with a noble parapet of broken bottle-glass. The garden lay on the opposite side of the road from the little house where its owner lived with his daughter and son-in-law, and possessed a solid wooden gate, locked at night with a padlock. On either side of it were flourishing orchards; at the back ran a deeply rutted land, still muddy—for the summer, up to the last few days, had been a wet one.

"That there gate," said Mr. Puffett, "was locked last night at nine o'clock as ever is, an' it was still locked when I came in at seven this mornin'; so 'ooever done it 'ad to climb this yer wall."

"So I see," replied Lord Peter. "My demon child is of tender years; still, I admit that he is capable of almost anything, when suitably inspired and assisted. But I don't think he would have done it after yesterday's little incident, and I am positive that if he had done it, he'd have said so."

"Reckon you're right," agreed Mr. Puffett, unlocking the door, "though when I was a nipper like 'im, if I'd 'ad that old woman a-jorin' at me, I'd a-said anythink."

"So'd I," said Peter. "She's a friend of my sister-in-law's, said to need a country holiday. I feel we shall all shortly need a town holiday. Your plums seem to be doing well. H'm. A pebble path isn't the best medium for showing footprints."

"That it's not," admitted Mr. Puffett. He led the way between the neat flower and vegetable beds to the far end of the garden. Here at the foot of the wall was a border about nine feet wide, the middle section of which was empty except for some rows of late-sown peas. At the back, trained against the wall, stood the peach-tree, on which one great, solitary fruit glowed rosily among the dark leafage. Across the bed ran a double line of small footprints.

"Did you hoe this bed over after my son's visit yesterday?"

"No, my lord."

"Then he hasn't been here since. Those are his marks all right—I ought to know; I see enough of them on my own flower-beds." Peter's mouth twitched a little. "Look! He came very softly, trying most honorably not to tread on the peas. He pinched a peach and bolted it where he stood. I enquire, with a parent's natural anxiety, whether he ejected the stone, and observe, with relief, that he did. He moved on, he took a second peach, you popped out from the potting-shed, he started like a guilty thing and ran off in a hurry—this time, I am sorry to see, trampling on the peas. I hope he deposited the second peach-stone somewhere. Well, Puffett, you're right; there are no other footprints. Could the thief have put down a plank and walked on that, I wonder?"

"There's no planks here," said Mr. Puffett, "except the little 'un I uses meself for bedding-out. That's three feet long or thereabouts. Would yer like ter look at it, me lord?"

"No good. A little reflection shows that one cannot cross a nine-foot bed on a three-foot plank without shifting the plank, and that one cannot at the same time stand on the plank and shift it. You're sure there's only one? Yes? Then that's washed out."

"Could 'e a-brought one with 'im?"

"The orchard walls are high and hard to climb, even without the additional encumbrance of a nine-foot plank. Besides, I'm almost sure no plank has been used. I think, if it had, the edges would have left some mark. No, Puffett, nobody crossed this bed. By the way, doesn't it strike you as odd that the thief should have left just one big peach behind? It's pretty conspicuous. Was that done merely to point the joke? Or—wait a minute, what's that?"

Something had caught his eye at the back of the box border, some dozen feet to the right of where they were standing. He picked it up. It was a peach; firm and red and not quite ripe. He stood weighing it thoughtfully in his hand.

"Having picked the peach, he found it wasn't ripe and chucked it away in a temper. Is that likely, Puffett, do you think? And unless I am mistaken, there are quite a number of green leaves scattered about the foot of the tree. How often, when one picks a peach, does one break off the leaves as well?"

He looked expectantly at Mr. Puffett, who returned no answer.

"I think," went on Peter, "we will go and have a look in the lane."

Immediately behind the wall ran a rough grass verge. Mr. Puffett, leading the way to this, was peremptorily waved back and was thereafter treated to a fine exposition of detective work in the traditional manner; his lordship, extended on his stomach, thrusting his long nose and long fingers delicately through each successive tuft of grass, Mr. Puffett himself, stopping with legs well apart and hands on knees, peering anxiously at him from the edge of the lane. Presently the sleuth sat up on his heels and said:

"Here you are, Puffett. There were two men. They came up the lane from the direction of the village, wearing hob-nailed boots and carrying a ladder between them. They set up the ladder *here;* the grass, you see, is still a little bent, and there are two deepish dents in the soil. One man climbed to the top and took the peaches, while the other, I think, stood at the foot to keep guard and receive the fruit in a bag or basket or some-thing. This isn't a case of larking youngsters, Puffett; from the length of the strides they were grown men. What enemies have you made in your harmless career? Or who are your chief rivals in the peach class?"

"Well, there," said Mr. Puffett, slowly. "There's the Vicar shows peaches, and Dr. Jellyband from Great Pagford, and Jack Baker—he's the policeman, you know, came when Joe Sellon went off to Canada. And there's old Critch; him and me had a dispute about a chimbley. And Maggs the blacksmith—'e didn't 'arf like it w'en I wiped 'is eye last year with me veg-etable marrers. Oh, and Waggett the butcher, 'e shows peaches. But I dunno as any o' them 'ud do me a turn like this 'ere. But see 'ere, me lord, 'ow did they *get* peaches? They couldn't reach 'em from the top of the ladder, nor yet off the wall, let alone sitting on them there bottles. The top o' the tree's five foot below the top o' the wall."

"That's simple," said Peter. "Think of the broken leaves

and the peach in the box border, and consider how *you* would have done it. By the way, if you want proof that the robbing was done from this side, get a ladder and look over. I'll lay you anything you like, you'll find that the one peach that was left is hidden by the leaves from anybody looking *down* on it, though it's clearly enough seen from the garden. No, there's no difficulty about how it was done; the difficulty is to put one's hand on the culprits. Unfortunately, there's no footprint clear enough to show the complete pattern of the hob-nails."

He considered a moment, while Mr. Puffett watched him with the air of one confidently expecting a good conjuring trick.

"One could make a house to house visitation," went on his lordship, "and ask questions, or search. But it's surprising how things disappear, and how people dry up when asked direct questions. Children especially. Look here, Puffett, I'm not at all sure my prodigal son mightn't be able to throw some light on this, after all. But leave me to conduct the examination; it may need delicate handling."

There is one drawback about retreating to a really small place in the country and leaving behind you the stately publicity of town life in a house with ten servants. When you have tucked in yourselves, and your three children, and your indispensable man and your equally indispensable and devoted maid, both time and space become rather fully occupied. You may, by taking your husband into your own room and accommodating the two elder boys in his dressing-room, squeeze in an extra person who, like Miss Quirk, has been wished upon you; but it is scarcely possible to run after her all day to see that she is not getting into mischief. This is more particularly the case if you are a novelist by profession, and if, moreover, your idea of a happy holiday is to dispose as completely and briskly as possible of children, book, servants, and visitor, so as to snatch all the available moments for playing the fool with a congenial, but admittedly distracting, husband. Harriet Wimsey, writing for dear life in the sitting-room, kept one eye on her paper and the other on

Master Paul Wimsey, who was disembowelling his old stuffed rabbit in the window-seat. Her ears were open for a yell from young Roger, whose rough-and-tumble with the puppy on the lawn might at any moment end in disaster. Her consciousness was occupied with her plot, her subconsciousness with the fact that she was three months behind on her contract. If she gave an occasional vague thought to her firstborn, it was only to wonder whether he was hindering Bunter at his work, or merely concocting, in his own quiet way, some more than usually hideous shock for his parents. Himself was the last person he ever damaged; he was a child with a singular talent for falling on his feet. She had no attention to spare for Miss Quirk.

Miss Quirk had tried the woodshed, but it was empty, and among its contents she could find nothing more suspicious than a hatchet, a saw, a rabbit-hutch, a piece of old carpet and a wet ring among the sawdust. She was not surprised that the evidence had been removed; Bredon had been extraordinarily anxious to leave the breakfast-table, and his parents had shut their eyes and let him go. Nor had Peter troubled to examine the premises; he had walked straight out of the house with that man Puffett, who naturally could not insist upon a search. Both Peter and Harriet were obviously burking inquiry; they did not want to admit the consequences of their wickedly mistaken system of training.

"Mummy! Come out an' play wiv' me an' Bom-bom!"

"Presently, darling. I've only got a little bit to finish."

"When's presently, Mummy?"

"Very soon. In about ten minutes."

"What's ten minutes, Mummy?"

Harriet laid down her pen. As a conscientious parent, she could not let this opportunity pass. Four years old was said to be too early, but children differed and you never knew.

"Look, darling. Here's the clock. When this long hand gets to *that*, that'll be ten minutes."

"When *this* gets to *that*?"

"Yes, darling. Sit quiet just for a little bit and look after it and tell me when it gets there."

An interval. Miss Quirk had by this time searched the garage, the greenhouse and the shed that housed the electric plant.

"It isn't moving, Mummy."

"Yes, it is, really, only it goes very, *very* slowly. You'll have to keep a very sharp eye on it."

Miss Quirk had reached the back parts of the house itself. She entered by the back door and passed through the scullery into a passage containing, among other things, the door of the boot-hole. In this retreat, she discovered a small village maiden, cleaning a pair of very youthful boots.

"Have you seen—?" began Miss Quirk. Then her eye fell on the boots. "Are those Master Bredon's boots?"

"Yes, miss," said the girl, with the startled look peculiar to young servants when suddenly questioned by strangers.

"They're very dirty," said Miss Quirk. She remembered that Bredon had worn clean sandals when he came in to breakfast. "Give those to me for a moment," said Miss Quirk.

The small maid looked round with a gasp for advice and assistance, but both Bunter and the maid seemed to be occupied elsewhere, and one could not refuse a request from a lady staying in the house. Miss Quirk took charge of the boots. "I'll bring them back presently," she said, with a nod, and passed on. Fresh, damp earth on Bredon's boots, and something secret brought home in a pail—it scarcely needed a Peter Wimsey to put two and two together. But Peter Wimsey was refusing to detect in the right place. Miss Quirk would show him.

Miss Quirk went on along the passage and came to a door. As she approached it, it opened and Bredon's face, very dirty, appeared round the edge. At sight of her, it popped in again like a bolting rabbit.

"Ah!" said Miss Quirk. She pushed the door briskly. But even a child of six, if he can reach it and is determined, can make proper use of a bolt.

• • •

"Roger, darling, no! Shaking won't make it go any faster. It'll only give the poor clock tummyache. Oh, look, what a dreadful mess Paul's made with his rabbit. Help him pick up the bits, dear, and then you'll see, the ten minutes will be up."

Peter, returning from Mr. Puffett's garden, found his wife and two-thirds of his family rolling vigorously about the lawn with Bom-bom. Being invited to roll, he rolled, but with only half his attention.

"It's a curious thing," he observed plaintively, "that though my family makes a great deal of noise and always seems to be on top of me" (this was, at the moment, a fact), "I never can lay hands on the bit of it I want at the moment. Where is the pest, Bredon?"

"I haven't dared to ask."

Peter rose up, with his youngest son clinging, leech-like, to his shoulder, and went in search of Bunter, who knew everything without asking.

"Master Bredon, my lord, is engaged at present in altercation with Miss Quirk through the furnace-room door."

"Good God, Bunter! Which of them is inside?"

"Master Bredon, my lord."

"I breathe again. I feared we might have to effect a rescue. Catch hold of this incubus, will you, and hand him back to her ladyship."

All Miss Quirk's coaxing had been impotent to lure Bredon out of the furnace-room. At Peter's voice she turned quickly.

"Oh, Peter! Do get the child to come out. He's got those peaches in there, and I'm sure he'll make himself ill."

Lord Peter raised his already sufficiently surprised eyebrows.

"If your expert efforts fail," said he, "will my brutal threats have any effect, do you suppose? Besides, even if he *were* eating peaches, ought we, in this peremptory way, to suppress that natural expression of his personality? And whatever makes you imagine that we keep peaches in the furnace-room?"

"I know he's got them there," said Miss Quirk. "And I

don't blame the child. If you beat a boy for stealing, he'll steal again. Besides, look at these boots he went out in this morning—all covered with damp mould."

Lord Peter took the boots and examined them with interest.

"Elementary, my dear Watson. But allow me to suggest that some training is necessary, even for the work of a practical domestic detective. This mould is not the same colour as the mould in Puffett's garden, and in fact is not garden mould at all. Further, if you take the trouble to look at the flower-beds, you will see that they are not wet enough to leave as much mud as this on a pair of boots. Thirdly, I can do all the detective work required in this family. And fourthly, you might realise that it is rather discourteous of you to insist that my son is a liar."

"Very well," said Miss Quirk, a little red in the face. "Fetch him out of there, and you'll see."

"But why should I fetch him out, and implant a horrible frustration-complex around the furnace-room?"

"As you like," said Miss Quirk. "It's no business of mine."

"True," said Peter. He watched her stride angrily away, and said:

"Bredon! You can come out. She's gone."

There was the sound of the sliding of iron, and his son slithered out like an eel, pulling the door carefully to behind him.

"You're not very clean, are you?" said his father, dispassionately. "It looks to me as though the furnace-room needed dusting. I'm not very clean myself, if it comes to that. I've been crawling in the lane behind Mr. Puffett's garden, trying to find out who stole his peaches."

"*She* says *I* did."

"I'll tell you a secret, Bredon. Grown-up people don't always know everything, though they try to pretend they do. That is called 'prestige,' and is responsible for most of the wars that devastate the continent of Europe."

"I think," said Bredon, who was accustomed to his father's meaningless outbursts of speech, "she's silly."

"So do I; but don't say I said so."

"And rude."

"*And* rude. I, on the other hand, am silly, but seldom rude. Your mother is neither rude nor silly."

"Which am I?"

"You are an egotistical extravert of the most irrepressible type. Why do you wear boots when you go mud-larking? It's much less trouble to clean your feet than your boots."

"There's thistles and nettles."

"True, O King! Yes, I know the place now. Down by the stream, at the far end of the paddock. . . . Is that the Secret you've got in the furnace-room?"

Bredon nodded, his mouth obstinately shut.

"Can't you let me in on it?"

Bredon shook his head.

"No, I don't think so," he explained candidly. "You see, you might feel you ought to stop it."

"That's awkward. It's so often my duty to stop things. Miss Quirk thinks I oughtn't ever to stop anything, but I don't feel I can go quite as far as that. I wonder what the devil you've been up to. We've had newts and frogs and sticklebacks, and tadpoles are out of season. I hope it isn't adders, Bredon, or you'll swell up and turn purple. I can stand for most livestock, but not adders."

" 'Tisn't *adders*," replied his son, with dawning hope. "Only very nearly. An' I don't know what it lives on. I say, if you will let me keep it, d'you mind coming in quick, 'cos I 'spect it's creeped out of the bucket."

"In that case," said his lordship, "I think we'd better conduct a search of the premises instantly. My nerves are fairly good; but if it were to go up the flue and come out in the kitchen—"

He followed his offspring hastily into the furnace-room.

"I wish," said Harriet, a little irritably, for she strongly disliked being lectured about her duties and being thus prevented from attending to them, "you wouldn't always talk about 'a' child, as if all children were alike. Even my three are all quite different."

"Mothers always think their own children are different," said Miss Quirk. "But the fundamental principles of child-psychology are the same in all, I have studied the subject. Take this question of punishment. When you punish a child—"

"*Which* child?"

"Any child—you harm the delicate mechanism of its reaction to life. Some become hardened, some become cowed, but in either case you set up a feeling of inferiority."

"It's not so simple. Don't take any child—take mine. If you reason with Bredon, he gets obstinate. He knows perfectly well when he's been naughty, and sometimes he prefers to be naughty and take the consequences. Roger's another matter. I don't think we shall ever whip Roger because he's sensitive and easily frightened and rather likes having his feelings appealed to. But he's already beginning to feel a little inferior to Bredon, because he isn't allowed to be whipped. I suppose we shall have to persuade him that whipping is part of the eldest son's prerogative. Which will be all right provided we don't have to whip Paul."

There were so many dreadful errors in this speech that Miss Quirk scarcely knew where to begin.

"I think it's such a mistake to let the younger ones fancy that there is anything superior in being the eldest. My little nephews and nieces—"

"Yes," said Harriet. "But one's got to prepare people for life, hasn't one? The day is bound to come when they realise that all Peter's real property is entailed."

Miss Quirk said she so much preferred the French custom of dividing all property equally. "It's *so* much better for the children."

"Yes; but it's very bad for the property."

"But Peter wouldn't put his property before his children!" Harriet smiled.

"My dear Miss Quirk! Peter's fifty-two, and he's reverting to type."

●   ●   ●

Peter at that moment was not looking or behaving like
fifty-two, but he was rapidly reverting to a much more ancient
and early type than the English landed gentleman. He had,
with some difficulty, retrieved the serpent from the ash-hole,
and now sat on a heap of clinker, watching it as it squirmed at
the bottom of the bucket.

"Golly, what a whopper!" he said, reverently. "How did
you catch him, old man?"

"Well we went to get minnows, and he came swimming
along, and Joey Maggs caught him in his net. And he wanted
to kill him along of biting, but I said he couldn' bite, 'cos you
told us the difference between snakes. And Joe bet me I
wouldn't let him bite me, an' I said I didn' mind and he said,
Is it a dare? an' I said, Yes, if I can have him afterwards, so I
let him bite me, only of course he didn' bite an' George helped
me bring him back in the bucket."

"So Joey Maggs caught him in his net, did he?"

"Yes, but I knew he wasn't an adder. And please, sir, will
you give me a net, 'cos Joe's got a lovely big one, only he was
awfully late this morning and we thought he wasn't coming,
and he said somebody had hidden his net."

"Did he? That's very interesting."

"Yes. May I have a net, please?"

"You may."

"Oh, thank you, Father. May I keep him, please, and what
does he live on?"

"Beetles, I think." Peter plunged his hand into the bucket,
and the snake wound itself about his wrist and slithered along
his arm. "Come on, Cuthbert. You remind me of when I was
at my prep. school, and we put one the dead spit of you into—"
He caught himself up, too late.

"Where, Father?"

"Well, there was a master we all hated, and we put a snake
in his bed. It's rather frequently done. In fact, I believe it's
what grass-snakes are for."

"Is it very naughty to put snakes in people you don't like's
beds?"

"Yes. Exceedingly naughty. No nice boy would ever think of doing such a thing. . . . I say, *Bredon —*"

Harriet Wimsey sometimes found her eldest son disconcerting. "You know, Peter, he's a most unconvincing-looking child. *I* know he's yours, because there is nobody else's he could be. And the colour's more or less right. But where on earth did he get that square, stolid appearance, and that incredible snub nose?"

But at that instant, in the furnace-room, over the body of the writhing Cuthbert, square-face and hatchet-face stared at one another and grew into an awful, impish likeness.

"Oh, Father!"

"I don't know what your mother will say. We shall get into most frightful trouble. You'd better leave it to me. Cut along now, and ask Bunter if he's got such a thing as a strong flour-bag and a stout piece of string, because you'll never make Cuthbert stay in this bucket. And for God's sake, don't go about looking like Guy Fawkes and Gunpowder Treason. When you've brought the bag, go and wash yourself. I want you to run down with a note to Mr. Puffett's."

Mr. Puffett made his final appearance just after dinner, explaining that he had not been able to come earlier, "along of a job out Lopsley way." He was both grateful and astonished.

"To think of it being old Billy Maggs and that brother of his, and all along o' them perishin' old vegetable marrers. You wouldn't think a chap cud 'arbour a grievance that way, would yer? 'Tain't even as though 'e wor a-showin' peaches of his own. It beats me. Said 'e did it for a joke. 'Joke?' I says to 'im. 'I'd like to 'ear wot the magistrate ud say to that there kinder joke.' 'Owsumdever, I got me peaches back, and the Show bein' termorrer, mebbe they won't 'ave took no 'arm. Good thing 'im and they boys 'adn't 'ave ate the lot."

The household congratulated Mr. Puffett on this happy termination to the incident. Mr. Puffett chuckled.

"Ter think o' Billy Maggs an' that good-fer-nothin' brother of 'is a-standin' on that there ladder a-fishin' for any peaches with young Joey's stickle-back net. A proper silly sight they'd a-bin if anybody'd come that way. 'Think yerselves clever,' I says to Bill. 'W'y, 'is lordship didn't only cast one eye over the place afore 'e says, "W'y Puffett," 'e says, " 'ere's Billy Maggs an' that there brother of 'is been a-wallerin' all over your wall like a 'erd of elephants." ' Ah! An' a proper fool 'e looked. 'Course, I see now it couldn't only a-been a net, knockin' the leaves about that way. But that there unripe 'un got away from 'im all right. 'Bill,' I says, 'you'll never make no fisherman, lettin' 'em get away from you like that.' Pulled 'is leg proper, I did. But see 'ere, me lord, 'ow did yer come ter know it was Billy Maggs's Joey's net? 'E ain't the only one."

"A little judicious inquiry in the proper quarter," replied his lordship. "Billy Maggs's Joe gave the show away, unbeknownst. But see here, Puffett, don't blame Joe. He knew nothing about it, nor did my boy. Only from something Joe said to Bredon I put two and two together."

"Ah!" said Mr. Puffett, "an' that reminds me. I've got more peaches back nor I wants for the show, so I made bold to bring 'arf-a-dozen round for Master Bredon. I don't mind tellin' you, I did think for about 'arf a minute it might a-bin 'im. Only 'arf a minute, mind you—but knowin' wot boys is, I did jest think it might be."

"It's very kind of you," said Harriet. "Bredon's in bed now, but we'll give them to him in the morning. He'll enjoy them so much and be so pleased to know you've quite forgiven him for those other two."

"Oh, *them!*" replied Mr. Puffett. "Don't you say nothing more about them. Jest a bit 'o fun, that wos. Well, good-night all, and many thanks to your lordship. Coo!" said Mr. Puffett, as Peter escorted him to the door, "ter think o' Billy Maggs and that there spindle-shanked brother of 'is a-fishin' for peaches with a kid's net a-top o' my wall. I didden 'arf make 'em all laugh round at the Crown."

Miss Quirk had said nothing. Peter slipped upstairs by the

back way, through Harriet's bedroom into his own. In the big
four-poster, one boy was asleep, but the other sat up at his
cautious approach.

"Have you done the deed, Mr. Scatterblood?"

"No, Cap'en Teach, but your orders shall be carried out in
one twirl of a marlin spike. In the meantime, the bold Mr.
Puffett has recovered his lost treasure and has haled the criminals up before him and had them hanged at the yard-arm
after a drum-head court-martial. He has sent you a share of
the loot."

"Oh, good egg! What did *she* say?"

"Nothing. Mind you, Bredon, if she apologises, we'll have
to call Cuthbert off. A guest is a guest, so long as she behaves
like a gentleman."

"Yes, I see. Oh, I do hope she won't apologise!"

"That's a very immoral thing to hope. If you bounce like
that, you'll wake your brother."

"Father! Do you think she'll fall down in a fit an' foam at
the mouth?"

"I sincerely hope not. As it is, I'm taking my life in my
hands. If I perish in the attempt, remember I was true to the
Jolly Roger. Good-night, Cap'en Teach."

"Good-night, Mr. Scatterblood. I *do* love you."

Lord Peter Wimsey embraced his son, assumed the personality of Mr. Scatterblood and crept softly down the back
way to the furnace-room. Cuthbert, safe in his bag, was
drowsing upon a hot-water bottle, and made no demonstration as he was borne upstairs.

Miss Quirk did not apologise, and the subject of peaches
was not mentioned again. But she may have sensed a certain
constraint in the atmosphere, for she rose rather earlier than
usual, saying she was tired and thought she would go to bed.

"Peter," said Harriet, when they were alone; "what *are* you
and Bredon up to? You have both been so unnaturally quiet
since lunch. You must be in some sort of mischief."

"To a Teach or a Scatterblood," said Peter with dignity,

"there is no such word as mischief. We call it piracy on the high seas."

"I knew it," replied Harriet, resignedly. "If I'd realised the disastrous effect sons would have on your character, I'd never have trusted you with any. Oh, dear! I'm thankful that woman's gone to bed; she's *so* in the way."

"Isn't she? I think she must have picked up her infant psychology from the woman's page in the *Morning Star.* Harriet, absolve me now from all my sins of the future, so that I may enjoy them without remorse."

His wife was not unmoved by this appeal, only observing after an interval, "There's something deplorably frivolous about making love to one's wife after seven years of marriage. Is it my lord's pleasure to come to bed?"

"It is your lord's very great pleasure."

My lord, who in the uncanonical process of obtaining absolution without confession or penitence, had almost lost sight of the sin, was recalled to himself by his wife's exclamation as they passed through the outer bedroom.

"Peter! Where is Bredon?"

He was saved from having to reply by a succession of long and blood-curdling shrieks, followed by a confused outcry.

"Heavens!" said Harriet. "Something's happened to Paul!" She shot through her own room on to the Privy Stair, which, by a subsidiary flight, communicated with the back bedrooms. Peter followed more slowly.

On the landing stood Miss Quirk in her nightgown. She had Bredon's head tucked under her arm, and was smacking him with impressive though ill-directed energy. She continued to shriek as she smacked. Bredon, accustomed to a more scientific discipline, was taking the situation stolidly, but the nursemaid, with her head thrust out of an adjacent door, was crying, "Lor', whatever is it?" Bunter, clattering down from the attic in his pyjamas with a long pair of fire-tongs in his hand, pulled up short in observing his master and mistress, and, with some dim recollection of his military service, brought his weapon to the present.

Peter seized Miss Quirk by the arm and extricated his son's head from chancery.

"Dear me!" he said. "I thought you objected to corporal chastisement."

Miss Quirk was in no mood for ethical discussion.

"That horrible boy!" she said, panting. "He put a snake in my bed. A disgusting, slimy snake. A snake!"

"Another erroneous inference," said Peter. "I put it there myself."

"You?" *You* put a snake in my bed?"

"But I knew all about it," put in Bredon, anxious that the honour and blame should be equitably distributed. "It was all his idea, but it was my snake."

His father rounded upon him. "I didn't tell *you* to come wandering out of your bed."

"No, sir; but you didn't tell me not to."

"Well," said Peter, with a certain grimness, "you got what you came for." He rubbed his son's rump in a comforting manner.

"Huh!" said Bredon. "*She* can't whack for toffee."

"May I ask," demanded Miss Quirk with trembling dignity, "*why* I should have been subjected to this abominable outrage?"

"I fancy," said Peter, "I must have been suffering from ingrowing resentment. It's better to let these impulses have their natural outlet, don't you agree? Repression is always so dangerous. Bunter, find Master Bredon's snake for him and return it carefully to the furnace-room. It answers to the name of Cuthbert."

AFTERWORD

by John Curran

The year 1920 is the generally accepted dawn of the Golden Age of detective fiction. Sherlock Holmes was then still appearing in the pages of the *Strand Magazine* and the last collection of his investigations, *The Case-Book of Sherlock Holmes*, was published in 1927; G. K. Chesterton's Father Brown was still solving mysteries and saving souls. Agatha Christie and Freeman Wills Crofts published their first titles, *The Mysterious Affair at Styles* and *The Cask*, respectively, in 1920, and before the end of the decade Margery Allingham, Anthony Berkeley, John Dickson Carr, and Ellery Queen would also publish their first detective novels. This was the era in which the puzzle dominated, and fair play to the reader in the presentation of information and clues was of paramount importance. Almost simultaneously in 1929, the British detective novelist Father Ronald Knox and S. S. Van Dine, the American creator of Philo Vance, formulated their rules for the creation of detective fiction: No clue could be withheld from the reader. The detective could not pick up "a mysterious object" at the murder scene without telling the reader exactly what it was. Secret passages, poisons unknown to science, evil Chinamen, twin brothers (or even sisters), and "supernatural agencies" were all forbidden. All of the information pertinent to the only correct solution to the crime had to be given to the reader. The question of romance within the covers of a detective story was a contentious one—Van Dine ruled it out of court without discussion while Knox remained diplomatically silent on the matter. And in 1923 Dorothy L. Sayers published *Whose Body?*

Born in June 1893 in Oxford, where her father, Rev. Henry Sayers, was headmaster of Christ Church Choir School, Dorothy L. Sayers was, like her great contemporary, Agatha Christie, educated at home. At the age of sixteen, she attended Godolphin College and in 1912 went to Somerville College, Oxford, one of the first all-women colleges, from which she graduated with a First Class Honors degree in French. Her first proper job, in 1922, was as a copywriter at the advertising agency S. H. Benson, a background she was to put to good use over a decade later when she wrote *Murder Must Advertise* (1933).

In January 1924 Sayers gave birth to a baby boy, John Anthony. This event, far more shocking a century ago than can now be appreciated, remained a well-kept secret until long after Sayers's death. After an unhappy love affair, she had found solace with one Bill White who, on learning of her condition, disappeared. Nobody at Benson realized her situation —a two-month leave of absence was not questioned—and she successfully kept the baby's existence a secret while her cousin, Ivy Shrimpton, raised him. John Anthony was "good friends" with Sayers for most of his adult life, although he never lived under her roof. In April 1926 Dorothy married "Mac" Fleming, a freelance writer as well as a painter and photographer, twelve years her senior; as his health deteriorated —he had been gassed during the Great War—Dorothy became the major breadwinner.

It would seem that nothing nobler than economic necessity was the motivation behind her decision to write a book. She had some experience of professional writing—she had already published poetry, and, more surprisingly, written film scenarios—before beginning her first detective novel, *Whose Body?* in 1921. Published two years later, it sent forth her aristocratic sleuth, Lord Peter Wimsey, to solve the mystery of an unidentified corpse, clad only in a pair of pince-nez, found in a bath. In creating this immortal character she endowed him with some of the advantages Fate had denied in her own life. Wimsey, with an enviable address in Piccadilly—note the similarity of "110A Piccadilly" to Sherlock Holmes's "221B Baker Street"—was a lord with a manservant, a wealthy bibliophile with a wine cellar, a superb musician, and a gifted linguist; later, he was a happy husband with an intelligent and strong-minded wife and, ultimately, a family. If, as is claimed, Sayers, to their joint detriment, fell in love with Wimsey, can you blame her? So confident was she of his success that she embarked on Wimsey's second investigation, *Clouds of Witness*, even before *Whose Body?* was published.

SAYERS THE DETECTIVE NOVELIST

In a 1937 essay on the genesis of *Gaudy Night* Sayers wrote: "When in a light-hearted moment I set out, fifteen years ago, to write the first 'Lord Peter' book, it was with the avowed intention of producing something 'less like a conventional detective story and more like a novel.'" Although she admitted that *Whose Body?* was "conventional to the last degree," she felt that "each successive book of mine worked gradually nearer to the sort of thing I had in view." Its immediate successor, *Clouds of Witness*, begins very much as a conventional Golden Age detective novel with a mysterious death at a secluded shooting lodge in Yorkshire. As the investigation proceeds, it transpires that many of those present night have secrets, none more so than Wimsey's brother, Gerald, Duke of Denver. The novel culminates in an unexpected revelation during the most dramatic murder trial in the genre.

Unnatural Death (1927), the title of which is not the least clever element, contains one of the most sinister characters in the entire Sayers output. And the method of the murder—the discovery of which is trickier than the identity of the villain—is chillingly plausible. In *The Unpleasantness at the Bellona Club* (1928), that bulwark of British male society, the gentleman's club, is exposed to gentle—and sometimes not so gentle—mockery as Wimsey uncovers nefarious deeds within its walls and among its members. And the plight of returned First World War veterans is also a potent element in a plot that turns on a question of timing.

The Documents in the Case (1930) is noteworthy for a variety of reasons. It is Sayers's only non-Wimsey novel, it is her only coauthored novel, and, as the title suggests, it is told in the form of letters rather than a straight narrative. It was her collaborator, Robert Eustace, a doctor, who suggested the scientific idea at the heart of the plot. Darker in tone than the Wimsey novels—probably because of Lord Peter's absence—and with a smaller than usual cast of characters, it concerns a poisoning in a remote cottage. Although Sayers herself was disappointed with it, the novel remains a fascinating experiment.

Sayers introduced Harriet Vane in *Strong Poison* (1930) and allowed her and Wimsey to embark on a three-book courtship culminating in marriage in *Busman's Honeymoon* (1937). This is the longest—and, some would argue, the most wearisome and embarrassing—courtship in the annals of detective fiction. Detective-fiction purists contend that this type of romantic relationship—between detective and suspect—has no place in a detective story. Other sleuths have managed to meet, court, marry, and produce children without any of the soul-searching in which Peter and Harriet indulged. Ngaio Marsh's Roderick Alleyn met and married (offstage) Agatha Troy; Margery Allingham's Albert Campion and Amanda Fitton meet, marry, and produce a son—between *Sweet Danger* (1933) and *Traitor's Purse* (1941)—with much less agonizing.

Five Red Herrings (1931) is for lovers of the clue-and-alibi story. Set in Galloway, an area of Scotland well-known to

Sayers from regular holidays, it has a wonderful gimmick to tantalize those readers who like to play the game alongside the detective. After a member of an artist's colony is found dead near his easel, Wimsey, without taking the reader into his confidence, notices something odd about the scene. In order to underline her adherence to fair play, Sayers inserts a paragraph in which she assures readers that they have all the information necessary to come to the same conclusion as Wimsey. And so they have.

> "What would we be lookin' for?" [Sergeant Dalziel] demanded, reasonably.
>
> (Here Lord Peter Wimsey told the Sergeant what he was to look for and why, but as the intelligent reader will readily supply these details for himself, they are omitted from this page.)

It's not a spoiler to say that a possible title for the novel, suggested by Sayers, was *There's Something Missing*.

Murder Must Advertise (1933) draws heavily on Sayers's experience at Benson as Lord Peter, working incognito, joins Pym's Publicity to investigate the death, some time earlier, of a copywriter. Apart from the ramifications of a clever plot, the reader learns more about office life in the years between the wars than could be garnered from a dozen social histories. Opinion is equally divided as to whether Sayers's best novel is *The Nine Tailors* (1934) or *Gaudy Night* (1935), and a compelling case could be made for either. The former contains yet another example of Sayers's resourcefulness at inventing imaginative murder methods—earlier, both *Unnatural Death* and *Strong Poison* had shown similar ingenuity—and settings; the background of campanology was unique in the world of detective fiction. *Gaudy Night* is a fascinating glimpse into the rarefied, pre-Second World War atmosphere of all-women education—again drawn from firsthand experience—coupled with an exploration of the vexed (even eighty years ago) question of woman's place in society, the family, and academia.

This, surely, is the book that Sayers hoped would be "less like a conventional detective story and more like a novel."

But my favorite Sayers novel remains *Have His Carcase* (1932). While on a walking-holiday to recover from the broken heart sustained before and during *Strong Poison*, Harriet Vane discovers a dead body in a pool of blood, as a result of throat-cutting, on the beach at Wilvercombe. With admirable sang-froid she searches the corpse, takes photos, collects evidence, and walks four miles to raise the alarm, after which she calls a newspaper and dictates—no mobile phones or laptops—her story. Is it any wonder that Lord Peter loves this woman? And surely these opening chapters bear out P. D. James's contention that a body found in civilized, peaceful surroundings has a much more powerful and dramatic impact than one found in a back alley. Part of the plot of *Have His Carcase* is predicated on a piece of now well-known medical lore, and the clues, all eleven of them, are not just mentioned but, in some cases, brought to the reader's attention again and again. No accusations of cheating can be levelled at the era's leading advocate of the fair-play rule. But while the detective plot is ingenious, the characters' portraits—middle-aged Mrs. Weldon and her search for love, pathetic itinerant barber Mr. Bright, as well as the doomed Paul Alexis—are masterly.

It must be admitted that Lord Peter's swan song, *Busman's Honeymoon* (1937)—which began life as a stage play the previous year—is disappointing when considered as detective fiction. Called unequivocally, by its author, "a love story with detective interruptions," it is exactly that. And the interruptions are not convincing. Raymond Chandler, in his famous—some would say infamous—essay "The Simple Art of Murder," was scathing. "This is what is vulgarly known as having God sit in your lap; a murderer who needs that much help from Providence must be in the wrong business."Although I make it a point of principle to disagree with anything, and everything, Chandler wrote about classic detective fiction, I find myself reluctantly siding with him here.

Long after you have finished reading them I guarantee that certain scenes—chilling, dramatic, hilarious, poignant—from the Lord Peter novels will stay with you. Who could forget the scene on the moors in *Clouds of Witness*, so reminiscent of *The Hound of the Baskervilles*; or the sacrosanct atmosphere of the gentleman's club, as it is contaminated by *The Unpleasantness at the Bellona Club*; or Wimsey as Harlequin in the fountain at Dian de Momerie's party in *Murder Must Advertise*; or the biblical flood at the climax of *The Nine Tailors*; or the blood-soaked interruption to Harriet's idyllic reverie in *Have His Carcase*; or the fate of the magnificent, hand-carved chess set in *Gaudy Night*; or the sinister Mrs. de Forrest trying to seduce Wimsey in her Mayfair flat in *Unnatural Death*; or Miss Climpson's stage-managed séance in *Strong Poison*; or the multi-transport, alibi-testing journey that climaxes *Five Red Herrings*?

It is slightly disillusioning to realize that after the 1939 appearance of the short-story collection *In the Teeth of the Evidence*, Sayers wrote no more crime fiction. (The 1972 collection *Striding Folly* consisted of three final short stories: "The Haunted Policeman," "Striding Folly," first published in 1939, and "Talboys," written in 1942.) Thereafter, she turned her not inconsiderable attention to religion and Dante. She wrote *The Zeal of Thy House* (1937) and *The Devil to Pay* (1939), both plays with religious themes, and, more controversially, *The Man Born to Be King*. This ground-breaking cycle of twelve plays for BBC Radio, broadcast in 1942, told the story of Christ in contemporary language. It provoked endless correspondence between the BBC and Sayers as she defended her artistic integrity. Its reception, however, was enthusiastic, and the entire enterprise was considered a triumph, both for religious broadcasting in general and for Sayers personally.

Her next focus of attention was the famous Italian writer of the Middle Ages, Dante Alighieri. In August 1944, as the sirens sounded over London during the Second World War, Sayers grabbed a book to pass the time in the air-raid shelter and discovered that it was Dante's *Inferno*. This was not her first contact with the writer, but the masterly combination of Italian poetry and religion that consumed her in that shelter inspired her to undertake a translation. The first volume, Dante's *Hell*, appeared in 1949, with *Purgatory* coming out six years later; she was still working on *Heaven* at the time of her death.

Apart from the main series characters, Sayers also created lesser, but no less memorable, minor characters. Lord Peter's manservant, Mervyn Bunter—even the name is inspired— makes an appearance in all of the novels and in some of the short stories. As imperturbable as Wodehouse's immortal Jeeves, he can offer sartorial advice and prepare a gourmet meal just as well as he can make discreet enquiries or take crime-scene photographs.

Inspector Charles Parker of Scotland Yard is that rare example of a policeman in Golden Age detective fiction not portrayed as totally dependent on the clever amateur. Intelligent, honest, and hardworking, he meets Lady Mary, Wimsey's brother, in *Clouds of Witness*. Ill-advisedly, she had been involved with the victim, and Parker, instrumental in solving the case, embarks on a romantic relationship, which continues, mainly offstage, through a few novels, eventually leading to marriage by the time of *Have His Carcase*. Solid, sensible, likeable, and very much his own man, as indeed he needs to be, he and Peter also form a close bond.

In *Unnatural Death*, where she makes her first appearance, Miss Alexandra Katherine Climpson is described by Wimsey as "my ears, my tongue and especially my nose. She asks questions which a young man could not put without a blush." Because Wimsey feels that middle-aged women and their natural curiosity and resourcefulness are wasted, he sets up a typing bureau, known as the Cattery, installs Miss Climpson at its head, and calls on its services when involved in inquiries where men might fear to tread. Miss Climpson herself carries out just such an investigation into the death of Rosanna Spearman in *Unnatural Death*, and she makes a further appearance in *Strong Poison* when she plays an important, albeit very entertaining, role in clearing up the mystery of Philip Boyes's death. Throughout her investigations on Lord Peter's behalf, she displays a resourcefulness belied by her appearance and demeanour, both of which disguise a mind with a clear-sighted outlook on her fellow men and—crucially in *Unnatural Death*—women.

Although Montague Egg, a little-known Sayers creation, appears in less than a dozen short stories, all of his investigations are neat puzzle tales, turning usually on a small but clever point. As a salesman of fine wines Egg travels the country, involving himself in crime as frequently as salesmanship. He has a saying for every occasion, culled from his salesman's handbook, and although it says nothing of his crime-solving abilities, his number-one maxim is "to serve the public is the aim of every salesman worth the name."

SHORT STORIES

Taken overall, the Lord Peter short stories are arguably less interesting than those without him. Perhaps because he needs a book-length appearance to be properly appreciated, *Lord Peter Views the Body*, the first collection, is best read at intervals; like vintage wine, the stories need to be savored rather than gulped. That said, lovers of the more abstruse crosswords should not miss "The Fascinating Problem of Uncle Meleager's Will"; "The Queen's Square," "Absolutely Elsewhere," and "The Necklace of Pearls," from later collections, are typically clever detective stories. But some of the non-Wimsey stories—"Hangman's Holiday" and "In the Teeth of the Evidence" each contain a mixture of Wimsey and non-Wimsey stories—are among Sayers's best. "Suspicion" and "The Fountain Plays" are both wonderfully clever suspense stories; the former has been filmed and dramatized for stage and radio. The whimsical "An Arrow o'er the House" and "The Milk Bottles" and the thoughtful "Dilemma" and "The Man Who Knew How" show Sayers's mastery of the crime—as distinct from detective—short story. "Blood Sacrifice," her contribution to *Six Against the Yard*, is a psychological study with dark criminal overtones. Montague Egg, whose very unobtrusiveness, like a certain Miss Marple, is his strength, is seen at his best in "Murder in the Morning" and "The Professor's Manuscript."

SAYERS AND THE DETECTION CLUB

Although the exact details of the origin of the famous Detection Club are, somewhat appropriately, shrouded in mystery, there can be little doubt that Sayers was hugely influential in its foundation. In her introduction to their first collaborative novel, *The Floating Admiral* (1931), she explains: "It is a private association of writers of detective fiction in Great Britain, existing chiefly for the purpose of eating dinners together at suitable intervals and of talking illimitable shop." As Sayers's description observes, membership was confined to writers of detective fiction, as distinct from thrillers, crime stories, or spy stories; only authors of novels with a logical process of deduction from clues honestly presented to the reader were eligible for consideration. Prospective members had to be proposed, and Sayers devised an elaborate ritual for induction into the club, involving ceremonial robes and darkness lit by candles, with Eric the Skull (filched, according to legend, from one of the teaching hospitals) lending an appropriate macabre element to the proceedings. And, most important, an oath; happily acting as mistress of ceremonies, Sayers extracted promises from prospective candidates:

> Do you promise that your detectives shall well and truly detect the crimes presented to them, using those wits which it may please you to bestow upon them and not placing reliance on, nor making use of Divine Revelation, Feminine Intuition, Mumbo-Jumbo, Jiggery-Pokery, Coincidence or the Act of God?
>
> I do.
>
> Do you solemnly swear never to conceal a vital clue from the reader?
>
> I do.
>
> Do you promise to observe a seemly moderation in the use of Gangs, Conspiracies, Death-Rays, Ghosts,

Hypnotism, Trap-Doors, Chinamen, Super-Criminals and Lunatics; and utterly and forever to forswear Mysterious Poisons unknown to Science?

I do.

As can be judged, the oath, while lighthearted in tone, was also explicit in outlawing anything in a detective story that could be considered cheating: unknown poisons, coincidence, feminine intuition, gangs, and conspiracies. All these militated against the fairness between writer and reader that was, in effect, the basis of detective fiction. Despite the fact that she had produced no fiction for the last twenty years of her life, Sayers was president of the Detection Club from 1938 (and the death of the first president, G. K. Chesterton) until her death. The presidency was subsequently accepted—on condition that she would never have to make a speech—by Agatha Christie.

In order to maintain a healthy financial position, the Club undertook to produce collaborative titles. Their first ventures were two radio plays, *Behind the Screen* (1929) and *The Scoop* (1930), followed by the novels *The Floating Admiral* (1931) and *Ask a Policeman* (1933) and a themed short-story collection, *Six Against the Yard* (1936; *Six Against Scotland Yard* in the United States). Sayers was involved in all of these ventures and would seem to have been the mastermind behind most of them. Surviving correspondence attests to the fact that it was she who coordinated the scripts for the radio plays and was the name best known to—and feared by—the BBC during the productions of each. BBC executive J. R. Ackerley referred to "the terrific vitality, bullying, and bounce of that dreadful woman Dorothy L. Sayers"; this fractious relationship was revisited some years later during production of her scripts for *The Man Born to Be King*. Each of the Detection Club ventures involved variations on the game-like qualities of Golden Age detective fiction. *The Floating Admiral* was written by thirteen writers, each contributing a chapter—and a proposed solution, although unseen by their successor—and passing it onto the next collaborator. Exhibiting her customary thoroughness, Sayers's proposed solution and notes ran to almost twenty pages, half as long as her actual chapter. In *Ask a Policeman* (1933), six writers "swapped" detectives to solve the murder of newspaper baron Lord Comstock in Hursley Lodge. So Sayers wrote of Anthony Berkeley's Roger Sheringham while Berkeley took on (brilliantly, it should be noted) Lord Peter Wimsey. *Six Against the Yard* was very different from its predecessors: Six writers each devised a "perfect murder," and Superintendent Cornish, a real-life former policeman from Scotland Yard, examined each story to spot the flaws in each "perfect" plan. Sayers took great offense at his criticism of her very clever story, "Blood Sacrifice."

SAYERS AS EDITOR

At the request of Victor Gollancz, her publisher, Sayers edited the anthology *Great Short Stories of Detection Mystery and Horror* in 1928, and it remains to this day a model collection. Her forty-page introduction was one of the earliest attempts to trace the origins of the detective story and to discuss in detail the influence that Edgar Allan Poe had had on the genre. She analyzed five—other critics counted only three—of his short stories and identified in them ideas and themes that continue to dominate detective fiction to the present day. She wrote cogently of developments since Poe's day, discussing trends and ideas in then-current detective fiction, and presented the stories in the anthology under specific headings: "The Police Detective," "The Intuitive Detective," "The Scientific and Medical Detective," and even "The Comic Detective." Although many of the writers she discussed are long forgotten, her analysis of their plots—whether good or bad—remains a model of literary criticism. Because it was as a literary form that Sayers wanted detective fiction to be considered, it remained her earnest hope that "the modern detective story [will be] compelled to achieve a higher level of writing and a more competent delineation of character." Ironically, in view of the Wimsey-Vane relationship that would begin two years later in *Strong Poison*, Sayers complained that "some of the finest detective stories are marred by a conventional love story irrelevant to the action and perfunctorily worked in. . . . Far more blame-worthy are the heroes who insist on fooling about after young women when they ought to be putting their minds on the job of detection." How often must those words have come back to haunt her.

Almost a decade later she edited the more compact, but no less impressive, *Tales of Detection* (1936), also with an erudite introduction. Although shorter than its predecessor, it was, even as the Golden Age drew to a close, no less notable in discussing the developments since the earlier collection. She sounded more confident in her assessment of the future of detective fiction and felt that, although writers could "now handle the mechanical elements of the plot," they had yet "to discover the best way of combining these with a serious artistic treatment of the psychological element, so that the intellectual and the common man can find common ground for enjoyment of the mystery novel."

SAYERS AS REVIEWER

For two years, between June 1933 and August 1935, Sayers reviewed crime fiction for the *Sunday Times*. More than 350 titles were discussed in her column, which, in turn, meant that she read, on average, three books a week, every week, throughout the period. And during those years she also published *Murder Must Advertise, The Nine Tailors,* and *Gaudy Night*. Although many of the titles she reviewed were by well-known authors such as Agatha Christie, Ellery Queen, R. Austin Freeman, and Georgette Heyer, it is noticeable how many of the names she discussed have completely disappeared. Through this column she is credited with boosting the career of one of the greatest names of the period between the wars, John Dickson Carr, when she gave him a rave review for *The Mad Hatter Mystery* in September 1933. She wrote: "Mr. Carr can lead us away from the small, brightly-lit stage of the ordinary detective plot into the menace of outer darkness . . . in short, he can write. This is the most attractive mystery I have read for a long time." Her praise appeared for years on reprints—not just of *The Mad Hatter Mystery* but other Carr books as well.

On December 17, 1957, after a day of Christmas shopping in London, Dorothy L. Sayers returned home to Witham and collapsed at the foot of the stairs, where she was found the next morning. The more sensational papers could not resist a headline—DETECTIVE NOVELIST FOUND DEAD AT FOOT OF STAIRS—about a woman who had been a force in British life for almost half a century. Whether as novelist, short-story writer, essayist, editor, historian, or reviewer, Sayers was a towering figure in the development of the detective story. Her contribution to the genre, in an impressive range of capacities, was immeasurable. Although her career as a detective novelist spanned a mere fourteen years—from *Whose Body?* (1923) to *Busman's Honeymoon* (1937)—she continued until her premature death to contribute to the promotion and acceptance of the literary form with which her name is forever linked.

DOROTHY L. SAYERS

Dorothy L. Sayers is the author of novels, short stories, poetry collections, essays, reviews, and translations. Although she was a noted Christian scholar, she is most known for her detective fiction. Born in 1893, she was one of the first women to be awarded a degree from Oxford University. Her first book featuring Lord Peter Wimsey, *Whose Body?*, was published in 1923 and over the next twenty years more novels and short stories about the aristocratic amateur sleuth appeared. Dorothy L. Sayers is recognized as one of the greatest mystery writers of the twentieth century. She died in 1957, but her books continue to enthrall readers today.

READ ALL THE LORD PETER WIMSEY AND HARRIET VANE MYSTERIES

STRONG POISON

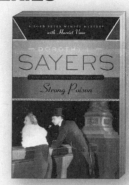

ISBN 978-0-06-219620-0 (paperback)

"A model detective story. . . . Fascinating."
—*New York Times*

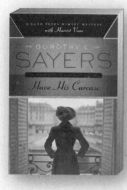

HAVE HIS CARCASE

ISBN 978-0-06-219654-5 (paperback)

The second Lord Peter Wimsey and Harriet Vane mystery, a classic of the genre from a writer often called the greatest detective novelist of the Golden Age.

GAUDY NIGHT

ISBN 978-0-06-219653-8 (paperback)

"*Gaudy Night* stands out even among Miss Sayers's novels. And Miss Sayers has long stood in a class by herself."
—*Times Literary Supplement* (London)

BUSMAN'S HONEYMOON

ISBN 978-0-06-219657-6 (paperback)

"*Busman's Honeymoon* has everything—mystery, comedy, love, and drama—all served up in Dorothy Sayers's best style." —*New York Times*